Rosanna Battigelli loved Mills & Boon romances as a teenager and dreamed of being a romance writer. For a family trip to Italy when she was fifteen, she packed enough Mills & Boon novels to last the month! Rosanna's passion for reading and her love of children resulted in a stellar teaching career, with four Best Practice Awards, and she also pursued another passion: writing. She has been published in over a dozen anthologies, and since retiring, her dream of being a Mills & Boon writer has come true!

Michele Renae is the pseudonym of award-winning author Michele Hauf. She has published over ninety novels in historical, paranormal and contemporary romance and fantasy, as well as writing action/adventure as Alex Archer. Instead of writing 'what she knows', she prefers to write 'what she would love to know and do'. And, yes, that includes being a jewel thief and/or a brain surgeon! You can email Michele at toastfaery@gmail.com, and find her on Instagram @michelehauf and Pinterest @toastfaery.

Also by Rosanna Battigelli

*Captivated by Her Italian Boss
Caribbean Escape with the Tycoon
Rescued by the Guarded Tycoon
Falling for the Sardinian Baron*

Also by Michele Renae

Art of Being a Billionaire miniseries

*Faking It with the Boss
Billion-Dollar Nights in the Castle*

Fairy Tales in Maine miniseries

Cinderella's One-Night Surprise

Discover more at millsandboon.co.uk.

REUNITED WITH THE TYCOON NEXT DOOR

ROSANNA BATTIGELLI

JET-SET NIGHTS WITH HER ENEMY

MICHELE RENAE

MILLS & BOON

All rights reserved including the right of reproduction in whole or in part in any form. This edition is published by arrangement with Harlequin Enterprises ULC.

This is a work of fiction. Names, characters, places, locations and incidents are purely fictional and bear no relationship to any real life individuals, living or dead, or to any actual places, business establishments, locations, events or incidents. Any resemblance is entirely coincidental.

Without limiting the author's and publisher's exclusive rights, any unauthorised use of this publication to train generative artificial intelligence (AI) technologies is expressly prohibited. HarperCollins also exercise their rights under Article 4(3) of the Digital Single Market Directive 2019/790 and expressly reserve this publication from the text and data mining exception.

® and TM are trademarks owned and used by the trademark owner and/or its licensee. Trademarks marked with ® are registered with the United Kingdom Patent Office and/or the Office for Harmonisation in the Internal Market and in other countries.

First published in Great Britain 2025
by Mills & Boon, an imprint of HarperCollins*Publishers* Ltd,
1 London Bridge Street, London, SE1 9GF

www.harpercollins.co.uk

HarperCollins*Publishers*, Macken House, 39/40 Mayor Street Upper, Dublin 1, D01 C9W8, Ireland

Reunited with the Tycoon Next Door © 2025 Rosanna Battigelli

Jet-Set Nights with Her Enemy © 2025 Michele Hauf

ISBN: 978-0-263-39684-3

08/25

This book contains FSC™ certified paper and other controlled sources to ensure responsible forest management.

For more information visit www.harpercollins.co.uk/green.

Printed and Bound in the UK using 100% Renewable Electricity at CPI Group (UK) Ltd, Croydon, CR0 4YY

REUNITED WITH THE TYCOON NEXT DOOR

ROSANNA BATTIGELLI

MILLS & BOON

To all the loved ones we have lost,
and the memories we will never lose.

Especially for Ma, Dad, Pina, Nelda, GG, Grampsy
from Nova Scotia, and our beloved Alain.

We love you, we miss you,
and you're always in our hearts.

CHAPTER ONE

A PASSENGER'S SNEEZE a few seats behind her startled Angel from her all-too-brief nap. She straightened in her seat and inhaled and exhaled deeply. She couldn't help shivering a little from the anticipation of reaching Halifax. The flight from Toronto wasn't an especially long one—three hours—but it had been delayed twice, set to arrive finally at 7:00 p.m. instead of early afternoon.

Angel had been looking forward to arriving at the Halifax airport early, picking up the rental car she had booked and proceeding leisurely up the scenic coast to her destination: a quaint B&B still another four hours away in the French Acadian fishing village of Chéticamp Island, off the northwest side of Cape Breton Island. Her Gramsy's B&B. Known by the same name.

A sharp prickle beneath her eyelids made her turn to the window to conceal any tears from the other passengers across the aisle, several of whom were also sitting up and checking their watches or phones. There was nobody in the two seats next to her, yet she was afraid to give in to her vulnerability in public. She bit her lip, refusing to let surface those unbridled emotions, even if they *were* silent tears.

Her grandmother's B&B was imprinted in her mind: a two-story lemon-yellow saltbox with sea-blue-and-white-striped canopies over the top-floor windows and front door. Red, coral and yellow begonias interspersed with purple trailing verbena and the startling yellow-green of potato vine spilled over each of the white window boxes.

The wide steps leading up to the front entrance welcomed guests with splashes of color from the flowers in each glazed ceramic pot on either side. Petunias of all shades, their bright blossoms encircled by a lacy foliage border of dusty miller. You couldn't help but catch your breath at the floral wonder that greeted you and led to the front door and roomy wraparound deck.

Whenever Angel had visited Gramsy in previous summers, she always paused at the entrance gate to take in the picture-perfect scene of the house set against a cloudless, baby blue Atlantic sky and the deeper hue of the Gulf of Saint Lawrence. Walking up to the double front door, she would inevitably catch the mouthwatering scent of one or more freshly baked pies: apple or blueberry, and most certainly, her favorite, wild berry pie. Moments later, she would be nestled in Gramsy's warm embrace, and promptly ushered into the farmhouse kitchen for a generous slice— or two—of steaming pie topped by a scoop of creamy vanilla ice cream.

Angel blinked to stem the wave of emotions evoked by the memories. *Sadness. Regret. Guilt.* All feelings that she knew would intensify once she was actually on Gramsy's doorstep. And in the days after, concentrating on what she would have to do.

Her thoughts dissipated at the pilot's announcement of their imminent landing. Yawning, Angel tucked her magazine into a compartment of her handbag and focused on the twinkling city lights as the plane descended.

Minutes later, she was at the rental car office with her

suitcase, wondering why it was taking so long for the employee to call up her booking.

"I'm so sorry," the middle-aged man finally said with a shrug. "Your booking seems to have been canceled."

Angel blinked. "That's impossible. Why would I cancel it? In fact, I called your office last week to confirm my booking." She heard her voice rise an octave. "I need a car. *Now.*" She turned as she sensed another person moving next to her.

"There's no need to panic," a deep voice announced. "I can explain."

A voice with a Scottish brogue. Angel looked up to connect the voice to the impossibly tall man next to her. Her head was level with his chest and as she craned her neck farther to meet his glance directly, a muscle pulled and she involuntarily raised her hand to her neck with a grimace. *Really?* she thought. *Now?*

She took a step back, trying to ignore the soft thudding of her heart, as her gaze locked with ocean eyes that had enchanted her in the past with alternating hues of teal and blue green. Enchanted her until the rose-colored glasses she had been wearing had finally faded when he decided not to return to the island ten years ago.

Gabe. Gabe McKellar, the owner of the estate next to Gramsy's property and B&B.

How had *he* managed to get her booking canceled? Just because he was a celebrated Michelin-starred chef who delighted Gramsy and the islanders with his permanent return, what made him think he could overstep like this? Why was he here in the first place?

Angel's stomach twisted. She was tired and emotional, and the last thing she expected was to not have a rental car at her disposal and to have Gabe McKellar show up, declaring that he could explain why her booking had been canceled.

She glanced back at the employee with a frown. He shrugged and gestured for Gabe to continue.

"I was instructed to pick you up personally to take you to Chéticamp," he said calmly, looking at her unwaveringly as he stroked his groomed beard.

Angel felt her jaw drop. "By whom? And why?" She crossed her arms and stared up at him defiantly.

Gabe held her gaze without blinking. "By your Gramsy," he said, lowering his voice. "I'll explain further on our way to the B&B." He reached for her suitcase. "May I?"

His mention of Gramsy was the last thing Angel had expected to hear. Her heart began to hammer loudly and she bit her lip. "Look, Angel, I know it's been a long time since…since we—"

"Since you left the island," she said coolly. "Actually, I was going to say it's been a long time since we chased each other around your Gramsy's apple trees." He grinned, showing perfect teeth.

Angel blinked. She had met Gabe over the many summers she had visited her maternal grandparents, "Gramsy" and "Grampsy," at their B&B in Chéticamp. He was their neighbor's grandson visiting from Scotland. She was seven when she had first met him, and Gabe ten, with a shock of curling black hair and a penchant for challenging her to a race, whether around the trees or along the sandy shore of their stretch of island. He had stopped coming to the island ten years ago, only to return permanently three years back. After ten years, here again was that black-haired boy—man now—smiling at her as if nothing had happened between them.

Nothing had happened between them.

Angel's jaw tightened. How could he even bring up the past at a time like this? Feeling her cheeks burn, she turned to the employee self-consciously, but to her relief, he was assisting another customer.

"I'm sorry," Gabe said gruffly. "Can we start over? It's been a long time and... I'm very sorry for the loss of your Gramsy," he said more softly. He started to extend his hand, then let it drop. "Welcome back to Nova Scotia, Angel."

Gabe was all too aware of Angel's brown eyes blurring when he expressed his condolences.

"Thank you," she said, and quickly turned away to dab at both eyes before facing him again.

"May I?" He reached again for her luggage and she nodded curtly before following him to the exit doors.

From the look of Angel's furrowed brows and pursed lips, she obviously had mixed feelings about the situation. She must be curious about *him* being designated to meet her at the airport and drive her back to the B&B, while also trying to process the recent passing of her grandmother, her *Gramsy*—who was known and beloved by most islanders, and who'd left a lasting impression on anyone fortunate enough to have booked and stayed at her B&B.

When Gabe reached his Range Rover, he opened the passenger door for Angel and when she was settled in, he proceeded to place her luggage in the trunk. She must not be planning to stay long on Chéticamp Island, he mused, if the weight of her suitcase had anything to do with it.

"You must be tired," he said, starting the ignition. "Look, Angel, why don't you just sit back, relax and even nod off if you want to. There's plenty of time tomorrow to meet and talk about your grandmother's wishes and—"

"Are you a lawyer, too?" she said bluntly.

Gabe glanced at her, his foot still on the brake. "No, I—"

"Well, then, I'll wait to talk to her lawyer, if that's okay."

Gabe caught the glint in her eyes before proceeding to exit the airport parking lot. A look that made it clear that he was treading on sensitive territory. That her grandmother's business was none of *his* business.

He nodded. "No problem. Are you hungry? Would you like me to stop for anything?"

"No thanks," she said gruffly. "Look, Gabe, I don't know why *you* were sent to pick me up, but after the almost seven-hour flight delay, I'm beat. I...didn't mean to be rude," she added more softly. "I just can't process anything more tonight." She yawned into her hands before adjusting her seat to a reclining position. Leaning back, she closed her eyes, her hands clasped in her lap.

Gabe gazed at Angel for a few seconds before concentrating on merging into the highway traffic, and once he was comfortably in his lane, he glanced over again at the granddaughter of the woman who had been like a grandma to him, too. In fact, he had also called her Gramsy. She had insisted on it.

His parents owned the property next to Gramsy's, a two-acre piece of prime land that was settled by the McKellars, his father's Scottish ancestors, centuries earlier. They were among the fifty thousand Highland Scots who settled on Cape Breton Island in the late eighteenth and early nineteenth century. Gabe's parents had business interests in Scotland, but they made sure to return yearly to what they considered to be one of the friendliest places on earth. Gabe was their only son, and bringing him to Nova Scotia and Cape Breton Island for a month every summer became a tradition that Gabe always looked forward to. He loved watching the waves of the Gulf of Saint Lawrence froth and darken in a storm, while he was safe inside the reinforced Tudor-style estate his grandfather had commissioned to be built in the 1950s.

Angel's yearly summer visit to Chéticamp had coincided with his visit up until ten years ago, when he was accepted at Le Cordon Bleu in France. He distinguished himself during his culinary training and was offered several apprentice and sous-chef opportunities afterward in Italy and Switzerland, resulting eventually with the opening of his own restaurant, Maeve's—named after his mother—in Edinburgh. His dedication and innovative dishes resulted in the granting of his first Michelin star, after which his success flourished and he no longer needed his parents' financial support. He only returned to Chéticamp after the tragic death of his parents in a car accident, needing time to process their passing as well as his recently broken engagement.

In the last three years since he moved permanently to Chéticamp, he had opened a second restaurant and gained another Michelin star. During that time, Angel hadn't visited at all.

Gabe glanced over at Angel. Her long lashes rested above cheekbones that were flushed. Her mouth was no longer pursed, and her rhythmic breathing confirmed his suspicions that she was sleeping. *It hadn't taken long.* He noticed her pulse in the curve of her neck, and something stirred in his chest. She looked so lovely, with her shoulder-length auburn hair framing her heart-shaped face.

She had blossomed into a beauty. Not that she was unattractive when she was young. At ten years of age, he had met her at a tea party at Gramsy's. A party Gramsy had planned specifically to try to get the seven-year-old Angel out of her shell. So, she had invited him along with his parents, as well as a girl named Bernadette, the granddaughter of her friends farther down the coast.

Gabe recalled noting the difference between Angel and Bernadette. Angel was shy, quiet and reserved, with pigtails or braids tightly in place, and wearing a brightly colored sundress, while Bernadette was a free spirit with long, strawberry blond hair and freckles, flitting about in T-shirt and shorts, doing pirouettes and cartwheels around the adults, and interrupting their conversation to add a lengthy and spirited story of her own. He liked them both, and by the middle of her vacation, Angel too was more relaxed and allowed herself to join in the races that he and Bernadette made a part of every encounter. A couple of times, when Bernadette couldn't join them, he and Angel had spent hours together, riding their bikes along the Chéticamp Island roads, their baskets loaded up with sandwiches and fruit for their inevitable picnic later on a huge, flat outcrop at one section of the beach, in full view of Gramsy's B&B.

They would eat silently, watching the waves rise up and cascade over the beach, the soft, swooshing sound mingling with the cries of the gulls overhead. Angel would stop eating and always made the comment that the foam spreading over the sand reminded her of the lacy hem of a wedding dress. The dress of a princess, she had added dreamily, before biting back into her sandwich. And afterward, she would pull one of her books—often a fairy tale—out of the basket behind her bike seat, and be completely absorbed for a while, leaving him to build sandcastles and delight in seeing a rogue wave knock it over and splash him in the process. She would join him in collecting unusual shells strewn along the coast, and sometimes they would trade one for the other's.

Ultimately, Gramsy would call out to them from the

back deck. A slice of pie and milk later, and Gabe would then run or ride back to his summerhouse.

For Angel's birthday on August 17—which always fell during both their visits—Gramsy would have a small birthday party for her, inviting Gabe and Bernadette. Gabe would bring a gift and include a special shell that he had found. On the inside, he would print his initial in permanent marker. He would always be pleased by Angel's delight over the shell, and it became a tradition to add to her shell collection on her birthday.

When she turned sweet sixteen, he gave her a heart-shaped shell he had found washed up on the beach after a storm a few days earlier. It was a delicate pink that reminded him of the flush in Angel's cheeks, especially when she was adamant about something. He brought it home, cleaned it and put it in a special box. It had a tiny hole and could be made into a pendant, but he was too shy to offer it to Angel like that. He presented it to her after a stroll on the beach rather than in front of everybody at her birthday dinner.

Gabe was surprised that these memories were resurfacing. *Again.* He wondered if Angel recalled such details. *Probably not.* Was she still a dreamer, perhaps wondering if one day *her* prince would sweep her away? He glanced over at her. She was missing the beauty of the splashes of gold and orange against the darkening sky. For a moment, her eyelids fluttered, and he wondered—*hoped*—that she would wake up and catch it before it dissipated. *And so they could talk.*

Instead, she inhaled deeply and shifted to the side closest the window, her hands intertwined. No ring on her left hand, he noted before turning his attention once again to the highway. It would be about four and a half hours before they reached Chéticamp Island. His drive to Halifax airport hadn't seemed that long, with a stop at his restaurant in Inverness and then a leisurely dinner at one of his favorite restaurants at the Halifax harbor before heading to the car rental place to pick up Angel.

He had canceled the car rental a couple of days earlier, when Gramsy's lawyer went over the instructions she had left specifically for him, written months earlier, but only to be revealed to Gabe shortly before Angel's arrival.

He took a deep breath and exhaled slowly. The week ahead was undoubtedly going to be a hard one for Angel, being her first return in three years, and having missed Gramsy's last days. *She's worked so hard as a teacher in Toronto these past ten years,* Gramsy had told Gabe during afternoon tea one day when he stopped in to check on her. *And taking special courses over the last three summers. She deserves a break.* She had gone on to wistfully tell Gabe that although she missed Angel's visits, they chatted and video called regularly.

A slight pattering against his windshield confirmed the earlier weather report. Steady rain throughout the night, with increasing winds and likely a series of thunderstorms, due to the tropical storms gathering momentum in the Gulf of Mexico and swirling their way up the Atlantic coast to the Maritime Provinces.

He stole another glance at Angel. She still had a sprinkling of light freckles on her face, and her lips were—

His head snapped back to the traffic. He could not let himself be distracted by the lips that had granted him his first kiss…

The intermittent flash of the approaching car's headlights alerted him that police were up ahead. He checked his speed and concentrated on staying within the safe speed limit instead of conjuring up memories that should remain buried.

The first part of the lengthy drive to Chéticamp and Gramsy's B&B was to get to the Canso Causeway that connected mainland Nova Scotia to Cape Breton Island. It would take two and a half hours from the airport to the causeway. After that was crossed, the road snaked along the western flank of the island to almost the northern tip. It was beautiful and scenic during the day in fine weather, but in inclement conditions, especially with reduced visibility at night and during a storm, it could get downright risky. Gabe was prepared to stop on the way if need be, and from the sudden pelting, it seemed more than likely that they would have to do so. He reduced his speed, surprised that Angel hadn't budged. Of course, she was exhausted from the ordeal of the long delay at the airport, and most likely from the anticipation of dealing with Gramsy's affairs once she arrived.

A flash of lights from a truck zooming closer and then passing him, sending an unwelcome spray against his window, made his heart jolt and he swerved. *Too close for comfort.* He clenched his jaw. "*Damn idiot!*" he muttered as he edged back in his lane, causing Angel to slide against his right shoulder. The motion did not wake her up, though, and he had no intention of trying to do so.

Her proximity unsettled him. With her breath fanning his arm and the lilac scent of her perfume wafting up to him, it felt as if she were a girlfriend he was bringing home after a date.

The guy racing by had unsettled him, too, as he could have ended up skidding off the road to prevent a collision with the truck, endangering his life and Angel's.

Fortunately, by the time they arrived at the causeway, the rain had subsided, and Gabe continued north to Highway 19, which would snake its way parallel to the coastal waters of the gulf and turnoff at Chéticamp Island Road, a road along a sandbar that led to Chéticamp Island. With any luck, they would arrive at Gramsy's B&B before the predicted thunderstorm.

He had picked up a few groceries earlier and left them in the fridge and on the counter for Angel. Being Gramsy's closest neighbor, he had often looked in on her to see if she needed anything, and she had found it more convenient to entrust him with a key in case she lost hers or was upstairs, having a nap. Two months ago, when he was returning with Gramsy's mail at her request, he entered to find her pale and gasping for air at her kitchen counter.

Knowing it would take much longer to wait for the paramedics to arrive, he helped her into his Range Rover and drove to the emergency department at the Chéticamp Community Health Centre. She underwent a series of tests, which confirmed that she had suffered a small stroke. A month later, having accepted her invitation for tea, he walked over with a bouquet of wildflowers from his own garden, only to find her napping on her swing that looked out over the bluff to the beach.

His heart had stopped when he realized she wasn't napping. He called the paramedics immediately. After the vehicle sped away, he sat down on the swing and let the tears flow at the loss of the dear woman who had always treated him like a grandson.

The memories of that day made his eyelids prickle. He blinked rapidly, needing his vision to stay clear. At that moment, Angel woke up and gazed up at him, and realizing she was nestled against him, quickly jerked away and sat upright.

"Sorry about that," she murmured with an embarrassed laugh. "You should have shaken me off." She checked the time on her phone and groaned. "Still two hours away." Peering at the winding road ahead, she said, "Any chance of stopping for a coffee and a sandwich? I'm feeling hungry now. All I had on the plane was a bag of roasted almonds and water."

Gabe nodded, relieved to shelve his memories. "A gas station and diner are coming up soon. Can you survive till then?"

The corners of her mouth lifted. "I guess so. Just warning you, though. Don't be alarmed at the sound of my stomach grumbling. It usually frightens small children and animals."

Gabe couldn't help laughing. "I'm neither a child nor an animal, so I should be fine."

"Well, I warned you," she murmured, averting her gaze.

CHAPTER TWO

FIFTEEN MINUTES LATER, Gabe pulled into the mostly empty parking lot of an all-night diner. The Cabot Trail Diner, open only a year, Gabe mentioned, but always busy during the day and evenings. Angel looked around, liking the retro vibe with its booths on the periphery of the room, and round pedestal tables arranged around the center, their padded chair seats and backs a variety of '50s-style colors: red, mint, teal, coral and yellow.

Gabe chose a booth, and to Angel's dismay, her stomach grumbled loudly as she surveyed the menu. Gabe pretended to jump back in his seat. She felt her cheeks flushing, and she looked around self-consciously.

"You were right," he said teasingly. "It's a good thing that there are no children on the premises at this hour."

Angel didn't reply. The flash of his eyes and smile were disconcerting in the bright light of the diner. He was no longer the cute, twenty-three-year-old guy next door to Gramsy. With his straight nose, strong jaw and closely shaven mustache and beard—and perfect lips—Gabe had become drop-dead gorgeous. In the ten years since Angel had seen him, the lanky frame of his youth and young adulthood had changed to a physique that only dedicated workouts could produce, she mused, as he took off his all-weather jacket and rolled up his shirtsleeves, revealing his sculpted arm muscles and broad chest and shoulders. A small patch of curly hair peeked out of the open V of his shirt, and sensing his eyes on her, Angel averted her gaze quickly and focused on her menu.

When the waitress came over and greeted them, accusing Gabe of "being a stranger," he apologized with a chuckle. "Meet my friend Angel," he said. "Angel, Heather."

Heather grinned and took their order. A turkey and brie on rye for her, and a chicken clubhouse for Gabe. "Wanna split an order of fries?" he said. "They pile them on."

"Um, sure." Angel said, glancing from him to Heather, who she was sure was gazing at her with curiosity. "Oh, and a coffee, please, with milk."

"Ditto," Gabe said. "But black for me. I need to stay awake for the rest of the way."

Heather's eyebrows arched at Gabe, but she didn't comment. "It won't be long," she said, taking their menus and walking away.

Angel looked past Gabe to the framed posters on the wall, featuring the stars of the '50s: Lucille Ball, Doris Day, Rock Hudson, Elvis and more. She was too embarrassed to look at Gabe directly. He had introduced her as his *friend*, even though they hadn't seen each other for ten years. Yes, they had been childhood friends for a few weeks over two decades' worth of summers, but how could he still consider her a friend? From the way the waitress had glanced from Gabe to her, she must have wondered if they were more than just friends… Angel excused herself to go to the ladies' room. Hopefully it wouldn't be long before their food was ready. A wave of fatigue washed over her. And sadness over the reason for her trip. She just wanted to get to Gramsy's and curl up in the four-poster bed in the spare bedroom Gramsy kept for her and her alone. The three other bedrooms were designated for the B&B guests.

She couldn't wait to get there. And spill the tears that had been building up during the flight. She looked at herself in the mirror. Hair a little skewed, eyeliner blurred, shadows under her eyes. Cheeks still flushed. She ran a comb through her hair, wiped away the smudges and, taking a deep breath, returned to their table, which already held two steaming cups of coffee.

"Good timing," Gabe said, as Heather approached with their orders. She set the bowl of fries between them.

"Now, don't fight over them." She grinned. "There's plenty for both of you." She met Gabe's gaze. "Ketchup and vinegar are coming," she chuckled. "Enjoy."

Angel was glad that there was minimal talk between them as they dug into their sandwiches. Gabe gave a thumbs-up after taking a few bites and Angel nodded. He squirted a corner of his side of the fries with ketchup and vinegar. Angel did the same with only the ketchup. When they bumped fingers as they reached for a fry, their gazes met. "After you, Angel," he said. "Just leave me one or two."

Was he always such a teaser? Yes, he *had* teased her when they were kids. Gentle teasing, not mean. At first, she had been too shy to give it back to him, but as she got older, she'd sometimes initiate and he would just laugh. "Okay," she said brightly, and impulsively pulled his entire bowl toward her. "Will do." She deliberately dipped one of her fries in his pool of ketchup and then plopped it in her mouth, while staring at him boldly.

He let out a deep laugh that drew the attention of the other customers. Heather sauntered over. "Wow, Angel.

You must be pretty special for Gabe to turn over all his fries to you," she chuckled. "He's pretty proprietorial about them."

Angel shrugged. "He said for me to just leave him one or two," she replied innocently, before choosing one of his longest fries and plopping one end into her mouth. Heather and Gabe laughed and Heather shot Gabe a knowing look before walking away to greet new customers.

"Just kidding," Angel murmured, sliding the bowl back in the middle. "Go crazy. I'm full."

"I appreciate your generosity," he said. "I'm *not* full."

Angel sipped her coffee as Gabe finished the rest of the fries. Despite her protests a few minutes later, Gabe insisted on taking the bill. "My pleasure," he said when she thanked him with a sigh of resignation. "Happy to keep your growling at bay."

Heather thanked Gabe for his generous tip and they rushed back into the Range Rover, the returning rain starting to gain momentum. In the car, Angel kept her eyes on the road ahead. There were many dark and narrow stretches, and she didn't want to distract Gabe. Even when bushes appeared on either side of the road, Angel was all too aware that to the west of them was the steady companionship of the Gulf of Saint Lawrence, which eventually led into the Atlantic Ocean. "Music okay?" He glanced at her briefly.

"Uh, sure," she said. Perhaps listening to some quiet music would help relax her. She settled back in her seat and closed her eyes. The strident notes of a fiddle made her start and her eyes flew open. Glancing at Gabe, she saw that he was moving to the lilt and rhythm of the music, and smiling, his fingers tapping with both hands on the wheel. It didn't take her long to recognize the Natalie Mac-

Master tune. She had seen MacMaster perform "David's Jig" at a concert in Toronto when she had graduated from university. Angel had fallen in love with fiddle music and took every opportunity to go to fairs where fiddlers were featured, especially Cape Breton fiddlers like Natalie and Ashley MacIsaac.

Well, it was not the classical music she had somehow expected Gabe to play, but it was certainly distracting. She found herself tapping her fingers on her thighs, and every once in a while, Gabe would glance her way with a smile, and she would involuntarily smile back. An hour went by surprisingly quickly, and when he turned the music off to inform her that they were approaching Inverness, she felt a twinge in her chest. In another hour they would be arriving at Chéticamp and then crossing to Chéticamp Island. And Gramsy's B&B.

Of course, it was no longer operating as a B&B. Gramsy was the only person who had operated it since her husband died ten years earlier. Her beloved Grampsy, Angel thought, an image of his kind blue eyes, fine white hair and ready smile flashing in her mind.

Gabe turned down the music. "We'll be passing by my restaurant shortly," he said casually. "I studied the culinary arts in Europe and operated my first restaurant in Edinburgh as owner and executive chef. After my parents passed, I returned to Chéticamp Island to take care of the family property. I needed some time away after... their accident."

Yes, Gramsy had tearfully told her all this. "I'm very sorry for your loss." Angel said.

"Thanks," he said huskily. "I ended up staying longer than I first planned, and your grandmother was very supportive." He shot a glance at her. "She helped me a lot in my grief."

Angel bit her lip. *That was Gramsy.* Everybody who knew her always had something to say about her big heart, how she went out of her way to help anyone in need. Gabe had been fortunate to have Gramsy next door to him during such a sad time of loss. Her eyes blurred and she quickly wiped them. Despite her mixed and sometimes resentful feelings toward Gabe these past ten years, she had felt for him and for his parents, who had both been so kind to Angel over the years.

"I'm sorry," Gabe said. "I shouldn't have brought this up."

"No, it's okay," she assured him. "So, you decided to stay?"

"Not right away. I returned to Edinburgh after a month and for the next six months I went back to work." He paused as the rain intensified. When it subsided, he took a deep breath. "Life was very empty without my parents," he said, his voice breaking slightly. "There were too many memories—albeit good ones—but they saddened me. I found myself getting very distracted at the restaurant. Not a good thing for a Michelin chef," he said, shaking his head. "I toyed with the idea of moving to Cape Breton Island, and I finally did. Three years ago. And I opened my second restaurant two years ago. In Inverness." He slowed down as a transport truck zoomed by.

"Yes, Gramsy had mentioned that. And the fact that you've earned a second Michelin star." Angel was surprised that Gabe would open up to her now about such a sensitive time. "Did you sell your restaurant in Scotland?"

"My talented sous-chef is now running it as executive chef while I'm away. I fly out every month or so to check operations."

"What's the name of your restaurant there?"

He met her gaze. "Maeve's." He smiled. "My mother's name."

Angel couldn't help smiling back at his tone of affection. *A loving son.* And he had named his restaurant in Inverness Mara's, after Gramsy. When Gramsy had told her that, and how humbled she felt at having been an inspiration for Gabe over the years, Angel had realized just how much of a connection existed between her and Gabe. Angel had been happy for Gramsy, too, having the support of Gabe, but in all honesty, she had felt a twinge of jealousy at times, knowing that Gabe had the privilege of Gramsy's company and she didn't, teaching full-time, and then too busy with her additional courses to visit Gramsy these past three summers. It made the latent sense of guilt she felt spring up again.

Both Gramsy and Bernadette had shared details of the opening night at Mara's, and how touched Gramsy had been at Gabe's address, thanking her along with his parents for his success as a world-renowned chef.

Gabe stared straight ahead after seeing the sudden look of dismay on Angel's face. Had he said too much? Perhaps he should have been more careful with what he had revealed about himself. There was so much more he wanted and needed to tell Angel, but spilling it in the Range Rover after her tiring flight delay was neither the time nor the place.

Now, they were nearing his restaurant in Inverness, near Cabot Links, one of the world's best golf courses. With the attraction of golf and the scenic ocean views, Mara's had been an instant success when it opened two years ago. "There it is, in the distance." He pointed to a series of rugged cliffs and an architecturally stunning building perched on a flatter stretch of the coastline. "It's hard to see clearly with this rain pelting down, but you can make out the name in lights."

Angel leaned close to the window to try to get a better look. Even when he had redirected the car to continue back on the main road, Angel was still looking out, her arms crossed tightly. And saying nothing.

Seeing Gramsy's name in lights had undoubtedly affected her. It had moved him when he had first seen it. And perhaps she was wondering why Gramsy's business was *his* business. He knew a lot more about Angel than she knew about *him*, simply because he had spent the last three years next door to Gramsy, enjoying many cups of tea and slices of pie or oatcakes with her, and a weekly dinner. From Angel's body language, he sensed he would have to take care in the way he revealed things to her.

"Look, Angel," he said to her back, "there's plenty of time tomorrow and in the week ahead to fill you in about everything. The main thing is that you're here, and shortly we'll be at the B&B." He deliberately avoided saying "we'll be at Gramsy's."

Angel turned away from the window. "I'm tired," she said, in a voice that sounded defeated.

Gabe felt a rush of empathy for her, remembering his feelings after his parents had died. She must be exhausted and overwhelmed. "Don't worry, we're almost there," he said gently, reaching out to tap her arm reassuringly.

She stiffened slightly and he sighed inwardly, turning his gaze back to the road.

As he drove, his thoughts turned back to the grief of his parents' death.

And his broken engagement.

He and Charlotte had dated for four months in what

could only be called a "whirlwind" relationship, and were engaged for two months. He had met her at a prestigious charity event she had held at his restaurant, and she had actually been the first one to initiate a second meeting. And then a third. After a few more "meetings," they both agreed that they were officially dating.

She was a high-end real estate agent in Edinburgh, negotiating sales and acquisitions of multimillion condos and the occasional heritage estate. She was impressed with the status of his restaurant and, he discovered later, the economic status of his family. He was initially impressed with her seeming generosity toward charitable causes and, to be honest, with her confidence and beauty. Eyes turned when she walked into a room, drawn to her flaming red hair and glossy red lips. She wore designer clothes, and with her statuesque height enhanced by stiletto heels, people often thought she was a famous model or actress.

Unfortunately, what he believed was genuine about her turned out to be simply a veneer. In the weeks following their official engagement party, an elaborate affair in a Scottish castle, Gabe started to see signs that Charlotte was mostly preoccupied about herself and her needs. A charity event she hosted usually resulted in some benefit for herself, mostly publicity and an increase in clients.

A month into their engagement, Gabe's parents died in a tragic highway accident after their fortieth anniversary cruise, and his life changed instantly. He was overcome with shock, grief and loss, feeling as if he were in a small, rudderless boat in an angry, turbulent ocean. He was overwhelmed with everything he had to do: identify his parents, handle the funeral arrangements and manage his father's business affairs, or designate people who could.

He had no time for flamboyant parties and other social

events. In fact, he wanted to hide from the world and try to make sense of what had happened. He ultimately had to take a leave from his restaurant.

Charlotte expressed her sympathies and tried to comfort him, but she couldn't break through the wave of sadness that often submerged him. The outings and trips that she suggested would help him get out of the dark hole of grief, she insisted.

But he wasn't ready. Grief was a process she didn't understand. And it became obvious she wasn't prepared to wait for him to go through the process.

When his doorbell rang one day and he opened it to sign for a package personally addressed to him, he thanked the employee, tipped him and then opened it inside, expecting a sympathy message.

He was right. It was a message from Charlotte, saying she was sorry to have to break their engagement, but she couldn't deal with "the darkness he was stuck in." And she had returned the solitaire in its box.

Gabe realized he was a couple of minutes away from the B&B. When at last he came down the lane and turned into Gramsy's driveway, Angel straightened, unbuckled her seat belt prematurely and leaned forward to look at the house. Gabe had turned on some indoor lights and the front door lamp lighting up the pathway and steps before he left for the airport. When he came to a stop, Angel burst into tears.

CHAPTER THREE

Angel gratefully took the couple of tissues that Gabe offered her and wiped her face. "Sorry," she murmured.

"You don't need to apologize, Angel. It was only natural that arriving here would trigger your grief."

"Just seeing the lights on and how beautiful the place still is…and knowing Gramsy won't be there to…welcome me…" She felt fresh tears spill onto her cheeks. "It's just too much." She sniffed and wiped her cheeks and nose.

She continued to stare at the house and was glad that Gabe wasn't rushing her out of the car. After a few minutes, she turned to him, "Okay, I'm ready to go in."

He nodded. "I'll get your luggage." He went around to open Angel's door and moments later they were at the front door.

Angel looked past Gabe's shoulder to the bluff and beyond, but it was too dark to see the waters of the Gulf of Saint Lawrence. She could hear the rush of the waves, smell the salt-tinged air and the faint scent of fish emanating from the churned-up waters. The wind had picked up since they had left the diner, and she could hear it rustling the wild grasses bordering the property.

She took a deep breath. She had missed this place, and most of all, Gramsy.

Gabe unlocked the door with a key he said Gramsy had given him, and gave Angel a spare key.

"I'll be okay now," she said, her voice wavering. "Thanks for getting me here."

Gabe nodded, a corner of his mouth lifting. He placed her suitcase inside. "Oh, I almost forgot, I have a bag of homemade muffins I picked up on my way to get you at the airport. I thought you might enjoy them in the morning. I'll go and grab them."

She grudgingly had to admit that Gabe had been very thoughtful, not only with stocking the fridge and turning the house lights on, but also getting her something for breakfast.

"Thanks, I owe you," she said.

Gabe gazed at her for a few seconds. "You don't owe me anything," he said gruffly. "Good night, Angel."

She nodded, afraid that if she replied, she'd burst into tears again, thinking how lonely it would be, the very first night she'd be sleeping in the house without Gramsy.

He left and Angel returned to the kitchen. Feeling somewhat deflated, she plopped down on the cushioned seat of the breakfast nook. She gazed at the familiar decor of the spacious kitchen: the lemon yellow Arborite counters, the deep farmhouse sink with Gramsy's homemade curtains hiding the shelves underneath, the massive oak china cabinet that had belonged to Gramsy's grandmother and in which she proudly displayed plates passed down from their French Acadian ancestors.

There was history here. The history of her ancestors. Her heritage.

A place that soon she'd have to sell. She had no choice. A sob escaped from her lips before she could suppress it.

She suddenly realized that she hadn't heard Gabe

starting the car. She hurried to the door window. He was crouched down, inspecting one of the back tires. The only illumination he had was from the porch light. She opened the door, and he looked up.

"Flat," he said. "I'll get it replaced in no time at all and then I'll be out of your hair," he joked.

She shrugged. It was on the tip of her tongue to suggest he walk back to his property and take care of the tire in the morning, but he had already disappeared to get his tools in the trunk. She went back to the kitchen, any previous vestige of fatigue gone. She eyed the kettle. Perhaps a cup of chamomile tea would help relax her and help her sleep tonight...

Angel was startled as an ominous roll of thunder reverberated around her, followed moments later by large raindrops that slammed the large picture window like projectiles. Her thoughts turned immediately to Gabe. He'd be getting drenched.

She rushed to the front door as a series of lightning flashes illuminated the sky and the rain soaking Gabe. Opening the door quickly, she called out, "Gabe! Come inside!"

Gramsy would surely have extended the hand of friendship and invited Gabe or anyone else in, out of the rain. How could she expect him to walk back to his place in this kind of weather? It wasn't as if their homes were the traditional distance apart, like city homes. Each of their properties was a couple of acres, and walking from the B&B to Gabe's estate was downright dangerous under these conditions.

He sprinted over and closed the door behind him. "Good timing," he said wryly. "If the weather forecast is correct, things are going to get even nastier in the next few hours." As if on cue, the wind shrieked through a partially opened window in the kitchen and Angel ran to close it. She grabbed a roll of paper towels and mopped up the water on the sill and floor.

She quickly returned to the foyer, then glanced at Gabe, standing in the foyer, his hair and shoulders dripping. The paper towel roll in her hand wouldn't do.

"Um, why don't you hang up your jacket here in the foyer, and then grab a towel or two in the washroom and dry your curly locks. I'll put on some tea."

Did she just say "curly locks"? Good lord.

His eyebrows lifted and his mouth curled in amusement. "I thought you'd never ask," he quipped, removing his shoes.

When he returned, the kettle was whistling, and she had the mugs and muffins out on the breakfast nook by the picture window overlooking the gulf. The only view they had, though, was of the rain still battering the windowpanes.

He sifted through the boxes of tea Angel had set out, his blue-green eyes narrowing as he contemplated his choices. Angel's heart did a flip, his damp hair and T-shirt evoking memories of swimming together and then returning to this very nook for a snack and a cool drink.

With Gabe sitting across from her, as he had done countless times before, Angel felt surprisingly at ease. And relieved, to be honest, not to be alone in Gramsy's house. Not because she was afraid; it was just that being there by herself would somehow make the emptiness of the place more palpable.

Things would be different in the light of day. Not that her feelings of sadness and emptiness would magically disappear, but at least the light might mitigate her sense of loneliness and grief.

"Hmm, I'll have the wild blueberry tea," Gabe said with a smile across from her. He surveyed the muffins. "Lemon cranberry, blueberry, carrot and oatmeal raisin. After you, miss."

"Easy choice. Lemon cranberry. And you?"

"Carrot. I can't resist the cream cheese icing. It tastes like the cake Gramsy..." He paused, and Angel could see from his furrowed brows that he wasn't sure if he should bring up memories about Gramsy, in case it incited more tears.

"Used to make," Angel said lightly. "I had forgotten about that." She peeled off the paper and bit into her muffin. "Very good. Thanks."

Gabe nodded. "Well, they *were* supposed to be for breakfast. By the way, I picked up some bread, eggs and milk for you earlier. All in the fridge."

"Thanks, and for the apples and bananas on the counter, too. That was nice of you."

"I'm generally a nice guy," he said with a crooked smile. He ran one hand through his hair. "My curly locks are pretty dry now," he said wryly. He plopped the last bite of his muffin in his mouth and stood up. "Thank you for the tea." He glanced at his watch. "I'd better get going."

Angel's gaze flew to the round clock on the wall and she did a double take. It was almost midnight. "But it's still raining."

"It's a warm rain. I'll be fine."

She put her hands on her hips. "I'll not be responsible for you getting struck by lightning, Gabriel McKellar."

His brows arched at her use of his full name. "I jog every day," he said, unable to stop himself from grinning. "I'll just jog faster. Besides, it looks like the thunder and lightning have stopped." He put on his jacket and reached into his pocket. Handing her his business card, he said, "Call me if you need anything, Angel. Anytime."

"I hope you get some rest," he said, his tone now serious. "I'll be in touch." Gabe opened the door and a violent swirl of wind and rain hurled the door back along with a deafening roll of thunder. Letting out a cry, Angel grabbed Gabe's arm as he grabbed the handle and shut the door quickly.

The wind had whipped his hood back and her gaze went from the hair she had caressed more than once ages ago to the teal eyes that could sometimes be as enigmatic as the dark gulf waters. She realized her hand was still clasping his arm and she started to pull it away, but he stopped her, taking her hand in his.

Her heart stood still as he searched her face, and then started drumming when their gazes locked.

"Okay, that settles that, then." He inhaled and exhaled deeply. "I'm afraid I'm going to have to ask you if there's room at the inn for me tonight," he said gruffly, his Scottish brogue sending a flutter through her.

Gabe watched Angel processing his words: her eyebrows lifting, her mouth dropping open and then closing, her intense brown eyes and the touch of her hand in his sending shock waves through him. "Let me rephrase that. If you insist on barring me from leaving, I can just camp out on the living room couch, if that's okay."

Angel shook her head as if coming out of a trance. She forced herself to pull her hand away from his. "No. I mean yes, of course it's okay. And no, not on the couch, for goodness' sakes. Gramsy would not approve. You can take either one of the guest rooms with an en suite upstairs." Her gaze flew to the puddle at his feet. "Stay right there. I'll grab some towels."

He watched her disappear into the bathroom past the foyer and reemerge with two large towels. He removed his jacket and shoes and used one towel for the floor and one for his face and hair.

She reached over to lock the door and then turned on the light of the stairway leading to the bedrooms. "I'm sure there's everything you need up there." Her brows furrowed. "Gramsy provided guest robes in the B&B rooms. You can—um—change into one of them and use the upstairs laundry room if you need to."

"Thanks. I really appreciate it." He smiled. "I'll thank you properly with a meal at my restaurant. Whenever you're up for it."

Angel held up a hand. "No worries. You don't have to." She turned slightly. "I'll just check out a few things down here and then… I'll be calling it a night." She gestured toward the stairway. "The guest rooms are the first ones on the right at the top of the stairs. Good night."

"Good night, Angel." He watched her return to the kitchen.

Upstairs, he found the luxurious robe, hanging ready for the next guest. He put it on, reminded of how efficient and thoughtful Gramsy had been as a B&B hostess. There was no need that her guests might have had that *she* hadn't thought about first. And generously provided, as promised on her website. Not just the usual items that might have been forgotten, like toothbrushes and toothpaste, but other things that provided a special touch: a welcome basket with snacks and drinks, a plush towel that they could leave with, that she had embroidered with their initials, discount coupons for attractions and restaurants, including his, and a souvenir book about the special attractions of Chéticamp and Cape Breton Island. It was no wonder that many of her guests returned. Or spread the word. The guest rooms were very rarely unoccupied.

His hair dry and his jeans hanging over the towel rack in the washroom—he didn't want to start the dryer at this late hour—Gabe walked to the large window of the bedroom and gazed out toward the gulf. The boughs of the apple trees on the property were swaying wildly. Intermittent flashes of lightning revealed the undulating wild grasses and the churning waters, with whitecaps forming and collapsing. Such weather wasn't uncommon at this time of year, a result of the seasonal storms south of the border and swirling off the coast of Florida. Unfortunately, it was a rough start to Angel's return to Chéticamp.

Yawning, he sauntered away from the window, removed his robe and settled comfortably under the covers of the king-size bed. He turned off the lamp on the night table and stared up at the ceiling. It had been a full day for him, not just because of the long drive to the airport and then back, but also because of the anticipation of meeting Angel again. He had not seen her in person in ten years, but he still recalled times spent with her and her friend Bernadette. Gramsy had mentioned her countless times since he'd moved back to the island.

He knew that Evangeline was the name she was given at birth, but her parents tended to shorten it to Angel most times. *Unless they were being serious with her,* Gramsy laughed, *and giving her time out.*

While enjoying a cup of tea with Gramsy, she always seemed to find a way of bringing up Angel and would proudly show him photos of her, past and present. He learned about her graduation from teachers college, her new apartment and the additional courses she was taking these past three years. So, he knew exactly what she looked like since he had last seen her ten years ago. She was beautiful. Beautiful with sad brown eyes that reminded him of the innocent gaze of a fawn. They were eyes that reflected her grief for her beloved grandmother. And there was something more that he had glimpsed in their depths. Regret, and possibly guilt.

Gramsy had told him that Angel felt bad about staying away for the past three summers. "I miss my darling girl," she told Gabe, "but I understand, and I told her that."

Gabe could understand Angel's feeling remorseful for not being around in the last years of Gramsy's life. He had felt similar regrets when his parents had passed, wishing he had spent more time with them instead of being so wrapped up in his restaurant. The sad thing for Angel was that she had finally booked her flight and visit to Chéticamp Island after finishing her extra courses, but Gramsy's heart had given out a couple of weeks before Angel's arrival.

A series of squeaks in the oak floor alerted Gabe to Angel's presence in the hall outside his room. And then a door opening and closing. The last thing she'd probably expected was to have her childhood playmate and first boyfriend sleeping under the same roof on her first night back.

He closed his eyes. He was kind of glad it had turned out that way. Perhaps his presence made Angel's first night at Gramsy's a little bit easier for her.

Gabe turned to one side and flipped over his pillow. Ordinarily, he didn't have a problem getting to sleep right away once his head hit the pillow. He just hoped Angel would be able to sleep well in the few hours left before sunrise.

CHAPTER FOUR

ANGEL TURNED ON the light switch of her bedroom and set down her suitcase. She slowly scanned the room that Gramsy had always reserved for her: The wallpaper with its delicate design of roses against a soft leaf green background; the cushioned window seat from where she could reach out and grab a Granny Smith apple from the edge of one of the massive trees that had been planted decades earlier by her grandparents; the antique white four-poster bed with its light pink bedspread and a folded quilt over the footboard that Gramsy had recently finished, each square consisting of a piece of Angel's clothes from summer visits over the years. In one of their last chats before Angel went on her cruise, Gramsy had proudly shown her the quilt and Angie had been moved to tears.

And now her eyes blurred again. She wiped them with a corner of her shirtsleeve. "Oh, Gramsy," she murmured, "I wish you were still here. I'm going to miss you so much." She walked over and sat on the edge of the bed, pressing the quilt against her cheek. She sniffled as her gaze fell on the plush toy lying next to the pillow sham. Her white, well-loved unicorn, with its shiny horn and rainbow-colored mane and tail. Angel couldn't help laughing. She had called it "Magic" and she had slept with it often as a child, after Gramsy had read her a bedtime story, and even later, when she was reading fairy tales by herself after Gramsy had kissed her good-night and gone to bed.

Angel sighed. The flight delay, meeting Gabe, the drive and all her thoughts and emotions throughout the day and night had left her exhausted. She had to try to get some sleep, strange though it might feel with Gabe in the room across the hall.

She fished out her nightgown from her suitcase, and after changing she flicked off the light and slipped under the covers. Sleep eluded her but she kept her eyes closed and tried to focus on listening to the rain and wind thrumming against her windows. Images of Gabe flashed in her mind despite her best intentions: The height of him as she craned her neck to meet his gaze at the car rental office; his teal-green eyes softening when he mentioned Gramsy's carrot cake; his upper body swaying to the fiddle music while driving; his damp hair with its curling ends; and those enigmatic ocean eyes as he asked if there was room for him at the inn.

And then imagining him in a guest robe...

The sunlight flooding her room woke Angel up. She squinted and waited until her eyes had adjusted somewhat and then opened them fully. Her gaze flew to the window. Droplets of rain dotted the panes, but there was no active rain that she could see.

Angel checked the time on her phone. *What? How could it be 9:10?* She scrambled out of bed. Was Gabe still here? She caught sight of herself in the dresser mirror. If he was, she could *not* go downstairs until she showered and felt more human. She grabbed the robe hanging on the back of her door. It brought a lump to her throat, knowing Gramsy had put it there in anticipation of her arrival, along with the fresh towels on the long, cushioned bench at the foot of her bed.

She opened her door slightly. Gabe's door was half open. Had he left? Debating whether she should make a dash to the bathroom, the sound of clinking dishes and cutlery downstairs answered her question. She stepped into the bathroom separating her room from Gramsy's and rushed through her shower. After briskly towel-drying her hair, she tied the bathrobe tightly around her waist and opened the door. Startled at the sight of Gabe coming up the stairs, she froze, self-conscious about her disheveled hair and robe.

"Good morning, Angel," he said pleasantly, as if it were perfectly natural to be meeting her coming out of the shower. He paused on the second last step. "I hope you slept well."

"I did, thanks," she said. "Longer than I thought I would. Um… I'll be down shortly."

He nodded. "I hope you don't mind? I took the liberty of getting a few things together for breakfast. I was just coming up to see if you…if everything was okay."

Angel wasn't sure how she should respond. Gabe was obviously quite comfortable in Gramsy's house. She wasn't sure *she* was as comfortable with having him linger in the spaces she thought she would be lingering through alone, going from room to room and coming to terms with Gramsy's absence. But she had no intention of being rude and asking him to leave, given his generosity in taking the time to drive all the way to the airport to pick her up and bring her here. Besides, he would probably leave right after breakfast to deal with his flat tire. "I'm fine." *For the moment.* "I'll be down in a couple of minutes."

She walked into her room without waiting to hear him

reply and closed the door firmly. Her heart was thudding. During the time that Gabe had stood there with his muscled arms crossed, his hair damp too, his T-shirt and jeans fitting him perfectly, she actually felt that he belonged there even more than she did. A strange feeling, and a perplexing one.

There were a lot of questions she wanted—*needed*—to ask him, but she would have to find the right time to do so. *Not today.* Today she just wanted to be alone in the house with her feelings and memories of Gramsy.

Angel opened her suitcase and sifted through the few clothes she had decided to bring: some casual, and a couple of more formal items for the reception that would be happening in two weeks' time in memory of Gramsy. It was her friend Bernadette who had called with the devastating news of Gramsy's passing. They had talked and cried over shared memories for at least an hour, and Bernadette had told her that she would drop in the day after Angel arrived in Chéticamp.

She would call Bernadette later, she decided, as she fished out a pair of fuchsia Capris and a pale yellow eyelet blouse and quickly changed. She brushed her hair back in a ponytail and added a bit of blush to her pale cheeks.

The welcome aroma of coffee greeted her as she walked downstairs. She noticed Gabe's gaze sweeping over her as she entered the kitchen and, feeling her cheeks ignite, she wished she hadn't even bothered to use blush.

Gabe had the breakfast nook set up with breakfast dishes, juice glasses, milk jug and mugs. He filled a mug and handed it to her.

"Thanks," she said. "I can't start my day without coffee."

"Enjoy." He smiled. "And shortly, breakfast will be

served." He gestured toward a pan on the stove and a bowl beside it.

Angel watched him as he proceeded to make scrambled eggs, bacon and toast. Her mouth started to water as the aroma of bacon pervaded the kitchen.

"Is there anything more tantalizing than the smell and sound of sizzling bacon?" He grinned, and a few minutes later handed Angel a plate with a generous portion of both eggs and bacon, a couple of tomato slices and two slices of toasted and buttered sourdough bread. "Enjoy. I'll make mine and join you in a minute." He took a drink of his coffee and turned again to the stove.

"Thanks, I will," she said, and after her first few bites, "Why does food always taste better when someone else makes it?"

Gabe chuckled. "I don't know. Especially since I'm usually the one making the food."

It was obvious that Gabe was very much at home in Gramsy's kitchen. Gramsy had mentioned his treating her with one of his signature dishes every so often. Angel couldn't help wondering if Gabe currently had a girlfriend that he enjoyed cooking for. He must be attached; she couldn't imagine that someone with his striking good looks and culinary expertise could be single.

A couple of minutes later, he was eating across from her. She gazed at his left hand. *No ring.* But that didn't necessarily mean anything. And not that it was any of her business.

"Is something wrong?"

Angel realized that she had stopped eating and Gabe had caught her staring at his hand. "Um, no, I was just thinking…" she murmured and promptly turned her attention back to the remaining food on her plate.

"About what?" Gabe persisted.

"Um…" What could she say? That she was wondering if he was married or with someone? "I was thinking about calling Bernadette," she said quickly. It was true, after all. "She said she would come by later."

"Ah, my sister from another mother," he said jokingly. "She keeps me in line, that one."

"As someone should," she blurted.

Gabe laughed. "Now you sound like her. That's a compliment," he added quickly with a wink. "Bernie's a true Cape Bretoner, speaking her mind. And often."

He rose. "Well, I should be going before my mouth gets me in more trouble," he said. "I need to look after that tire. But first, I want to thank you, Angel," he said. "For allowing me to stay at the inn.'"

Angel set down her fork. "It wouldn't have been very nice of me to have you walk—or jog—to your place in such bad weather. Gramsy wouldn't have approved. Anyway, thank *you* for making breakfast," she said. "I should have set my alarm."

"No worries, Angel. I always enjoy cooking." He started to walk away and then stopped to gaze back at her. "I imagine you want to stay put and settle in today. When you're ready to go over a few matters Gramsy wanted me to discuss with you, just call me or text." He gestured toward the counter where she had left his card. "What about the lawyer?" She felt herself tensing.

"We'll tackle things with him later. It doesn't have to be today. Or tomorrow. It's important that I talk to you first."

He was being enigmatic and Angel wasn't motivated to pry for more details. Not now. Maybe not even later today. She would see how she felt after reconnecting with Gramsy's house on her own.

"Good luck with your car," she said casually. "I'll let you know."

Gabe nodded. "If you're up for a good walk, you're also welcome to meet me at my place. When you're ready." Without waiting for her to answer, he strode across the kitchen to the foyer. Moments later, he was gone.

After replacing his tire with the "donut" in the trunk, Gabe drove straight to the auto repair shop to have the tire replaced with a new one. On the drive home, he reflected on the feelings Angel must be experiencing. He understood perfectly that she needed time to process being back in Gramsy's home. With Gramsy gone, it was no longer operating as a B&B, as the only staff had been Gramsy as owner, manager and cook; a younger woman whom Gramsy had hired after Angel's grandfather died to do the cleaning and housework relating to the B&B; and a gardener to maintain the property. Everything else, Gramsy had managed on her own.

So, Angel didn't have to worry about having to deal with guests. The "Gramsy's B&B" sign was still up, but word of Gramsy's passing and the closing of the place had circulated in and around the community.

What Angel didn't know—yet—was that Gramsy, discovering that she had some health concerns a year ago, had been astute and forward-thinking, making plans and updating her will. She had decided not to let Angel know about her irregular heartbeat and subsequent tests, angiogram and, ultimately, three stents until Angel arrived at the beginning of August, when her last course was done. Sadly, her heart hadn't lasted that long.

He would have to explain all this to Angel, and why Gramsy had confided in *him* instead of her.

There was a lot that Angel didn't know about him.

Their lives had intersected many times over the years when Angel returned to the island in the summer. His summer visits were often spent bicycling over to Gramsy's. She was an awesome neighbor and had invited him and his parents for dinner quite regularly, and they had done the same. On one occasion, his parents couldn't make it but sent him, and Gramsy had handed him an apron and encouraged him to help make the meal.

He smiled at the memory of sautéing Digby scallops and adding chopped parsley and lemon zest, and drizzling them with some of the lemon juice, and a shot of white wine or chicken broth. The next time, she had him help her with all the steps of making rappie pie, which she told him was the national dish of Nova Scotia and Prince Edward Island Acadians.

Gramsy enjoyed his company and encouraged his culinary curiosity and appreciation for island traditions. And because she hadn't been blessed with a grandson, she mentioned with a twinkle in her eye, she was happy to symbolically adopt him as her grandson. *So now I have two grandkids,* she chuckled. *And you can call me Gramsy, too.*

Gabe didn't really know how much Gramsy had told Angel over the years about him. He imagined he'd soon find out.

He stepped out of the Range Rover and once inside his house, he strode to the floor-to-ceiling living room window, where he could gaze out at the stretch of beach and Gramsy's adjoining property. The sky was a palette of blues and grays, with a smattering of small white clouds. The gulf waters reflected the same hues, and although the wind had calmed from the evening before, it was still ruffling the waters enough to produce whitecaps.

Turning away from the window, his gaze fell on a framed photo of his parents on the coffee table. It had been taken at their thirtieth-anniversary dinner. Gabe sank back on the dark brown leather sectional and felt a lump begin to form in his throat. He felt their loss acutely, and when he'd returned to Chéticamp Island, Gramsy was there for him, enveloping him with all the love and support that he needed in his time of grief and mourning.

And now she was gone, too.

He understood how vulnerable and lost Angel must feel now. Gramsy had told him that Angel had lost her father from a stroke when she was twenty-one, and her mother had passed from cancer five years ago. Gramsy was her last living relative, and they had been very close. And Angel, like him, had no siblings she could turn to for support.

He hoped that she would continue to accept the support he was ready to give her.

CHAPTER FIVE

Angel did the few breakfast dishes by hand. As she watched the soapy water swirl down the drain, she felt the absence of Gabe disquieting. Which was strange, given that she had initially wanted to be alone in Gramsy's home. Drying her hands, she sighed and glanced around. It was going to be hard, going from room to room, reminiscing about times spent here. But it was something she had to do. *Wanted* to do. She wanted to cling to every memory, lock it securely in her heart and mind. In fact, she planned to take a photo of each room, to remember how it was when Gramsy was alive, since she would have to ultimately sell the place.

That would be a sad ending to Gramsy's B&B, a fixture in the community for decades. Angel hoped that maybe there would be someone local who might be interested in purchasing it and continuing to operate it as a B&B.

Selling it would break her heart, but she had no other option. She couldn't see herself packing up and moving from her Toronto neighborhood to relocate to Cape Breton Island and take over the B&B. Much as the place held treasured memories since her childhood, there was no way she could just give up her teaching job and start a new life on the East Coast. *Year-round.*

Sighing again, Angel scanned the kitchen, probably

her favorite room in the house. The room that diffused Gramsy's mouthwatering breakfast scents up to her bedroom and lured her downstairs. The kitchen island where Gramsy let her help with making her many varieties of cookies and fudge, not to mention her oatcakes, pies and puddings.

This triggered a particular memory: racing around the apple trees on the property with a visiting neighbor—*Gabe*—and then the two of them using a broom to knock down some of the ripe apples. After filling the sturdy wicker baskets Gramsy had supplied them with, they raced back to her kitchen, and later that evening, they enjoyed a slice of pie fresh out of the oven, with a scoop of vanilla ice cream on top.

And then, while Gramsy relaxed in her favorite recliner, she and Gabe would pretend to own the B&B and cook for the guests. Angel blinked. When was the last time she had even conjured up *that* memory? Well, part of it had come true, with Gabe becoming a renowned chef and cooking not only at his restaurants, but for her in this very kitchen. As for her owning the B&B, she couldn't see that happening.

Angel sauntered into the living room, eyeing the soft, sage green couch where she had loved to curl up on with a book. It looked out onto the gulf and was the perfect spot to feel cozy in during a summer storm. She gazed at the corner bookshelf that still held all of Gramsy's books and some of her own. *Classic Fairy Tales. Anne of Green Gables. Heidi. The Secret Garden.* And later additions: *Little Women* and a number of Agatha Christie and Jane Austen novels. Gramsy never booked guests during Angel's stays, but any other time, they were welcome to read any of the books in this common room.

Her gaze fell on the spine of a book gifted to her on her sixteenth birthday: *Evangeline*, Henry Wadsworth Longfellow's epic poem published in 1847, chronicling the expulsion of the Acadians in Nova Scotia by the British and New England authorities from 1755 to 1764. She had been moved by the story of the French farmers and fishermen of the area being deported from Acadie, and in particular, the heartbreaking separation of an Acadian girl, Evangeline, from her beloved fiancé, Gabriel, and her search for him for years before reuniting with him on his deathbed.

Angel had wept over their sad destiny, and she wondered at a love so strong that would compel a woman to spend years searching to find her lover. She was captivated by the 1920 bronze sculpture of Evangeline in the Grand-Pré National Historic Site in central Nova Scotia on one of her subsequent summer visits, and had reread the poem so many times that certain passages remained in her memory. She had also driven along the scenic Evangeline Trail, the historic route through the Annapolis Valley, where the French first settled in North America, and ending in Yarmouth on the southwest coast of Nova Scotia.

Angel felt goose bumps on her arms now at her recollection of the first lines of the poem: *This is the forest primeval. The murmuring pines and the hemlocks, Bearded with moss, and in garments green, indistinct in the twilight, Stand like Druids of eld, with voices sad and prophetic... Loud from its rocky caverns, the deep-voiced neighboring ocean Speaks...*

Angel sighed and sank into one corner of the couch. When she was younger, her parents had told her that they had named *her* Evangeline, moved by the spirit of the fictional character who symbolized the deportation and the fortitude and persistence of the Acadians. Since her mom and dad always considered her their "little angel," the name stuck early on, and Angel only heard her parents call her Evangeline when they were being firm with her about something.

We have our own Evangeline and Gabriel, she'd overheard her mom say to Gabe's mother over tea at Angel's birthday when Maeve had spotted the book in the living room. She and Gabe had just finished having cake and were heading out for a stroll on the beach.

What was that all about? Gabe had asked her when they had reached the beach.

Angel told him about the Acadian lovers and their destiny as they walked, and for a few moments he was silent. When he stopped suddenly, she gazed up at him and the look in his eyes made her heart begin to hammer softly. He had never looked at her that way before. And then he had fished a box out of the back pocket of his jeans and handed it to her.

"Happy birthday, Angel."

She opened it wordlessly and lifted out a heart-shaped pink shell with a tiny hole in it. She turned it over and saw his initial, as he marked other shells he had given her. But next to this initial, he had inscribed an *x* and an *o*. Underneath the shell was a delicate gold chain. He attached the shell to it, and she let him place it around her neck. Her heart was racing now, and as he turned her gently around and leaned forward, she found herself looking up to meet his kiss. A sweet kiss that took her breath away. And then another, and another.

Angel stood up abruptly, berating herself silently for resurrecting memories that ultimately generated feelings of sadness and loss. She proceeded to walk through every room on the main floor, recalling instead a special memory that involved Gramsy. Sometimes she laughed out loud, and sometimes a few tears slipped out. She continued her tour on the second floor, through the guest rooms and, finally, to Gramsy's room.

Angel sat on the corner of Gramsy's bed. And was flooded. Memories of running into the room in the morning and jumping into bed with Gramsy. Tickling her when Gramsy pretended to be sleeping still. She placed her palms on the quilt Gramsy had made and looked around at all the familiar things that made this room so special: the antique dressing table with the round mirror where Angel had sat while Gramsy brushed Angel's long hair with a silver brush; the huge wardrobe that reminded Angel of the one in *The Lion, the Witch and the Wardrobe*; and her bookshelf with all sorts of intriguing titles.

What was going to happen to all these treasured belongings of Gramsy? And the B&B?

Angel felt a surge of anxiety. She put a hand up to her heart, which had started to race. Lying back on the bed and closing her eyes, she focused on doing her deep-breathing exercises to help her relax. When her anxiety had diminished, Angel turned on one side and hugged Gramsy's pillow.

"I love you, Gramsy," she murmured, her heart heavy. "I'm going to miss you."

The sharp ring of the doorbell startled her, and she jumped up, momentarily disoriented. She glanced at her watch and realized she had drifted off. She rushed downstairs.

Had Gabe forgotten something? Her heart thumped at the thought of seeing him again. When she reached the foyer and peered through the side window, the sight of the figure standing at the doorstep made her eyes prickle. She flung open the door and fell into the embrace of her longtime friend Bernadette, whom she hadn't expected until later.

"Oh, Angel, I'm so sorry about Gramsy," Bernadette said, her voice catching in a sob.

Angel nodded and let her own tears flow for a few moments. "I know," she sniffed. "I feel so bad I didn't get back in time—"

"Angel, Gramsy wouldn't want you to feel bad," Bernadette said, squeezing Angel's shoulders. "She understood why you were away. And she was so looking forward to your visit this summer." She gave Angel another hug. "Who was to know that her beautiful heart would give out?" She shook her head sympathetically. "These things are out of everyone's control…"

"I know," Angel said, wiping her eyes. "Come on, let's go in."

She made tea while Bernadette sat at the island and caught her up with news of her family and work. She was head waitress at Making Waves, a popular seafood restaurant on the northwest coast of Cape Breton Island. She had moved to Halifax for a few years, working for her certification in the restaurant and hospitality industry, and had recently moved back to Chéticamp.

From the first time they had met as children, Angel and Bernadette had become fast friends, and when Angel was back home, they became pen pals and looked forward to reuniting for a few weeks every summer. "Mmm, peach," Bernadette said, and smiled. "You remembered."

Angel nodded and sat across from her. "Of course. How could I forget anything about my peachy friend?" They both laughed and Angel was glad for these moments of levity, and grateful that she would have Bernadette close by this week.

"Okay, now tell me more about your *friend*," Angel said.

Bernadette had been dating a real estate agent for the last three months. Ross Grant was an islander and very successful at his job. Bernadette had shared that he was a widower with no kids. Sadly, his wife had passed suddenly from a rare heart condition five years earlier.

Her eyes widened at Bernadette's grin. "Wait, what? Are you two serious?"

Bernadette's eyes seemed to sparkle. "I… *Yes!* He's not like any of the guys I dated in the past. He's thoughtful, smart, funny and—" she winked "—as cute as hell."

"I'm so happy for you, Bernie," Angel cried, rushing over to give Bernadette a tight hug. "I can't wait to meet him."

Bernadette nodded. "You will tonight. He and I are taking you out for dinner."

Angel's smile faded. "I…um… That's very kind, but I don't think I'm up to going out in public. Sorry."

Bernadette reached out and clasped Angel's hand. "Don't apologize. I understand. Okay, how about I order and have it delivered here?"

Angel couldn't help but concede at Bernadette's hopeful expression. "Sure, I can handle that." She narrowed her eyes deliberately. "Besides, I have to meet this man of yours and make sure he's worthy of my bestie."

Bernadette laughed. "By the way, Angel, how did everything go with Gabe yesterday? He stopped by the restaurant a couple of nights ago and told me he would be picking you up."

Angel shrugged nonchalantly. "Yeah, he took it upon himself to cancel my car rental and meet me himself," she said. "He said he was following Gramsy's wishes."

Bernadette nodded. "I'm not surprised. Gabe and Gramsy have gotten pretty close over the years, especially after his parents died."

Angel frowned. She remembered feeling sad when Gramsy had shared the news of the terrible accident that had claimed the lives of Gabe's parents. They had always been very kind to her. "I'm sure that Gramsy would have been a great support for him," Angel murmured. "She was always like a mother hen to anyone in the community who was grieving, making meals and comforting them in any way she could."

"Yup," Bernadette nodded. "And Gabe never forgot it." Her phone trilled and she read the text. She quickly replied and then put the phone down. "It was Ross—" she smiled "—asking about you. He said he'd order and meet me here. You and I don't have to do a thing."

"That's very kind. Thanks. He scores a point in my books," she teased.

"What about Gabe?" Bernadette countered.

Angel threw her a puzzled look. "What do you mean?"

"Did he make any sort of impression?" Bernadette said casually. "I mean, you haven't seen him for ten years."

"What kind of impression was he supposed to make? I mean, I did notice he was impossibly tall…"

"And?"

Angel put a finger to her temple and tapped it, as if trying to remember. "Oh yes. He had two eyes and ears, a nose and a mouth." She stared pointedly at Bernadette. "What's your point, Bernie?"

Bernadette shrugged innocently. "I just wondered if you had noticed how good-looking he is."

Angel's lips twitched. "No," she replied emphatically.

"Liar," Bernadette shot back with a grin.

Gabe decided to go for a jog after ending a long business call to his restaurant manager and acting executive chef in Edinburgh. He changed into a long-sleeved hoodie and sweatpants, and moments later he was breathing the fresh ocean air and enjoying the brisk wind that was prevalent at this time of year. It wasn't the aggressive wind of the night before, and if the week's weather forecast was to be believed, the wind would again rise up and show its less pleasant side, influenced by the yearly hurricane activity swirling off the Florida coast.

For now, it was perfect jogging weather. He usually went for at least five miles every morning, depending on how busy his day was. His restaurant opened for lunch, but his shift started at 5:00 p.m., so he usually arrived at three to prep for the evening with his sous-chef and staff.

As he passed his property and continued along the coast in the direction opposite Gramsy's land, he wondered how Angel was doing. He knew from his chat with Bernadette a couple of days ago that she would be dropping by to be with Angel today. He had also told her that he would be picking up Angel at the airport. Bernadette's eyebrows had shot up and he explained that when Gramsy learned the details of Angel's flight schedule a month ago, she told him that she didn't want Angel driving for hours after her flight.

My poor girl will be exhausted enough after finishing her course. Gramsy had advised him to cancel Angel's car rental—she had the confirmation number that Angel had given her, along with her flight schedule—and to just show up. And then she texted him a recent photo of Angel.

Gabe had looked at the photo often in the weeks preceding the day of Angel's flight. It hadn't been the first photo Gramsy had shared with him, proclaiming her pride for her only granddaughter. He had seen photos of Angel over the years: wearing braces in her teen years; beaming in her sea-green prom gown, her hair done up, with tendrils on either side of her cheeks, standing next to her smug-looking date; graduating from university and teachers college; and countless birthdays.

During his teatime visits with Gramsy, their conversation would inevitably veer to Angel's accomplishments with her students, and other events in her life.

Like her dates.

Angel would probably be embarrassed, to say the least, that Gramsy would have shared any details about her dates to him or anyone else. Not that any of those meager details had been worthy of embarrassment.

Gramsy had simply dismissed the guys based on what Angel had told her. Which wasn't much, she complained to Gabe with a laugh. *He was too arrogant. He ate like a slob. His gaze wandered to other women.* In their last teatime together, Gramsy had expressed her hope that now that Angel had finished her special courses, she would hopefully go out more and find a special guy.

The recent photo was the only one Gramsy had texted to him, and he couldn't help scrolling to view it every day. The sun was shining on Angel's dark auburn hair, and she was laughing, her bright red lipstick matching her top above rolled-up jeans and bare feet. It was taken at a beach northwest of Toronto, Gramsy told him.

Angel's dark brown eyes looked almost teasing, and Gabe wondered if the person taking the photo was someone special that maybe Angel hadn't told Gramsy about.

An inner voice warned Gabe to put a halt to those thoughts. This was a sad and sensitive time for Angel. Gramsy wanted him to be there for Angel and to help her with the decisions that had to be made around the B&B. Angel was vulnerable and Gramsy trusted *him* to see that her affairs were carried out the way she intended.

Gabe checked his watch and saw that it was time to turn back. The wind was starting to pick up and the sky was changing from hues of blue to gray. He took a drink from his water bottle and then headed back. When he was about a quarter of a mile from his place, he caught sight of someone walking along the beach, just past his property. A few minutes later, he realized it was Angel. He slowed down and stopped a few yards away. He had worked up a sweat and took a moment to grab a small towel in his hoodie pocket to wipe his brow. He breathed in and out deeply, hoping to slow his pulse, which he knew wasn't just the result of his jog.

"Hi, Angel."

"Hello."

Gabe nodded. Up to now, she had never called him by name. An image flashed in his mind of the photo of Angel that Gramsy had texted to him. Her eyes weren't sparkling now and she wasn't laughing, but he still found her beautiful. She was wearing fuchsia Capris and a yellow blouse, and her hair was up in a casual ponytail. A natural beauty.

"Are you starting or ending your walk?"

"Ending. Bernadette came by for a bit and then kindly offered to get some groceries for me."

He nodded. "Nice of her. Can I offer you tea or a refreshing drink at my place, since we're practically on my doorstep?"

CHAPTER SIX

GABE'S TEAL-GREEN eyes were mesmerizing. His hair was windswept and damp, and yes, even in his hoodie and sweatpants, Angel couldn't deny that he was good-looking. *Damned* good-looking.

But she had no intention of letting him know that she thought that about him. And she really shouldn't take him up on his offer. She still felt vulnerable and wasn't ready to show her feelings again to Gabe. Bursting into tears when they arrived at the B&B had been regrettable, and she couldn't be sure that any mention of Gramsy while they were having tea wouldn't incite the same response.

She had to try to curb her emotions, at least when she was with Gabe or the lawyer. How could she make rational decisions about Gramsy's affairs if she allowed herself to be openly overwhelmed with grief? The meeting with the three of them was scheduled for the day after tomorrow, and Angel meant to present a staunch demeanor. She had to be strong. She needed some time before then to condition herself for the meeting. If she had to cry and break down, she would do it in the privacy of Gramsy's house. And with Bernadette, with whom she had had a connection for years.

"Angel?"

Startling, she realized that she had been staring beyond

Gabe at the undulating waters of the gulf. She shifted her gaze back to him. "Um, thanks, but I'll have to pass. I need to—"

"You don't need to explain, Angel." He scanned the sky. "From the look of those clouds and whitecaps, I think we may be in for another blast of bad weather." He started to turn away. "Take care."

She nodded and kept walking. A sudden gust of wind sent up a spray of sand. She shielded her face as she headed for the path to Gramsy's. The first onslaught of rain followed moments later and at the rumbling of thunder, she started to run. Her foot made contact with something protruding in the sand. She catapulted forward and cried out as she felt a sharp item puncturing her lower leg as she landed unceremoniously on the beach, her face grazing the sand.

She winced as she shifted her position and managed to sit up.

"Don't move, Angel," Gabe said, reaching her. "Did you hit your head?"

"I—I don't think so. It happened so fast." She brushed the sand from her face. "My leg—" She gasped at the gash on her blood-splattered limb.

Gabe frowned. "Here, let me wrap that up for now." He pulled a small towel out of his hoodie pocket and tied it around the wound and her calf. "I'll clean it up at the house. Sit tight for a minute." He scanned the beach sand around her and extracted a piece of driftwood with a nail sticking out of it and a tattered piece of cloth attached to the head of the nail. "A kid's sailboat," he said, shaking his head.

"I think I'm okay to get up," she said, the rain starting to seep through her clothes. She moved her legs to make sure she hadn't twisted anything.

"Let me help you." Gabe bent over her and supported

her shoulders and elbow as she tentatively stood up. "Okay, tell me if it hurts when you put your weight on it."

"I'll be fine," she insisted. She took a step forward but when she put her weight on her injured leg, she faltered and reached for Gabe's arm. She looked down and saw that the towel was blood-soaked and the rain was making the blood run down her leg in rivulets.

"Take this," Gabe ordered, handing her the driftwood.

Seconds later, he had scooped her up and was striding quickly to the path leading to his property. Her cheek brushed against his chest as he carried her up the slope to the path that led to the manicured lawn at the back of his house. After setting her down gently, he opened the door and she gingerly stepped inside.

He pulled a chair over to where she stood. "Have a seat and I'll grab some towels and tend to your cut."

Angel was about to say she could look after it herself if he could just supply her with a few bandages, but he was gone before she could open her mouth. She sighed.

She had no choice but to rely on Gabe. Again.

He returned with a face towel and a large bath towel that he placed over her shoulders. He waited until she had towel-dried her hair and arms, and then, kneeling by her chair, he removed his towel from her calf and proceeded to clean the area around the cut with cotton pads. "Sorry if this stings," he said, moistening a fresh pad with alcohol.

She winced, gritting her teeth as he gently dabbed the cut. He squeezed an antibiotic cream over the cut and then wrapped a strip of gauze around her calf.

"Okay, now to get you dry." He stood there looking at her quizzically. "Actually, I'm pretty wet now, too." He pulled off his hoodie, revealing a black T-shirt. "I'll grab you something you can wear while you dry your clothes.

The dryer's in the next room." He strode across the room to a set of stairs.

Angel let out a pent-up sigh. What happened to the quiet day she had planned to spend at the B&B, reflecting on memories and processing Gramsy's loss? It seemed the more she wanted to be alone, the more the universe contrived to do the opposite, throwing her and Gabe together.

She glanced around at what was obviously the family room, with an oversize dark chocolate leather sectional and a couple of recliners, a live-edge coffee and side tables, and a sleek floor-to-ceiling fireplace with built-in bookshelves on either side. On one side of the room was a well-stocked bar area with leather stools and a mini kitchen. The room had been designed, like Gramsy's and other homes on this side of Chéticamp Island, to highlight the view of the waters of the Gulf of Saint Lawrence. A few magazines and newspapers were scattered on the coffee table along with a couple of hardcover books. The white wood walls and the steel elements around the high glass windows gave the room a cottage industrial look. Even with its masculine features, the room had a warm feel to it.

Ordinarily, Angel would be drawn to the bookshelves, being an avid reader and always curious about what others liked to read. But in wet clothes and with a gash on her leg, she wasn't about to move off the chair.

Gabe's footsteps drew her gaze back to the doorway where he reemerged with a plush cotton robe.

"Do you think you can manage throwing your wet clothes into the dryer?" He glanced at her leg. "If not, I can—"

"I can do it," Angel said crisply, reaching for the robe without looking at Gabe directly. "It shouldn't take long, and then I'll get out of your hair."

***

Gabe left the room and went upstairs, deciding to have a quick shower before changing. That should give Angel enough time to get her clothes dried. He'd drive her back to Gramsy's, as it was raining even harder, and even if it wasn't, he didn't think she'd want to walk the distance with her injured leg.

The hot shower felt good after being in wet clothes. As he shampooed his hair, his thoughts kept returning to Angel. She seemed hesitant around him, as if she didn't want to have to depend on him. Being an only child, like him, she was probably very independent and used to doing things and making decisions on her own.

Or maybe she was reluctant to be at ease with him until she met with him and the lawyer to find out how he figured in Gramsy's affairs. Perhaps she'd even be more wary once she found out that he had been privy to Gramsy's condition and she hadn't been.

Angel would be hurt, of course. And he couldn't blame her. But he hoped that she would be willing to listen to him explaining how and why Gramsy made the decisions she did, and why she had trusted *him* to be the one to talk to her, and be involved with the lawyer to settle Gramsy's affairs.

Gabe rinsed off and wrapped an oversize towel around his hips. He towel-dried his hair, then headed to his walk-in closet and chose a Cape Breton T-shirt and casual cargo pants to change into. Checking the time, he didn't think Angel's clothes would have dried yet, so he decided to head down to the kitchen and see what he could whip up for dinner.

Even though Angel had said that she would "get out of his hair" after drying her clothes, maybe she would consider staying for dinner. He scanned the contents of his fridge and pantry and wondered what Angel's food tastes were like, beyond sandwiches like the ones they had enjoyed at the Cabot Trail Diner. Did she like simple meals with basic ingredients, or did she have gourmet tastes? If she decided to stay, should he make a simple lemon pasta dish topped with sautéed mushrooms and shaved Parmigiano? Or chicken cordon bleu with roasted lemon rosemary potatoes and an arugula salad?

From the main kitchen at the opposite end of the house, Gabe heard the faint sound of the dryer door being open and shut a few moments later. The laundry room was at the far end of the main floor, next to the family room that they had first entered.

He shook his head. Chances were, she'd want to get out of his hair, not stay for dinner. He closed the fridge door and put on a kettle. *She might appreciate a cup of tea, though*...

When Gabe returned to the family room, Angel was standing by the fireplace, scanning the bookshelves. She turned when she heard his footsteps on the oak floor.

"Thanks for the use of your dryer," she said. "I left the robe on the hook behind the door."

"You're welcome. And no worries. I have a few more upstairs," he said, smiling. "How's your leg?"

"Sore, but I'll be fine. I should be getting back to Gramsy's."

The whistle of the teakettle drew both their glances to the kitchen. "I thought you might like a cup of tea?" Her brows lifted and she hesitated but he didn't move, his gaze locking with hers.

"Sure," she said finally. "Thanks."

CHAPTER SEVEN

"Here's to Gramsy!" Gabe lifted his mug.

Angel hesitated slightly before lifting her mug of tangerine lemon tea to clink it with his. She looked around as she sipped her tea. The kitchen was an eye-stopper, eclipsed only by the stunning view of the Gulf of Saint Lawrence from what had to be custom-built windows. A chef's kitchen, with its massive six-burner range and double oven, and oversize steel refrigerator. The gleaming pomegranate-colored cabinetry was stunning. She had never seen such a vibrant color in any kitchen decor. The white quartz island, with its waterfall edges, black farmhouse sink, built-in butcher block and six cushioned steel stools, was impossibly long, and Angel couldn't help imagining the intimate dinner parties Gabe must entertain, perhaps alongside a special lady.

She cut off those thoughts swiftly. She might as well take the opportunity to ask him some questions. She set down her mug and stared at it for a few moments before fixing him with a direct gaze. "Okay, Gabe, I need you to clarify a few things for me."

Gabe's brows lifted at the mention of his name. She was well aware that she hadn't used it before. The main reason she had avoided it was because it put them on a familiar level—like in the past—and she wasn't comfortable with that. And now, it had just slipped out.

"What would you like to know, Angel?" He gazed at her steadily.

He had no problem using her name.

"I was going to wait until we went to the lawyer's, but I'd like to get some things straight about Gramsy." She bit her lip. "I know you've been looking out for her since you moved back. Did you know that she had health issues? And if you did, why didn't you let me know? I'm sure Gramsy would have given you my contact number."

Gabe rubbed his chin. "She found out she had an irregular heartbeat about a year ago. She told me this a few months later, when she was finally scheduled to have an angiogram." He inhaled and exhaled deeply. "I encouraged her to tell you, Angel. More than once. And again when she had to undergo the procedure to get stents put in for the three blockages revealed by the tests." He shook his head. "But she started to get agitated and insisted that she didn't want to worry you while you were teaching, and that she'd let you know once you finished your courses and flew back here." He threw up his hands. "I didn't want to agitate her further. I drove her to the hospital, she had the procedure and stayed overnight, and then I drove her home the next day."

Angel blinked, trying to digest everything Gabe had said. "Did anyone else know? Bernadette didn't mention anything."

"No, I didn't tell anyone, and the only other person Gramsy told was her lawyer, when she went to…"

"Review her will?" Angel said softly.

Gabe nodded.

"She must have been worried about her health," Angel said, her heart twisting.

"I have to tell you, Angel, Gramsy never seemed worried about it. She was just worried about *you* and wanted to ensure that her affairs were in order. She actually met with her lawyer every year to review things, even before she found out about her irregular heartbeat."

Angel leaned forward to put her elbows on the table, and cupped her chin with both hands.

"She was so excited when you booked your flight, Angel. And up until two weeks ago, when I…when I found her, she was looking good, feeling good and in great spirits." He reached across to put a sympathetic hand on her arm. "She passed peacefully, on the swing your Grampsy made for her, looking out on the gulf."

Gabe's words and the image they evoked broke the dam building up inside her. As the tears started to stream down her cheeks, she rose from her chair and turned away. She heard Gabe's chair scrape the floor, and seconds later he was facing her.

"I'm so sorry, Angel," he said huskily, encircling her shoulders with one arm.

She found herself closing the circle and falling against him, not caring about their past, just needing a caring embrace at that moment. When both his arms tightened around her, she sobbed against his chest. Other than Bernadette, there was nobody on whom she could unload her grief, and she knew that there were many tears that were still pent up inside her.

When one of Gabe's hands reached up to cup the back of her head, Angel felt a surge of something familiar run through her. A feeling of being protected, cared for and cherished even, despite the fact that Gabe couldn't possibly feel those kinds of emotions for her now.

But he had in the past when they were young…at a local playground where a tourist had teased her—for losing her balance coming off a slide and falling flat on her face—before running off. She had burst into tears, feeling humiliated, and Gabe had rushed to her side, helping her up, gently brushing the sand and tears off her face and putting a protective arm around her to comfort her.

It didn't matter now. It was obvious that Gabe had cared for Gramsy in many ways, and Gramsy had trusted him implicitly, and that made her feel some kind of connection with him.

Sniffling, she moved her head off his chest. "Sorry for the deluge on your shirt," she said gruffly.

"Don't ever apologize for your tears, Angel. They have to come out. That's part of the grieving process."

She nodded and looked at him through her blurred vision. "Thanks for being there for Gramsy over the years. I really should get back now." She wiped her eyes. "And thanks for the tea."

"My pleasure."

The rain had diminished to a light drizzle. Gabe drove her back in the sleek silver Porsche that was parked next to his Range Rover. When he pulled into Gramsy's, Angel saw Bernadette at the front living room window. She could only imagine what was going through Bernadette's mind as she witnessed Gabe opening the door for Angel and offering his hand to help her.

Bernadette opened the front door before they did. She looked closely at Angel. "Is everything okay? Why are you limping?"

"I'll tell you inside," Angel said. At that moment, a Jeep pulled into the driveway behind Gabe's Porsche.

"It's Ross," Bernadette said, her face lighting up. "With pizza."

They watched as Ross climbed out of his Jeep with two large pizza boxes and a gift bag. "Everyone come in," Bernadette said. "I'll introduce you inside."

Ross smiled at Angel and Gabe and entered first, handing the pizzas to Bernadette. Gabe turned to Angel.

"I'll say goodbye, Angel. I want to talk with you about a few other things Gramsy shared with me, but it can wait until tomorrow." He gestured at his Porsche. "You'll have to tell Ross to kindly move his Jeep."

Bernadette reappeared and heard him. "There's plenty of pizza for all four of us. Come on, you guys. Let's eat it while it's hot."

Gabe glanced at Angel.

She snapped out of her thoughts. The least she could do was to invite him in. "Yes, of course. You're welcome to join us, Gabe."

Bernadette nodded and went back in.

"After you," Gabe said, gesturing with his hand.

Angel stepped forward, faltering at a sharp twinge in her calf.

Gabe immediately reached out to encircle her and prevent her from falling.

Angel felt another twinge, only this one was closer to her heart.

Bernadette introduced Ross to Angel and Gabe, and after Ross expressed his sympathies to Angel, Bernadette ordered him and Gabe to sit and chat in the living room while she had a word with Angel in the kitchen. From Bernadette's frown, Gabe could see that she was reacting to Angel telling her about her leg injury.

A few minutes later, Angel joined them in the living room, choosing to sit at a recliner. Bernadette brought out plates and the pizzas, and set them on the large rectangular coffee table between the two couches. She asked Ross to fill the glasses on the island with the wine he had brought.

"Cheers, everyone." Bernadette raised her glass. Everyone leaned forward to clink glasses with each other. "Let's toast to Gramsy."

Gabe caught Angel's gaze and held it. "To Gramsy." He wondered if this would incite fresh tears, but this time Angel just smiled briefly at him and nodded. When everyone had helped themselves to pizza, he reached for a couple of slices of the Pizza Bianca, with its "white" sauce of olive oil, cheese and fresh rosemary.

"Mmm, this is really good. Maybe I should consider opening another restaurant that just serves pizza," he chuckled.

"Do you remember the first time Gramsy let the three of us help her make pizzas?" Bernadette said, gazing from Gabe to Angel.

Gabe and Bernadette exchanged a look and then burst out laughing. They were both the same age, and Angel would have been seven and they ten at the time.

"Gramsy left us to join Gabe's parents and my grandma out on the back patio. Gabe started to brush the sauce onto the first pizza and I was in charge of the second pizza. *You*—" Bernadette pointed accusingly at Angel "—started sampling the ingredients, popping a mushroom into your mouth, and then a slice of pepperoni, and on and on."

"And when I told you to stop eating all the ingredients on the pizza, you took offense and decided to dab my face with the brush," Gabe said, smirking. "I called you a brat—teasingly, of course—then Gramsy came in and you played the innocent. Just like now."

Everyone laughed as Angel's mouth dropped and she

crossed her arms, raising her chin in defiance. "I object to my childhood reputation being tarnished in such a manner." She sniffed and reached over to get the last piece of the Pizza Bianca at the same time he did.

"You can have it," Gabe told her, his lips twitching.

"Is that your way of finally making up for calling me a brat?" She took a bite and stared at him, her eyes narrowing.

Gabe couldn't help chuckling. "Okay, let's go with that." He picked up his glass of wine on the coffee table, and as he was swirling it, he could feel the relaxed vibes in the room. The shared memories and laughter had obviously helped set a lighter tone to the evening. It was good for Angel to have moments like this to help balance the more difficult and grief-filled occasions that were sure to arise.

For him, too.

The loss of Gramsy hit him at different times. She had truly been family to him. He hadn't had the chance to tell Angel how much Gramsy had meant to him, but he would when the time was right. When they were alone. Right now, the four of them were at ease with each other and with sharing a meal. The thought occurred to him to treat them to dinner at his place or his restaurant. He smiled, remembering something Gramsy had mentioned to him over the years: *I love my friends and cooking for them, and my friends can always feel that love in my cooking.* That love extended also to Gramsy's B&B guests, whom she treated like family.

The thought of family choked him up. Even though he had just met Ross and hadn't seen Angel for ten years, Gabe felt a closeness with the group. A familiarity, with Gramsy at the heart of it.

He looked up and realized he was alone in the room with

Angel. Bernadette and Ross were in the kitchen, Ross leaning over the island while Bernadette made coffee. Angel was looking at him quizzically.

"I'm sorry," he said huskily. "My mind wandered off for a moment." He glanced at his watch. "I should probably head back home."

Bernadette heard him from the kitchen. "Oh no, not until you have dessert, Gabriel McKellar." She lifted up a tray. "I made these especially for Angel, even though it's nowhere near Christmas."

Gabe lifted his eyebrows. "Pork pies? How can I resist? One of Gramsy's specialties." They were one of his favorite traditional Cape Breton desserts that usually surprised tourists with their misnomer. Gramsy always made some for him during his summer visits, and of course at Christmas these past three years. It was rare for him to only have one or two of them. His mouth watered just at the thought of the buttery tarts with their filling of dates and brown sugar, and a creamy maple frosting on top.

"I'll make tea for anyone who wants it, Bernie," Angel said, getting up.

"You sit down, miss. Ross and I can handle it. Besides, you have a boo-boo. Sit down and relax."

Angel threw up her hands. "I'm not helpless," she protested. "I can still walk." She sat back down and shook her head at Gabe. "She's so bossy," she murmured.

"I heard that!" Bernadette called out.

"I love you," Angel returned with a grin. She gazed back at Gabe, and for a moment, her words seemed to linger in the air between them. Then she looked down and brushed something Gabe couldn't see off the couch.

A few moments later, they were all back in the living room, having tea or coffee and oohing and aahing over the pork pies. Ross was the first one to leave shortly after, explaining that he had an early meeting with another Realtor whose client was interested in a summer property on Cape Breton Island. Bernadette walked him to the front door and their murmurs and brief silence before the door clicked open seemed to intensify the awkward silence now between him and Angel.

Bernadette came back and gave them both a parting hug. "I have the early shift tomorrow," she said. "Try to get a good sleep, Angel. Bye, Gabe."

After she left, he turned to Angel. "Now that I've been fed and fortified, I think I'll call it a night, too."

Angel hesitated a moment before nodding and he couldn't help wondering, from the uncertainty in her gaze, if she wanted him to stay a bit longer.

Like he did.

CHAPTER EIGHT

Angel unwrapped the gauze bandage around her calf. The cut was no longer bleeding but she placed a fresh bandage over it before returning to her bedroom. She sat on the edge of her bed and pulled back the quilt and top sheet.

Tonight she didn't feel as bereft. Being with Bernadette and meeting the guy that was putting stars in her eyes had distracted Angel from the heaviness of her grief. Ross had been kind and attentive, and genuine, as far as Angel could see. He hadn't seemed like a stranger at all. Angel couldn't wait to tell Bernie how happy she was that they had found each other.

And what about Gabe?

In less than two days, she had experienced a flurry of emotions in his company. Irritation and confusion at their initial encounter, embarrassment at napping against him on the way to Gramsy's and a surge of grief and tears at the first sight of the house. This morning, surprise that Gabe made breakfast for her, and later, another wave of sadness and more tears, this time against his chest, for goodness' sake. And tonight, she even found herself laughing. The apprehension she'd felt at first at Gabe's joining them had dissipated as they sat around the coffee table, enjoying the pizza and easy banter.

There *were* a couple of times, though, when her and

Gabe's gazes had locked, albeit briefly, that she had felt something aflutter in her chest. Something familiar. Something that came and went almost immediately. Had she imagined it?

Perhaps it was just a physical reaction to the way he looked. Those teal-green eyes were not hard to look at. And it was certainly not hard to listen to him talk, with his deep Scottish brogue. The way he rolled those *r*'s.

Angel couldn't help wondering if he had a woman in his life. Three years ago, Gramsy had been excited to share that Gabe was moving permanently to the family estate on Chéticamp Island. Months earlier, she had expressed her sadness over his parents' death, and how bad she felt for Gabe. They had been good friends over the years, and she would miss their summer visits.

Gramsy had also added that it was a pity that Gabe not only had to deal with the loss of his parents, but also with the breakup with his fiancée. It was just about the time she had broken it off with the guy she had been dating for three months.

She had met Colin Baxter at the high school where he taught drama, and was director of the *Beauty and the Beast* production the school was putting on for the elementary schools in the north end of the city. Angel's kindergarten students loved the performance and on their way out, she thanked "Mr. Baxter" and told him that she hoped the school would continue to do such wonderful plays. He shook her hand, thanking her for the feedback, and Angel felt that the handshake lasted much longer than it should have. When he finally let go of her hand, she smiled, feeling awkward, and quickly shepherded her children outside and back into the waiting bus.

A week later, Colin called her school during lunch and

asked to speak with her. He asked Angel if she would be interested in meeting him. If she was, he would call her at the end of the school week. Angel hesitated at first and then said okay, trying to sound casual, but inside, her emotions were causing her heart to flutter and her cheeks to burn. She said nothing to her colleagues, though, reluctant to mix her personal life with her professional life.

The excitement of the anticipation of the first meeting and then the next, and the ones to follow, made the days and weeks pass quickly, with her and Colin getting together on either Friday or Saturday evenings for a date. As time went on, Angel wondered if he was going to introduce her to his parents. Missing her own parents, she was curious about Colin's family and mentioned it a few times to him. He promised Angel that she would eventually meet them, but something always seemed to come up to prevent this from happening.

The week before Christmas, on a Friday, Angel invited Colin for dinner at her apartment. She prepared a meal of his favorite foods: spaghetti and meatballs, Caesar salad and Key lime pie. Before dessert, he excused himself and while he was in the washroom, his cell phone dinged. On her way to get the pie, Angel happened to look down at his phone and froze when she saw the text: Are you going to be much later at school? Liam wants you to tuck him in.

She faltered, feeling as if she had just been punched in the stomach. She knew then why he kept procrastinating about meeting his parents.

When Colin came back to the table, Angel was still standing there.

"Is everything okay?" he said, coming over to kiss her on the cheek.

Angel stiffened and turned away. "You got a text," she

managed to say before starting to gather up the dishes on the table. *And a wife and kid.*

He frowned and left her side to pick up his phone. Seconds later, he turned to her with a sigh. "Look Angel, I can explain…"

She glared at him. "Don't bother. Now I get why you didn't want me to meet your parents. I feel sorry for your wife and your son. They don't deserve a person like you." She put up a hand when he opened his mouth. "Get out of my house, Colin. *Now!* I'm sorry I ever trusted you. And don't even *think* about calling me again!" And when he grabbed his jacket and was walking to the door, she called out, "I can see why you're in drama. You know perfectly well how to be two-faced."

After he left, the first thing Angel did was to block him on her phone and then she sank down on her sofa and let the tears flow. She felt betrayed, manipulated, used. And *stupid.* She barely slept that night, tossing and reviewing their dates together, and berating herself for trusting him. For falling for his charm, his good looks and his consideration of her—and his—work obligations during the school week, suggesting that a Friday or Saturday evening would work best for them both.

Angel held honesty in the highest order in a relationship and he had failed miserably on that count. She shuddered at the thought of how long their relationship might have continued if she hadn't seen that text.

She spent Saturday in her pajamas, ignoring the dishes still on the table. When she opened the fridge and saw the pie she had made for Colin, she wished she had taken it out and flung it at him. Sighing, she put on her dressing gown and brought it to the elderly couple in the next apartment, their eyes lighting up when they saw it.

How could she have been fooled for three months? She'd wondered for days. Had she missed other signs?

Yes, she had. Colin had been enthusiastic about an investment that had yielded him thousands of dollars, and he had encouraged Angel to buy in. She should have been more prudent in vetting the company, but she was busy with report cards, and she had blindly trusted Colin with her money. She vowed never to be so gullible in the future.

The loss of her entire contribution still rankled.

By the following Saturday after breaking it off with Colin, Angel vowed not to spend any more tears over him, and to focus on her job and the kids she loved to teach. After Christmas, she decided that once the school year was over, she would pursue her goal of taking additional qualification courses to increase her teaching options. This kept her busy for the last three summers. No time for dating.

Happy when she had finally reached her goal and completed her last course, Angel booked her flight to Halifax and didn't waste any time letting Gramsy know. Her happiness was short-lived when Bernadette called to tell her the sad news of Gramsy's passing.

Angel got into bed. She shut her eyes and made herself think of good memories of Gramsy. Ones that would make her smile or laugh instead of crying. Thinking about Colin had brought back bad memories. She wanted to forget him and just think about her beloved Gramsy.

Except that somehow, each good memory that her mind called up included Gabe in the picture.

Gabe bent his head against the wind as he strode to his Porsche, the rush of the waves of the nearby gulf even more audible in the still of the night. He breathed in the crisp air, never tired of the sound or scent of the ocean, no matter the season.

Despite the sad fact of Gramsy's absence, he felt that the tone of the evening had been upbeat, with the sharing of funny memories and good food. He liked the sound of Angel's laugh, and the fact that she could join in with the teasing remarks. He wondered how things would be now if their lives hadn't gone in different directions ten years ago.

Gabe was glad Bernadette was there tonight. He had always liked Bernadette, and over the years, he thought of her as being like a sister. There was never any pretense with Bernie, and her spirited—and sometimes mischievous—ways, at least when they were younger, made him think of the tales his mother told him when he was young about the fabled Cape Breton fairies that lived in a *sitean*, a fairy hill, where they enjoyed music and dancing. It was Gramsy who had actually told him, that first summer he had visited, that the name of nearby Inverness was actually "The Fairy Hill."

Gabe envisioned Angel as a more guarded fairy, but one that showed her strong spirit when she needed to, like when he had shown up at the car rental office and she demanded to know if he was a lawyer. She had a tender and sensitive side, too, openly displaying her grief over the loss of Gramsy.

At home a couple of minutes later, Gabe went into his office and rifled through a few envelopes to retrieve the letter he had received from Gramsy's lawyer, requesting that he and Angel meet with him once she arrived. Gabe had confirmed the appointment for the day after next, thinking that Angel needed a couple of days to herself before dealing with Gramsy's legal affairs. The letter briefly outlined Gramsy's wishes: that the lawyer disclose them in the presence of Angel and Gabe, and that, a week or so later, a small reception in her memory be held at her B&B for her closest friends. The lawyer would provide more details at the meeting.

Gabe actually knew a little more than Angel did, simply because Gramsy hadn't wanted to distract Angel during her teaching and summer courses, talking about her will. He and Gramsy had become very close, especially in the last three years since he moved back to Chéticamp Island. Gramsy had told him often that he had always been like a grandson to her, that he had helped her in countless ways over the years and that his concern for her and his not-so-subtle checking up on her to see if she was okay had warmed her heart. She always looked forward to having tea with him in the afternoon before he headed to his restaurant, and she would inevitably serve him whatever she had made for the B&B guests, whether it be scones, muffins or a piece of pie.

And, of course, she'd always mention Angel, her eyes lighting up when she'd declare that she loved Angel to the moon and back. After Gramsy's stent procedure, she told Gabe that she was thinking about the future and what to do with her B&B after she passed, and she earnestly hoped that he and Angel would be on board with her wishes. And if they weren't, she said, laughing mischievously, she would have to enlist the help of the fairies over in "Fairy Hill" to get them to see it her way. Gabe felt a wave of sorrow grip him. Gramsy was the closest person to him besides his parents, and at moments like this, thinking about times they had spent together and the trust she had put in him, the grief he felt would resurface. His grief for his parents had been overwhelming, especially in the first year after their tragic passing, but in the last two years, it had been tempered by the love and caring Gramsy had shown to him. And now that she was gone, he felt her absence deeply. If he had felt like an orphan three years ago, he felt that same sentiment now.

Gabe strode across his room to the large bay window overlooking the waters of the gulf. This fresh grief brought back memories of how alone he felt when his fiancée left. Charlotte had been unable and unwilling to deal with his lingering sadness over his parents' senseless death. Since moving to the island, he'd had plenty of time and space to process their relationship, and to see the cracks that had been there from the beginning. He could understand that he had been partially responsible, having put up an emotional wall between him and Charlotte, sensing that she was incapable of truly understanding what he was going through, as she had never lost anyone in her family. He was willing to take the blame for that, but he didn't regret it, because it had allowed him to see that Charlotte lacked the empathy and compassion he needed at the time. She couldn't deal with his heartbreak and with having to give up their social activities to "dwell in this dark place" he'd found himself in.

It was a blow at first, and it felt like the world was crumbling around him. Hearing a few weeks later from his sous-chef that Charlotte was seeing someone anew, Gabe felt the yoke of guilt slide off his shoulders. She was not the right person for him, never had been, and even though it had taken a tragedy for him to see that, he was relieved that it was over.

Yawning, Gabe headed for his bed. He would give Angel a call tomorrow and arrange a time where they could talk. *Alone.* He needed to at least share with her what Gramsy had told him. She had a right to know, and then they would be on a level playing field going into the meeting with the lawyer.

Gabe felt the gulf breeze from his open window fanning his face and upper body. Breathing deeply, he closed his eyes and thought about Angel, most likely trying to get to sleep herself.

"Sweet dreams, Angel," he murmured. "I'll see you tomorrow."

CHAPTER NINE

Angel woke up to the sound of a text. She reached over to grab her phone and squinted at it. *Gabe*.

Good morning, Angel. I was wondering if you might want to take a drive around and see what's changed in the area. And…we can talk more about a few things before the meeting with the lawyer tomorrow.

Angel sat up and stared at the phone for a few moments.

Angel? Are you there?

Uh, yeah, sorry, I just woke up and…and I'm not fully functioning until I have my first coffee.

Oops, sorry to interrupt your sleep.

That's okay.

Can I call you instead of texting?

Um…okay.

Seconds later, she answered Gabe's call. "Hello again."

"Hi. I hope you don't mind me calling. I prefer to hear a human voice, either by phone or in person."

Angel's thoughts flew to the text she had seen on Colin's phone. "I agree, actually. Although a text can be very illuminating about a person."

"And subject to interpretation," Gabe said. "Communicating with someone face-to-face is always the best option, whenever possible. So, do you—"

"Sure," she said lightly. "You can come by in half an hour?"

"Will do. I'm just near the end of my jog. I'll be there after my shower."

"Um…okay. If I'm not ready, just let yourself in. And you might as well make me a coffee."

In the shower, Angel wondered what had gotten into her, taking such a sassy tone with Gabe. She liked his unchecked reaction: that deep laugh, and even though she couldn't see it, she imagined the look of surprise in his eyes. Knowing he was showering at the same time she was gave her a funny feeling. And why did she feel shivers of anticipation running through her under the hot shower spray? *Did Gabe feel some kind of anticipation, too?*

She rinsed the rose-scented lather off her body and stepped out onto the plush bath mat. She dried herself briskly with an oversize towel, replaced her leg bandage with a new one and then wrapped the towel around herself while drying her hair.

Afterward, Angel opened the bathroom door tentatively. The welcome scent of percolating coffee wafted up the stairs. *Just like when Gramsy was alive.* Somehow it made her feel that Gramsy would approve.

She inhaled deeply and then dashed into her room to get

dressed. She decided on a pair of black jeans and a soft, sky blue pullover. She gave a last glance at herself in her dresser mirror, decided to add a touch of blue eye shadow and then, ignoring her unmade bed, headed downstairs.

Gabe looked up, the coffeepot in his hand. He continued to gaze at her while she descended and arrived in the kitchen, sitting at the island opposite him.

"Good timing, Angel." He smiled, pouring her a cup. "And good morning. Your cut is better, I hope?"

He had selected two mugs that Angel had bought for Gramsy at a local pottery studio. Each was a swirl of blues and white, evoking for her the image of the waves of the gulf, tinged with the foam of whitecaps.

"Good morning," she said, "and yes, my leg's better." She took a sip of her coffee. "Thanks for indulging me. It always—"

"Seems to taste better when someone else makes it," he laughed. "Is that a not-so-subtle hint for me to indulge you with breakfast, too?"

Angel shook her head, feeling a warm rush in her cheeks. "Not at all. I wouldn't have such lofty expectations."

He raised an eyebrow.

"I'm happy with a coffee to get me going. And then, maybe in a bit, we can stop for brunch or lunch somewhere."

"Of course." Gabe's eyes crinkled as he smiled. "Gramsy mentioned once or twice that she always made sure you were well-fed, or else—"

"Or else what?" Angel frowned, crossing her arms.

That laugh. Again.

"'Or else your usual angelic temperament might change.'

Her words, not mine," he said defensively, holding out his hands.

"Really!" Angel said imperiously, raising her chin. "What else might dear Gramsy have told you about me?"

"Do you really want to know? And remember, I'm just the messenger."

"Spill!" she said sternly, narrowing her eyes.

Gabe sputtered as he was drinking his coffee. He swallowed quickly and struggled to keep a straight face.

"Who *are* you?" she demanded, trying to restrain herself from smiling. "And what kind of details would my beloved Gramsy disclose to you?"

Gabe hesitated as he stared at her, tapping a finger over his lips. "It's all good, I promise," he said finally, a gleam in his ocean eyes. "You're smart, you're beautiful, you're a good cook, you're a great teacher, you're kind, you're—"

"Enough!" Angel put up a hand. "I don't need to hear any more." She looked down at her coffee. "I'll finish this and then we can go."

Angel's cheeks had turned pink, reminding Gabe of Gramsy's summer peonies. They looked just as soft as the petals, too. She looked up suddenly and their gazes locked. She *was* beautiful, and from her reaction, he wondered if perhaps she wasn't used to hearing an avalanche of compliments. Or maybe it made her uncomfortable because *he* was saying the words.

Minutes later, they were passing the bluffs, the grasses mingled with white, pink and yellow wildflowers swaying in the wind. The Porsche's windows were down, and Angel was transfixed on the view, her hair flying up around her and the scent of her floral perfume tickling his nose.

They passed Chéticamp Island Beach and Gabe put on

some relaxing classical music, sensing that Angel did not want to be distracted from the views as she reconnected with the island. As he drove along Chéticamp Island Road, he decided to take the Cabot Trail north. He never tired of the stunning views of the North Atlantic Ocean and the impossibly steep cliffs and woodland promontories on Cape Breton Island's northwest coast. Knowing that there was a chance of showers in the afternoon, he wanted Angel to enjoy the trail in its full splendor while the sun was out. He would suggest going to Inverness that evening.

When Angel rolled up her window a while later, he did the same. "This is God's country," she murmured. "I've missed it. The wind, the waves, the heights. *Everything.*"

From his occasional glances in her direction, he could see that she was enjoying not just the views, but the music, too. When Pachelbel's Canon in D came on, she paused from her sightseeing to smile at him. "One of my favorites," she said, before leaning back in her seat, occasionally closing her eyes and swaying gently to the melody.

As he headed toward Pleasant Bay, Gabe turned off at a lookout point. "I thought we could stop and enjoy the scenic view from here for a few minutes. Shall we?"

He stepped out and went around to open Angel's door.

"Thanks," she said and walked to the guardrail. "Absolutely breathtaking."

Gabe watched her as she scanned the sky—now streaked with white wisps—and the massive woodlands jutting into each other, with the Gulf of Saint Lawrence visible between their clefts. A bald eagle, with its distinctive white head, soared majestically across the sky in the distance. "Breathtaking indeed," he said as she turned and caught his gaze.

"This is so different from living in the city," she said. "So calm."

"Would you ever move here from Toronto?"

"I'd lose my seniority." She shrugged. "But I do recall a teacher on my staff moving to the west coast, and saying that she'd lose her seniority, but her experience would be recognized for salary purposes."

"Gramsy mentioned you taking extra courses these past three summers. Was it to get your principal's designation?"

Angel laughed. "No, no, no. I *love* being in the classroom. I was taking additional qualification courses, namely, advanced French immersion in order to get my Certificate of Bilingualism. Which I *did*."

"Félicitations, Ange! Sois fière de toi-même."

Surprise flashed across her face at his "Congratulations, Angel. Be proud of yourself." "*Merci beaucoup*," she replied with a smile. "Your French is good."

"I've learned a few select phrases since moving permanently to Chéticamp Island, with its French Acadian heritage," he chuckled. "I'm getting better. I should keep practicing, though."

"*Mais, oui, monsieur*," she said teasingly.

They both laughed, and the way Angel's eyes were sparkling in the sunlight made something catch in Gabe's chest. "Okay, let's continue on, *mademoiselle*. I don't know about you, but I'm thinking we should stop for a bite soon."

"Sounds good," Angel said. "I just want to take a couple of photos first."

Gabe nodded and opened her door before getting into the driver's seat. He smiled as he saw her taking a selfie against the backdrop of the highlands and gulf.

As he continued driving a few minutes later, Gabe couldn't help thinking how remarkable it was that sadness and happiness could coexist. He and Angel were both grieving the loss of Gramsy in their own way; yet, they had managed to experience moments of happiness and beauty.

Together.

Being with Angel was so different from being with Charlotte. He hadn't observed any sign of an inflated ego, or a sense of entitlement. And he hadn't seen any evidence of snobbery or pretension, being from a big city. Angel was simply being herself, as she had always been in the past... "Oh, there's the Rusty Anchor!" Angel said, pointing. "My mouth is watering, just thinking about the food I had there with Bernadette the last time I was here, before doing the whale cruise tour."

"Lunch there, then?" Gabe laughed. "It'll be breakfast, too."

"Let's do it! I'm starving."

"I've never been disappointed with any of the restaurants I've been to on the island," Angel said. "The fish and chips are the best, wherever you go." She bit into a sweet potato fry. "Mmm-mmm."

"I agree," Gabe said. He'd ordered the same, "Cape Breton Style Fish & Chips." "Since we're talking about delicious restaurant food, I'd like to invite you to my restaurant tonight."

"In Inverness?"

Gabe nodded, his lips twitching. "We can fly to my restaurant in Scotland another time." He looked around. They had arrived before lunch and although only a few tables were occupied, he knew that soon the restaurant would be filled with tourists dropped off by bus during their tour of the Cabot Trail. Now would be the best time to talk to Angel about Gramsy's wishes. "Coffee and dessert, Angel?"

"Oh yeah," she laughed. "I spotted strawberry shortcake on the menu."

"Perfect. I'll have the same."

After the waitress took their order, Gabe leaned forward. "Angel, are you okay with discussing Gramsy's wishes?"

Angel sighed. "I have no choice, really. Look, I know Gramsy trusted you as a friend and neighbor. And she really did think of you as a grandson, Gabe. So—" she gazed at him steadily "—I want to hear whatever you have to tell me."

"Okay. First of all, you are Gramsy's only heir, and so her entire estate, including the B&B, goes to you. She told me this about a year ago."

"But she didn't think it important enough to tell me," Angel murmured, frowning.

"She didn't want you to worry needlessly. And she wanted to be proactive about her decisions. Decisions that would impact your life."

"Well, I'll have no choice but to sell the B&B," she said, her face slumping into her hands. "I can't just pick up and move to Cape Breton Island."

Gabe surveyed her for a few moments. "Would you sell it to me?"

CHAPTER TEN

"What? Really?" Angel blinked. "What would you do with it?"

"I can think of a few things. For one, I could keep it as a guesthouse for any out-of-town chefs in training for my restaurant in Inverness. Or I could keep it running as a B&B in honor of Gramsy, after hiring the right people to handle the various responsibilities."

Angel was stunned. "Wow. I don't know what to say."

"You don't have to say anything right now, Angel. I know it's a lot to take in. I just want you to know that you have options, and whatever you ultimately decide to do, I'm here to support you. And I'll be with you at the lawyer's, as per Gramsy's request."

Gabe's eyes held concern, as did his voice, and yet, Angel felt a sudden surge of anxiety. And pressure. It wasn't Gabe's fault; he was just presenting the reality of the situation. It was just too much to think about right now. The drive so far on the Cabot Trail had been a distraction, keeping her mind off her grief over Gramsy's passing, and subconsciously, it must have been a welcome coping mechanism. But like it or not, she had to accept that Gramsy was gone, and that these practical matters had to be dealt with. By *her*.

Something didn't sit right with her about the situation.

She picked at her fries, unable to look at Gabe directly. He wanted the B&B. Is that why he had been so pleasant and accommodating with her? Perhaps he thought that if their friendship of the past were to resume, he could get a better deal when she sold it to him.

The memory of Colin swindling her gave her a sinking feeling in the pit of her stomach. Perhaps he hadn't even invested the money and used it for himself instead. He had shown up one evening wearing a Rolex watch, and although he said it was pre-owned, the price he paid must still have been exorbitant…

She couldn't be sure about him, and now she couldn't be sure about Gabe's motivations. How could she trust Gabe, anyway? On her sixteenth birthday, he had told her he had feelings for her after he had given her the shell and gold chain. She had believed him but the sweet promise of a relationship in the future faded after he returned to Scotland and she to Toronto.

Gabe finished his degree in business and then was accepted into a prestigious culinary academy, a dream he had always had. Angel pursued her dream of becoming a teacher. They exchanged emails for a while, both apologizing for the lapses of communication, but eventually those dwindled while they each fulfilled their passions.

And sadly, the spark they had felt on the beach never progressed to a flame. How could it, with the ocean between them, and Gabe not being able to return to the island for years? All she was left with were the memories of his kisses and his gift.

Angel inhaled and exhaled deeply. Gramsy had obviously trusted Gabe, but could she? In one way, she was dreading the meeting with the lawyer, simply because it would be one step closer to the limited time that she had on the island to deal with things before flying back to her life in Toronto.

She stifled a sob just as the waitress arrived with their coffees and strawberry shortcakes. The restaurant was suddenly swarming with a tour group chatting excitedly as they settled at a number of tables. Neither she nor Gabe talked while they ate, and after a few bites, Angel put down her fork. "I'll have to take this home."

Home. Funny that she would call it that. She had never thought of it as *her* home. Yes, it had been her home away from home for a few weeks every summer since as far back as she could remember, but it was always Gramsy's home. And now it was her temporary home while she settled Gramsy's affairs.

Gabe called their waitress over to pay the bill.

As soon as they were both in the Porsche, Angel turned to Gabe. "Thanks for lunch and…for the drive. I'd like to go back to Gramsy's now." She wanted to be alone. Alone to think, to cry and to think some more about the future of the B&B without Gramsy. And without *her*.

Gabe raised an eyebrow and was about to say something, then just nodded.

After driving for about twenty minutes, he glanced briefly at Angel. "I'm sorry if I upset you, talking about the future of the B&B."

Angel bit her lip. "I know I have to face the reality of the situation. I just got overwhelmed."

"That's understandable, Angel," he said. "It's a lot to take in." He paused to concentrate on the road as a series of transport trucks zoomed by.

Angel studied Gabe's profile. He had a straight nose and strong jaw, his trim sideburns connecting with his sculpted beard. His mustache was impeccably trimmed above his lips. He was a man who obviously cared about his appearance. *And there must be plenty of women who cared about his appearance also.*

"*Stop it*," she told herself, and when Gabe turned to her with raised eyebrows, she realized that she had actually spoken.

"Sorry," she blurted, feeling her cheeks burn. "I wasn't talking to you."

Gabe pulled over onto a side street and parked. "Angel, I think that we should postpone dinner at my restaurant. Save it until after the lawyer's meeting tomorrow, or another day. Why don't you take the rest of the day and evening to relax. We can talk tomorrow."

Angel met his steady, blue-green gaze. She didn't want to go out for dinner at Gabe's restaurant—at least, not tonight—but on the other hand, she wanted to know more about his interest in Gramsy's B&B. "I think we should postpone it, too. I would rather stay home and talk more there." She heard Gramsy's voice telling her on more than one occasion to give people the benefit of the doubt. She should at least hear Gabe out, listen to what he had to say with an open mind.

Gabe nodded. "Okay, then, Angel. How about I whip up something for dinner and we can talk more after that. Since my fridge and pantry are stocked, why don't you come over to my place?" His eyes crinkled at the corners as he smiled. "I make a mean lobster mac and cheese. It's one of my favorite comfort foods."

Angel blinked. Lobster mac and cheese was one of *her* favorite foods. In fact, Gramsy always made it for her on the first and last day of her yearly summer visit. *Had Gramsy shared this information with Gabe on one of his visits to her place for tea?* She eyed him suspiciously. "Did Gramsy tell you—"

Gabe laughed. "She did. But she also made it for me a few times when I was young, after I finished some chores or errands for her. And eventually, she showed me how to make it. I must have been twelve. Now I make it at least once or twice a month." He cocked his head at her. "What do you say? I can stop at Chéticamp Fisheries on the way home."

Angel's eyes widened. "My mouth is watering already. I'd be crazy to pass up a chance to have lobster mac and cheese. What can I bring?"

"Yourself and your appetite," he laughed. "Nothing else. Okay, that's settled. *Allons-y?*"

"*Oui*, let's go."

Gabe's smile lingered as he drove back onto the Cabot Trail and headed south to Chéticamp. "Mind if I put on some music again?"

"Not at all," Angel said. She settled back in her seat and closed her eyes as the mellow notes of a harp gently broke the silence. She had always loved the relaxing effects of Celtic music, and often listened to it while meditating or doing yoga exercises. And often, after returning from a hectic drive in rush-hour Toronto traffic, she unwound by running a hot bath with rose or lavender-scented Epsom salts, and listening to one of her favorite Celtic CDs. She found the harp melodies especially soothing, and when she couldn't sleep for nights after discovering Colin's duplicity, she played the tunes in a loop until finally succumbing to sleep.

Gabe's smooth driving, combined with the peaceful music, gave Angel a sense of calm, making the previous wave of overwhelm she had experienced begin to dissipate. As she felt the tension in her shoulders lighten, her eyes opened, connecting with Gabe's. He turned his attention quickly back to the highway, but not before Angel noticed the gentleness in his gaze.

A look that caused a warmth to spiral through her body and her heart to melt a bit, despite her intentions of staying on guard. Since Colin, she had kept her heart locked, frozen to any possibilities of a serious relationship. She closed her eyes again, hoping the heat in her cheeks wouldn't betray her feelings should he turn to look at her again.

What are your feelings? an inner voice whispered.
I like him.

Angel let out a long breath she had been holding in. Yeah, she liked him all right.

Gabe was glad Angel hadn't turned him down when he'd invited her to dinner at his house, although he would have understood if she had chosen to stay at Gramsy's, a place that held special meaning and memories for her. The fact that she wanted to talk more about the B&B was a good thing.

Her reaction at the restaurant had taken him aback at first, wondering if she had assumed the worst about his intentions. That he was trying to manipulate her in some way so that she would sell the B&B to him. He had felt a twinge of hurt, but with Angel's enthusiasm for his lobster dinner, his spirits had returned.

And he was more than happy to be able to cook for her. Cooking was his happy place, always had been. Sharing his culinary creations with others made him even happier. It was too bad that cooking for Charlotte hadn't quite given him the warm fuzzies he expected. She had preferred to dine in his restaurant rather than having him cook for her at his place. It had puzzled him at first, but as the months went by, he realized that she needed to be in public to be noticed, and to notice people noticing *her*. Being the girlfriend and then the fiancée of the Michelin-starred chef Gabriel McKellar looked good on her and she wanted to be seen with him at Maeve's, and out and about in general.

Gabe was not exactly a recluse, but socializing six days out of the week was a bit much. More than a bit much. He didn't like the pressure he was starting to feel with Charlotte expecting him to end his evenings at his restaurant with an alternating group of her friends, friends she had invited to dine there. Of course, he was grateful to her for recommending Maeve's to her associates, but after the intensity of working with his crew to prepare his signature dishes night after night to a clientele that expected the best, all he wanted to do was to go home and relax.

He glanced quickly at Angel. She seemed more relaxed now, her lips curved in a slight smile, her fingers moving with the harp strains. His gaze reverted to traffic, but the image of the soft curve of her lips kept breaking into his thoughts.

He forced himself to think about the dinner he'd be making. The only thing he needed to pick up was the lobster. The fresh-catch season was actually over, but customers could still obtain them from local distributors during the year, as the lobsters were kept in holding tanks. As a restaurateur, Gabe made lobster dishes that were renowned not only on Cape Breton Island, but throughout the Maritime Provinces. He was proud to support the local island fishermen who worked to ensure the ethical and sustainable practices of lobster harvesting.

His restaurant in Inverness was packed every evening except Sunday and Monday, when it was closed. There were many return customers whose preferences ranged from his lobster chowder, chili and rolls to his Gramsy-inspired lobster mac and cheese. He was proud to feature traditional island dishes but also experimented with new creations, using local products and plants, many of which were grown in his year-round temperature-controlled greenhouse situated on his restaurant property.

He'd have to bring Angel there for a tour.

He stopped himself. Why was he thinking of making any kinds of plans with Angel? She wasn't here for a tour or anything of that nature. She was here for one reason only: to see Gramsy's last wishes honored. And, as the lawyer would explain in more detail tomorrow, to have a simple gathering of close friends at the B&B. Gramsy had confided in him that when she was gone from this "island paradise," she wanted a plain and simple send-off in her own home. *With my darling Angel and some of your cooking, dear Gabe, and fiddle music, of course.*

Gabe smiled at the memory but at the same time, he felt a prickle behind his eyelids. He was going to miss that funny, quirky, amazing, lovely, generous and affectionate woman who had become family to him. The best kind of family, with a heart as big as the hearth in her home.

He blinked hard and was relieved to see the Chéticamp Fisheries sign come into view. "We're here," he said briskly, and when Angel started, he apologized for his loud tone. "It doesn't exactly go with gentle harp music." He turned off the ignition. "Want to join me?"

Angel shook her head. "No, I'll just feel guilty seeing them in their tanks." She shrugged. "Better just to wait until you serve me your mac and cheese."

"Oh, *I'm* going to serve you, am I?" he teased.

She blinked, opened her mouth to say something and

then just laughed. "Well, since Gramsy isn't here to spoil me with her famous cooking, and *you* are probably the only person she shared her recipe with, I'm sure she would expect you to carry on her tradition and—"

"And spoil you?" He stroked his beard thoughtfully. "Hmm. I'll have to give this some serious thought." He flashed her a smile and got out of the vehicle. When he looked back as he was opening the door to the building, Angel was still looking at him.

And yes, she was still smiling, too.

CHAPTER ELEVEN

Angel watched as the door closed behind Gabe. She immediately pulled down the car visor to look at herself in the mirror. Just as she thought. Her cheeks were flushed a cranberry red. *She* was the initial cause, she acknowledged, with the silly words that had popped out of her mouth. *Better just to wait until you serve me.*

And he had just flown with it. The teasing glint in those ocean eyes and the flash of his perfect teeth when he smiled had ignited something inside her that she hadn't felt with anybody. Not even Colin. She flipped back the visor and took a deep breath in and out, hoping the flush would subside by the time Gabe returned to the Porsche.

Mercifully, Gabe focused his attention on driving for the rest of the way back to Gramsy's.

"Dinner at six okay?" he said as she turned to get out of the car.

"Sure," she said, nodding. "Um, why don't I bring dessert? I'm sure Gramsy's pantry is stocked."

His mouth twitched. "If you insist. Angel food cake, perhaps?"

Angel rolled her eyes. "Maybe devil's food cake would be more appropriate."

"Touché." He grinned. He glanced at the sky. "Looks like rain again. Shall I pick you up at five thirty?"

"Even if it does rain, I'm not made of sugar," Angel scoffed. "I'll walk over, thanks."

Gabe waited until Angel was inside before driving away. She checked the time and then the walk-in pantry. All the main baking ingredients were there, and when she peeked into the upright freezer in the pantry, her heart twinged to see all the containers and items Gramsy had made and labeled: half a dozen pie crusts, chili, seafood chowder, tea biscuits, blueberry scones, a variety of soups and breads and assorted meats, fish and seafood and poultry.

"Oh, Gramsy," she sighed, "I wish you were here with me." She closed the freezer door and walked to the built-in corner cabinet where Gramsy kept her various recipe binders.

All the binders would be precious keepsakes of Gramsy's legacy, her personal collection of tried-and-true recipes from over three decades. Angel wouldn't even think of returning home without them. She pulled out a pink binder labeled "Desserts" from the half dozen on the bottom shelf. Flipping through the pages of Gramsy's handwritten recipes, Angel stopped at one that caught her eye: butterscotch pie, and next to the title were the words *One of Gabe's favorites*. So the guy had a sweet tooth!

She scanned the list of ingredients and checked to see if she had all of them. *Okay, butterscotch pie it will be.* She returned to the freezer to take out one of the piecrusts and set it on the kitchen island before gathering all the ingredients for the filling and meringue.

It wouldn't take long to make, but it needed to cool down a couple of hours before serving. Which would take her close to the time that Gabe had indicated for dinner. *Perfect.*

Gabe was making a decadent lobster dish that *she* loved

and she would be making and bringing over a decadent dessert that *he* loved.

Angel flipped through more of the binder and saw many of Gramsy's notations, including *her* favorites and ones that the B&B guests particularly liked. Next to the title *Chocolate Pudding Cake*, Gramsy had written *Angel and Gabe loved it!* And she had drawn a heart around their names, with the date.

Angel's heart drummed gently. She had been eight then. And Gabe eleven. She stared at the heart around their names. Angel was glad that Gabe had been close to Gramsy. Not just distance-wise, but emotionally. It comforted her to know that Gramsy had enjoyed teaching Gabe how to cook, and that he had shown his appreciation by naming his new restaurant after her.

And now he wanted to buy Gramsy's B&B.

Angie shook her head. Things were moving so fast, but she didn't want to think about it now. She flipped back to the butterscotch pie recipe. *Okay, Gramsy, let's hope I can make you proud...*

It wasn't as complicated as she first thought. She finished covering the pie with the meringue and slid it into the oven to bake for ten minutes.

Yes! It looked and smelled heavenly as she removed it and set it on the counter to cool. With a satisfied smile, she headed upstairs. She had plenty of time to have a shower or even a bath, and contemplate Gabe's query about selling the B&B to him.

It had never even occurred to her that he would be interested in buying Gramsy's place. And Bernadette hadn't mentioned anything of the kind, either. As Angel soaked in her lavender-scented bubble bath, she couldn't help feeling ambivalent about it. Selling it so quickly seemed somehow like a betrayal to Gramsy. *It should stay in the family.*

Angel sighed. Gabe *was* family for Gramsy. If *she* couldn't uproot and move to the island, then wouldn't selling it to Gabe make the most sense? She shivered and added more hot water so she could soak a while longer. Closing her eyes, she tried to imagine what it would be like to return to the island and *not* stay at Gramsy's. The property had been a part of her life for as long as she could remember. It would be bittersweet to leave it in someone else's hands. Even if it was Gabe.

And what if he followed through with keeping the place as a B&B? Who would run it? Cook and clean?

That's not your concern. But if he keeps it running, you'll have a place to return to.

Would she want to? Be a guest in a place that had been her home away from home?

Suddenly remembering that she had to refrigerate the butterscotch pie, Angel pulled the plug and stepped out of the bathtub. She tied her terry cloth robe around her and headed to the kitchen.

Moments later, when Angel was putting on the kettle for tea, the first fat plops of rain hit the kitchen window. The weather forecast of intermittent rain throughout the week was turning out to be true. She watched as it intensified. The views from this side of the house were so dramatic during a good storm. With her mug in hand, she walked to the living room and sipped her cranberry lemon tea while gazing at the waters of the gulf.

The rumbling of thunder and darkening skies leant a mysterious and romantic air to the place, Angel always thought, while the aroma of Gramsy's barley soup or crab cakes—or anything else, for that matter—permeated the whole house.

The memories that flooded her made her smile and at the same time brought a twinge of sorrow. There would be no more of Gramsy's cooking, no more treasured books, no more chats.

The sky seemed to darken even more at that moment, and when lightning flashed moments later in a stunning display, Angel knew the storm was about to get much worse. Again.

So much for walking over to Gabe's with the pie...

Gabe called Angel to tell her that he'd drive over to pick her up in a half hour. "I wouldn't want lightning to strike you or the dessert you've made," he said.

"I will graciously accept the ride," she said. "Unlike myself, my dessert *is* made of sugar."

He laughed. "Oh, I know at least one person who has referred to you as 'sweet.' In fact, I believe I heard her call you 'honey' a few times as well."

"Jeez, let me take a wild guess. Was it Gramsy?"

"You got it. And I think she was a pretty good judge of character," he added on a more serious note.

There was a long silence. "I better go and get ready, then," Angel said lightly.

"Okay, see you in two shakes of a lamb's tail."

He heard her laugh softly before hanging up.

Gabe strode into the kitchen to check the lobster mac and cheese casserole in the oven and then headed for the shower. He thought about how, in every exchange with Angel, something she said made him smile or laugh. He could still see the serious side of her, too, as serious as the eight-year-old who was determined to beat him in a race around the apple trees on Gramsy's property. She had some spunk in her, too. It was evident even when she was young, having the audacity to brush pizza sauce on his face.

After towel-drying his hair, Gabe changed into a pair of grey trousers and a light blue shirt. Casual and comfortable. Just like he hoped their dinner would be.

He checked the time, not wanting to keep Angel waiting. He put on an all-weather jacket and grabbed a golf umbrella in the entrance before dashing into his Porsche.

Moments later, he was at Angel's door under the oversize umbrella. Angel appeared in a bright yellow raincoat with a matching sou'wester hat and knee-high flower-designed rain boots. He couldn't help smiling, having seen Gramsy in that getup many times.

Angel's dessert was protected in a red plastic container that she was holding tightly. "Now you've captured my curiosity," he said, holding the car door open for her. "Can you give me a hint?"

"Hmm," she said, smirking. "Okay. Corn and liquor."

"Really? Let me think…a dessert made with corn and liquor?" He frowned. "I've been going through every dessert I can think of, and every dessert Gramsy made, and I'm coming up with *nada. Zilch.*" He turned into his driveway and turned off his Porsche's engine. He gazed at her quizzically. "Would you be so kind as to provide me with one more clue?"

Angel laughed. "Sure. Sea foam."

Gabe gazed at her for a moment. She looked so damn cute, grinning under that floppy hat. She looked like she belonged on the island. A true Acadian. He couldn't imagine Charlotte ever allowing herself to appear in anything so down-to-earth. If it wasn't recognizably designer, she steered clear away from it.

"Well? Have you figured it out?" Angel said, arching her eyebrows.

Gabe started. He had been staring at her. He wrinkled his nose. "I'm stumped."

A triumphant laugh. "All right, I guess I won't pick you as a partner on a game show. Okay, let's start with corn. Corn on the cob. What do you put on it?"

"Butter." Gabe narrowed his eyes. "Butter cookies! With rum!"

Angel made a harsh buzzer sound. "Not butter *cookies*."

Gabe stroked his beard. "Butter fudge?"

"No, silly. Think of a kind of liquor. *Your heritage*."

"Butter...butter scotch? Butterscotch!"

"Butterscotch *what*?" She cocked her head imperiously at him. "'Sea foam' is my last clue."

Gabe tapped his lips with his index finger.

Angel feigned an impatient sigh. "What looks like sea foam on top of butterscotch—"

"Meringue!" he said triumphantly. "It's butterscotch pie, right?"

"Finally!" she returned, rolling her eyes.

He grinned. "I'm in heaven. You're an angel, Angel."

Angel shook her head and covered her face with her hands before spreading her fingers to look at him. "And you're a goof," she said, and climbed out of the car.

Gabe laughed and followed her to the front door, not bothering to open up his umbrella. He'd have to change, but he didn't care. The rain was refreshing and the exchange he just had with Angel had felt so easygoing and *natural*. Her teasing had charmed him. Captivated him, as if time had stopped in the world around them so they could have these lighthearted moments together.

As they stepped inside his house, Gabe wondered if

Angel felt the same. He caught his reflection in the large foyer mirror and his lips twitched. His hair was plastered on his forehead and rivulets were running down his cheeks. Was it his imagination, or were his eyes unusually bright? And his senses were tingling in a way that he had never felt before. Including the sense that Angel was gazing at him curiously. "I'll take your rain gear," he said, holding out his hand.

She set down the dessert container on the foyer side table and handed him her raincoat and hat. She had dressed casually, too, with a pair of burgundy pants and a white cotton blouse with flared sleeves. He smiled at the sight of her multicolored polka-dotted socks.

Angel caught his gaze. "One of my junior kindergarten students gave them to me as a gift on the last day of school," she said brightly. "A little girl called Tessa. Her father said she saw them at the dollar store and wanted to get them for me." She laughed. "She chose seven pairs to last me the week. By the way, Mr. McKellar, I'm getting hungry and you're a wet mess."

Gabe glanced at the mirror. "I am, aren't I? I'll just go up and change," he said. "In two—"

"Shakes of a lobster's tail."

He burst out laughing. "Good one, Angel. Okay, make yourself at home. I'll be back in a few minutes to check the mac and cheese. Oh, and go ahead and put your 'corn liquor sea foam' creation in the fridge. By the way… It's one of my favorite desserts." Grinning, he leaped up the stairs two at a time.

CHAPTER TWELVE

Angel watched Gabe practically fly up the curving staircase, his hair and pant legs soaked. She shook her head and proceeded to saunter through the elegant foyer and spacious living area that connected to the kitchen and formal dining room. Angel breathed in the mouthwatering scent of the lobster mac and cheese and hurried to place her dessert in the fridge. Moving into the dining room, Angel saw that Gabe had set the table. A bottle of wine was chilling next to two goblets, and the elegant gold-rimmed tableware was a perfect match with the rest of the decor.

With nothing to do but wait for Gabe to return, Angel sauntered back to the living room and sat at one of the couches. She picked up a magazine on the coffee table and casually flipped through the pages until the heading of one article and the opposite page caught her attention.

"Michelin-Starred Chef Opens Mara's in Inverness."

She went on to read how Gabe had decided to return to Chéticamp permanently after losing his parents, and how his new restaurant paid homage to the French and Acadian history and culture, and featured his take on the traditional dishes of the area. The opposite page showed Gabe in his chef's hat and jacket, standing behind a table showcasing a number of his featured seafood and local dishes. The article explained how some of the dishes had their origins with the Indigenous Mi'kmaq peoples. She read on, and when she came to the paragraph explaining his decision to name his restaurant after Gramsy, Angel felt her eyelids prickle.

Everything came back to Gramsy.

Hearing Gabe's footsteps on the stairway, she hurriedly wiped her eyes and set down the magazine.

"I hope you're hungry," Gabe said, smiling as he joined her. His gaze flew briefly to the magazine before returning to her.

Angel nodded. "I almost started without you. That would have left you only with the butterscotch pie."

He laughed. "I should know by now to expect the unexpected to come out of your mouth. Now, let's head to the dining room so I can get some food into you."

Angel's gaze swept over him as he walked away. He had changed into black linen pants and a teal shirt with sleeves rolled up mid-arm. His hair was slightly damp, curling at his nape, and his eyes, matching his shirt, made her pulse quicken.

She followed him in, and moments later Gabe had poured the Chardonnay and they clinked glasses. "To Gramsy," he said huskily. He drank and set down his goblet. He gestured at her steaming plate. "Enjoy."

Angel savored her first mouthful and sighed. "I have missed this." She had a few more forkfuls and then paused to sip her white wine. Its delicate, citrusy tones paired perfectly with the creamy lobster meat, cheese and corkscrew-shaped pasta. "I'm sure Gramsy is smiling, wherever she is." She dabbed at her lips with her napkin. "Thank you, Gabe."

"My pleasure. There will be plenty left over for you to take home."

"Maybe," she said slyly. "Maybe not."

Another deep laugh.

"I can see now why Gramsy said she never had to worry about food going to waste while *you* were visiting."

Angel shrugged. "Her fault for making such delicious meals. And now I'll have to start making her recipes on my own," she added wistfully. "I'll need another suitcase to bring home all her recipe binders."

Gabe gazed at her for a moment. "Unless you reconsider and relocate *here*."

Angel finished swallowing another delicious forkful. "I can't see that happening. I have my job, my apartment, my friends…*everything* in Toronto. I don't really have a choice."

Gabe's brows furrowed. "Couldn't you get a teaching job here? Make new friends and have your friends from Toronto visit? From what I've experienced the couple of times I've been in Toronto, it's a pretty fast-paced existence."

"I'm used to it. Kind of," she said, her mouth twitching. "I'm north of the city. Downtown is another matter."

Gabe refilled her wineglass.

"Don't get me wrong," she sighed. "Living here would be a dream. I'll have to consider it when I retire."

"So you're fine with selling the B&B?"

Angel put down her fork. "Like I said, I don't have a choice." She gave Gabe a measured glance. "I thought about it more once I got home after lunch today. If I have to sell it to anyone, I might as well sell it to *you*. I'm sure Gramsy would approve."

"You don't think she'd prefer it if *you* stayed?"

Angel blinked. "Oh, of course. But it wouldn't be the same without her." She took a sip of her wine and looked up to see a sheen in Gabe's eyes.

"You're right," he said softly. "It won't be the same without her."

Angel felt a twinge in her heart. Up until now, she had only really thought about her own grief at losing Gramsy. But it was obvious that Gabe felt just as bereft without the woman who had been a grandmother to him. It hit her that they were united in their grief and she felt a sudden urge to comfort him. "I'm sorry for your loss of Gramsy, Gabe. She loved you."

Gramsy had never kept her feelings for Gabe a secret, and since his move to Chéticamp, those feelings had become stronger. Angel noticed Gabe's Adam's apple bobbing and he cleared his throat, visibly moved.

"And I, her," he said gruffly. He stood up. "Shall we move to the living room for dessert? I'll grab the pie."

Angel nodded and pulled back her chair. As she entered the living room, she turned to see Gabe pressing his fingers to his eyes before grabbing the oven dish with the remaining mac and cheese. His gesture of emotion made a rush of warmth spread across her chest. At the same time, it somehow made her want to cry.

She felt a twinge of guilt. Perhaps she had misjudged him and his intentions.

A couple of minutes later, Gabe entered with her pie, two plates and forks, and a pie server. He cut a generous wedge for both of them and then sat down next to her before taking his first generous forkful.

"This. Is. Amazing." He sighed and gazed at her appreciatively. "I'm in heaven." He proceeded to dig in again. "You're not taking home any pie leftovers," he said, his gaze both teasing and challenging.

She burst out laughing. "Go crazy, Gabe. Have it for breakfast."

"If there's any left by then," he said. "I might just help myself to a midnight snack."

Her lips twitched. He was like a little kid wanting to raid the fridge while everyone was sleeping. Only there was nobody else who was sleeping in the house with him. At least not regularly, as far as she knew. And he wasn't a kid. She pictured him getting out of bed, hair tousled and just wearing boxers, and heading to the fridge. "Wh-at? Sorry?" She started, her cheeks burning as she realized she had been daydreaming.

"I said, Angel, that the rain has stopped and the sun is breaking through the clouds. Feel like going for a walk on the beach to work off some calories? Not that you need to work anything off," he added quickly.

Angel wondered if it was wise to say yes. Did she want to be walking side by side with someone who had managed to pull on her heartstrings several times tonight? Just his suggestion now had made her pulse quicken. *Again.*

She really should say no, thanks and just go home. She could walk back. But as Angel met his gaze, something in those mesmerizing green depths made her knees feel weak. "Sure," she blurted before she could stop herself. And she said it a little too breathlessly for her own liking.

"I'll just put the leftovers in the fridge and take care of the dishes later," he said. "Let's go before the sun disappears. Get your stuff and we'll go out back."

A few minutes later, they were on the beach. The gulf waters were still active, cresting and collapsing, but the breeze was warm. He breathed in its salty scent and glanced at Angel, who was absorbed in scanning the beach in front of her for shells or stones washed up by the surf. He couldn't help smiling at the picture she made, wearing Gramsy's raincoat and boots. She had brought her sou'wester again, just in case. It dangled from her hand as she walked, her gaze intent on the beach sand. Occasionally, she bent down to pick up a shell, rinsing it at the edge of the surf before shaking it and putting it in her raincoat pocket. It was just like the collecting they had done in the past. Suddenly she shrieked as the surf rushed up her boots, and she tried to step out of it but the force of the waves knocked her back. He lunged forward to prevent her from falling, and as she fell against him, he circled her waist with his arms and held her firmly while the surf receded. The new and spicy scent of Angel's perfume wafted up to him with the breeze as strands of her hair brushed his jaw. For a few seconds, he felt a sensation that he hadn't felt for a long, long time. *Desire.* His heart pounded as she turned to regain her footing and he pulled her even closer.

Angel looked up at him breathlessly and the memory of their kiss on the beach on her sixteenth birthday came back to him, accompanied by a piercing regret that he had let his studies and ambition for culinary school take precedence in his life once he'd returned to Scotland. They were an ocean apart, and the fledgling communication they had initially with each other had eventually ceased.

Was Angel thinking about that time on the beach? The kisses that had kept him up that night? Looking at her intense brown eyes now, he wanted nothing more than to taste her kisses again. The sound of the incoming surf broke into his thoughts and they both leaped away from the water's edge to avoid the surge.

They continued walking silently, the sky darkening as clouds shifted to block the sun. Along with the rushing surf were the intermittent cries of seagulls and the warbling sounds of roosting cormorants. Gabe could kick himself that he had missed his chance with Angel long ago and he knew it was unrealistic to think that they could recapture those moments and start over. She would be leaving soon, and both their lives would go on, just like before. There was no denying his attraction for Angel, but he couldn't start something that would just be coming to an end shortly. The back of Angel's hand brushed his momentarily, and he had to stop himself from taking her hand in his. He jerked his hand away and felt like a heel when she caught his reaction.

"I better be getting back," she said abruptly. "But don't let me stop you if you want to keep working off those calories."

Gabe cursed silently, hoping she didn't think he had recoiled at her touch. "No, I'll head back, too. The lawyer's meeting is bright and early. I'll pick you up at eight thirty."

Angel kept a wider distance between them as they walked back. The wind had picked up and she put on her sou'wester and hurried ahead, her shoulders hunched. When they arrived at his place, Gabe asked her to wait for a moment while he grabbed his keys. "I was just kidding about keeping the rest of the butterscotch pie," he said. "I'll pack it up for you."

Angel put up her hand. "No, it's all yours. And no need to drive me, since it's not raining, and my leg is fine. Good night." She gave him a half smile before walking away. "Oh, and thanks for a great meal," she called out without turning to face him.

He *had* offended her. *Damn!* He watched her as she disappeared from view. It would be awkward if he tried to catch up to Angel and apologize. What would he say? That he had moved his hand away from hers simply because he actually *wanted* to hold her hand? Uh, no. It sounded ridiculous and inappropriate. She probably had enough on her mind with the upcoming lawyer's meeting. He didn't need or want to complicate things for her. There was no use even hinting to her about his feelings when she had been very clear that she would be returning to Toronto—

He shut those thoughts down and turned to go inside. He hoped that Angel would sleep well tonight, although he wasn't so sure *he* would.

CHAPTER THIRTEEN

Angel glanced sideways at Gabe as he drove. He had arrived at her door at precisely 8:30 a.m. She offered him coffee, but he politely declined, saying he had been up since five and had had his fill. He had shadows under his eyes and seemed less relaxed than previously, although he still opened the car door for her and made small talk about the weather.

"I hope you slept well?" He turned to gaze at her and she blinked in embarrassment.

"Uh, not bad," she lied. She had tossed, turned and tossed some more throughout the night, her thoughts alternating from the lawyer's appointment to the evening with Gabe. The dinner had been pleasant, the food delicious, but the way he had jerked his hand away from hers when they accidentally touched while walking on the beach left her with a strange feeling in her stomach.

She didn't know what to think. *He* was the one who had suggested they go for a walk. Was it normal for him to have that kind of reaction from his hand simply brushing against hers? She had been feeling mellow from the two glasses of wine she had enjoyed, one more than her usual, and when Gabe prevented her from falling and steadied her with his strong arms, she had felt lightheaded and her heart started beating erratically as his breath fanned her neck and the side of her face. She had almost wanted the moment to last longer.

Almost? an inner voice prompted.

Okay, so I was having a physical reaction to a guy who's freaking gorgeous and whose mouth was inches away from mine. That's perfectly normal.

Angel felt her cheeks burn. She pressed the lever to roll down the window and breathed in deeply.

"I can turn on the air-conditioning if you'd like," Gabe said.

"That's okay. I'd much rather the fresh Maritime air."

"Enjoy it while you can," he said, a husky edge to his voice.

"I wish I could bottle it up and take it with me," she sighed. "Along with some other things I love about this place…"

"Hmm," he said. "It will never leave you, even if you do go back."

If. Gabe hadn't said *when*. Was he thinking or even hoping that she would change her mind about relocating?

With a sinking feeling in the pit of her stomach, she drank in the views as Gabe drove, wanting to store them forever in her memory.

"Well, here we are, Angel. You'll like Tom. He's easygoing, honest, professional and will help in any way he can."

Moments later, Gabe introduced her to Thomas Applebee and she shook his hand warmly. "It's nice to meet you, Thomas, even under the circumstances."

"Please. Call me Tom, although your dear Gramsy insisted on calling me Tommy." He chuckled. "She was the only one I let get away with it." His smile faded. "I'm so sorry for your loss, Angel. We're all going to miss her." He gestured for her and Gabe to sit in the plush chairs opposite his large mahogany desk. His office was in a historic building that also housed a store featuring Acadian antiquities and a collection of artisanal Chéticamp hooked rugs.

Angel nodded. "Thank you. And thanks for all you did to help Gramsy with her legal affairs."

Tom gave her a grateful smile. "That's very kind of you. She did reward me generously with one of her delicious pies or loaves whenever we met." His mouth turned down. "She spoiled me."

"As she did all of us," Gabe said, nodding.

Tom opened up a portfolio and took out a document. "As you know in the letter I sent to both of you, Gramsy wanted you both at the reading of her will. If there's anything you want me to clarify as I go on, please let me know."

Tom waited until they both nodded and then pushed up his glasses before proceeding with reading the clauses slowly.

As Angel was Gramsy's sole living relative, she would inherit Gramsy's estate, with several expectations: that a donation be made every year to the cultural museum to keep the Acadian culture in the area alive; that a scholarship in her name be handed out by Gabe yearly at the Culinary Institute of Canada in Charlottetown; and that a reception for her be held at the B&B for her close friends and neighbors after the legalities of her estate were finalized.

Tom looked up from the document. "Gramsy wanted some time to go by before friends gathered. She wanted the mood to be celebratory and, quote, 'not a downer.'" He smiled but his eyes were sad. "She requested that you and Gabe receive friends informally at the B&B and not in a stuffy room at a funeral home. Friends could drop in and share memories and enjoy fiddle music and Gabe's cooking."

Angel wanted to cry and laugh at the same time. "I guess it's just as well that Gabe is in charge of the food," she said, her mouth twitching.

Gabe turned to her. "Hey, you can make the pie you made for us last night. Gramsy would love that."

Tom glanced from Gabe to her, his brows lifting.

"Um, I guess," Angel said, feeling the heat in her cheeks. She braced herself to ask Tom a question that had been niggling at the back of her mind. "In the letter you sent a couple of weeks ago, you said that Gramsy had wanted to proceed with…with the—" She choked up.

"With the cremation immediately," Tom finished sympathetically. "Those were her wishes, Angel." He reached out to put a comforting hand on her arm. "She wanted to make things as easy for you as possible." He glanced at Gabe. "And she had Gabe order an urn that she picked out herself online."

Angel met Gabe's gaze through blurred vision. "Gramsy was more forward-thinking than I thought."

Gabe held out the box of tissues on Tom's desk. "She sure was," he said gruffly.

"She ran the B&B with spreadsheets and had faithful followers on social media." He exchanged glances with Tom and then Tom said quietly, "I'll bring the urn to the B&B when you have the reception in her memory…"

At this point, Angel couldn't control the tears from spilling over her cheeks. She grabbed a few more tissues and wiped her eyes and face.

"Is there anything more, Tom?" she said, taking a deep breath.

"Yes, one more very important thing." He flipped a couple of pages before looking up. "Gramsy was aware that your life is in Toronto. She always dreamed that one day you might want to consider moving to Cape Breton Island and, specifically, Chéticamp Island. So, although she bequeathed you the B&B, she stipulated that, should you decide to sell it, that you give Gabe McKellar the first right of refusal, since she considered him family."

He paused, glancing from her to Gabe, letting them process the information.

"Okay, now here's what Gramsy added more recently. Knowing that you would certainly return to Toronto after the service, Angel, she would like you to rent it to Gabe for a year—if he's willing—while you have the year to think about it. That way, he can see if it will work out for him to buy it in the future, and you will have time before you make a permanent decision." He cleared his throat. "Gramsy didn't provide details, but simply said that the rent would help make up for a financial setback you unfortunately experienced a few years ago."

Angel felt her cheeks burn. She had told Gramsy about her failed investment with Colin. She took a deep breath. Would she be okay with Gabe potentially running the B&B for a year? She would have to be very clear about him upholding Gramsy's expectations on running the place. In any case, this arrangement would give her some breathing space and time to ultimately make a final decision. But would Gabe be willing to give it a go?

Tom tapped his pen against the document. "She said, and I quote, 'I love them both and I have every confidence that my Angel and Gabe will figure it all out.'"

Angel squeezed her eyes shut to prevent more tears from flowing. "This is a lot to think about. Do I...we have to decide and sign now?"

"No, of course not, Angel. Take your time." He handed her a business card. "Call or text when you're ready. Or if you have any other questions."

She nodded and stood up. "Thanks, Tom." She shook his hand and gave him a grateful smile. "I'll do that."

Gabe turned to Angel as she was putting on her seat belt. "Is there anywhere you need to go before heading back to the B&B? I'd be happy to drive you."

Angel's brows lifted. She checked the time on her phone. "Actually, I wouldn't mind if you dropped me off at Making Waves. Bernadette texted me this morning to meet her there for lunch. It's still a bit too early for that, but I can always grab a coffee while I'm waiting for her to go on her break. I have to think about everything Tom said." She turned away to gaze out her window.

"Sure." He drove out of the parking lot. "Angel, do you want to talk about the B&B? Just to clarify something… I had no idea that Gramsy would make that request of you."

Angel swiveled in her seat. "I think Gramsy meant well, but I think it just makes everything more complicated." She threw up her hands. "I just don't know what to do. I thought I would sell, and I would be fine with selling to *you*, but do I want to wait a year before things are settled? I'll be heading back to Toronto in less than two weeks."

Gabe pursed his lips. Angel really wanted to sell and be gone. *No strings attached.* He felt a twinge in his stomach. He, too, was puzzled as to Gramsy's conviction that he and Angel would "figure it out."

"I want to go back in a day or two to see exactly how Gramsy worded things in the will," Angel said decisively. "I'm sure there's an escape clause, or whatever you call it, so we don't have to wait a year to finalize things." With a hopeful smile, she leaned back and relaxed in her seat.

Moments later, the stylized sign bearing the words *Making Waves* appeared and Gabe turned into the restaurant parking lot. He had barely come to a stop and Angel already had her seat belt off. "Thanks for the ride," she said as she let herself out of the Porsche. She closed the door before he could reply and walked briskly toward the restaurant.

Gabe had hoped Angel would invite him to join her, at least for the time that she'd be waiting for Bernadette to get off for lunch. They could have talked more about Gramsy's wishes.

A couple of young adults walked by Gabe's silver Porsche and gave him a thumbs-up in admiration. He smiled and nodded and moments later drove out of the parking lot. It had been on the tip of his tongue to ask Angel if she'd like a ride back home, but she obviously had worked out something with Bernadette. It was early, but he decided he might as well head to his restaurant in Inverness.

The parking lot was empty when he arrived, but in a half hour or so, guests would be hard-pressed to find a vacant spot. Mara's was as popular at lunchtime as it was in the evening. He let himself in and grinned at the surprised looks from his sous-chef and staff when he strode into the kitchen.

"You can't stay away, eh, McKellar?" Chris Fox said teasingly as they moved into the dining room. Gabe had hand-picked him as sous-chef for Mara's after dining in a restaurant in Montreal where the young chef was getting acclaim for his traditional yet innovative dishes. After chatting with him several times and discovering that Chris was from Cape Breton, Gabe made him an offer to join him at Mara's. Chris jumped at the chance to return to the island, and since his return, had reunited with a high school girlfriend and married a year later. Customers had nothing but great things to say about him, and Gabe was grateful that their culinary paths had crossed and that now they were good friends to boot.

"You know I love you, Foxy," Gabe laughed. "Actually, I had business in Chéticamp and I thought I'd stop in for lunch."

"Well, make yourself at home." Chris smiled and glanced at his watch. "We open in exactly twenty-five minutes. Can I get you a coffee in the meantime?"

"No rush. I have things to mull over."

Chris eyed him closely. "Hmm. You sound serious. Does this by any chance have to do with the B&B and Gramsy's granddaughter?"

"You're a smart cookie, Foxy," Gabe said, shaking his head. "We'll chat about it another time."

Chris gave a mock salute and nodded, "Okay, boss. I better get back to the kitchen before the staff revolts."

Gabe strode over to a booth and slid to the spot near the window overlooking the seaside dunes and North Atlantic Ocean. The waves resembled flowing ribbons of blue-and-green silk along an endless golden beach. He never tired of taking in the panoramic beauty of this and countless other scenic spots on Cape Breton Island. He couldn't imagine any other place he'd want to live in.

Gabe shifted his gaze to the dining room with its gleaming mahogany bar and tables and plush tartan-upholstered booths. Large prints of scenic locations in the Highlands captured during various seasons graced the walls. His gaze rested on one scene of the Cabot Trail that reminded Gabe of the spot where he had stopped with Angel before stopping for lunch at the Rusty Anchor. The memory of Angel gazing in wonder at the view of the sweeping Highlands with the ocean backdrop caused a twinge in his chest. The sensation of knowing that she was as moved by the panorama as he was had somehow made him feel closer to her.

One of the scenes showed the Highlands in their brilliant autumn colors, the melding of red, orange and yellow resembling a rich carpet or quilt. People came from all over the world to see the stunning views of the Cabot Trail and Highlands throughout the year, but the epic autumn views were especially sought out.

He started as a waiter approached with a mug of coffee. "Thanks, Jeremy," he said, flashing a smile.

"Can I bring you a menu?" Jeremy said, his eyes twinkling.

"If I don't know my menu by heart by now, we're in trouble," Gabe laughed. "I'll wait for the official opening and just have a bowl of chowder and a couple of biscuits, and then I'll disappear until I'm back for my shift."

After Jeremy left, Gabe checked his phone. No messages. What was he expecting? A note from Angel? He inhaled and exhaled deeply. Why was he thinking about her so much? He took a drink of his coffee and then stared out the window again.

You don't want her to leave.

Gabe blinked. This random thought shook him. No, he *didn't* want Angel to leave. There was something about her, something familiar yet undiscovered, that was tugging at him like an invisible magnet. They had popped back into each other's lives again after ten years, their link being Gramsy and her property, of course, but now, with Gramsy gone, they both had only their memories, and the property.

Gabe started at the sound of people entering the restaurant. His thoughts were interrupted by approaching footsteps. He turned, expecting Chris or Jeremy with his seafood chowder, but the person a few feet away was the last person in the world he expected to see.

Charlotte, his ex-fiancée.

"Hi, Gabe," she said with a tentative smile. "I was hoping I'd catch you here…"

CHAPTER FOURTEEN

BY THE TIME Angel finished her cup of coffee, Bernadette had completed her morning shift. She set down the menu and gave Angel a warm hug before sitting across from her. "What do you feel like ordering, breakfast or lunch?"

Angel scanned both sides of the menu. "Hmm, let me see. What do you recommend?"

Bernadette laughed. "Everything! I'm surprised I haven't gained fifty pounds since I started working here!"

While they enjoyed Bernie's favorites—lobster roll and blueberry grunt—Angel filled her in on the meeting with the lawyer.

"Why would Gramsy want to make things more complicated?" she finished plaintively.

Bernadette shrugged. "I guess she wanted to give you a chance—and time, Angel—to consider making such a big decision in your life. And obviously, she trusted Gabe to look after the place until you ultimately decide. It's a win-win for both of you, really."

"But I don't have to wait a year to make up my mind. Much as I'd love to live here—who wouldn't? —relocating is not a viable option." Angel shook her head. "I don't know. I guess I'll have to just bide my time until the year has passed."

"It will fly by, Angel. Why don't you come back for a visit during Christmas or spring break?"

Bernadette checked her watch. "I have time to drive you home," she said. "Unless you've made an arrangement with Gabe—"

"No, I haven't. I'd appreciate a ride, Bernie." She reached out to take the bill from the returning waiter, but Bernadette snapped it up. "My treat, Angel. You can get it next time."

As soon as Bernadette dropped her off at home, Angel went upstairs to lie down. She hadn't mentioned to Bernie that her head had begun to throb. She took a headache pill and partially closed the wooden blinds but left the window open, feeling relaxed by the sound of the rushing waves breaking on the beach. Stretching out on her bed, Angel tried to focus on deep breathing, but her thoughts kept meandering from the lawyer's meeting to Gabe, and from Gabe to Bernadette.

"Oh Gramsy," she murmured. "I'm so overwhelmed..."

She rolled to one side and hugged her pillow. *You're complicating things,* an inner voice intruded into her thoughts. *Just sign the papers, have the reception for Gramsy and then go back to your life in Toronto, your world. A year will go by fast enough, as you always find when you're teaching. And if you want to return to Chéticamp during the Christmas or spring break, what's stopping you?*

"Gabe," she murmured. *He* was the one stopping her from having peace of mind now, so how could she expect anything different if she returned? How could she switch off the currents that seemed to run through her when she was near him? Currents that only *she* felt, obviously. She couldn't forget the way he had jerked his hand away from hers when they had brushed against each other on the beach.

He was interested in the B&B, not her.

Angel put her fingers up to her temples. She could feel the throbbing of each pulse. "Stop thinking!" she admonished herself. Her thoughts were neither productive nor inspiring.

She squeezed her eyes shut. She hadn't been looking for a man, and what were the chances that she'd feel sparks for Gabe again when she returned to Chéticamp? Someone she had played with as a child, for heaven's sake, and who had given her hope on her sixteenth birthday only to stay away for ten years? Life wasn't fair. Then the universe had thrown Colin her way, which ended up being a total bust, and now Gabe was literally next door to her and figuring in her life in more ways than one.

Ways that she had to ignore, with the hope that he wouldn't haunt her thoughts after she returned to Toronto.

Gabe was speechless for a moment, his gaze taking in the perfectly coiffed, perfectly dressed and perfectly manicured woman he had spent a whirlwind six months with—including two months of engagement—before she broke things off. *What was she doing here, halfway around the world from Scotland? It was a long way to travel just to apologize. If that was her intent.*

He stood up. "Charlotte. It's…uh…been a while." He tried to muster a smile, but couldn't.

"Gabe, I'll understand if you don't want to talk to me." She tossed back her long, red hair. She was a burst of color, with the flared sleeves and pant legs of her green jumpsuit adding the touch of sophistication always displayed in her wardrobe choices.

He pursed his lips. "It's been three years, Charlotte."

She raised a sculpted eyebrow. "I'm very aware of that, Gabe. So… May I sit for a few minutes?"

Gabe inclined his head and gestured at the empty seat across him. As Charlotte settled in her seat, he felt a strange sensation running through him. He looked up and saw Chris approaching with his seafood chowder and biscuits, and swiftly put up his hand and shook his head. Chris glanced quickly at Charlotte and then gave Gabe a slight nod before returning to the kitchen. Chris would have recognized her from photos Gabe had shared with him. Photos Gabe deleted from his phone when he got home.

Charlotte's green eyes were fixed on him. They were actually brown, but she sometimes changed the color of her contact lenses to match the outfit she was wearing. Gabe had found it somewhat disconcerting at times, gazing into black, blue, hazel or green eyes over the time they were with each other. He rarely saw her brown eyes. Or natural brown hair. When they were dating, she was a strawberry blonde, but changed to a deep auburn red after they were engaged.

She cleared her throat. "Gabe, this is long overdue."

He cocked his head at her and said nothing.

"I… I really should have contacted you much earlier." She waited for him to reply, and when he didn't, she tapped the table nervously with her glossy red fingernails and eyed him squarely. "To apologize. *Sincerely*."

Gabe wondered how he should reply. *It's kind of too late, don't you think? Why bother, Charlotte? I've gone on with life.* Or: *Why did you bother to come all this way? You could have called or texted…three years ago.*

He frowned. "I've moved on, Charlotte." He looked away from her to the waves chasing each other toward the shore.

"I actually tried to contact you a year ago," she said softly.

Still too late. He turned his gaze back to her.

"I stopped in at Maeve's and I was told you had relocated to Cape Breton Island. I gave up, not having the nerve to call or text."

"You gave up on me two years earlier when I needed your support," Gabe said quietly.

"Look, Gabe. What I did was inexcusable. *Insensitive.* Unforgivable, really." She shook her head, her brow creasing. "I'm sorry I wasn't able to be there for you. I was selfish, I wasn't patient with the grieving process you were going through." She bit her lip and tried to blink back tears. She reached for a handkerchief and dabbed carefully at her eyes.

He opened his mouth to reply but she held up her hand.

"No, please let me finish, Gabe. I have a client who wants to purchase property here, so I thought I'd take the chance to come in person to apologize to you. I want to let you know that I'm sorry I didn't have the empathy I should have had when you were grieving." She threw up her hands. "I had never lost anybody until my dad died six months ago. Now I can only imagine how painful it must have been for you to lose both your parents at the same time. I should have been more understanding, more patient with your grieving process." She took a deep breath. "I'm truly sorry for having caused you even more grief. I couldn't live with myself if I didn't try to make amends."

"I'm really sorry for your loss, Charlotte," Gabe murmured. "Your dad was a great guy."

Charlotte nodded. "Thanks, Gabe. He was a great guy and a wonderful father." She wiped her eyes again. "You know, he was really upset at me when I told him that I had broken things off and that we were no longer together." She shook her head. "He said I had let a good man get away."

Gabe felt a twinge in his chest. He gazed at Charlotte helplessly. The past was past, and there was no changing things now.

"I can see that now, Gabe." Charlotte intertwined her hands as if in prayer. "Can you find it in your heart to forgive me?"

Gabe let out a breath he'd been subconsciously holding in. His thoughts were racing as fast as his pulse. He gazed out the window and the image of Angel at the beach beside him popped up in his mind. Another twinge. In less than two weeks, she'd be gone.

He turned back to meet Charlotte's hopeful gaze. "I've forgiven you, Charlotte. I don't hold any grudges."

She blinked, almost as if she couldn't believe what he was saying. "Thank you. Would you be willing to give us another chance, Gabe?" she said softly, her green eyes glistening.

CHAPTER FIFTEEN

ANGEL'S EYES FLUTTERED OPEN. Disoriented, she stared at the ceiling for a few seconds. And then she remembered lying down after Bernadette drove her home.

She reached for her phone on her night table and checked the time. *How could it be after four?* She'd nodded off for over two hours. Running her fingers through her hair, she strode to the washroom to freshen up.

Feeling more revived in the kitchen after drinking a glass of orange juice, Angel tried to decide whether to go through Gramsy's cooking binders or to just inspect each room and make a list of the items she couldn't part with. Either task would take a chunk of time, and now that the sun was streaming through the windows, Angel was tempted to leave both tasks for the next rainy day. She might as well take advantage of the sun and heat while it lasted, and go for a relaxing swim. She would cook up something for herself after that, if she even felt hungry at all. She was still full from lunch with Bernadette.

Angel had brought the suitcase she had originally packed before getting the news that Gramsy had passed. It had a couple of bathing suits in it, summer wear, a few dressy items and, now, a special dress for the reception for Gramsy. Sifting through it, she pulled out a tangerine one-piece bathing suit and quickly changed into it. She packed an oversize towel in her beach bag, her beach hat and a bottle of sunscreen after applying it to her face and body.

Since Gabe would be working at his restaurant, she'd have a long stretch of beach to herself. It was rare to have people wander toward their end of the island, and Angel was looking forward to having some alone time. She decided to bring along a beach chair and, just as she did whenever she visited in the past, a book and a couple of locking bags for any stones and shells she collected.

With a shiver of excitement, Angel put on her swimsuit cover-up and beach shoes, and headed down to the beach. The sun and heat had intensified during the day and it felt good after the bouts of wind and rain. She lifted her face and gazed at the endless expanse of azure sky. Not a cloud in sight. She breathed in the salt-tinged ocean air and exhaled slowly, feeling the last vestiges of stress from the morning start to dissipate.

Angel set down the folding chair and her other items. The water would be cold—it always was in the summer—so she'd go for a walk first and get toasty warm before diving in for a swim. After grabbing her shell and stone-collecting bags, she began her walk. The gentle and repetitive swoosh of the waves nudging the shore was comforting as she scanned the beach sand for her treasures. She stayed close to the water's edge so she could rinse off any shell or stone before slipping it into one of her bags. She loved the way the colors of the rocks would pop when rinsed. As a child, she would imagine that they were ocean jewels that she had discovered, their shiny hues resembling some of the vibrant colors in her box of crayons. Gramsy had kept her prized collections over the years, displayed in various bowls and dishes around the B&B.

And she had kept the heart-shaped shell Gabe had given

her, only to shove the box in a corner of her bedroom closet after communication between them had dwindled and then ceased.

Angel straightened and turned to look at the house that she had been coming to for almost three decades. Her summer visits to Gramsy had been her birthday gift from her parents. Sometimes they accompanied her, but their work schedules did not always allow them to take holidays at the same time. So sometimes she traveled with one parent, and sometimes alone. Angel had no problem traveling alone. Whether they went by train or plane, she always enjoyed the journey.

A series of raucous cries diverted her attention, and she turned to see the descent of a black-and-white seabird on the water. A common murre, with its distinctive black head and body, and white underside. She was wistful as she watched it, wondering what it would be like, not having all this to return to in the summer. Gabe's estate came into her peripheral vision and she turned to gaze at its multiple gables, upper-floor decks and huge scenic windows. The groomed path from the home to the shoreline brought back memories of Gabe helping her as she limped into the house after injuring her leg. And then her mind became flooded with images of moments with Gabe.

Angel shook her head and walked briskly on, focusing on thoughts about the reception to celebrate Gramsy's life. She wanted to go through the photo albums on the bottom shelf of one of the living room bookshelves and compile photos to put into a slide presentation on her laptop. She could have it running on a loop while friends popped in to pay their respects. And in the next couple of days, she'd make some cookies, scones and loaves to serve with coffee and tea.

By the time Angel turned around and returned to her beach chair, she was sweltering. She poked around in her bag for a hair elastic and swept back her hair into a ponytail before taking off her cover-up. She eyed the undulating waves, and knowing it was better to dash into the water instead of inching into it slowly, she gave a whoop and ran for it.

She gasped at the first impact of the water, but she continued immersing herself, head included. She came up to the surface and treaded water while getting used to the exhilaratingly cold-water temperature. She knew that the initial numbness would gradually fade after her body acclimatized. When it did, she swam parallel to the coastline for a bit and then floated, loving the gentle buoyancy of the waves.

The sun on her face and the silky water cradling her body filled her with a sense of peace and relaxation. *What a gift to have the waters of the Gulf of Saint Lawrence practically in Gramsy's backyard.* Angel breathed in the fresh breeze and wished she could float for hours. She was tempted to close her eyes, and she did, briefly, but she knew she had to stay attentive, or she'd be transported too far from the shore. She was a pretty good swimmer, but she wasn't about to get overconfident with the deeper waters.

Angel reverted to swim mode for another stretch and then turned back toward Gramsy's neck of the beach. When her feet touched bottom, she proceeded to walk her way out of the water. Squinting in the sun, she saw a figure approaching on the beach. She wiped her eyes and the figure came clearly into view.

Gabe. Wearing swimming trunks and with a plush towel draped over one shoulder. She stopped, well aware of the water dripping from her shivering body and still too far to grab her beach towel.

* * *

Gabe felt an erratic drumming in his chest at the sight of Angel emerging from the water in her iridescent orange swimsuit. He hoped she hadn't noticed his fleeting gaze sweeping over her seconds earlier. The last thing he wanted was for her to feel uncomfortable with him.

"Hi, Angel," he called out casually, also coming to a stop.

"Hi," she said, and strode swiftly to her beach chair to grab her towel and drape it around herself.

He was still a few paces away but he didn't advance. "I guess we both got the same memo—'Sun's out; go for a swim.'"

Angel held the towel tightly against her. "I thought you would be at your restaurant. Not that it would matter if you weren't. I mean—"

"I was at Mara's earlier…with someone I knew. And then I decided I needed a quick break before returning for the evening."

Gabe had been taken aback by Charlotte's appearance and even more so by her wanting to know if there was still a chance for them. He had excused himself for a few moments and had sought out Chris privately to briefly explain the situation. Chris had generously offered to take his evening shift so Gabe could deal with his ex-fiancée, and Gabe was genuinely touched, but he told Chris that he wouldn't return as early as he usually did, but he'd still be in for the evening shift. Returning to the booth, he suggested taking Charlotte to a nearby park to have a more private conversation. She agreed.

Gabe didn't want to think about their discussion now. He just wanted to cool off with an invigorating swim before heading back to Mara's. However, he hadn't expected to see Angel here. "I hope you don't mind if I go for a quick swim? I don't want to intrude on your privacy…"

"This isn't my private beach," she said, sitting on her chair with her towel still around her. "Go for it." Her gaze dropped to his chest before quickly shifting to her bag to grab a book.

Gabe glanced at the title: *Fairies and Fables of Cape Breton Island*. His mouth twitched. "I recognize that book. You would read it on the bluff the summer that we—"

"You remember that?" Angel stared at him incredulously.

"I do," he said, unable to hold back a smile. "After reading about the fairy dances, you were bound and determined to spot them on their fairy hills."

"I was a kid. Kids believe in magic." She shrugged. "I saw the book in my room and was curious." She opened it and looked intently at the illustration next to the title page.

Gabe took the hint. "Enjoy the read. Or reread. Maybe it'll make you believe in magic again." He walked toward the water and tossed his towel far enough on the beach to avoid the surf's reach. When he glanced back at Angel, she was still looking at her book. He turned, but not before catching her looking up from the page.

Feeling a surge of heat spiraling through his body, Gabe made a run for the bracing waters and dived in without hesitation.

CHAPTER SIXTEEN

Angel was embarrassed that Gabe had caught her watching him. She wished she could quietly leave but she was reluctant to show him that his appearance had affected her. She set the beach chair in the lounging position and put on her cover-up. Lying back, she started reading her book, but thoughts and images of Gabe kept shattering her concentration. The last person she had expected to encounter on the beach was Gabe, looking like "Mr. August" in a firefighter calendar.

How could she stop the fluttering in her chest? And why was her body betraying her? She told herself that it was normal to admire a perfect physique, whether it belonged to a man or a woman.

But her reaction wasn't normal.

Just looking at Gabe gave her a rush that she had never experienced with anyone else, not even Colin. Yes, she had been attracted to Colin, but her nerve endings hadn't sparked when she saw him, like they did with Gabe. And any superficial attraction she had felt for Colin had dissolved instantly when she found out that he was married.

So why did she tingle all over, blood pulsing through her veins, feeling a yearning that coursed from her core upward when she was around Gabe?

Because maybe you want him?

Angel closed her book with a snap, and stared at it in shock. How could she be having these crazy thoughts? The sun must be getting to her. She looked up, her heart jolting wildly as Gabe emerged from his swim. She couldn't pull her gaze away. He bent to reach for his towel, his arm muscles flexing. He shook it out and towel-dried his hair before quickly running it over his body.

She averted her gaze when he wrapped the towel around his hips and started walking toward her. Stopping a few paces away, he said, "Mind if I join you for a minute?"

Angel cleared her throat and gazed up at him. "No problem."

It was more than a problem.

Even a minute was dangerous. The more time she was around Gabe, the more she realized that something was chipping away at her convictions. The conviction that she had to sell the B&B and return to Toronto. The belief that she couldn't possibly have serious feelings for Gabe. Again. Feelings that went beyond just wanting to enjoy his body…

Angel didn't want to even formulate the words in her mind. Because it wasn't ever going to happen. She'd be crazy to believe for even a minute that it would.

Gabe laid his towel on the beach parallel to her lounge chair and stretched out on it, his hands tucked under his head as he looked up at the sky. "Would you like to have dinner at Mara's tonight?" he said casually.

Angel's heart skipped a beat. She leaned over slightly and her book slipped out of her hands onto the sand between her and Gabe. She reached over to get it and gave a yelp as she leaned too far and found herself tumbling over herself, ending up pressed up against Gabe with his arms flying out involuntarily to help her.

The impact took her breath away as she lay against him, his arms bracing her.

She didn't move, and neither did he.

"Are you okay?" Gabe murmured, his mouth brushing against her temple.

What was happening? She shifted slightly and his teal-green gaze was on her, his brow furrowed in concern. His mouth, oh so close. Angel couldn't speak, and for a moment she wondered if she had banged her head and was rendered speechless with a concussion. Was she imagining the intensity in his eyes? The desire? The sensation of their bodies pressed together was…breathtaking. Her mouth opened in wonder and Gabe promptly kissed her. *Slowly*. Tenderly. And when she started to respond to his touch, he cradled her head with one hand and his kiss became more passionate.

When he pulled away, his breath ragged, alarm bells rang in her mind.

"Are you okay?" he huskily repeated his earlier question. "Did you hurt yourself?"

Angel shifted away from him, her mind a jumble of emotions. "I… I'll be okay." She cringed as she stood up. "I'm more embarrassed than hurt." She put her book in the bag and closed up the lawn chair.

"Don't be, Angel," he said gruffly. "It was an accident. And I'm very sorry. I got caught up in the moment." He rose. "I should go and get ready for my shift." He shook out his towel and wrapped it around his waist. "I'd really like you to check out Mara's, Angel. I'll be busy with an engagement dinner tonight, but I guarantee you'll love the food." Angel hesitated for a moment, wondering how wise this would be. She had let herself get carried away with Gabe and now she was regretting it. Their attraction had been mutual, yes, but the reality was that she was still leaving Chéticamp Island. She couldn't afford to get tangled up with Gabe physically or emotionally. She'd have to make it clear to him that her focus for the remainder of her time on the island was to get things ready for Gramsy's reception.

In any case, if she went to Mara's with him, she'd be dining alone, which would be safe. Then she'd take a cab home, instead of waiting for him to finish his shift. "Okay, I did want to check out Mara's before I left," she said casually, heading to the path back to Gramsy's.

"Great. Can I come by and pick you up in about forty minutes?"

His words followed her as she walked away, and she was pretty sure his gaze was following her, too.

Gabe watched Angel for a few moments before heading to the path back to his place. His heart was still hammering against his chest. Angel had literally fallen into his arms, and he had responded automatically, his senses instantly charged by the feel of her face and body touching his.

He should have shown more control…

But his instincts had taken over, overwhelming him with all the feelings that he had kept locked up inside him: protectiveness, desire and the need for human connection. *Connection with a woman. Physically and emotionally.*

When his lips brushed her temple, the feel of her soft skin ignited him instantly. Feeling the length of her body against his had sent him into another realm. He didn't have to say anything to reveal how his body was responding. The way she had gazed at him, eyes and mouth open, had done him in. He wanted to hold her, taste her lips, feel her heart beating against his.

Their kisses hadn't been the sweet ones shared on her

sixteenth birthday. These were the passionate kisses of two adults wanting more, needing more.

With the feel of the sun on his body and the sensual sound of the rushing waves, Gabe had lost himself in the moment. Time stood still when he kissed her, and feeling her responding had inflamed him even more. When a niggling voice in his mind warned him that things could get out of control for both of them, he'd reluctantly pulled away. In an unexplainable way, he felt responsible for Angel while she was on the island, and the weight of the reason she was here in the first place had brought an abrupt halt to his passion.

After stepping inside, Gabe threw the beach towel in the laundry room and headed upstairs.

He checked the time and then headed for the shower, his thoughts alternating between Angel and Charlotte. Before they both reappeared in his life, he had mainly focused on one thing: his restaurants. He took his role and reputation as a Michelin-starred chef seriously, and working at his profession took up most of his time, especially since he flew back to Scotland regularly to check on operations at Maeve's.

Charlotte.

Her appearance at Mara's had shocked the hell out of him. And her apology and desire for reconciliation even more. Noticing the restaurant starting to fill in, he wanted to find a more private space to talk. They left Mara's, with several curious gazes directed mostly at Charlotte. The tongues of the regulars would be wagging, no doubt. He had laughed on several occasions when Bernadette told him that he was Inverness County's most eligible bachelor, and that his Scottish brogue and handsome beard had the single ladies sighing and vying for his attention.

Which is why he had mostly avoided attending the year-round local *cèilidhs*, rollicking nights of fiddle music and dancing, whether in a hall, barn or other community space. Not that he didn't enjoy this Celtic tradition; it was just that he hadn't been motivated to engage in that kind of fun as a single person. Perhaps he'd change his mind when he was lucky enough to find the right person to go with, he told Bernadette with a smirk.

And how will you meet anyone if you're always cooking in your restaurant or home, Chef? Bernadette had challenged him good-naturedly. *You have to get your Scottish buns out there, laddie.*

Gabe had opened the side door of his Porsche for Charlotte and drove to the nearest park. It felt awkward to have her in the front seat, especially since Angel had been the only woman—other than Gramsy—who had occupied that spot since he had moved to the island. And the awkward silence between him and Charlotte intensified his unease.

He was thankful for the hot weather, which meant they could sit at one of the shaded park benches instead of staying in the car. When they arrived, there were only a few people strolling or jogging on the grounds.

When they were both seated, Charlotte tossed her hair back and looked at him with a rueful smile. "I'm sorry for just showing up like I did, Gabe. But I couldn't take the chance that you would refuse to see me." She sighed. "And I really wanted—*needed*—to apologize for abandoning you in your time of need." She shook her head. "Your forgiveness means a lot to me."

Gabe rubbed his jaw. "I'm not a saint, Charlotte. I was upset when I got your note and ring. More than upset. Shocked. Hurt. Disappointed. And maybe angry for a while. But I was dealing with enough grief over losing my parents." He looked away, his jaw tensing.

"I'm sorry."

He held up a hand. "It's done with, no need to apologize again." He met her gaze. "Life went on."

"I missed you, Gabe."

Gabe couldn't bring himself to say "I missed you, too." Maybe because he had been too numb at the time to miss her.

"We had something once, Gabe. I think we could have something better now." She put a hand on his arm briefly. "I want to try to make it up to you, if you let me." She blinked, trying to hold back tears. "Unless there's someone in your life…?"

Gabe almost wanted to laugh. How was he supposed to answer that? *Um, kind of, but she's about to leave, so there's no chance of anything developing.* "Not really," he said, "but—"

"You don't have to explain," she said. "Gabe, I want to earn back your trust. All I'm asking is for you to give me a chance. I'm here for a week on business and then I have another week off for myself. Maybe we could get together some evening this week?" Her green eyes were hopeful. "I've changed, Gabe. In the ways I needed to change."

"I've changed, too, Charlotte," he said quietly. "I just don't think we can go back in time."

She shook her head. "We wouldn't be going back, Gabe. We'd be going forward. Like you said, the past is done with."

Gabe inhaled and exhaled deeply. Charlotte looked as attractive as she had in the past, but there *was* something different about her. Her humility, for one. Could he entertain the thought of giving her a chance? Trust her again?

He was being honest when he told her that he had forgiven her. But forgiving didn't mean forgetting.

"One day at a time, Gabe."

He started. It was almost as if she had read his thoughts. "I don't want to give you false hopes, Charlotte." He glanced at his watch. "I need to head back home. I have things to do before I get ready for my shift tonight."

She gazed at him for a few seconds, then nodded. "I'll have lunch at Mara's and then I'll take a cab back to my hotel."

"May I offer you a ride?" he said lightly.

She smiled. "You may."

When they arrived at Mara's, Charlotte turned to Gabe. "*Tapadh leat*," she murmured and squeezed his hand before letting herself out. "I think I'll go in for a bowl of the seafood chowder. I checked the website and saw that it's a favorite with customers."

Gabe couldn't bring himself to reply to their Scottish Gaelic "Thank you." He smiled politely and nodded, and when she entered the restaurant, he left immediately for home, intending to decompress with a refreshing swim before his shift.

Only he hadn't imagined encountering Angel on the beach—

And now, as he showered, Gabe tried to suppress images of Angel from his mind and concentrate instead on the evening's menu at Mara's.

But his mind wouldn't let him.

CHAPTER SEVENTEEN

WHY HAD SHE said yes to going to Mara's with Gabe?

And how could she face Gabe again after what had happened between them? She shook her head. No, she couldn't see him again. At least not so soon. She turned off the blow dryer and set it down before pacing around her room in her bathrobe. What excuse could she use?

Before she could think of anything, her cell phone rang. Her nerves taut, and wondering if that was Gabe now, she picked it up. Bernadette, on her last break.

"Thank goodness it's *you*!"

"What's the matter, Angel? Did something happen?"

"Um…yes! And I'm embarrassed to tell you about it, Bernie, but if I don't, I'll burst."

"Oh my gosh, what is it?"

Angel gave Bernadette an edited version of what occurred between her and Gabe. "And I said yes to going to Mara's with him tonight. He's working, though, so I wouldn't exactly be sitting across from him all night trying to keep my mind off his body. I really should text him and cancel. He could be here any minute and I'm not even dressed."

"Angel! Listen to me. You don't want to miss the chance to eat at Mara's. If you're that uncomfortable with Gabe after what happened, why don't I meet you there once

I'm done here? That way, you won't be alone and if Gabe does have time to join you, it will be less awkward with me there. And Gabe won't mind."

"I don't know, Bernie…"

"Angel, really, we're in the twenty-first century. What happened was an accident and then you both succumbed to temptation. At least partially." She laughed. "Which is totally understandable, with both of you being pretty cute, if I may say so. And it's not like it's going to go anywhere, with you leaving in a week and a half…"

"You're right," Angel said swiftly. "It isn't."

"Okay, then. I'll see you in a bit."

"But—"

"No *buts*, Angel. Now go and get dressed. Love you!"

Angel stared at her cell phone for a few moments, then strode to her closet and looked at the limited items she had brought for this trip. She decided on a silky midi dress with tulip sleeves and a scattering of pink and apricot vintage roses. She had liked the feminine look of it, with its fitted waist and flared skirt. Feminine but not provocative.

She didn't want to give Gabe any ideas.

At the sound of tires on the driveway, Angel took a last glance in the mirror and hurried downstairs to put on a pair of ivory lace-up sandals. She rose just as Gabe rang the doorbell.

She opened the door and gave Gabe a tentative smile.

"Hi, Angel. You look very nice," he said casually. "I hope you don't mind if we jet it to Mara's?"

With his crisp white shirt and black trousers, Gabe looked very nice, too, but she couldn't bring herself to repay the compliment.

"Not at all," she said, grabbing her handbag. He strode to open the door of the gleaming silver Porsche for her and waited until she was seated. "Oh, your hem is hanging out," he said, and bent to tuck it inside the car. His hand brushed hers as she did the same. Their gazes met for a few seconds and a sizzle went through her as she tried not to let her gaze slip to his lips. He straightened and shut the door.

On the drive to Mara's, he put on some fiddle music. "That always gets me in the cooking mood," he said with a half grin.

"Somehow, I don't think you need any help to get you in the mood. For cooking," she added hastily. She turned to look out her window, sure that her cheeks were as pink as the roses on her dress.

"You're right," he said, turning down the music. "I love cooking, no matter the time of day or night. And I love cooking with the changing seasons we're lucky to have as Canadians."

"What's your favorite?" Angel said, glancing back at him.

He chuckled. "That's a hard one. I have my specialties for each season. Let me see. Summer is the most abundant one, with fresh fruits and vegetables from our restaurant gardens. And I love fall, where I imitate the colors of the Highlands and the Cabot Trail with my autumn dishes. Winter is a cozy season, perfect for comfort food—" he smiled at Angel "—like lobster mac and cheese."

"You mean you made me a winter dish?" Angel said, feigning disapproval.

"That's an all-season favorite," he laughed. "And you loved it, admit it."

Angel smirked. "And spring?"

"Spring literally puts a spring in everyone's steps. Everyone's out walking, so I keep things light and I experiment with combinations. Cape Breton meets Tuscany, for example. *Aragosta fiorentina.*"

"Pardon me?"

"Lobster florentine, with arugula instead of spinach, and a creamy lemon and fennel sauce over fettuccine."

"That's light?"

"Touché! Okay, maybe not as light as some of my other dishes. I try to please all tastes," he said, the corners of his eyes crinkling as he smiled.

"You still haven't said which season is your favorite," she said as he turned into the restaurant parking lot and drove into the space marked *RESERVED FOR CHEF GABRIEL*.

"You're going to try to pin me down, eh?" Gabe said teasingly, turning to her. His brows furrowed, as he probably realized the double entendre of his words.

She wanted to melt in her seat.

"Winter's my favorite," he said huskily. "I love to cook when it's snowing outside and while listening to Christmas music, both at Mara's and at home. Having a cozy dinner by my fireplace wearing my reindeer pajamas. And eggnog and Cape Breton pork pies for dessert. *Or butterscotch pie*."

Angel pictured herself sitting by the roaring fire with Gabe, wearing her candy-cane pajamas. A cozy season they'd never share.

She gave him a half-hearted smile and turned to open the car door. Why did her heart suddenly feel heavy?

Angel stopped to gaze at the stylized sign bearing Gramsy's first name. Gabe waited beside her. "Do you like it?" he said.

"I do," she replied without shifting her attention from the sign. "I like the way the *M* drops down and becomes a set of waves, with more waves above, directly underneath the rest of her name. Very appropriate. She loved the water and always said she was living her dream when Grampsy built their house on Chéticamp Island." Her voice cracked and she paused and quickly wiped her eyes. "I'm sorry."

Gabe took a step forward so he could face Angel directly. "You don't have to be," he said softly. "Gramsy meant the world to you. And to me. Of course you're going to feel her loss, especially when you're at her place, or when you're reminded of her in some way." He smiled. "She liked the sign, too, but she liked the food in here even more."

Angel laughed. "Of course she did. Now you know where I get my love of food." She gestured toward the front door. "So let me in, Chef, before I huff and I puff and—you know the drill."

"You're funny," he said. "Have you ever considered doing stand-up?"

"I already do. In my classroom," she said, her lips twitching.

Gabe burst out laughing. "Your kids must love you." He pressed the code into the panel by the front door of the restaurant and a buzzer sounded. He opened the door for Angel, and moments later they were in the dining room.

"By the way, Gabe, I was talking to Bernadette and she said she would join me, since you'd be cooking away. She said you wouldn't mind."

"Oh, she did, did she?" He feigned a frown. He supposed he shouldn't feel disappointed. It was unfair of him to expect Angel to dine alone, although he had intended to join her intermittently throughout the evening, especially when she took her first bites of every course. Well, it was probably safer this way. He seemed to keep putting his foot in his mouth whenever he was with her. "Of course I wouldn't mind. Bernadette is the sister I never had." He chuckled as he led Angel to the booth he had occupied earlier. "She's bossy at times, and brutally honest, but I love her. She has a heart of gold. I'm sure you know she has a gig singing and playing guitar two or three times a month at ceilidhs all over Cape Breton Island. The venues are always packed when people know she's performing. Everyone loves her."

"She's easy to love," Angel said. "And funny, I always thought of her as the sister *I* never had."

"Well, speak of the little devil now," he said, glancing out the window. "I just saw her car pull in. It's still too early to open, but I'll let her in and you two can chat while I slave away in the kitchen."

"*You're* funny now," Angel said.

He shrugged and a couple of minutes later he was back with Bernadette. "And now, ladies, I'll have Jeremy come out and offer you some drinks." He turned to Angel. "I'll return in a bit to introduce you to my sous-chef."

Gabe walked briskly to the kitchen. Shortly, he'd switch to chef mode, but while he was donning his white Lafont jacket in a side room, he could allow himself the indulgence of thinking about how lovely Angel looked. *A natural beauty.* And maybe one with a little bit of fairy magic to bewitch unsuspecting chefs with.

If someone had told him a week ago that he'd be falling again for Angel, *and* that his ex-fiancée would be arriving from Scotland and trying to reconcile with him, he would have seriously questioned their sanity.

What was it that people said when confronted with several challenges at once? *It never rains but pours.*

He had some decisions to make, the first being whether

or not he should let Angel know about his feelings for her. Not the physical ones. She was already aware of those. But would it even make a difference? Convince her to maybe stay for the rest of the summer and at least see if there was a chance to make it work? That is, if she even *had* any deeper feelings for him.

He sighed. The complicating factor was her teaching. And right now, she couldn't see herself relocating.

And then there was Charlotte, hoping to reignite their relationship. Could he find a way to trust her again? Could he entertain the thought of giving her the benefit of the doubt if there was no way forward with Angel? But how fair would it be to Charlotte, though, to have her waiting on the sidelines while he explored possibilities with Angel?

He wasn't a cad and he had no intentions of playing with their lives. The only thing he could do was to be honest with each of them about his feelings. The question was, whom would he talk to first?

Gabe checked his watch. No more time to think about either Angel or Charlotte. He had some serious cooking to do.

CHAPTER EIGHTEEN

ANGEL LIFTED HER wineglass. "To Gramsy," she said, before clicking her glass with Bernadette's.

"To Gramsy," Bernadette said solemnly.

"Very nice," Angel said after tasting the wine.

"Somebody must be trying to impress you," Bernadette said with a teasing smile.

Angel frowned. "Why do you say that?"

"That happens to be an extremely expensive wine. I know, because it was served at Mara's soft opening for a small group of Gabe's friends, including me and Gramsy."

"Well, I'll only have one glass, then."

"I'm sure Gabe's not going to make you pay, silly. He *did* invite you here, right?"

"Yes, but—"

"Angel, I know he wanted you to enjoy a dinner at the place he named after Gramsy. Enjoy the experience." She leaned across the table conspiratorially. "Is he a good kisser?" she said, lowering her voice.

"Bernie!" Angel looked around self-consciously. "It happened so quickly—"

"And? Come on, you barely gave me any details on the phone. And you've never held back in the past about Colin or any of your other boyfriends."

"Gabe is not my boyfriend. And you make it sound like I had an endless supply of guys in my life. Which I did not!"

"Okay, okay, but from your flushed cheeks, I'm going to infer that he was a great kisser."

"Bernie, you're incorrigible!" Angel said, and laughed at Bernadette's feigned pout. "Okay, I admit it, but it was my fault for falling down and practically landing on top of him."

"Well, you obviously made an impression on each other. *Literally*." Bernadette grinned.

"It doesn't mean anything, Bernie. And it won't happen again. I'm leaving in a week and a half, remember?"

Bernadette sighed. "I wish you could stay longer. Why don't you extend your trip? Then maybe, you and Gabe—"

"Did I hear my name? Bernie, are you telling tales about me? You know the penalty for that is doing the dishes." Gabe laughed as he approached their booth, followed by his sous-chef, whom he introduced to Angel.

"Nice to meet you, Chris." She smiled and shook his hand.

"The pleasure is mine." He placed his other hand over hers. "I'm sorry for your loss, Angel, and I hope you take comfort in knowing how much Gramsy meant to us here and in the community."

She nodded. "Thank you. I do."

He left and Angel met Gabe's gaze. She wondered if he had heard any of her earlier comments or noticed her gaze inadvertently traveling down the length of him as he approached, drop-dead gorgeous in his white chef's jacket and tailored black trousers.

From the corner of her eye, she could see Bernadette watching them. She gave her a gentle kick under the table.

"Ow!" Bernadette blurted.

Gabe turned to her. "Are you okay?"

"Uh…yeah. Just a cramped muscle in my leg. I'll just walk it off. Be right back."

Angel hoped her burning face didn't give her away.

"Have you had a chance to look at the menu?" Gabe's gaze reverted to her.

She hadn't even glanced at the menu.

"Or would you like it if I surprised you with the selections for your dinner tonight? Perhaps choosing some of Gramsy's favorites?"

"Oh! Sure, why not? Actually, I think that would be very nice." She looked away from him as the memory of what his chest looked like under his jacket made her catch her breath.

"Okay, I'll get right on that."

But he didn't move, and she looked up at him questioningly.

"I'm glad you came, Angel," he said huskily. "I—" He caught sight of Bernadette returning. "I hope you enjoy what I make you."

He met Bernadette on his way back to the kitchen and they exchanged a few words.

"Did he tell you that he's surprising us with his dishes?"

"Yes, I told him I was good with that." Her eyes narrowed. "Did you and Gabe talk about anything else? I figured that's why you kicked me under the table."

"Really? You thought I was giving you a hint to leave?" Angel shook her head. "No, I just noticed you staring at the both of us with that dazed look of wonder, and I wanted you to stop. You didn't have to yell."

"You got me on the shinbone, girlfriend. I almost jumped out of my seat."

"Aw, I'm sorry, Bernie."

"No, you're not," Bernadette laughed. "Now come clean. Did you feel something special when you two collided?"

Angel sighed. "I won't get any peace until I answer, so okay, yes, I felt *something*. And I'm sure he did, too. Something purely physical, nothing else."

Bernadette raised her eyebrows. "Are you sure it was just physical? I was observing the way you and Gabe looked at each other. Call me a romantic fool, but I thought there was something more than just a physical vibe between you two."

Angel was relieved to spot Jeremy walking with a tray toward them. She was reluctant to further analyze her or Gabe's feelings, physical or otherwise, with Bernadette. At least not at the moment.

Jeremy set two parfait glasses in front of them. "Enjoy your appetizer, Chef Gabriel's Inverness shrimp parfait. Chef will check on you shortly."

Angel met Bernadette's gaze after their first taste. "Amazing." The melt-in-your-mouth lime mousse with slivers of lemon zest complemented the grilled shrimp beautifully. "Great taste, Gramsy," she murmured.

They had enjoyed a few mouthfuls when Gabe returned. "I hope the parfaits are to your liking, ladies?" His gaze went from Bernadette to Angel.

"Delicious," Angel said. "I could have this every day."

Bernadette nodded. "Ditto."

Gabe smiled approvingly. "Great. I passed test number one." His gaze remained fixed on Angel. "A few more to go."

Angel dropped her gaze and hoped her cheeks wouldn't betray her reaction to what she perceived as Gabe implying something else…

When Gabe left, Bernadette nudged Angel. "I knew it."

"Knew what?" Angel raised an eyebrow as she bit into a shrimp.

"There is something going on between you two. Gabe couldn't take his eyes off you."

"Oh, come on, Bernie. He was looking at you, too."

"Yeah, for a nanosecond. His eyes were practically smoldering when he was talking to you."

Angel couldn't help laughing. "Bernie, have you considered writing a romance? You have the imagination for it!"

Bernadette was about to answer when her cell phone dinged. She reached into her handbag and read the text. After replying, she set it down on the table and sighed. "Ross is tied up tonight," she said. "We were going to get together after dinner and play some board games. In fact, we were going to ask you to join us."

"So what happened?"

"Well, I knew he was meeting with an out-of-country Realtor this afternoon. She's on Cape Breton Island to scope out properties for a high-powered client. Apparently she has a personal connection here. Anyway, she wanted Ross to take her to see some of the higher-end properties for sale this evening. He texted to see if that was okay with me."

"Aw, how considerate." Angel smiled. "You're a lucky gal, Bernie."

"And Ross is even luckier." Bernadette grinned. "So how about I drive you to my place and we can see who has board game supremacy?"

Angel hesitated. "Maybe another time, Bernie. I think I'll just have an early night tonight. But thanks. Oh, here comes our next dish."

Jeremy approached and set down two bowls of steaming seafood chowder.

"Chef Gabriel sends his regrets. A large group with a reservation for the private room has just arrived and he'll be extremely busy for the next while. He said he'll try to get back before the end of your dinner."

Angel nodded and smiled. She wasn't about to show her disappointment that Gabe wouldn't be stopping by their table. She could feel Bernadette's gaze on her, but she focused on tasting her chowder.

Chock-full of lobster meat, scallops and a variety of other fish and seafood, it was the best chowder Angel had ever tasted. *He'll make his future wife very happy one day.*

The unbidden thought shocked her. Why was she even thinking such things?

Gabe focused on making a series of his signature dishes for the large group celebrating a wedding engagement. He had just finished making a special surf 'n' turf platter for Angel and Bernadette, but couldn't spare the time to check in on them at their booth.

While Gabe and his team worked in sync, images of Angel inevitably popped up in his mind, but he had to swiftly nudge them aside. He didn't want to compromise the quality of his dishes due to lack of concentration. He would process his thoughts and feelings later, once he was back home.

Gabe strode to the private room to congratulate the engaged couple. The group clapped when they saw him, and the couple and several family members thanked him enthusiastically for his fabulous dishes and the complimentary bottles of champagne.

He continued into the main dining area, looking forward to seeing if Angel and Bernadette had enjoyed their dinner. They were chatting over coffee and dessert, his "Maritime Berry Pavlova."

"We haven't stopped raving about our dinner tonight, Gabe," Bernadette said, "You set the bar pretty high. I may have to get Ross to take some cooking lessons to keep me happy."

Gabe laughed. "Tell him not to bother with lessons. Just have him take you *here* for dinner." He winked as he caught Angel's gaze.

"I'm good with that," Bernadette declared with a thumbs-up.

They all laughed. Bernadette turned to Angel. "If you're ready, I'll get the bill and then we can head out."

"The bill is covered, Bernie. My treat tonight." Gabe put up a hand as Angel and Bernadette started to protest. "I own the place. I can do what I want." He smiled directly at Angel. "And Gramsy would approve."

"Gabriel McKellar, you're the best," Bernadette said, sliding out of the booth to give him a hug. She turned to Angel, who had risen also. "Are you still wanting to head home?"

"I am," Angel said. "But I'll take you up on the board game challenge another night." She glanced at Gabe. "Thank you for a wonderful dinner. It's very kind of you to cover it."

"It's my good deed of the day," he replied. "And you're very welcome." He turned to Bernadette. "I'm done for the night and Chris will close up, so I'll drive Angel home."

"Oh! Okay," Bernadette said swiftly, oblivious to Angel's surprised expression. "I guess that makes sense, since you're next door to each other." She gave Angel a hug. "Talk tomorrow, okay?"

After she left, Gabe looked at Angel. "Don't go away," he smiled. "I'll be right back."

Once he had deposited his chef's jacket in the side room to be sent to the dry cleaners, Gabe went into the kitchen to pack up a generous wedge of the pavlova for Angel and to thank Chris and his team for another excellent night.

He returned to find Angel in the same spot, tapping her fingers on the table. He handed her the see-through container. When she saw what it was, her eyes lit up.

A flicker of pleasure ran through him. Perhaps the adage about the way to a man's heart could be reversed. And then an inner voice told him not to be foolish. *It would take much more than food to get to Angel's heart.*

"I'm glad you enjoyed my humble offerings tonight," Gabe said as he started up the Porsche.

"I can see why Gramsy spoke so highly of the restaurant. And *you*."

Gabe shot her a surprised glance. "I didn't know I was the subject of your conversations."

"Only very rarely," Angel said in a serious tone.

Gabe caught her teasing grin as she looked out the window. "Ah. She also mentioned *you* once or twice in the last three years," he returned with a smirk. "Hey, instead of driving you home right away, Angel, I'd like to show you a special spot in the Highlands that I doubt you've been to. And if you have, I'm sure you'll still enjoy it. Sound good?"

"Uh, I'm kind of tired, Gabe. I was intending to just go home and hibernate after eating so much. *Your* fault."

He laughed. She was always making him laugh. "You'll wake up pretty quickly once you see where I'm taking you. Trust me."

She hesitated, her brow creasing.

Those last two words had just popped out of his mouth.

Maybe she had trust issues like he did. Gramsy had hinted that Angel had been deceived by a guy she had dated for months. *She broke it off pronto,* she told him approvingly. *My Angel deserves someone better.* Gramsy hadn't revealed the nature of the guy's deception, and Gabe hadn't probed. But now he had to consider whether Angel's hesitation was connected to her past experience with the guy. And with him.

"I suppose I can vary tonight's itinerary slightly," she said. "If it's a short detour. Otherwise, I *will* fall asleep and you'll have no choice but to carry me over Gramsy's threshold. And trust *me*, I weigh much more *now* than when I walked into Mara's." She cocked her head and smiled ruefully.

The image of carrying Angel in his arms sent a current of desire through him. He kept his eyes on the road, not wanting her to see his feelings reflected in his gaze. Things might be different if she was considering a move to the island, but with her future clearly back in Toronto, any attraction he might feel for her, both physical and emotional, could not be encouraged.

CHAPTER NINETEEN

Despite the lively music, Angel felt her eyelids drooping. Had it only been this morning that she and Gabe had seen the lawyer? The emotion of hearing Gramsy's will, meeting Gabe again on the beach and practically smothering him, and then dining at Mara's had pretty well taken up all her mental and emotional reserves. She allowed her eyes to close and the music to drown out her thoughts. She would process things tomorrow, after what she hoped would be a restful sleep.

Though she probably shouldn't have agreed to extending the day with a ride to goodness knows where. Was it wise to be in such close quarters with a guy whose kiss earlier had woken up some part of her that had been numb?

She stifled those thoughts and, keeping her eyes closed, concentrated on the music and the motion of the Porsche as Gabe picked up speed. Minutes later, she felt the car veer to the right and her eyes fluttered open. She squinted to try to see where they were going, but all she could make out was a ribbon of road against a sheer cliff topped by dense woodlands. As the road wound itself around the Highlands, Angel shivered. It was one thing to take the Cabot Trail by day, but by night, the immensity of it was even more daunting, with its cliffs skirting the ocean. She squeezed her eyes shut, feeling lightheaded. "Are we there yet?" she said, her voice cracking.

"We are arriving at the lookout…in five, four, three, two, one." He stopped the car. "You can open your eyes, Angel. And step out of the car. You'll want to see this."

Gabe was staring at her, the corners of his mouth lifting. He jumped out of the Porsche and held her door open. As far as she could see, they were in total darkness, except for the Porsche's interior light. She stepped out of the car and when the door closed and the light went off, she reached for Gabe's arm in alarm, her eyes trying to adjust.

"Now look up, Angel," he said.

She gazed upward and her mouth fell open. She had never seen so many stars in the night sky. Millions and millions. Some tiny, some large, some seeming to twinkle. The Milky Way, the constellations. She stared in awe. Was that Venus? Or Sirius, the brightest star? She did a 360-degree turn. The sheer beauty of it made her eyelids prickle. She blinked and gazed at Gabe. "I've *never* seen a sky like this. *Ever.* Are we still on earth?"

Gabe laughed softly. "I can't imagine being any closer to heaven than this."

"Wow, I can't get over it. I could stare at the sky all night." She tilted her head up again and as she started to turn, she faltered and Gabe's arms shot out to prevent her from falling. His hands on her bare arms made her catch her breath and when their gazes met, all she could see were stars reflected in his eyes.

"I wanted you to see this before you returned to Toronto," he said huskily. "To remember the beauty of this place, even at night."

Angel swallowed. "I'll never forget this." *And you.* An ache was spreading in her chest as it hit her what and whom she would be leaving behind when she left. The place that had been home to her for a part of practically every summer since she was a kid. Home and a place of magic, with fairy hills and fiddles, and lifetime friends like Bernadette. And maybe the promise of something more with Gabe.

Was it some stellar force that was drawing her closer to him? Making her want to kiss him again? Ignoring all the warning bells in her head, she closed the short distance between them and had barely murmured her thanks when his hands shifted to draw her into his embrace. Their cheeks brushed against each other briefly and she heard Gabe draw in his breath before their lips met.

Angel threw caution to the wind and returned his kiss readily, pressing her hands against his broad back. His hand reached up to cradle her head and she shivered with pleasure as his lips trailed kisses down her neck slowly and made their way back to her mouth. They finally drew apart as a cool gust of wind swept over them.

"I better get you home," Gabe murmured, his eyes searing into hers.

"Why?" Angel said breathlessly.

"Because you're dangerous. And the stars aren't helping."

"It's your fault for bringing me here."

Gabe stared at her for a moment and then, without warning, swept her up in his arms and swung her around. She gave a yelp that seemed to echo into the Highlands and clasped her hands around his neck.

"Aye, you're right," he drawled, his Scottish brogue sounding even sexier. "And I rightly take all the blame." He set her down gently. "But I can't let you bewitch me any further, or we'll be both sleeping under the stars tonight."

Angel's heart gave a jolt. He was right. If they didn't leave now, any sanity that she still had would leave her. And the stars wouldn't help.

* * *

Gramsy's words came back to Gabe as he drove. *My Angel deserves someone better.* Gramsy had trusted him to help Angel through the process of settling her estate, and he didn't want to do anything to jeopardize that trust. Yet he had allowed himself to be swept away by Angel, once on the beach, and now, under the stars. And from what he had seen and felt, Angel had willingly capitulated to the chemistry between them as well.

They were both vulnerable, having lost Gramsy. And maybe the natural human instinct was to connect with someone who had or who was experiencing similar emotions. But did the feelings that had emerged between him and Angel fall under that category?

It doesn't matter. You can't allow them to go any further.

Gabe felt a twinge in his chest, knowing he had to repress his feelings for Angel in the time that she had left on the island. Keep her at arm's length.

Not an easy task, considering that they had to work things out about the sale of the B&B.

He glanced over at Angel, but she was looking out her window. Not that she could see much in the dark. He wondered if perhaps she, too, had come to the conclusion that it was best to not encourage their budding feelings.

Like it or not, he'd have to come to terms with this reality, as well as the situation that was brewing with Charlotte. Somehow, he had the impression that she wasn't going to give up so easily. She had flown across the world to clear things up with him, for heaven's sake. Could he just casually dismiss her, let her know that it was too late to try to fix things? That it was finished three years ago? He had told her he'd moved on. But he didn't want to think any more about Charlotte now, with Angel sitting next to him. Doing so almost felt like a betrayal to Angel.

The silence between them was getting to him. Had he offended her in some way? Disappointed her?

"Do you want to talk, Angel?" He glanced over at her briefly. "About the meeting with the lawyer. Or *anything else*?"

She inhaled and exhaled deeply. "I don't know. I'm so… mixed up about things."

"About selling the B&B?"

"Hmm. Partially. A part of me wants to cling to it physically, and to all the memories it holds. Another part of me feels guilty that I haven't been back for three years, missing out on Gramsy's last years." Her brow furrowed and she looked away.

When she glanced back at him, she was blinking away tears.

"Angel, Gramsy was proud of you for being such a dedicated teacher, taking those summer courses to benefit your students. She wouldn't want you to feel guilty."

"She probably should have left something to you, having helped her so much."

Gabe took the exit into Chéticamp. "Angel, I owe a debt of gratitude to Gramsy. She inspired me to become the chef that I am. That was her gift to me, along with treating me like a grandson, and I'll never forget it. That's why I wanted to honor her by having a restaurant built in her name." He chuckled softly. "I'm not lacking for anything, Angel, and when Gramsy asked me if there was anything I wanted, I told her that she had already given me everything a grandson could want. Her love and attention. *Her recipes*," he added with a smile. "So don't feel bad or guilty about anything. The B&B is rightfully yours."

Angel didn't reply and looked ahead while they passed the familiar spots on Main Street, Le Gabriel Restaurant and Evangeline's, places she had often been to during her summer visits, their names evoking Longfellow's epic poem that she had read several times.

"But Gramsy also knew that if you intended to sell," he continued, "I would want the B&B. She knew how much it meant to me, too." Gabe turned at the beach sign and, a few minutes later, came to a stop in Gramsy's driveway. "If and when you're ready, Angel," he said, meeting her gaze, "just name your price and I'll empty my piggy bank."

His heart lifted when she laughed softly.

"You make me laugh, even when I don't want to."

"I don't mind being laughed at." Gabe grinned. *Or kissed*, he wished he could tell her. He also wished he could reach over and give her a reassuring hug.

A sudden ring startled them both, and their gazes shifted to Gabe's cell phone in the open console between them. The caller's name was visible to both of them. *Charlotte*.

"I'll say good-night," Angel said quickly, letting herself out of the Porsche.

"Hold on, Angel," Gabe called out, but she was already at her doorstep. Frowning as the cell phone kept ringing, he watched Angel disappear into the house. "*Damn*," he muttered, and picked up his phone.

CHAPTER TWENTY

Angel locked the door and moments later heard Gabe leaving.

Charlotte. So there was a woman in his life.

But why did that name ring a bell? Where had she seen or heard it before?

Gramsy. Yes, Gramsy had mentioned the name when she was telling Angel about Gabe's tragic loss of his parents and his breakup. That was three years ago.

She remembered feeling for Gabe, even though she hadn't seen him for ten years. Angel felt a knot in her stomach. They were still in touch with each other.

She stared at the container she was holding with the piece of pavlova. She had contemplated having it as a bedtime snack, but her appetite had faded, her stomach too jittery. She strode to the kitchen to put the container in the fridge. Too tired to even think of running a bath, she brushed her teeth, changed into a teddy and got into bed.

Angel flipped her pillow over and turned on her right side to stare out her window at the stars. She breathed the night air deeply, trying to calm her racing thoughts.

Up until seeing Charlotte's name, Angel had been replaying in her mind the scene of Gabe and her gazing at the sky, brimming with a zillion stars that she was sure were sprinkling their magic over them. Gabe's magical kiss had led her to have crazy thoughts and feelings. Thoughts about what it might be like if she stayed longer in Chéticamp. Just a few weeks, to see if the returning spark she felt for Gabe—and that he seemed to reciprocate—would ignite into something more serious. It was crazy. Crazy to have even allowed her mind to veer into these danger zones. Crazy because Gabe obviously still had a connection with his ex-fiancée.

So why did he kiss me? And in a way that was far from casual...

Her heart twisted. Maybe Gabe and Charlotte were a thing again. And *she* had just been a diversion.

Just like she'd been to Colin.

Her eyes started to prickle. She felt hurt, used. Embarrassed by the way she had responded to Gabe's kisses. She turned over on her left side so she wouldn't see the stars. Earlier, they had tricked her into thinking that there was *something* between her and Gabe.

And Gabe had played along.

Angel let the tears flow. It was her fault for letting her guard down, and Gabe was equally to blame. She just didn't know how she was going to face him in the time she had left before flying back to Toronto. There was still the terms of the B&B to finalize, but maybe she could go and see the lawyer herself and sign the necessary papers without Gabe being there. She didn't even want to think about the reception to honor Gramsy at the B&B. Tomorrow, when her head was clear, she would figure out how to deal with that.

Angel flipped the pillow over to the dry side and closed her eyes, concentrating on imagining every room in the B&B, and thinking of the items she wanted to bring back with her or have shipped to Toronto. Tomorrow she would go and purchase some packing boxes.

And the first thing she'd pack up were Gramsy's recipe binders.

Angel's eyes flew open when she realized that the train sound she was hearing was the sound of Bernadette texting. She reached for her phone and squinted to read the message.

Are you up? I have coffee and croissants, right outside your door.

Coming!

Angel slipped out of bed, put on her robe and hurried downstairs. When she opened the door, Bernadette gazed at her with raised eyebrows.

"Late night, Angel?" Her mouth twitched.

"It's not what you think," Angel said, grabbing the bag of croissants. *"Not. At. All."* She opened the door for Bernadette. "Come on in. Coffee first, talk after."

A few minutes later, sitting across from each other at the island, Angel frowned at Bernadette. "Aren't you supposed to be at work?"

"It's Saturday, remember? I'm working the afternoon shift. And hopefully afterward, I'll finally get to see Ross."

"What do you mean, *finally*? Where has he been?"

"He's been spending a lot of time with that out-of-country Realtor I mentioned the other day, showing her properties for her uber-rich client from Edinburgh."

Something clicked in Angel's memory. She put down

her half-bitten croissant, her throat suddenly feeling dry. "The one who has a personal connection here?"

"Good memory. Yeah, why?"

Angel felt a twinge in her chest. "Did Ross mention her name?"

"No. Angel, you look really pale. Did you not sleep last night?"

"Not much, no. Can you do me a favor, Bernie? Text Ross and just ask him the name of the Realtor. I think she's—"

"Oh my gosh. Are you thinking what never crossed my mind until now?" Bernadette set down her mug. "That she's—"

"Gabe's ex-fiancée," Angel blurted. "And I think they're back together."

Bernadette shook her head. "I can't believe that. Any time I've met Gabe for coffee or lunch, he never mentioned Charlotte or even hinted at a reconciliation between them. This must be a coincidence. Ross has had other Realtors from the UK scoping out properties here."

"Bernie, when Gabe drove me home last night, he got a call. I saw the caller's name. *Charlotte*."

Bernadette's mouth dropped. She shook her head. "Okay, I'm texting Ross."

A couple of minutes later, she looked up from her phone, her eyes wide. "You're right, Angel. Charlotte's the Realtor he's been dealing with. He's on his way to pick her up at her hotel." She scrunched up her face. "She *is* looking around at properties for a client, but Ross said she was actually considering purchasing a property for herself on the island."

Angel felt as if someone had punched her in the stomach. "I don't think she's joking, Bernie," she said, unable to stop her voice from breaking.

Bernadette stared at her for a moment, eyes widening. "Oh, Angel, you've fallen for him again," she said slowly.

Angel's eyes blurred. "Yeah," she said bitterly. "You can call me 'a fallen angel.'" She wiped her eyes with the napkin from the croissant bag. "And a damn fool."

Gabe stared out the living room window at the beach, willing Angel to appear. She had left the car so abruptly last night. But what did he expect? She had seen the call come through, and if he were to guess, Charlotte's name might have thrown her off. Made her think that he and his ex were on closer terms than they actually were.

That is, if she even knew that Charlotte was his ex-fiancée.

He couldn't blame Angel if she thought he was a cad, kissing her when he was seeing someone else. He had wanted to clear up any misunderstanding right then and there, but she hadn't given him the chance.

Gabe gulped down the rest of his coffee, tired of his conflicting thoughts. They had interrupted his sleep several times last night and he needed to get his act together, especially since there was an invitation-only event at his restaurant tonight. He needed to be in top form, especially since his sous-chef had heard that an international food critic would be among the invited guests.

Pouring his second cup, Gabe went over the last conversation he had with Angel. It had touched him that Angel felt Gramsy could have left him something. What Angel didn't know was that Gramsy *had* left him something. Or rather, *someone. Her.*

Of course, Gramsy hadn't known that he would have

feelings for Angel. Or had she? Was that something that she had hoped would happen, that the two people she loved would connect—or reconnect—when she was gone?

The more Gabe thought about it, the more it seemed possible that Gramsy had drawn up her will in the way she had for that very reason. He knew she wanted Angel to think about staying in Chéticamp, and Gramsy was wise enough to consider that if Angel felt she had to sell, then she should sell to Gabe. And even wiser—or more cunning—to add the clause about Angel renting the place to him for a year, to give Angel a decent amount of time to really think about whether she wanted to let the B&B and property go.

A memory of Gramsy randomly showing him photos of Angel in the last two years made Gabe suspect now that her actions held a deeper motive. Gramsy knew how much he had suffered after his parents passed and after Charlotte broke up with him. She helped him through his grieving, and was always concerned about him. He would find someone worthy of him and vice versa, she had reassured him. And after treating him to fresh-out-of-the-oven oatcakes or scones, or a steaming seafood chowder, she would casually share her latest photos of Angel. It hadn't hit him then—perhaps his mind and heart were too numb with grief—but now, it seemed more than plausible that Gramsy was trying to be a matchmaker.

This thought made his eyes prickle. Not only had she shown him care and concern—and love—while she was alive, but even after passing, the terms in her will could pave the way for possibilities between him and Angel…

He was going to miss Gramsy dearly. She had been such a good person, not only to him but to her guests and neighbors. He wanted to honor her by doing all the cooking for the reception at the B&B, and he'd hoped to talk about his plans with Angel last night, but she left prematurely.

Perhaps he should make his way over to talk to Angel. Casually tell her that the call coming in last night hadn't meant anything to him. He had to be up front with Angel, explain that his ex-fiancée was in the area for business purposes, and that she was calling to arrange a coffee meeting with him, but that he had politely declined.

But would this even make a difference? Or was he setting himself up for another letdown?

Gabe set down his mug and was about to go upstairs to change out of his robe when the doorbell rang. His pulse spiked, thinking it might be Angel. Perhaps she felt bad for leaving so abruptly last night and was coming over to explain? He strode to the door, not wanting to risk her leaving if he first went up to get dressed.

He tightened the sash on his robe and opened the door. His welcoming smile froze on his face. It was Charlotte.

CHAPTER TWENTY-ONE

Angel strode to the living room and plopped down onto one of the recliners. Bernadette sat opposite her.

"Angel, you might have it all wrong, you know," Bernadette said half-heartedly.

Angel shot her a skeptical look. "Come on, Bernie, I'm not that naive."

"Why don't you talk to Gabe and tell him how you feel?"

"You've got to be kidding!" Angel frowned. "I'm not going to embarrass myself any more than I already have." She held up her hand. "I allowed myself to be fooled once. *Not* gonna happen again."

"You can't very well avoid him for the next few days."

"I'll try my best," Angel said decisively. "I want to go out and buy some packing boxes. Can you drive me and give me a hand packing up Gramsy's recipe binders?"

Bernadette sighed. "Well, don't pack up too much. Gramsy was a wise owl, figuring you needed time to really make up your mind about selling." A gleam came into her eyes. "So maybe there's hope that you will—"

"Bernie, I love you, but don't get your hopes up." She hugged Bernadette. "I'll still visit when I can, and you can come and visit me in Toronto."

"Angel, I love you, too, but don't get *your* hopes up," she said cheekily. "You know I'm not a city girl. I'm a proud

Cape Bretoner, and I wouldn't last long without my ocean air and water."

"Yeah, you'd feel like a fish out of water in Toronto," Angel laughed. "Look, Angel. Why don't I just take a run for the boxes, and you can get dressed and call Gabe or just go over?" She raised her hand. "No, I'm not crazy, if that's what you're about to say. I just think you might have overreacted to seeing Charlotte's name. She might have just wanted to say hello to Gabe. You're just fixated on the worst-case scenario because *you have feelings for him*. And you had a bad experience with Colin."

Angel waited until Bernadette finished talking. Her voice was gentle, not pushy, and hearing her say the words made them even more real.

Yes, she *did* have feelings for Gabe. Feelings that had resurrected from the time she was sixteen and had become exponentially stronger. And she didn't know what to do with them.

"He won't bite if you go over and be up front with him, Angel."

"And what exactly would I say?" She frowned, drumming her fingers on the island countertop.

"That you shouldn't have left so quickly last night, and that you'd like to talk. *Easy-peasy*. And then you apologize, he looks at you with his luminous blue-green eyes and holds out his hand. You take it and he pulls you gently into his arms, and—"

"Stop, Bernie!" Angel put her hands on her hips. "You are such a dreamer."

"Okay, maybe I am. But maybe you should start dreaming about possibilities, Angel. I see the way Gabe looks at you. Trust me, I haven't seen him look at any other woman that way. And believe me, a lot of women have tried to get his attention."

Angel let out a big sigh. "Okay, I'll… I'll think about it while I change."

Bernadette grinned. "I'll go find some packing boxes. We'll talk later." She strode to the front door. "And be prepared to give me details," she said, and winked back at Angel.

Angel changed into a pair of pale yellow Capri pants and a white T-shirt. As she was slipping into her running shoes, the first drops of rain tapped against the side window of the front door. Unperturbed, she grabbed one of Gramsy's umbrellas from the corner bin and her light all-weather jacket. *You have to make peace with the weather if you're a true Maritimer*, Gramsy told Angel during her visits. *You can't let a few raindrops stop you.* And they would work in the garden together, or walk the beach, or walk to a neighbor's for afternoon tea. Angel would always enjoy their outings, and sometimes Bernadette would join them. *And Gabe, too.*

Angel took a deep breath. Could Bernadette be right about Charlotte? And that Angel was creating unnecessary drama around seeing her name pop up on a call to Gabe? She supposed it *was* possible.

Suddenly she felt foolish. Her imagination had gone wild, and if Bernadette could see that she had feelings for Gabe, maybe Gabe had seen that also. Her heart began a quiet drumming. Was Gabe thinking about possibilities? Could *she* start dreaming about possibilities between them, too?

Any aspirations she'd had about Colin had disintegrated after his deception, and after that, she hadn't allowed herself to get close enough to anyone to allow dreams to nudge into her thoughts during the day or night.

Now, remembering how close she and Gabe had gotten on the beach and then under the stars sent a current of heat spiraling through her. She was grateful for the intermittent breeze that cooled her cheeks.

Doing some deep breathing, Angel started briskly toward the road that would take her to Gabe's, rather than the path to the beach. She gazed at the flower garden that ran across the B&B and the window boxes and the pots on the front steps, and her heart ached at the beauty Gramsy had created. The bursts of color reminded her of some of the paintings of Nova Scotia's Maud Lewis, who had left a legacy of her brilliant works, created in her tiny decorated house that now held a celebrated spot in the Halifax art gallery.

Flowers always uplifted Angel, and as she walked, she told herself to stay positive and to keep an open mind—and heart—about possibilities. The future wasn't clear to her, and she found that a little scary, given her penchant for having things under control—*her control*. But maybe she should let go a little and allow the universe to guide her, instead of *her* taking the reins all the time.

As she neared the estate, Angel felt a gust of wind swirl around her and her umbrella turned inside out. She tried to fix it but one of the spokes broke off. The gentle sprinkling of rain that had accompanied her this far quickly changed to a shower. Giving up on the umbrella, she made a run for Gabe's front door. By the time she reached it, her clothes were partially soaked and the rain was running down her hair in streams. Ordinarily, Angel would have been annoyed or distressed, but to her surprise, she felt neither emotion. She set down the broken umbrella and rang the doorbell. She was squeezing the excess water out of her hair when the door opened.

Gabe's eyes widened and then skimmed over her. He was wearing a bathrobe and slippers, and Angel felt embarrassed that she had caught him in this state.

"Is it my cab, Gabe?"

The voice preceded the woman, who, unlike Gabe, was fully dressed. Her red hair was long and silky, and her eyes were a startling green, matching her sleeveless sundress. Angel's heart plummeted. This had to be Charlotte.

As much as Angel wanted to run away, her shoes felt leaden. She stood under the front-door awning, and from the once-over Charlotte was now giving her, Angel could only imagine the picture she made.

Gabe glanced from Charlotte to her. "Angel—"

"Sorry, I should have called first. I just wanted to discuss the meeting with the lawyer," she lied, avoiding his gaze. At that moment, a cab turned into the driveway.

"I better grab my handbag," Charlotte said, and rushed inside.

Angel wasted no time in turning away. The cab slowed to a stop and Angel ran past it.

"Angel, wait, *please*."

Gabe's voice was urgent, but she ignored it, quickening her pace. Why had she let Bernadette convince her to go over to his place? What a complete and utter fool she was to have believed that she meant something to him.

She cringed at the thought of Gabe in his robe and the fact that Charlotte had spent the night with him. Her jaw clenched. *Fool me once, shame on him. Fool me twice, shame on me.* She wanted to scream and let out her sadness, anger, disappointment and regret.

By the time she reached Gramsy's, she was out of breath

and completely drenched, but she didn't go inside. She needed to walk out her disillusionment and frustration. The same horrible feelings she had experienced when she had found out that Colin was married.

Angel took the path down to the beach, and headed in the direction away from Gabe's place.

Now she was convinced there was no place for her on the island. No reason for her to ever reconsider a move. Absolutely no reason at all.

Gabe went upstairs to his room to change as soon as Charlotte left. It was unfortunate that Angel arrived at the moment she did, with him in his robe and Charlotte at his place. What she didn't know was that he was unaware that his ex-fiancée would show up uninvited. Charlotte explained that when she found out that Ross knew Gabe, she asked him for Gabe's address, saying that they were friends from the past and she had misplaced his contact information.

Ross innocently gave her the information and she arranged for a cab. When she arrived, she invited herself in and sauntered into the living room, claiming that she needed to talk to Gabe before she made her next move.

"I need to know if there's a chance for us, Gabe," she had stated bluntly after Angel left. "My business here ends in a couple of days, and then I have a week to myself. I am not going to stick around and waste my time if you're not interested."

You had a hard time sticking around in the past, Gabe wanted to say. He was silent for a few moments, choosing his words carefully. "Charlotte, I don't think small-town living on Cape Breton Island is the kind of lifestyle you want or need."

"I could fly back and forth to Scotland when I get bored," she said with a smile. "Like you do."

"Charlotte, I don't return to Scotland because I'm bored. I don't get bored here. I love this island and I love my life here."

She tossed back her hair and her green eyes narrowed. "Have you found someone? Is that why you're not interested?"

"Charlotte, even if I hadn't found someone, I wouldn't be interested."

She frowned.

"I'm not trying to be mean. It's just that our priorities are different. *We're* different. You deserve someone who wants the same things you do."

Her eyes widened. "Is it that woman who showed up like a bedraggled kitten on your doorstep?"

Gabe had to control his mouth. "Your cab is waiting," he said curtly. "And that woman has more heart in her little finger than most people." *Than you*, he wanted to add, but he didn't want to stoop to her level. He stared at her pointedly. "And yes, I love her and want to spend the rest of my life with her." *Even if she doesn't know it yet.*

Charlotte's sculpted eyebrows went up and her mouth dropped open. "Well, that settles that, then," she said, with a curt laugh. She turned to open the door. "Have a nice life, Gabe."

"I will," he said. "Thanks."

She gave him a look of resignation and let herself out. He wasted no time in going upstairs to change. He felt breathless as he dressed in a pair of jeans and hoodie. Breathless for voicing what he had, up to now, kept in his heart…that he loved Angel. Acknowledging it openly made him feel exhilarated, but he knew that at the moment, Angel was feeling anything but.

He had to go after her and make her understand that Charlotte had no place in his life, and that *she* was the one he wanted. He took the stairs two at a time and grabbed his all-weather jacket from the hall tree.

He drove to the B&B and rang the doorbell and, moments later, opened the door slightly and called out Angel's name. If she was out, she couldn't have gone far. He took a chance that she might be on the beach. He ran down the path and couldn't see anyone on his side of the beach, but he spotted a figure in the opposite direction. The rain and the ocean spray from the increasing winds blurred his vision so he couldn't be sure if it was Angel, but he was willing to take the chance.

He broke into a run. The wind kept whipping his hood off and he stopped trying to keep it on. The sound of the waves surging and cresting filled his ears. He could barely hear his own thoughts as he tried to formulate his words to Angel.

The figure was closer. He squeezed his eyes shut and then shielded them with his hands to have a better look. It *was* Angel. He felt his heart begin its drumming. "Angel!" he called out, but a cramp in his leg made him falter, and he felt himself collapsing on the beach as an intense pain gripped his calf. *"Damn!"* Gabe started to massage the area, but cringed at the pain. When he thought he wouldn't be able to endure it any longer, it suddenly subsided.

Gabe continued to rub the area, reluctant to stand up right away and risk getting another cramp.

"I suppose I should offer you a hand to get up...before you're washed out to sea."

Gabe twisted his head so sharply that he felt a burn

along a nerve in his neck. "Angel!" he said, his voice cracking. He stared up at her, with the rain streaming down her face and hair, and unconcerned about her drenched clothes. *An island girl.*

CHAPTER TWENTY-TWO

WHEN ANGEL HAD heard Gabe call, her first instinct was to ignore him and keep walking. But when she turned and saw him landing on the beach, her heart had jolted, thinking he was hurt and remembering how he had helped her when she'd injured her calf. Now she saw the look of relief in his eyes.

"Leg cramp," he said huskily. "I'm okay now. But thanks for offering to help." He ventured a smile. "I'll still accept a hand."

She hesitated momentarily and then extended her left hand. He pushed himself up and stood facing her without letting go of her hand. "Angel—"

"You don't need to explain, Gabe. I get the picture." She pulled her hand away but her gaze locked with his. "But I don't appreciate you taking advantage of the circumstances to lead me on." She bit her lip, recalling the swirl of desire his kisses had ignited. "It was dishonest, deceitful and just *wrong*, given the fact that you and your ex-fiancée are back together." She frowned. "I have no use for that kind of behavior. Or anyone who acts like that." Now that she had the chance, she wasn't going to keep her feelings to herself. She would let him have it. "Gramsy always spoke so highly of you. I guess she wasn't aware of this side of your personality," she said bitingly.

She paused, the rain mingling with the tears that were edging out. The waves breaking on the shore seemed to be extraordinarily loud. Usually, she loved the sound, but now, the cacophony just seemed to intensify the ache in her heart.

Gabe was looking at her intently but not making any attempt to reply. She smirked. Of course he had nothing to say. He knew she was right.

"It's too bad Gramsy wanted me to sell the B&B to you if I decided not to keep it," she continued, wanting to hurt him with her words, the way his actions had hurt her. "Under the right circumstances, I'd keep it myself and not sell it at all." She gave a bitter laugh. "But you can congratulate yourself for inching your way into Gramsy's heart," she said, her voice breaking. *And mine.* "I'll be packing up some of the items I want and leaving right after the reception in her memory. Oh, and you don't have to worry about doing any of the cooking or baking. I'll talk to Bernadette about ordering the food from Making Waves."

"Angel, stop. *Please.*"

She blinked at him, taken aback by the hurt in his eyes, and not feeling at all triumphant about it. He was as drenched as she was, and the rain had begun to intensify. He glanced beyond her shoulder and then back at her.

"Angel, please give me a chance to explain. I promise, you won't regret it. But standing here is ridiculous. The fairy hole is up ahead. At least it'll be dry."

Angel knew Gabe was talking about one of the sea caves in the area, a place that had held wonder for her as a child. Gramsy had taken her there and they'd had a picnic inside the cave, while watching the surf come roaring and crashing on the shore.

The fairy hole, tied to the sacred Mi'kmaq culture on the

island, was also a place where she, Bernadette and Gabe had ventured one summer while the adults were enjoying the garden party at Gabe's parents' place.

They didn't stay long, as the deep, dark recesses of the cave had frightened Angel, being the youngest. She imagined bats, trolls and even spooky fairies lurking in the depths. They hurried back and were met with stern looks and even sterner consequences for breaking the rules and wandering off. Gabe, being the oldest, was held responsible and was grounded.

But now the cave seemed a welcome respite. She nodded curtly and they both ran for it. A couple of minutes later, they were standing just inside. Angel glanced warily at the ceiling. There was no sign of bats at this time of day, thank goodness.

She caught Gabe's gaze and the amusement in his eyes, and she suspected he was recalling the incident when they were young.

"At least now I won't get grounded when we return," he said huskily.

"You should be grounded anyway," she said curtly.

"Touché," he said, and sighed. "Okay, Angel, now can I try to explain?"

She shrugged. "It doesn't matter."

"To me it does." He gazed at her intently. "Charlotte came to the island of her own accord. She did have business here and she did try to take the opportunity to see if there was a chance we could get back together. I made it clear that I wasn't interested."

"In your robe?" Angel's words slipped out.

Gabe's brows lifted and she knew that he'd guessed her implication.

"I wasn't expecting her to come to my place. In fact, I

had never given her my address. She got it from Ross, saying that she lost my contact information. She came over this morning. I had just taken a shower and when I heard the doorbell, I thought it was *you*. I didn't want to go and get changed and risk you not being there when I opened the door."

Angel blinked, her mind trying to process his every word. Could she believe him?

"Angel, I was finished with Charlotte three years ago. Yes, I was hurt when she broke off with me, but it didn't take me long to realize that we weren't right for each other. Look, she came to Mara's yesterday. She apologized for not being there for me when my parents died and she hoped we could reconcile. I accepted her apology. And… I thought you had no interest in seeing if there was a possibility that we could—"

"So you let her believe that there was a chance for a reconciliation?" Angel forced herself to ask the question.

"I said nothing, which I regret. Which is why she made a second attempt to push the issue. Just before you arrived on my doorstep." He smiled. "Looking like a beautiful, lost, drenched kitten that I wanted to rescue." He reached for her hand and squeezed it gently. "You bolted, and I wanted to run after you, but I had to change. *After* making it very clear to Charlotte that she was barking up the wrong tree." He took her other hand and gazed into her eyes. "I told her I loved you," he said softly. "But I should have told you that *first*."

Angel felt her eyes prickling. He loved her. And the leap of her heart confirmed what she knew deep down—that she loved him too. She blinked, wanting to believe him fully, but there was something she had to get out. "My boyfriend cheated on me, made me believe I was the only one in his life. Turns out he was married," she said. "I told him I never wanted to see him again." She looked at Gabe through blurred vision. "I could never be with a man I couldn't trust."

"And you thought I was taking advantage of you while I was involved with Charlotte." He nodded. "I get it. And I swear, Angel, as Gramsy is my witness up above, that you can trust me." He drew his arms around her. "I wouldn't risk lying and having Gramsy haunt me for the rest of my life." His chin grazed her cheek. "A life I want to spend with *you*," he murmured gently. "If you'll have me."

Angel shifted to meet his gaze, the dark green depths of his eyes mirroring the turbulent gulf waters. She felt a tremor go through her, anticipating what lay ahead for them. But could she make a permanent move to the island?

Gabe brought her hands to his lips and kissed them. "I love it here, Angel… But I love you more. We drifted apart in the past, and we can't let that ever happen again. If you want to stay in Toronto, I'll make my home there with you, and we can spend our summers here. I can always check in on Mara's, like I do with Maeve's." His eyes were bright as they pierced into hers. "You are my home, Angel."

Angel felt her heart do a flip at what Gabe was willing to give up for her. Her mind flipped, too. Relocating to Chéticamp wasn't as impossible as it had first seemed. So what if she lost her seniority? She could still teach with the same salary rate.

She had so much to gain here. And even if she didn't get a teaching job right away, she'd be happy getting reacquainted with the place that had enchanted her throughout the years, giving her memories to cherish. Only now, she could make new memories with the man she loved. Her Scottish Cape Bretoner.

Angel lifted her hand to tenderly touch his cheek. "The island has always been a part of my heart. But with you here, my heart is now full. I'm here to stay, Gabe." As her eyes began to prickle, she imagined Longfellow's Evangeline must have felt the same way when she was reunited with her Gabriel. She said as much toGabe and was startled to see his beautiful eyes misting.

"Only our story together will last a long, long time," he said huskily. "We found each other after again after ten years. No more searching. I love you, Evangeline. *My angel.*"

"I love you, Gabriel," she murmured, stroking his jaw. She reached into her pocket and fished out the pink heart shell and chain she had retrieved from her bedroom closet before heading to his place.

Gabe looked at it in wonder before placing it around her neck. He bent to kiss her. She wrapped her arms around his neck and allowed herself to reciprocate his passion, the rush of the waves and the salty breeze stirring her soul. She was exactly where she was meant to be, she thought, catching her breath to meet his gaze. On Chéticamp Island.

And in Gabe's eyes and heart!

* * * * *

If you enjoyed this story, check out these other great reads from Rosanna Battigelli

Falling for the Sardinian Baron
Rescued by the Guarded Tycoon
Caribbean Escape with the Tycoon
Captivated by Her Italian Boss

All available now!

JET-SET NIGHTS WITH HER ENEMY

MICHELE RENAE

MILLS & BOON

CHAPTER ONE

Number 8. Her lucky number. Peachy Cohen set the auction paddle on the empty folding chair beside her. Before her on stage, the Van Marks' Auction House manager oversaw the white-gloved crew bringing out the next painting to place on the block. Titled *Melancholy*, by French painter George Devereux, it had just been released from a private collection. It depicted a ghostly white Victorian-period woman sitting before a pianoforte while her startled and bereaved husband watched her create a haunting melody from the shadows.

It was this painting Peachy was here to bid on. And win.

Picking up her purse from the floor beside where she'd laid her cane, she ran her fingers over the Hermès silk scarf she kept tied to the handle—a good-luck talisman—then sorted through it in between glances at the competition in the seats around her. The usual suspects were bidding this afternoon in this subdued London salesroom. All of them men, save the one elderly woman in the back, her silver hair swept up in a stylish chignon and her choice in brick-red lipstick spot-on.

Peachy's employer at the Hammerstill Gallery—the notoriously grumpy Heinrich Hammerstill himself—had given her a want list of four paintings to win and bring back to the gallery. Each would be auctioned separately at various auction houses. None must end up in someone else's hands. Today's lot was the first of the four.

Pulling out her compact, she checked her makeup. Her lipstick needed a bit of retouching, so she pulled out a bold red lipstick and dabbed her lips. In the mirror, she took in those seated behind her. Silver chignon stood, preparing to leave. There were only two items remaining for bid. Many had already left the sales floor.

But there. Panic squeezed her heart. She hadn't noticed *him* earlier when assessing the room for competition. Must have walked in late. Or, more specifically, arrived just in time for the item he sought.

Peachy snapped her compact shut and set her purse on the floor. She'd swear, but that was no way to maintain her composure.

Krew Lawrence sat two rows behind her on the opposite side of the aisle. The man was a reality television personality, dubbed The Brain for his smarts and art knowledge. Lawrence was a shark at auction. Rarely did he lose a bid. He was one of three men who owned the London-based billion-dollar art brokerage The Art Guys. They were celebrities in the art world.

And where those men went…

With a surreptitious glance over her shoulder she spied the two-man film crew at the back of the room. Media were not allowed onto the sales floor, but apparently a television show had some clout. They had stationed themselves behind the last row of empty chairs. One held the camera, obviously filming. The other held a shotgun mic.

Smoothing a hand across her tightening stomach, Peachy blew out a calming breath. The Brain couldn't possibly have an interest in the painting she was here to win. But just in case…

She crossed her legs slowly, one hand slipping unobtrusively along her thigh to slightly inch up her red-and-white polka-dot skirt. A careful glide of her leg along the other should draw attention to the black patent-leather shoes that did not have a high heel but the straps gave them a sexy allure. This position was always taxing to her hip, which she'd injured years ago, but she would maintain it for the sake of her win.

With a calculated bow of her head, she twisted it to look over her shoulder. Lowered her lashes. Parted her lips…

Mr. Lawrence looked up from his phone. Directly at her. Mercy, he was handsome. Dark hair cut short on the sides and left a little longer on top emphasized his square face, and the trim beard further framed his handsome features, his straight nose. The telly did no justice to his shimmering green eyes or even that tiny mole above his eyebrow that danced as he frowned. He gave a tilt of his head as he studied her. *Surveyed* her.

She opened her mouth slightly. Jutted her chin. And then, crossing her fingers beneath the auction paddle, she turned to face the stage where the auctioneer detailed the provenance of *Melancholy*.

Had that sultry yet coy look been meant for him?

Krew noted the initial bid. A lowball. He never tossed out the first bid, knowing it was always wisest to first discern his competition. The auctioneer sought the next bidder and found it in the front row. Then another bidder. And then *she* lifted her paddle.

She wasn't going to win. And those sexy legs weren't going to help her either. He was impervious to female flirtation.

With a nod of his head, Krew bid. Everyone had their

bid style and the auctioneers at all the London houses were aware of his method. He couldn't be pressed to lift a paddle.

As the auctioneer sought another bid, Krew's eyes strolled along those long legs a second time. Sleek and bare, impossibly tantalizing. The shoes had thin black straps that crissed and crossed up her ankles. Caged in soft leather and tied as if a gift.

Krew's heart performed a sort of jump. Very odd.

The inner stutter alerted him to the auctioneer's prompt. Right. *Pay attention, Lawrence.*

He nodded to make another bid. Glanced to the film crew now standing to the side of the main floor. They were recording everything. And he was equipped with a lavalier mic pinned to his suitcoat lapel. Much as the television series "increased their socials," as The Art Guys' receptionist Maeve was wont to gush, he didn't care for the filming process. At least, not this banal, everyday kind of stuff. Nor did it please him that he was not allowed to direct or edit the content the crew captured. But Joss and Asher, his business partners, found great value in the show so who was he to argue the inconvenience of being followed 24/7?

This oil on canvas was lovely. Painted by a late-nineteenth-century French artist whose most popular works had been book illustrations, the majority of the canvas was dark, utilizing blacks, browns and deep umbers for mood, save for the brilliant creamy white tones of the female spirit seated before a very much alive and grieving man who had lost his wife. It was haunting. But not to Krew's taste.

It didn't matter that he cared little for the work. Krew needed to acquire this painting for a client: his father, Byron Lawrence. The Lawrence family was old money, and old art. Lots of both. To the point that if a family member did not admire art then a DNA test was suggested, not even facetiously. Krew's father had amassed an immense collection over his lifetime. It was an obsession. A vulgar display of wealth. But Krew would never suggest that to Byron, who measured his son's value by his bank statement and his ability to bring him yet another rare artwork.

Since forming The Art Guys eight years ago, Krew had helped Byron to procure a Rembrandt, a da Vinci and a Caravaggio.

The old man had divorced last year. For the third time. And his ex-wife, a Frenchwoman, had made off with some of Byron's prized pieces when she'd been clearing her things out of his home. Now Claudia was selling them, knowing it would drive her ex crazy. And she wasn't selling them all at the same auction house. Nor was she releasing info on the sales until a day or two beforehand. It was clear she wanted Byron to suffer the loss of the paintings slowly.

Krew had initially balked at being drawn into his dad's marital vendetta. But when Byron had pointed out the similarities between his third marriage and Krew's own brief marriage, Krew had agreed that a calculating woman should not be allowed victory after ruining a man's life so thoroughly.

His own marriage... Well, mistakes had been made.

So here he sat, his father's son in every aspect. Entitled art aficionado. Lonely heart. Unworthy of a real, true love. Eager to set the scales of justice to balance.

Thinking those descriptions of his father—and de facto, *him*—made Krew shake his head. Was he really such a pitiful case? No. He wasn't entitled, nor lonely. He had quite a good life. His work with The Art Guys made him happy. As for love? It wasn't that he felt unworthy of it, only... He wondered, was he even *capable* of true intimacy? He wanted love. He just wasn't sure how love actually worked emotionally. He'd never had a decent role model for it.

As his ears followed the exchange of bids, Krew's eyes again strayed to the slide of long, graceful fingers along thigh. That was a move a man should make, lingering on the softness of her skin, exploring the trek upward to that curvaceous—

The woman glanced his way. Krew narrowed his gaze. Something about her seemed familiar. That dress—red with white polka dots—hugged her every curve jealously. He didn't know her personally, but he was aware she was a dealer with a local gallery owned by Heinrich Hammerstill. Not The Art Guys' favorite dealer in London.

She didn't so much smile as make him a promise in the lush purse of her reddest-of-red lips. That promise tightened about Krew's heart, but nothing could storm the rampart into the tender center of a heart that, once broken, had pulled up armor.

Turning her attention back to the stage, a subtle shake of her head sifted her wavy charcoal hair in a sway. It wasn't long enough to reach her shoulders, and exposed a pale, swanlike neck.

With the bang of the auctioneer's hammer, the bidding came to an end.

Krew shook himself out of his observation of the woman. Wait. Had he won?

Gentle applause accompanied the auctioneer's announcement that Miss Cohen of the Hammerstill Gallery had won the Devereux.

Krew's jaw dropped open. He never lost a bid. And those in the business knew it.

He huffed and moved to adjust his lapel in frustration, then caught himself. If he placed a hand over the microphone he wore the crew would complain at the feedback.

With a graceful glide to stand, the woman picked up her

purse and turned to walk down the aisle. She was as steady as a gazelle gliding down the runway despite the fact she used a cane. She didn't lean on it heavily, as if she didn't actually need it for support. Curious.

Just as they came parallel, she winked at him. A triumphant smile followed along with a tilt of her head. An aura of crisp citrus perfume and sensuality sashayed along with her. So familiar...

Krew clutched his hands into fists. It felt as though he'd just been swept by a hurricane. This was bad form.

The man sitting beside him leaned in and muttered, "Tough luck, Mr. Brain. Don't take it so hard. She's a honeypot. That woman could have us all with a wink. Too bad she's broken."

Annoyed at the man's crass label, Krew countered, "You are the broken one, sir, to imply any human could be such a thing."

The old man huffed and crossed his arms over his chest.

Krew turned to look down the aisle, more as a means to distance himself from the rude comment. The woman had exited the room. The camera crew, now repositioned near the door, had obviously caught that sensual glide of triumph past her defeated opponent.

Krew had just...failed.

And the film crew had recorded it all.

CHAPTER TWO

Two days later Krew stood before his mirror, tying a Windsor knot in his purple silk tie. A knot that instilled feelings of success. After the lost bid the other day he needed it. But just the thought that he needed some sort of token or magical knot to aid his luck today disturbed him.

He was a confident man. Hell, confidence was 75 percent of the game. The other 25 percent was knowledge. Things always went his way. And if they didn't? He could generally buy his way into or out of whatever the situation demanded. But he never used money as a tool, lure or even bribe. He'd leave that to his father. Krew simply knew the art world well and had honed his skills at auctions and appraising. Not to mention he was an expert at spotting a forgery. Those skills gave him clout others respected.

He'd lost the *Melancholy* painting to Peachy Cohen. His reflection wrinkled a brow. What kind of name was Peachy? Was it even a real name? It alluded to sweet things and a sensual appeal. Which the woman had. In spades. He didn't want to admit it to himself, but he'd been distracted by her during the auction. She had been the reason he'd lost.

An irritating admission, as Krew Lawrence was not the type to be distracted by a sexy woman. He preferred his women more astute and even bookish. A woman who enjoyed numbers and finances, as well as being versed in the arts. It was Byron whose girlfriends and wives had been obsessed with celebrity sightings and fashion. Sexy on the outside, vapid on the inside. They didn't know art. And if pressed, they'd bring up artist names that he considered entry-level.

With a wince, he checked himself. How quickly he slipped into "Byron mode." Krew tried never to judge a person by their outer appearance and knew it was unfair of him to do so. Besides, he certainly would never place his mother in the same category as that cruel assessment of his father's past loves. Despite her moving out of his life when he was six, they still spoke once a month. She was the one who taught him there was much more beneath the skin, embedded in the very DNA of a person, that made every one of them a marvel. And thanks to his work with the public—through galleries, art events and charity soirees—he met many interesting characters and had expanded his knowledge of human nature beyond the Lawrence family's paternal legacy of "money equals power."

But such knowledge had not helped him avoid distraction at the auction.

Marvelous was the first word that came to mind to describe Miss Cohen. Followed closely by *dangerous*. Especially to a man who had difficulty knowing how to act around women, leery of making a wrong move thanks to his experience with his ex-wife, Lisa.

The last thing he wanted was to follow his old man's steps and go for wife number two. Byron collected women without a care; they were as much a prize to him as a Rembrandt or a Michelangelo. Yet at least Byron—he preferred Krew address him by his first name and not the sappy Dad or Father—was able to let go of the women. Not that he had a choice. They generally fled him. Along with a sizable settlement.

No, Krew would not follow Byron's lothario footsteps. He was done with relationships that might break a man's heart. His was tattered but the armor he'd pulled around it kept it functional. Though hookups were not his thing either. When a man had sex with a woman it had to be meaningful. He wasn't about to waste himself on surface attractions and one-night stands.

He tugged the tie knot to perfection. A Windsor was classic. Like Scottish whisky in a fine crystal decanter. Italian leather loafers. And a 1960s Aston Martin with the top down while cruising the countryside. Thinking of which, he really needed to get that out for a drive in the country.

Normally, he'd mark his rare loss as a bump on the road, but unfortunately, he could not. Krew had promised Byron he'd bring back all four paintings to fill those bare spots on the wall of the Lawrence estate. It was a matter of manly pride. Claudia must not be allowed to humiliate Byron in such a manner.

And Krew might finally get a sort of vicarious emotional closure for the cruel words Lisa had flung at him after she'd walked out of their divorce proceedings.

He hadn't been there for her emotionally? Well. That was neither here nor there now. So, onward.

The paintings on his list had originally been purchased by Byron through the Hammerstill Gallery over a period of a year. The Art Guys had just been getting started so they had been some of Byron's last purchases that hadn't gone through his son.

"Hammerstill," Krew growled at his reflection.

Why could The Art Guys not distance themselves from the Hammerstill Gallery? They'd never had a pleasant interaction with the man or his associates. Asher, one of Krew's partners at the brokerage, had last year gone toe to toe with the bombastic owner, Heinrich Hammerstill, over representing a prospective artist. Both had lost, and the artist had ultimately insisted on representation by their The Art Guys' talented receptionist, Maeve. That was a different story entirely.

The loss of *Melancholy* had cracked Krew's perfect record, but he was far from mortally wounded.

Three paintings remained on Byron's list and Krew had a spy in his pocket. Maeve, who was currently transitioning from full-time receptionist to a few days a week because she also owned a decor shop in the West End, had a flatmate, Lucy, who was related to Byron's ex-wife Claudia. Lucy Ellis was familiar to Krew as she'd recently become engaged to one of his most philanthropic clients, Conor Gavin. Lucy apparently wasn't close with Claudia, but she was following her on her private social channels, so he had an in to tracking the paintings.

The first auction had been a fluke. Miss Cohen couldn't possibly be at the one today. And if she were? He'd focus his attention on the auction block as if wearing blinkers. He had never let something so superficial as a pretty smile and sexy legs interfere in business before, and he wouldn't begin making a habit of it now.

And he had to remember these auctions were being filmed for an episode of The Art Guys. Any more mistakes would be recorded for the world to see, and that prospect was unacceptable to Krew. The last thing he needed was to be seen to fail so publicly. His father would never let him forget it.

Peachy adjusted the silk scarf tied on her purse strap as she waited for bidding to begin on the next lot. Mr. Lawrence was here again today, and looking delicious in a tailored suit that emphasized his straight shoulders and perfect posture. She had a photo of him on her vision board at home. He inspired her in so many ways. But never had she thought he'd be so devastatingly handsome in person. It was hard to suppress her blush at the thoughts that ran through her head around that man.

He hadn't bid on the previous six items. If he bid on the next painting she'd have to start becoming suspicious of his motives.

The canvases she sought were by different artists, painted in various time periods and styles, and were being sold at different auction houses. The only thing that tied them together was the seller, who had just released them after years of ownership.

Heinrich Hammerstill had taken a step away from auctions and even the sales floor over the past year, which was why she'd been sent to bid on the paintings instead. The man was in his seventies and age was not treating him fairly. He had breathing issues, took medications and was moodier than his usual grumpy self. Peachy sensed he would soon completely step away from the gallery, which could mean a move up to gallery manager for her. She had no designs on living in London permanently, but the increase in salary would mean an increase in the savings she had earmarked for a home of her own. She was so over her tiny studio flat in Mayfair. She wanted the independence of being a homeowner, with the stability and peace it would provide. Two things she'd never experienced growing up in her bohemian mother's household.

The Devereux painting Peachy had won the other day was now safely stored in a holding site away from the gallery, and Peachy and Heinrich were the only two who had access to it.

The hammer pounded and the audience jumped. Peachy looked to the stage. Krew Lawrence sat in the second row from the front, two rows ahead of her. Again he was on the aisle seat. He hadn't noticed her. Yet.

She needed to focus, and pray The Art Guys' budget for the piece was smaller than her own. The thought turned her stomach. The Art Guys was a billion-dollar enterprise. Those men had money, and the three of them were skilled, knowledgeable, charming and confident. Literal geniuses who had combined their expertise, they seemed to hold the world in their hands. And art was their forte.

The auctioneer briefly introduced the painting. *The Deluge* by Mongline, a painter known for his illustrations inspired by the Bible and literature, featured a Greek god holding his wife aloft as floodwaters swirled around them. Peachy liked the message that the man would risk his own life to save his wife's. So romantic. Also, the light in the work was ethereal. And, okay, there was also the fact that the man's muscles were nothing to sneeze at. Peachy would never say no to being hoisted over his shoulders!

The hammer pounded the block and she gripped her bidding paddle. *Time to bring home muscles.*

A handful of bidders thrust up their paddles, while others tugged an ear or winked as their bidding technique. The price rose quickly and Mr. Lawrence eventually tossed in his nod.

Peachy did have a bidding cap, but she'd spent less than expected on *Melancholy*, so when the bid exceeded that cap, she took a chance, factoring in the additional 20 percent the auction house added to the hammer price to cover their fees.

Someone coughed, startling her. She twisted to look over the crowd, for the first time noticing the camera crew. What was so interesting about an auction? Of all the episodes she had seen of The Art Guys on the telly, no time had been devoted to the boring auction floor. And she personally preferred the episodes that featured the one known as The Brawn where he traveled to exotic locations and did some wild adventuring to obtain rare artworks. Sure, he was a stud, but the location scenes were always the main draw for her.

Alerted by the auctioneer's voice, Peachy shifted out of her wandering thoughts and turned to raise her paddle. Mr. Lawrence twisted a look over his shoulder—that tiny freckle above his eye wiggled with an arch of his brow— then matched her bid. Another look from him. She winked. Lifted her paddle.

The Brain's eyes were so green. They reminded her of one of her favorite paintings...

The hammer banged the block with finality, closing the sale. Who had won? She'd seemingly bid last, yet she couldn't be sure Lawrence hadn't slipped in another nod to bid.

The auctioneer, with a wry twist of his mouth, nodded to her and announced she was the winning bidder.

Yes! She'd— Well, she wasn't sure how she'd won that one, but she wasn't going to argue. Or stick around. Even before the painting was lifted from the easel, Peachy rose and exited the salesroom, noting the camera lens followed her every step.

Stopping at the manager's desk outside the sales floor, she confirmed her gallery information and the address the painting was to be shipped to. As she waited for a receipt she spied Mr. Lawrence exiting the auction room. He wasn't staying for the Koons that was scheduled to be the final lot of the afternoon? A big-money dealer like him? Interesting. Surely he couldn't have only been interested in *The Deluge*? It had gone for less than a hundred thousand.

He glanced her way, did a double take, then with a smooth of his tie, lowered his head in a nod of acknowledgment and stuffed his hands in his trouser pockets, seemingly happy to wait for her to come to him.

She told herself it was just a strange coincidence that they'd bid on the same paintings twice in a period of three days. But she also wondered if he might be interested in the next two paintings on her list as well. It seemed unlikely. But she needed to know for sure.

Feeling in control, Peachy squared her shoulders and strolled over to meet him at the heavy brass exit doors where he'd paused.

Fully aware the camera crew lingered but ten meters from Mr. Lawrence, she kept her back to them.

The man must be crestfallen to have lost a bid—twice—given he was famous for his auction wins. But she also knew there was an opportunity here to gain his trust and find out why he was after the exact same paintings she was.

"Winner buys dinner?" she suggested lightly.

Mr. Lawrence turned to her, a sour look on his face. Such expressive brows. And that single freckle above the one that seemed to dance a protest to her standing so close to him. A girlish shiver rippled over her skin. Never had she dared to approach a cute guy in school. Even now, she usually relied on friends to set her up on dates. Standing up to a handsome and obviously smart man like Mr. Lawrence was new territory for her.

He glanced around the lobby as though checking to see no one witnessed their conversation and the camera was no longer rolling. The film crew had already captured the details of his loss in the auction room and it appeared he wasn't keen to give them more entertainment.

"I'd like to buy you dinner, Mr. Lawrence." She almost

said, *as a consolation*, but checked herself. Dashing a finger along her ear to sweep the hair away from her cheek, she tugged in her lower lip. A subtle move that attracted his gaze.

What are you doing? Flirting with the sexiest man alive?

"I, uh…" His gaze fell onto her mouth. A wince said he was feeling badly about the loss. "Yes," he said decisively, giving a tug to his tie. She did favor a Windsor knot, utilitarian as it was. "We should talk."

That sounded more businesslike and let-me-find-out-your-intentions than the friendly consolation meal she'd intended, but it was always best to keep one's enemies close. If he were indeed the enemy.

Peachy looked forward to sitting across the table from the man whose green eyes reminded her of the vivid glowing soul in *The Death of the Gravedigger* by Carlos Schwabe.

"Let's go to the bistro across the street," she suggested, and walked out ahead of him, confident he would follow.

CHAPTER THREE

Krew did not want to share a meal with the woman who had stolen the painting from him. Okay, she hadn't *stolen* it, but…well…she'd been using those long legs and a flutter of her lashes to distract him. Even sitting *behind* him, she had been a distraction. And then someone had coughed and he'd looked away from the stage for a moment and…

Really? Was he going with that feeble excuse? He wasn't a pushover. And yes, he did want to dine with her. Because he wanted to delve beneath the surface of Peachy Cohen. Explore her intricate brushstrokes and movement as if assessing a canvas. How else to truly discern her motives?

Following the waiter to a table, his eyes drifted to Peachy's curvaceous backside. Definitely some movement there. She wore polka dots again, this time white set against a deep blue fabric. Ruffles at her half sleeves and around the hem provided a kind of tease, tempting one to study all the curves they caressed. And why did she seem so familiar to him?

With a clear of his throat, Krew looked beyond the woman to the table, trying to focus his thoughts. One slip and he'd not claim a single painting on his list. That was, if she were after the same ones as he was. Two of them so far did indicate that she may have a list similar to his. Incredible. And strange. Agreeing to dine with her would at least give him a chance to try to decipher his opponent's next likely move.

They ordered wine and once she'd ordered her main she reminded him, "I'm buying, remember?"

Indeed? *Rub it in deeper, lady.* Krew skimmed his gaze over the menu, pausing on the most expensive item he could find. "The filet mignon."

The waiter left them with a carafe of water that glinted in the streetlights that shone through the window. It was midafternoon, yet the mizzle had settled, that London mix of mist and drizzle, turning the sky a brownish gray.

"A Windsor knot," she remarked, her eyes falling to his throat.

Krew straightened. Most would know the common knot.

"It's very professional," she offered. "But perhaps you should have opted for something a little more powerful today. A Trinity or Pratt?"

The woman evidently knew her knots. And she was right; the Pratt would certainly have proven more of a power booster. He should have gone with that one.

"Interesting suggestion, coming from the enemy," he muttered tightly.

"I won fair and square, Mr. Lawrence. Perhaps you got a kink in your neck and your bidding nod was off?"

Even more audacious. But also a little funny.

"You seem quite put off to be sitting across the table from me," she added. She pushed the button on her cane to retract it down to one-third its size and set it on the seat beside her. "I didn't force you here."

"I never pass up a free meal."

Her smile was so lush and confident. Red lips he could dream about for days. "I don't believe that for a minute. So what convinced you to agree? Are curious about me?"

"Hardly—" He caught himself. It wasn't like him to be so defensive. And he couldn't afford to start on the wrong foot if he were to glean any useful information from her. "Very well, I am a trifle curious. You're with Heinrich's gallery?"

"You know that, darling." She sipped the water. "Ask me something interesting."

Really? Like why was it he had difficulty maintaining a stoic facade when something so infinitesimal as the way her tongue collected a water droplet from the edge of the glass could stir his attention at a primal level?

Krew tugged at his tie. "May I ask about the cane?"

"Of course. I was injured years ago. It required a few surgeries to fix my hip. But I retained a middle-ear injury that messes with my balance. I can't make any fast turns or dashes because my proprioception is dodgy. The cane is for support, though I can walk fine, if a little slower, without it."

"I had noticed you possess a remarkable awareness of your— Well." He cleared his throat. If she only knew how he'd already mapped her curves… "The cane does not distract from your beauty."

She lowered her gaze. Blushing? Delicious.

But he was here for more than simple flirtation. "What's your interest in *The Deluge*? And for that matter, *Melancholy*."

"I have no interest."

He quirked a brow.

"I obtained the works for the gallery. And don't ask what my boss's interest is. Heinrich maintains a quirky collection. I know you're familiar with it."

"You do?"

"It wouldn't be wise for The Art Guys to not be familiar with all the local galleries and auction houses. I've been told you're the man to go to. The one who knows everything about… Well…" She smirked. "Word also tells you never lose an auction."

Krew curled his fingers about the wineglass just as the waiter arrived to offer refills. The glide of Peachy's long fingers over the top of her glass distracted. A slow, tactile summation. He swallowed and focused on his own glass.

"I wouldn't say *never*. We all have our off days," he said. "Hammerstill has a list, I take it?"

"Let's not talk about my perfidious boss. I'd prefer our dinner to be light and friendly. Can we agree to that?"

He shrugged, agreeing. Anything to keep her talking. He'd learn what he needed with patience.

"Tell me about yourself," she said, dipping her finger in the glass and then swirling it around the rim. "Why art?"

Was the woman aware that her every movement was a sensual lure? Well, of course. No one dressed like that and moved like a siren without knowledge that it would draw every male eye within visual distance.

It impacted Krew more than he was willing to admit, but so it would, given he was a details man who noticed more than most thanks to having grown up in a house filled with art and sculpture. His mother had been his most avid teacher. When she and Byron had divorced, Krew had been a mere six years old. He wished he and his mum were closer, but she now lived in Nebraska on a pig farm. Happy as can be.

Krew looked away from Peachy's glass, and that wet finger. She'd asked why he'd gotten into art. "Why not art? It's a lucrative business."

"One has to have a love for it to make such a fortune as you have, Mr. Lawrence. Or should I call you The Brain?"

"Please don't. It's a silly moniker the show's producers slapped on me." He glanced around the restaurant. The camera crew had not been allowed inside—it was difficult to get permission to film in public places at short notice—so for now he could relax. "I've enjoyed art of any kind since I was little. The walls in our estate were plastered with masterpieces, with barely any room between the frames. I started going to auctions with my dad when I was five, and Mum would quiz me on the masters as we strolled museums. I've never not known and admired art."

"I grew up with an artistic mum myself so I can understand that constant immersion in the arts. I can't imagine another profession…" She looked aside and winced. Krew sensed that had been a lie. But what was it she missed?

Their meals were delivered before he could ask. Peachy had ordered carbonara, which she daintily dug into. Her red nails flashed and a strand of dark hair fell over her lashes and across one eye, which she ignored.

"Where did the name Peachy come from?" Krew asked as a means to stop himself suggesting she push away the hair strand that he focused on like a beacon.

"It's on my birth record."

"That's your *real* name?"

"Of course." She looked up. Blinked at the rogue strand of hair. "You think it odd?"

"It is unique."

"And Krew is not?"

Fair.

Did a girl grow into a name like Peachy? Obviously she had. She embodied the name in her walk, her movements, the coy glances and graceful gestures of her hands. But he reminded himself that beneath the surface she was likely so much more than a pretty face. And the urge to uncover more about her intrigued him while also cautioning him. He couldn't know what he was up against.

"So what's next on your auction list, Peachy?"

She waggled her finger in a chastising manner as she finished a bite of food. "We're not talking business."

"I'd like to know as I apparently need to prep for my next auction if you're going to be there."

"I'm no man's competition."

"Well." She was and she wasn't. She'd already pulled off two successes to his detriment. Had he really lost to her because he'd been distracted by long legs and red lips? His father would never forgive him the idiocy. And at the same time, Byron would laugh and comment how his son was just like his old man.

He was not. Was he?

"What's *your* goal?" she asked, settling back in the booth and eyeing him over her wineglass.

His goal was simple: to obtain the paintings for his dad, clap his hands for a job well done... And, being honest, restore his dented ego by managing to metaphorically rescue his father's manhood/ego. Only then could he be satisfied and move on to the next job.

"Like...a life goal," she clarified. "What is it that motivates you, Mr. Lawrence?"

A deep question. What was her strategy?

"I'll tell you my goal," she said eagerly. "It involves two steps. The first of which is advancing at Hammerstill Gallery." She tapped her red nails against the water glass. The ting sounded as delightful as her voice. "I will be successful," she said, though he wasn't sure if she was telling him or herself.

"And part two?"

"Buying my own home. Maybe even a cottage in the country. I have dreams and they will come true. I even have a vision board. And you're on it!"

"I'm... Really?" He didn't know what to say to that. He had kept a vision board while growing The Art Guys so he knew the value of one but—he was on *her* board?

"You inspire me," she said. "You're talented, smart. So calm and classy."

"You flatter me." Sure, he'd become famous with the show, and he was accustomed to being recognized and even signing autographs. But this woman had been *inspired* by him? He'd not received such a genuine compliment before. "Owning a home is a good, solid goal. And life isn't worth living unless one takes on challenge. How does Heinrich feel about your desire to advance?"

"I've told him I'm interested in taking a larger role in the gallery. He's managed the place for decades, but he's ailing. I worry he hasn't many good years left. He's rarely at the gallery these days."

"Interesting." Krew hadn't been aware of the old man's decline in health. Not a surprise as interactions with Hammerstill were never pleasant and Krew tried to avoid them. The television show had once captured the older man berating Asher, whose moniker for the show was The Face, for being nothing more than a pretty boy. It had humiliated Asher. And Krew didn't take kindly to people bullying or trying to discredit those he cared about.

"So, your goal?" she prompted.

"I think I've achieved my goal of success with The Art Guys," he said.

"There's always something more to achieve. To aspire to."

He shrugged. "At the moment, I'm content."

And not willing to allow her in any further, much as he suspected she was trying to learn more about him than he could about her.

"Well." She wiggled on the seat and finally brushed aside that tantalizing strand of hair. "Then perhaps you have the universal human goal?"

"And what is that?"

"Why, to be loved, of course."

Krew set his utensil down with a clank on the plate. Peachy visibly flinched. He hadn't meant to be so demonstrative.

"You don't want love?" she asked with innocence.

"Been there. Done that. Wouldn't recommend it," he hastily blurted out. And at the same time he tossed his napkin over his plate, finished thoroughly with this intrusive conversation.

The sudden touch of her fingers to his hand startled him. Krew tugged away.

"Darling, you are skittish," she said. "And I've gone too far. Forgive me. I simply want to reassure you that we are not working against one another. You've nothing to fear from me."

Could she read his mind?

"I don't fear…" *Any woman.* Or did he? No, she threatened nothing about his career or manhood. As for his emotional needs… "Well, look, this has been—" not as helpful a conversation as he'd hoped and strangely, touching some rather intimate aspects of him he'd rather not acknowledge "—nice. But I should take off. I've work back at the office. Would you entertain an offer on *The Deluge*?"

"Absolutely not."

"Then I guess this is goodbye."

He stood and when she reached for his hand, he wasn't sure what she was going to do, so when the clasp happened he stared at it. Something electrical zapped at his very bones. It prickled in the best way possible. He'd never felt anything like it. Perhaps it was static from his shoes on the carpeting, he tried to tell himself.

The floor was tiled.

"Thank you, Mr. Lawrence. It's been lovely."

He pulled from her grasp, nodded and beelined for the front of the restaurant. There, he paid for the meal before leaving.

Once outside, he stepped close to the building to avoid the mizzle. That woman…annoyed him.

And—he studied his hand, still feeling a little tingly—she intrigued him.

The man was far too reserved for the sexy-television-star vibes he gave off. There was nothing and everything nerdish about him. But that tweed vest and his attempts to remain unfazed by her touches had told her so much. She was a tactile person and always dragged her fingers along the items on store shelves, or hedgerows, or racks of clothing in a shop. She liked to feel. To connect.

And Krew Lawrence was a man she wanted to connect with, even if he was a bit tense, and certainly protective of his true feelings. He didn't recommend love? Had he been hurt in a relationship? Possibly. But one bad experience shouldn't ruin a life. She'd meant it when she'd said love was a universal human desire. A need, even. She desired love. Who wouldn't? She sensed Mr. Lawrence required a tender touch. Or two. There was something very desirable about his stoicism. She'd not sat with such a calm and poised man before. It was very refreshing.

Yet, she mustn't allow herself to even consider them as anything more than rivals. Krew Lawrence represented the sort of man she had never been successful in befriending, let alone going beyond into something intimate. Smart, rich, walking an entirely different social level than her, and always on the lookout for nothing more than arm candy. A woman who would enhance his appeal but never interfere with the professional image he presented. Someone to be there for him in his bed, by his side as a decoration, but lacking her own deep thoughts and self-determination.

Of course, she was judging him harshly. But it came easy enough.

The one boyfriend she'd had in high school—they'd dated for a year—had moved to Australia to become a surfer, leaving her heartbroken but hopeful that she had so much life to live and boys and men to discover. At the time she'd thrown herself into her dance studies so not dating hadn't been an issue.

Yet she hadn't dated again until after her accident. Which had put a new twist on trying to relate to someone when she wielded a cane for balance. She'd found the men interested in her—mostly rich art collectors she met through the gallery—were either only in it for a quickie, or to try out a "wounded" woman. So deflating. Thus, she had no idea how real love actually worked.

Peachy lifted her chin. The move reminded her of what her mother had always said when her daughter was feeling less than able. "Darling, lift your chin. Be proud, or at least fake it. A good fake can get you through so much."

But Peachy was never fake. Thanks to her dancing background she knew how to hold herself, even if a cane was now required for balance. And that made it easier to fit in alongside the old boys' club frequently found at auctions, whose confidence was displayed in their stance. It hadn't been easy in the beginning. Their looks assessing her in seconds. The snide glances of the gentlemen making it clear they thought she belonged behind a cosmetics counter instead of in the high-stakes bidding rooms. Or the confusion they displayed when they could not parse the woman in a fitted dress and killer heels who also used a cane. She'd heard the whispers of *afflicted* and *broken*. That did not put her off. In fact, it fueled her desire to succeed. To prove to them all she belonged in their world.

Much as it tired her sometimes. Since losing dance, she'd had to find a way to feel as in her body as dance had once made her feel. That manifested in her fitted clothing and sexy outward appearance. It was her. And it was not. Would she ever be able to simply be herself? To not have to compete for a place in this world?

But even if she found the love and acceptance she craved, she knew that once found, it would never stay. Her mother was proof of that. So many men had waltzed in and then just as quickly out of Doris Cohen's life. Peachy wanted more than that. She wanted real love.

Peachy sighed and fussed with the silk scarf. A gift from her mum, it depicted a chorus of heavenly figures against a brilliant blue background. It inspired her and gave her hope, so she always kept it with her.

She suspected she had not seen the last of the indomitable man who wore the label The Brain. That she'd won the two paintings he had bid on clearly bothered him. Of course, it must have chinked his ego. But she would never sell to him. The paintings were now Hammerstill's property.

For now, she had to stay on task. And pack for Prague. Though part of her wished Claudia Milton had accepted the tidy sum for all four paintings Hammerstill had offered. But Claudia had refused, saying she wanted to enjoy seeing them auctioned off individually.

Strange. But people had their foibles.

And Krew Lawrence's foible was knotted in his ties. A tell that she knew she'd best pay close attention to.

CHAPTER FOUR

Krew strolled into The Art Guys' office in central London and thanked Maeve for the black coffee she handed him. Maeve always seemed to know, to the minute, when he'd walk in the door. Of course, it wasn't exactly difficult given he was always punctual, never landing in the office later than three minutes till the hour.

"I have info on your next auction," Maeve said, while typing away at the computer. Her pregnant belly hugged the edge of the desk and it made Krew smile. He knew how excited Maeve and his best friend, Asher, were to meet their little one. "Give me a few minutes to get everything in order," she added.

"Not a problem."

Hearing laughter echo out of Joss's office surprised Krew. Their resident Brawn didn't usually rise until well after the breakfast hour and if he made it into the office before noon he deserved a gold star.

"What's going on?" he declared to the world at large.

Maeve looked up and seemed to realize she was the only one there to answer. "He bopped in this morning to help Asher authenticate a Grecian urn. Both have been here an hour."

Stunned, Krew veered toward Joss's office. Both men greeted him heartily. Asher sat on the corner of Joss's desk, cracking that trademark charming grin that had earned him the moniker The Face. While Joss beamed at Krew.

Coffee unsipped, Krew cast a wondering gaze between the two men.

"Tell him," Asher said with a proud smile.

Joss, dubbed The Brawn for obvious reasons—Krew could never hope to achieve steel abs and biceps like his friend, even with his thrice-weekly gym visits—gave him a shy smile.

"What's going on? Has the world turned on its head? You two are here before 9:00 a.m. and both seemingly coherent? Asher, you never smile so early in the day."

"Joss has news."

News was always welcome. Had Joss nabbed a new client or artist? With a bounce to his step, Joss performed a shadowboxing move before stopping and with splayed hands announcing grandly, "She said yes!"

That could only mean that Ginny, the sweet librarian Joss had been traveling the world with on his work adventures, had said yes to marriage. The news was indeed grand.

"Congratulations, mate." Krew went in for a hug, and Joss met him with a firm back slap. Krew was thankful Asher had grabbed the coffee cup from him before it could spill.

"All right! You'll crush my tie." Krew stepped back from his friend.

"I'm getting married," Joss repeated. "To Ginny!"

"I had hoped it would be her and not some random stranger you picked up on the Tube." Krew took his coffee back from Asher. "Pints down at the pub to celebrate?"

"You know it." Joss nodded to Maeve, who entered the office. "What's our day look like, Maeve?"

"You'll have to schedule pints early. Krew leaves this evening for Prague."

Krew wasn't surprised when she announced the flight. She was always one step ahead of the three of them and kept the office running smoothly. She would be sorely missed as she would soon be leaving them to run her decor shop full-time, in addition to embracing motherhood. He doubted he would survive a new receptionist, but he supported her dream to own a business suited to her colorful and generous nature.

And her husband, Asher, wouldn't have it any other way.

"Prague is...?" he prompted.

"According to Lucy, the next painting has been placed for auction at the Arthouse," she said. "Tomorrow afternoon. Two o'clock sharp. I was able to book you a room just a quick stroll away from the auction house, but I wasn't able to get you an advance look. It's already been closed for viewing."

"That's fine. I don't need to see the work. My dad once owned the painting." He recalled the small work had hung in the gaudily decorated living room. Byron had acquired it perhaps eight or nine years ago, around the time The Art Guys was just establishing itself. "It's just a matter of getting it back so the old man can place it back on the wall to cover the unfaded portion of wallpaper revealed after it was taken down."

And restoring the old man's bruised ego.

The piece was a minor work by a seventeenth-century Chinese *shuimohua* artist and it featured a large flower in a jar. Thus the title: *Jar and Flower*. Not usually Krew's style, but he did admire it. His mother had been into the Chinese artists and had decorated their living room in the Asian style with all related artwork relegated there as it was acquired.

"You weren't able to get the first two paintings?" Asher asked.

There was no judgment in his tone, but Krew felt the unspoken assessment in his bones. He'd messed up. He'd lost. To a frustratingly, annoyingly, obstinate, *gorgeous* woman who he had best stop thinking about.

And yet. The way she'd stroked the back of his hand in the restaurant...

But then she'd had the nerve to ask him if he believed in love! Or something about love. No, his goal was not love. Much as he wouldn't shove it away if it dropped in his lap, Krew felt the pursuit of it could only end dismally. The Lawrence men were not meant to have love. They certainly didn't know how to *keep* love. If they'd even had it in the first place.

He shook the memory of Peachy asking him about love from his thoughts. "I have plans to make an offer for those two paintings that the buyer won't refuse. It'll all work out."

"Is that buyer a dealer with the Hammerstill Gallery?" Asher asked with as much vitriol as the name Hammerstill deserved.

"Yes, but it wasn't Heinrich. The old codger sent..." If he said an underling, then he'd be claiming that he had been bested by such. He'd not been bested. He'd simply been distracted.

Twice.

"Is the film crew trailing you for these buys?" Joss asked, saving Krew from having to label Peachy.

Krew nodded. "But I'm sure they'll give up. Probably won't make for good telly."

If he could convince the producers of that then those two lost sales would never be aired. And his ego could breathe a sigh of relief. It was bad enough he couldn't find happiness in his personal life, that he felt as though he were following in Byron's footsteps. Why show the world he was also stumbling in his professional life?

"I was talking to Chuck yesterday about a future show," Joss said. Chuck Granville was their producer. "He mentioned something about the crew being interested in following the woman who bid against you. She's gorgeous, apparently."

So they knew. Krew shrugged. "Just another dealer." But... "They're following her?"

"I think they want to add a salacious angle to this one."

"Mercy." Krew sat in Joss's office chair.

"You all right, mate?" Asher asked. "You lost twice. To the *same* woman. Is there—" he exchanged glances with Joss "—something we should know?"

"You got the hots for this woman?" Joss teased.

"I have no such thing," Krew insisted. "I was simply not on my game." He squeezed his eyelids shut. "No. I can handle this. I won't lose the next one. She won't be there. Why would she be? It was just a fluke that she was at the first two auctions."

On the other hand, if she were there again he would have an opportunity to see her, to talk with her. Take her in like the delicious piece of art she was...

"Uh-huh." Again, Joss and Asher exchanged looks.

And Krew could imagine what those looks meant. He'd shared much the same with each of them on occasion. Brewing a salacious story in their minds. Likely painting a picture of a torrid romance with the woman who had bested him.

"She's not my type," he felt compelled to say.

Joss raised his hands in placation. "Didn't say she was or wasn't. But just for reference, what *was* she like?"

Krew sighed. "I don't know. Beautiful. Attentive. Always…touching things. A soft voice, but powerful. And eyes that…undressed me."

Krew smiled at that one. And then he noticed the stunning silence in the room. When he looked up both men were staring at him with grins on their faces.

Finally, Joss splayed both palms outward. "Not going to touch that one, mate. What about you, Asher?"

"Perhaps we'll be announcing another wedding soon, eh?"

Both men laughed, and Krew, grabbing his coffee, quickly exited, leaving the jolly revelers to revel. They knew nothing.

Or did they?

Being on time wasn't her thing. Peachy had missed the call for first-class boarding and was literally the last person on the plane, having flagged down a transport cart because she could not run.

Blowing strands of hair from her eyes, she navigated to her seat, and when she was about to place her carry-on in the overhead bin, a man tapped her on the shoulder.

"Miss? Might we switch seats? There was a seating mix-up and me and my fiancée—" he pointed to the beautiful blonde sitting in the window seat next to Peachy's assigned seat "—were separated."

"Not a problem at all. Where are you sitting?"

"Up two rows. Let me get your bag for you."

"Thank you!" the fiancée called as Peachy allowed the man to move her bag and cane to a bin closer to the front of the first-class cabin.

Didn't matter where she sat. As long as it was business or first class she would be fine as a flight without free champagne was unendurable.

"Am I being punked?" her seatmate said as she sat next to him.

She turned to find Krew Lawrence looking up at her incredulously and laughed. "Oh, darling, this is truly fate."

"I don't believe in such nonsense," Krew said.

She pretended to be affronted as she sat next to him. "Don't be so disappointed. I'm sure I smell much lovelier than he did."

Krew's jaw pulsed as he considered the suggestion. Then he said, "By measures," and crossed his arms over his chest. "Tell me you're not headed to Prague for the Arthouse auction."

With a wiggle, Peachy made herself comfortable. Before crossing her legs, she slipped off her shoes. "I'm not headed to Prague for the Arthouse auction." She cast him a sweet smile and a wink.

He shook his head. "You're lying."

"I just told you exactly what you wanted to hear. You can't make demands of me and then get upset when I do as requested."

"I'm not upset. I'm just gobsmacked. The coincidences between us have been remarkable."

"Everything happens for a reason."

"Spare me your woo-woo philosophizing."

"Someone woke up on the wrong side of the bed this morning." He probably needed a shot of green juice, her favorite way to start the day. But nothing could match the kick in the feels she got from looking into his gorgeous green eyes. *Don't go all swooning teenager on him! Remember, he could never be interested in you for...you.* "I won't be a bother. I promise you won't even notice me sitting here."

"That's impossible when you look so—"

She smirked as he cut himself off from saying... What?

How did she look to him? Appealing? Pretty? Irresistible? Annoying? She'd take any of them, just so long as *he* noticed her. Because he was a man like no other. She barely knew him but her instincts pleaded for her to stick close. Learn him. And figure out why, for some reason, the universe wanted them to be in close proximity.

"Seems we have the same art interests of late." Which wasn't good for her bottom line despite him being intriguing. Was he after the same ink wash painting as she? What was going on? How could Heinrich's list be the same as Krew's? "Where's the film crew?"

"Already in Prague. Waiting for something..." He gestured futilely before them, seeming to seek the right word.

"Interesting? Exciting? Newsworthy?" she tried.

"Salacious," he spit out.

"Mmm." She wiggled on the seat. "I do love a bit of controversy, especially when it's salacious. Not you?"

"Apparently, thanks to my two failures in London—to a beautiful woman, no less—the producers are trying to put the two of us..."

Another extreme facial expression. He hated speaking it, she could tell. It must drive his astute, nerdy self mad. But he had dropped the word *beautiful*. She'd take that.

"Doesn't matter. I'm going to suggest those auctions be cut from the footage. It's not of interest to the show."

"Oh, I don't know. It does offer a glimpse into something most have never seen. That's always interesting. I would have never thought I'd find myself followed by a film crew simply because I've exchanged a few words with a man called The Brain. Such a lark."

"Did you forget dinner?"

How could she? The man had declared a personal vendetta against love. "You were supposed to allow me to pay for that."

She'd been surprised he'd picked up the bill, but also, not so surprised. The man was a gentleman. And she guessed his wallet was bottomless. Of course, he had also claimed part of her win with that move. Not cool.

"As the winner I wanted to buy you dinner."

"And as I fully intend to win the next one, I thought I'd get one step ahead and treat you."

He tugged at his tie. "The film crew is reading too much into this." He sighed. "It's all about ratings and views. Sexual tension makes for good television."

So the film crew thought that she and Mr. Lawrence had sexual tension? Delicious. Of course, she was attracted to the man who knotted his ties so tightly surely the oxygen supply to his brain was reduced measurably. But keeping him close and amiable would only help her cause. And that was more important than falling for his good looks and gentlemanly manner. She needed to keep him at a distance for the sake of another win, so she had best keep her silly thoughts of how handsome he was and how clear and gem-like his eyes were stashed in a deep dark closet. Distraction could prove her downfall.

On the other hand, a man could be manipulated with a flutter of lashes. A pout of one's lips. A glide of her naked leg along the other. That much she'd learned from her mother.

"Whatever you do," he said, "just stay away from me when the Daves are filming. We don't want it to appear as if anything untoward is happening."

"Darling, I never do untoward," she said with the slightest tease. "Only toward."

His grimace should tickle her but she didn't want to make

him angry. Or frustrate him any more than he already appeared to be. "Who are the Daves?"

"Dave Wilcox and David O'Shaunessy. Cameraman and mic operator. Standard minimal crew when not filming action scenes or high-traffic locations. I call them the Daves."

"Convenient if one has trouble remembering names." Which she did. She generally had to speak to a person and use their name a handful of times before the name fixed to her memory.

"Listen, darling." Peachy touched his arm. He didn't flinch as he had when she'd touched him in the restaurant, but he did keep an eye on her hand. Had he not been touched overmuch? Or maybe he was offended by *her* touch? "You're a dear man. A professional. As am I. I want to obtain a specific painting. I will have it. And no amount of *untoward* will win it for me. So don't you worry. This'll be a fair battle. Promise."

"Assuming we are both aiming for the same one?"

"The ink wash. *Jar and Flower*," she said.

He gave her a look of exasperation. So he *was* intent on the same painting. She didn't want to compete with this man. She wanted to befriend him. To get to know him better. To see if a few more touches could relax him.

"Sorry," she felt the need to say. "But I will have that painting."

The pilot announced they were taking off and to fasten seatbelts. Which would allow them a few hours for that getting-to-know-one-another session. Steeped with tension, as she suspected it would now be.

CHAPTER FIVE

ONCE IN THE AIR, Krew liked to go through his emails, research current sales and check for tips on works that may be going on the block. He maintained a corral of informants that included students, collectors, dealers and gallery managers; they never let him down.

However, as he tapped away on the laptop it seemed he wasn't going to be allowed the personal space to indulge in ignoring the beautiful woman to his right.

He looked down where her fingers rested on the crook of his elbow. Matte bloodred nails. Slender wrist. Soft skin that carried the faintest scent. Citrus? Orange, possibly. No, *tangerine*. Something he wanted to inhale and devour as if a juicy treat.

Krew cleared his throat and gave Peachy a pointed look. Head tilted against the back of the seat, she glanced at him. Long, lush black lashes fluttered over luminous brown eyes. Freckles dotted her high cheekbones and dashed the bridge of her tiny nose. A bit of whimsy to soften the turbo-sensuality that crafted Peachy Cohen into a dangerous opponent.

"Do you mind?" he asked carefully. He knew what the answer was going to be.

"Not at all."

Exactly.

If he were to shrug her off he felt it would be akin to

pushing away a kitten. No one did that. Even if the kitten had claws that she intended to whip out when the hammer met the block.

"Aren't the clouds dreamy when looking down on them like this?" she asked.

Krew looked out the window. They flew at twelve thousand meters altitude and the crisp blue sky boasted a few clouds that looked like marshmallows. Something he rarely afforded a moment to notice on the hundreds of flights he'd taken in his lifetime.

"Dreamy," he said in a lackluster tone, and refocused on the laptop screen. Maybe that would be her clue that he wanted to work undisturbed.

With an inhale for fortitude, her scent overwhelmed his senses. He marveled at the bright orangeness of it. Fresh fruit tingling on his tongue. Unique. Appealing.

Dreamy.

"You said your parents gave you a love for art?" she asked.

"Yes." He tapped away on the keyboard.

"I haven't always loved art. I wanted to be a dancer and I was part of a dance troupe when I was a teenager. What about you?"

"When I was a teen I worked at a gallery." He tried to type a sentence in an open email. "Janitor stuff."

Much to his father's horror. *Lawrence men do not do manual labor! We hire the laborers.* Despite being raised by old-money parents, Krew could never fully support that entitled attitude, so while he attended a private school, his after-school hours had been spent exploring the neighborhoods, meeting others his age and hanging out. Like a normal teenager. He didn't regret the exasperated admonishments from Byron either.

"I made friends with one of the dealers at the gallery where I worked," he provided, reminiscing. "He taught me about fakes and forgeries."

"Oh. Yes, I understand from the show that's your focus."

"I hate that fakes exist. That anyone would try to pass off an artwork for something it is not."

"I find it difficult to accept a lie as well. I've never run across a forgery while working at the gallery."

"That you know of. They are ubiquitous in the art world."

"Yes, unfortunately. But I don't think anyone has been successful in passing off my favorite artist with a fake."

"And which artist is that?"

"Alphonse Mucha was my first love."

Mucha was a nineteenth-century graphic artist who gained initial fame by designing posters for street advertising.

"He's a bit pedestrian for me, but I give the artist credit for bringing the Art Nouveau movement to a groundswell with clean lines, natural forms and ancient symbolism."

"The *Slav Epic* is intense," she said.

Agreed. The massive twenty-panel collection was a feat that Mucha created depicting his homeland and the strife of the Slavs via a mythological approach. Not at all commercial in nature. Certainly a masterpiece.

One of Peachy's fingernails slinked down his arm toward his wrist. Krew paused, fingers curled on the keyboard. Glanced aside at her big innocent eyes. *Not so innocent.* She was up to something. He almost said, *I have work. Do you not see?* but felt a punishing tug in his gut. *Don't be rude to the kitten, Krew.*

And really, his curiosity could not be ignored.

"Mucha is a mass market advertiser's dream." Closing the laptop, he tucked it aside and turned his back to the window, his body toward hers. "But let's talk da Vinci."

That choice seemed to agree with her as she tugged up one leg and readjusted her position to rest her elbow on the narrow armrest between them. Shoes on the floor, he saw that her bare toes were painted to match her fingernails.

"Yes, such an exquisite creator," she said. "The original Renaissance man. I would have loved to have known him. Do you think he was bisexual?"

Mercy. Why did every topic with her always seem to veer toward romantic interest and physical attraction? The woman would try his every nerve.

But for some reason, Krew decided to toss out his thoughts on the rumors that the Renaissance artist had both male and female lovers. Which eventually led to their discussion of the mechanical inventions the polymath artist had drawn. Items such as the parachute, the helicopter and even solar power could be traced to da Vinci's inventive drawings. They both marveled over his anatomical studies of animals and humans, and agreed that his Roman cartography dazzled. Finally, their conversation strayed to the obvious, his most famous works, the *Mona Lisa* and *The Last Supper*.

It made for invigorating discourse. Da Vinci had been Krew's first love and still was. And as Peachy bantered with his ideas and matched his knowledge on da Vinci, he found himself leaning in closer. Hanging on her every word. She knew about the experimental pigments da Vinci had used, which had suffered the effects of time worse than other paints. And that there was a hidden musical score within *The Last Supper*. Both had heard the melody played.

She also leaned closer to him. Her eyes were so bright. Her hands animated as she talked, and every so often that touch to his wrist or leg. As if she were anchoring herself. It didn't bother him so much as he thought it should.

After all, she could be trying to soften him up in order to

win another auction. No, it was simply an off-the-cuff conversation. Perhaps it was her manner. Or he hoped it was. Because he hated to believe that she could be a conniving woman who might have plans to stab him in the heart when opportunity presented.

His wife had done that. He hadn't been the same since.

And yet, he had to take half the blame for the failure of his marriage. Lisa had truly felt as though he had not been there for her, and he wouldn't discount her truths. The emotional side of a relationship was not an easy read for him.

When the pilot announced they'd landed in Prague, Krew straightened his shoulders, realizing he'd leaned forward to bow his head closer to Peachy as they'd chatted. Their conversation ended and he felt...disappointed.

Peachy sprang up and grabbed her bag from the overhead bin. "Have to catch a cab," she said. "I suppose I'll see you tomorrow afternoon."

"Yes, er..." She was leaving as if they'd not talked for over an hour about their most passionate art interests. Never had he enjoyed a conversation with a woman so much. Krew nodded, bringing himself fully back to ground, as it was. "Yes. At the auction. Best of luck."

She wandered off, and he leaned over and twisted to catch a glimpse of her sexy wiggle. Just before she stepped out of the first-class section, she glanced over her shoulder and winked.

Caught him!

Krew sat back and...smiled.

Half an hour later, Krew slid into the limo and thanked the driver. He didn't need to give a location. That was all taken care of by Maeve. He wasn't sure where he was staying, but

Maeve always choose the finest hotel in the city and something close to where he needed to ultimately be.

Drizzle coated the car windows as they pulled from the underground lot. He sat back and mused over the flight. They'd discussed da Vinci nearly the whole time. Rarely was he gifted the pleasure of talking about something he enjoyed so extensively. Art lovers abounded, but to chat more than a few minutes about any particular piece or artist was unusual.

Exhilarating.

He smiled. A sniff confirmed her perfume had permeated his suit fabric. And he didn't mind that at all.

The woman was so...in his face. Calling him *darling*. Always touching him. Yet, what did he know about women and their wiles? He'd thought he knew how to relate to a woman. Until he'd been told he could not.

His marriage to Lisa had lasted a year. They'd met in the National Gallery at a black-tie gala hosted by his father and his wife of the moment. Both had been fresh out of university and Lisa had come along with her parents; her mother the best friend of Byron's second wife. They'd quickly intuited their introduction had been a setup. It hadn't mattered. Krew had been captivated by Lisa's ease with speaking to anyone and everyone about anything at all. Most of the time winging it with little knowledge on the topic. She'd made him laugh. They'd dated for months. Lisa had dreams of starting a family and being a stay-at-home wife, and Krew had quickly asked her to marry him. Byron had been pleased when they'd announced their engagement. Said he'd selected well for his son.

Selected. Only now, when Krew looked back, did he realize just how calculating that selection had been. Pair him with the perfect wife, someone from old money, someone amenable to standing in the background while the husband remained a star in the spotlight. Someone who wanted to raise a family in the comfort of elegance, having her every need met.

Krew had thought he was in love with her. No, he *had* been in love with her.

Apparently, she hadn't been so in love with him. Or hadn't been able to tolerate a marriage in which she had not been emotionally satisfied. After a year she'd asked for a divorce. She needed more. A confidant. A protector. Someone who would listen and give feedback.

Rationally, he knew that was what marriage was about. Give and take. Sharing on an emotional level. If she would have said something to him, given him a chance, he would have tried.

Maybe they just hadn't been a good match. He should have known that having a wife *selected* for him could never promise him a long-lasting union. And yet, he had loved her. In his manner.

Months after the divorce, Byron had chuckled and said something like "It's your first try, son. You'll have another shot at it." Some role model his father had been.

With a wince, Krew tossed that memory aside. Or tried to. He hadn't been able to relax and enjoy himself in a relationship since that failed marriage six years earlier. On dates he always wondered if he was saying the right thing, appropriately catering to the woman's needs. That one statement from Lisa had thrown him off course. Apparently, she had lied about being happy during their marriage.

He hated lies. It was the reason why he vigilantly sought out forgeries. No one had the right to put something out there for others to enjoy knowing it was a fake.

The limo slowed as it drove past the long line of travelers

waiting in the light rain for a taxi. While he never flaunted his riches, Krew was thankful for the things money could afford him, like a driver when the weather was miserable. Out the corner of his eye, he spotted Peachy. Her hair shimmered with rain and she had no coat against the chill. Was she shivering?

"Stop the car."

The driver did so.

He told himself he was…keeping the enemy close. Not picking up a beautiful woman because it punched him in the heart to see her looking so miserable.

Krew opened the back door and called to Peachy. At the sight of him she perked up, collected her bags and slid inside the car.

"Darling, you are my angel," she announced effusively. She spattered him with raindrops while she shuffled her bags to the center of the seat. "I'm staying at the Marriott," she told the driver. "Unless…"

He tilted his head at her dramatic pause. The car started rolling again.

"Unless?" he asked.

She pushed aside a hank of wet hair from her lashes. Her lips were spotted with water droplets. He could reach over and brush them away…

"Perhaps we could share dinner again?"

"We've not determined who the winner will be yet," he said.

"Doesn't have to be a winner's dinner. I'm starving."

There was no denying he was also hungry. He'd intended to dine alone in his room, as was usual, but perhaps some company would be nice?

"My treat," she said, then directed the driver to take them to a restaurant.

"Your hotels are next to one another," the driver said in excellent English. "Someplace nearby?"

"Just take us to mine," Krew said. Then to Peachy he offered, "I like to settle in as soon as I arrive in a new city. We'll dine in my room."

"Nice." She settled back, crossing her legs and brushing at the dampness on the skirt that clung to her skin.

She smelled of tangerines and rain. And that was about the best scent ever.

CHAPTER SIX

ONCE IN THE lobby of Krew's hotel, he directed the valet to take Peachy's bags next door and see they were delivered to her room. He took control with an ease that excited her. Of course, she knew rich men were accustomed to having their needs met, and quickly. It was something she aspired to. Someday she'd make her first million and then be able to create the life she desired. Hell, she didn't even require a million for that dream. She had a good sum in savings. A few more years at the gallery, with a pay raise, was all that she required to go country bound.

"Do you want to freshen up before we dine?" Krew asked her.

She ran her fingers through her moist hair. When wet it curled, which she rather liked. "I'm good. You don't like the rain-drenched look?"

"You're gorgeous— Er, you look great." He proffered his arm for her. "My room then."

"Lawrence!"

Peachy turned to spy two men rushing toward them. The Daves. One held a camera, the other a microphone that was sort of gun-shaped but bigger and bulkier. Krew's sudden tight clutch on her arm directed her around behind him.

"Not now, guys," Krew said to the film crew. "The auction isn't until tomorrow. Are you filming, Dave?"

"You know we always do background shots," the man with the mic said. "We haven't been introduced. Miss Cohen?"

She was about to introduce herself, but Krew's hand at her waist stayed her. They were doing nothing untoward. And really, if he wanted to avoid *salacious* then tucking her away behind him was not helping his cause.

"Nothing to see here, Dave. David. Just helping out a fellow dealer. You know who Miss Cohen is." His hand slid into hers and he tugged her toward the lift as the doors opened.

The film crew followed.

"Tomorrow!" Krew waved them off and pulled her inside the waiting lift.

She had to catch her cane sharply against the floor to hold her balance. "They are persistent. Can't you tell them what to do? They are filming for *your* show."

The lift doors closed just before the Daves caught up with them.

"They don't need to film me walking to my room," he announced, pressing the top-floor button more than a few times.

Peachy stepped up beside him, shoulder to shoulder. She felt a little feisty after that tête-à-tête with the Daves. With a smirk, she asked, "Is this the salacious part?"

"Apparently so."

He looked down at her, his mouth parting, perhaps to admonish her? But then his sternness softened. His green eyes seemed to invite her to a place she could live in forever. If only he'd give her permission. Because she sensed he was a guarded man. And generally, that usually meant he'd been hurt in some manner. She certainly hoped it wasn't from a tragic love affair.

When the door opened they strolled to the end of the hallway and with a tap of his keycard the door opened to a wide space.

Peachy did adore a luxurious room. And this was top-of-the-line. She wandered in, taking notice of her reflection in the foyer mirrors. Loose waves of hair thanks to the rain. And her freckles always seemed to rise to the occasion whenever the weather was a bit nippy. She looked like a movie star caught in the rain who'd been rescued by the handsome protagonist.

And yet, she cautioned herself. She'd been invited into a man's hotel room before, though it never ended with her being satisfied. But she was willing to give Krew the benefit of the doubt.

Strolling through the spacious living area to the window, she looked out over the cityscape, capped by a dash of salmon and violet above a streak of bright gold from the setting sun. The Czech capital was known as the City of a Hundred Spires, and they certainly speared the sky everywhere. It had been called the Kingdom of Bohemia centuries ago, a title that reminded of her bohemian mum. Peachy intended to tour the city tomorrow before the auction and take it all in.

She swept up her arms and tilted back her head. "Hello, Prague, you sexy city!"

A turn caught Krew staring at her, open-mouthed, hands in his trouser pockets. Oh, how she wanted to muss his tidy hair. Tug loose that tie. Generally, loosen the entire man.

"I'll have the house special sent up?" he asked.

"Perfect."

"Is this your life?" Peachy strolled before the vast floor-to-ceiling window, wineglass—and bottle—in hand. She'd set her retractable cane on the coffee table. "Luxurious hotel rooms, limos and...generally getting whatever it is you wish?"

Krew set their finished plates on the serving tray and wheeled it toward the door. A fastidious man, she suspected he liked things kept orderly. He'd hate to get a peek at her studio flat. Housecleaning was not her forte, nor an interest. If she didn't trip over it, then it didn't require tidying. Another of her mum's traits she had inherited.

"It is." He took the bottle from her, drinking from it. Drinking straight from the bottle? So he wasn't as neat about some things. "I've earned the money. No reason I shouldn't enjoy the good life it brings me."

"I don't expect you to apologize. You wear the money well." Literally. That suit must have set him back, but it was worth every single pence on his long, lean and confident form. She leaned against the frame of the open terrace door. The rain had stopped and the humidity made her skin feel dewy. "The half Windsor knot is good for travel, yes?"

He touched his tie. "It's a simpler knot. How is it you know so much about men's neckties?"

"Knot tying, of all sorts, interests me. I suspect a person can read your emotions by the various ways you knot your ties." She touched his tie but resisted the urge to tug him closer. "Moss green silk. Not quite as clear and brilliant as your eyes."

He cleared his throat and stepped back. "Does it come naturally to you, Peachy?"

"What's that?"

"The flirtation. The bold way you move around men. From the driver to the doorman to the film crew, you were working it."

"I don't work it." Did she? Well. Not when it wasn't required as a defense mechanism.

And really, a woman wielding a cane was as far from bold as it got. Since losing dance and being forced to adjust to a body that no longer embraced an easy glide through the world, she did what she could to feel good about herself. Of course, her mother had been a big influence on self-care and loving the body one was in. So instead of drowning in the sadness of being changed from what she once was, she embraced her new body and the movement it still allowed her. She may not be as agile as she once was, but her clothing and attitude could distract any man from the cane she now carried.

"This is me," she said with a shrug. "And I'm going to take your suggestion that I'm bold as a compliment. I've always embodied, well…my body. However, it's a little harder now that I've a wonky hip to deal with. I'm also very tactile. More so since my injury. I've learned to be even more aware of my body as it moves through the world. If it bothers you…?"

"Not at all. And I meant it as a compliment. I've just never… You are unique."

"I doubt that."

"Oh, you are. Like a work of art."

"Thank you."

She wasn't one to dismiss a compliment. They were given so rarely. People were just getting…meaner, less caring. But not The Brain. He may have an astute exterior, but she suspected underneath the protective shield of suit and tie the man was as exhilarating as his love for da Vinci. And his calm aura was so compelling. He could stand firmly and protect a woman, as he'd done before the Daves. And he was also able to relax and flirt, just a little.

When he again smoothed a hand over his tie she noticed something. "Darling, you're missing a button."

"What?" He looked down.

Daringly, she slid a finger along the edge of his tie and pushed it aside. Like shifting aside a door that hid his heart. He tensed. "Right there. Oh. It's gotten lodged behind your vest. Let me get it for you."

She set her wineglass on a nearby table. "May I?"

His expression said so much. *Don't touch me.* Do *touch me. But tender your touch carefully.*

She slipped the pearl button out from behind his vest and held it up between two fingers, dashing her tongue across her lip as she studied it. "Let me sew it back on for you." She picked up her purse and fished out the small sewing kit she always carried.

"That's not necessary. I'll have the tailor reattach it when I get home. I have more shirts packed."

"Nonsense. I'm perfectly capable of sewing on a button." She threaded the needle and returned to stand before him. "Yes?"

He eyed the needle with suspicion. "You always carry that with you?"

She nodded.

"Very well. If you must."

"Darling, I must. You can leave your shirt on since it's only the second button. But first, let's get that tie off so I don't have to struggle around it."

Peachy loosened his tie, keeping her eyes on his. She'd learned knots years ago while she'd been laid up recovering after the accident. That year of reflection and courage-gathering she had taken to studying an assortment of things that interested her online and had mastered many odd skills. Knot tying, bird calls, color mixing—which helped with identifying certain artists that were similar—even embroidery. She'd sewed all her clothing since she was about ten, but now she could embellish with embroidery. If she couldn't dance... The new hobbies had distracted her from what she had lost.

"You sure you don't need me to take the shirt off?" He unbuttoned his vest.

Peachy eyed the base of his throat where the tie had been untangled. His Adam's apple bobbed with a swallow. She imagined gliding her finger down his throat. *Yes, please, take off the shirt.* Gliding down his chest. And then the belt. And the trousers. And...

Krew held her gaze for long moments. To know his thoughts might be too much. Secrets were delicious. She winked at him, not so much flirtation as a means to let him know she wasn't going to bite. He swallowed again and looked out the window. Nervous? Or simply aware of propriety? She wished he was not but on the other hand...yes, she preferred the feeling of safety she noticed when near him.

He smelled sweet, and a little dark. Expensive aftershave, but also subtle. As calm yet inviting as his eyes. And the confidence in his stance acted as a magnet. Already her body leaned toward his as she fussed with untangling the knot.

Tie hanging freely over his shoulders, he lifted his chin to give her free rein. This scenario forced her to stand close to him. And... Peachy slid her hand carefully inside his shirt to get a good working grip, the back of her hand gliding over his chest. So warm. And his heartbeats thrummed. Hard muscle tempted her to close her eyes and melt a little.

Focus, Peachy!

Right. She pierced the button and pushed the needle through the shirt fabric, pulling the long thread out. He'd missed some stubble under his jaw. She was about to point it out but decided it may drive the man of exacting ways batty. Mmm... Touching him sent shivers through to her bones. If her skin had felt dewy before...now other parts of her were getting just as dewy.

"Not very many people know how to perform such a simple task nowadays," Krew commented. "It's nice."

"I sew all my clothes," she countered as she worked.

"You do? That dress?"

"Of course." The navy blue dress was one of her favorite patterns. Cinched at the waist and fitted around her breasts and hips, with darts in the skirt to allow it to glide with her movement. "I like my clothes to fit perfectly. You're right, sewing is becoming a lost art. Some would even say the same of housekeeping, baking and gardening."

"You do all of that?"

"Not in my tiny studio. I barely have room to stretch on the easy chair without knocking my foot on the fridge. But I have big dreams."

"As you've mentioned."

Another stab of the needle through the button and she pulled the thread out behind the shirt tab. His breathing was steady. She closed her eyes again, realizing how calm he was. Her as well. It was so rare she felt immediately comfortable with a man like this.

"I grew up in a small house with my mother. We were best friends. But as I've matured I realize that having one's mum ask to go out on double dates with you and laughingly replay some of the more illicit details of her love life to you is not what I want. I need my own place. Freedom. Peace. Yes, I have the flat to myself, but it's like living in a closet. Someday I'll marry and have a family that lives in a cozy cottage in the countryside," she spoke her dreams out loud. "Big garden, handmade clothes for the little ones. Lots of baked treats. And plenty of room to stretch out and run barefoot."

"Seems achievable. But what about the hubby?"

"Hubby?"

"Yes, your universal goal for love must include a husband? If you've plans to live out in the country will he be a farmer?"

Cheeky of him. She'd never before been attracted to a man who smelled of livestock. Or who had muck on his shoes. There was nothing at all wrong with such a noble profession but she did have her limits.

"Oh, no. He'll be as driven as myself. Probably work in the city a few days a week, then home in the evenings, where I'll have dinner and cocktails waiting. Of course, we'll have art on the walls. Fancy cars in the garage. We'll live in luxury."

"Sounds like you'll be in need of a mansion."

"A cottage can be luxurious. A simple life can be elegant and rewarding."

"A simple life with expensive cars."

"Well, I do have my quirks. An Aston Martin is also on my vision board. Go ahead, you can call me silly for my extravagant dreams."

"Sounds…actually nice."

"Doesn't it?" She tugged the thread one last time and tapped the button. "Fixed."

He brushed the hair aside from her lashes and over her ear. The unexpected touch lowered his shield a little. Peachy stepped closer. He didn't take his eyes from hers. She traced a finger up the shirt to the base of his throat…

A knock on the door was followed by the call, "Housekeeping!"

"Come in!" Krew called.

"Nice," came from the two gentlemen who entered the hotel room. The camera's light flashed a tiny green LED.

Krew swore.

And Peachy nervously gripped Krew's shirtfront.

CHAPTER SEVEN

"Guys!" Krew closed his hand around Peachy's fingers and then realized how it probably looked. Standing so close. Touching one another. He tugged her fingers away from his shirt and pushed her aside to stand in front of her. He sensed she stumbled but caught herself while he made his quick move. "What the hell?"

Dave, the cameraman, was rolling. David stepped forward with the mic. "Just doing our job, Lawrence."

"By claiming you're housekeeping? I'm going to give the producer a call. This is getting out of hand."

"If that's the way you want to play it," David said. "Keep rolling, Dave. You signed the contract, Lawrence. You know what we can and can't do while filming an episode."

Krew smoothed a hand down his chest, fully aware of his unbuttoned shirt and hanging tie. Had she touched him any longer he may have had to kiss her. Not even *may*; he would have.

He lifted his chin to eye the men. Yes, he'd signed a waiver giving up rights to reject any content the producers may wish to air. But he'd not agreed to allow his personal life on the screen.

He glanced at Peachy. "You okay?"

She nodded. Rubbed a palm up her arm. Something twanged in Krew's chest at the sight of her visibly shaken.

"I should leave." She grabbed her purse and cane but had to wait for the Daves to part and allow her to pass.

"Guys, just let her go. She didn't sign any contract with you. You have no right to film her."

Realizing Krew had a point, Dave lowered his camera and both men stepped aside. Peachy left without another word.

Krew winced. That was not the way he'd wanted this evening to go. It was supposed to be a relaxing dinner. Maybe he'd get to know his competition a little better…and kiss her? He touched his shirt. The button felt like a direct connection to Peachy. His tie still hung loose. Yet he felt sure the footage would make it appear as though she'd been undoing his tie and— Hell.

"Listen." He scuffed a hand over his hair. "Guys. Can we agree that no one wants to follow me around on this fruitless quest? When the producer suggested this hunt for the paintings would make an interesting short feature that would give the viewers a look into Byron's collection, I thought it would too. But it's turned out to be a dead end. I didn't even win the first two auctions."

"Because you're distracted," David offered. Of the two of them, the mic man was the one Krew spoke to most often. He wasn't sure if Dave even spoke when he held a camera in hand. "By that bombshell."

"Don't call her that," he said defensively.

Peachy did personify the silver screen definition of a bombshell, all curves and sensual moves, red lips and lush, bouncy hair… But the label didn't feel right for her. She was so much more than what her outsides displayed. And he'd only just begun to learn what was within her.

"I'm calling Chuck. I'm sure he'll agree this is wasted footage."

"Give it a go," Dave said as they headed for the door. "But this is season three, mate, and you really need to kick things up a bit. A little romance action is just the thing."

"Rom—" The last thing a Lawrence man ever engaged in was *romance*. "I'm not performing for you idiots."

"You don't have to. It's apparent in the way you look at her. You're whipped, mate."

With that, the two exited the room. The door, on hydraulics, slowly closed, which allowed Krew to hear their laughter echo down the hallway. When the door finally slammed shut, he swore and kicked the base of a chair.

"I am not whipped."

He was just being cordial to a fellow art lover. They were both in town for the same reason. Why couldn't he meet with her, chat, get to know her better? Well, he didn't have to. He was perfectly fine sitting alone in his room, going over work on the laptop.

A dull, boring evening. Had he become such a stick in the mud?

Grabbing his tie, he slipped it from his collar. Then he fastened the button, securing the armor over his heart.

The following morning Peachy woke and took a shower. The green dress with cream polka dots and a thin lace trim had minimal wrinkling so she slipped it on. After scrunch-drying her hair, she stared at her reflection before applying makeup.

Last night in Krew's room she'd taken a step beyond dueling art dealers. She had not intended to engage in flirtation with him. But it had been fun. While it had lasted. Now she should focus on the job. Heinrich would be pleased if she managed to snag all four paintings. And, of course, that would be accomplished.

But there was something about Krew Lawrence and his exacting ties. The desire to crack his stoic demeanor could not be ignored.

They'd shared moments last night when he'd let her see beneath his steely exterior. And she liked what she saw. She had to wonder if he even knew what his softer side was like. He'd been so upset about the film crew catching them in a perfectly innocent moment.

Well. She supposed how it was presented on the telly could change the narrative from light flirtation to something salacious. She was all in for the tease, but she'd best watch herself around Krew. She was mixing business and pleasure. It could become a royal mess if she were not careful.

Applying lipstick, she pursed her lips, then winked at her reflection. She didn't want to get Krew in trouble with his coworkers or create a scandal. He'd used the word *salacious*. Was that what he thought spending time with her would be viewed as? Was that what her past lovers had thought?

She wanted Krew to think more highly of her. To see further than other men had seen, beyond her body and curves. She was so much more! She knew art and could hold a conversation with the smartest of art dealers. She wasn't just window dressing to draw buyers into the gallery, as she'd once overheard Heinrich mutter. And she would prove that by bringing back all four paintings.

Adjusting her hair, she grabbed her scarf just as her mobile rang.

"Mum?"

"Darling, I was just thinking of you so decided to call. How it's going with the auctions?"

She briefly wondered if Heinrich had prompted her mum to check on her progress. It was possible. Her mother denied it whenever she tried to wheedle the truth from her, but Peachy had suspected for years that the two had a thing going on.

"I've won the first two and the third is this afternoon."

"Wonderful! The paintings are secure?"

"They've been sent to Heinrich's holding site. He'll take them in hand."

"Oh, dear Heinrich. I'm a bit worried about him."

Tucking her cosmetics back in the travel bag, Peachy then wandered out to find her shoes. "Yes, he has seemed to slow down a bit. Hasn't been into the gallery much. How do you know what he's been like, Mum?"

"I spoke to him last night. He sounded morose."

Yes, the man wasn't his usual bossy self of late. Grumpy with a side of arrogance. Such a joy. "I wonder if he shouldn't go to the GP and have a good onceover. He's put on some weight and he winces when he walks."

"Now, darling, you mustn't be catty."

"It's not catty to notice a man is not top of his game. Haven't you noticed?"

"I, well…" If she replied, she'd reveal whether she had seen him. "How is your hip, darling? Has it been troubling you?"

Actually, she hadn't noticed much pain at all in the last week. She'd been so focused on the auctions. And a man with a propensity for a certain calm. And charming green eyes.

"I'm fine. Just, well, you know how auctions go. They can get intense."

"Darling, you are so loyal to the gallery. Always lift your chin."

"I do. Tell Heinrich I will be successful. I've got to run. Bye."

Tying the scarf to her purse, she stroked the silk. Her

mum always commented when she saw the scarf that she was such a dear to revere the gift. If Peachy won all four paintings she intended to celebrate by giving her mum something equally nice. And as for herself...

How to celebrate the win? Perhaps she'd begin looking at land listings. Really hone in on her dream and manifest by beginning the search for her future home. It was still little more than a dream, but that vision board didn't possess any power if she didn't activate it with real-world actions.

"Sounds like a plan."

Peachy headed out for the juice shop across the street. The hotel didn't offer much more than fresh-squeezed orange juice and she preferred to start the day with green juice. It kicked her system into go-get-'em gear.

Standing in the shop, waiting as they blended her juice, she perused the row of drinks lined along the counter for pickup and delivery, spying Krew's name, but misspelled as Kru. He drank green juice too? There was so much about that man to adore.

When her name was called, she pointed to his drink. "To be delivered across the street? He's my...boss. I can take it to him."

The clerk handed her Krew's drink, and winked, and she thanked him and headed out. Men always winked at her. She loved it. And she hated it. She was complex that way.

The streets and sidewalks were cobblestoned in a diamond pattern that created a work of art. With drinks in one hand and cane in her other, Peachy had to be cautious not to jab a toe into a raised cobblestone and go flying.

In the lobby of Krew's hotel, she immediately spied the film crew—if two guys could be considered a *crew*—and veered to the right before they might see her. She'd been annoyed last night when they'd barged into Krew's room, but not because of their audacity. At the sight of them Krew had literally shoved her aside. As if he couldn't bear to have her touching him. It had hurt her to be dismissed so rudely. And just at a moment when she'd felt they were starting to connect.

When the lift doors dinged and opened, she glanced over her shoulder to see one of the Daves had recognized her.

Swearing under her breath, she just caught a glimpse of the cameraman pointing his camera toward her as the heavy steel doors shut.

Rushing to Krew's door, she knocked. As he opened the door, she shoved her way in. "The Daves saw me."

"This is not wise, you coming here." He closed and locked the door behind her. "I didn't expect—"

She handed him the juice. "I was across the street and saw your name. I'm playing delivery person this morning. You like green juice?"

He sipped and nodded in satisfaction at the cool concoction. His shoulders lowered a notch. "No better way to start the day." He noticed she held the same drink. "Spinach, kale, apple, and…"

"Lemon," she continued, detailing her usual order. "With a touch of turmeric or ginger. Great minds, eh?"

Seeing his smile lessened her annoyance over last night's shove. He *had* stood before her after the dismissive move. Protecting her. Best she think of it in that manner as opposed to not wanting to be seen touching her.

Juice in hand, she wandered into his room and sat before the dining table, where his open laptop was in screensaver mode. Bright morning sunlight beamed through the open terrace doors and the scent of pastries from the same shop across the street spilled in.

"Yes, great minds," he said a little slowly. "So beyond

the juice, what brings you here?" he asked. "With film crew in tow."

"I tried to avoid them. They were camped out in the lobby."

As if on cue, someone knocked on Krew's door. He cast Peachy a roll of his eyes. She shrugged and mouthed, "I'm sorry!"

"The auction isn't until two this afternoon," Krew called. "I'll see you guys later."

"Ah, come on, Lawrence. You know the producer likes us to follow your day."

"Just making some notes on the laptop. Nothing exciting going on in here."

Peachy snickered behind another sip of juice. If only. She could think of a few exciting things to do with The Brain. One of them being to loosen that tight tie again. The man was too exacting. Rigid? No, he was more precise and organized than rigid. She'd seen the softness in his gaze when he looked at her.

"We saw Miss Cohen get in the lift."

"Is that so?" Krew called. He turned to wink at her.

Oh, yes, there was a bit of playful behind the gentleman's knotted silk.

"Listen, guys," he said to the closed door, "I'll head out for a bite to eat around noon. You can tag along to watch me try the local cuisine. Fair?"

After long moments, someone finally conceded, "Very well."

The two of them waited, listening for motion outside the door. When the distant lift dinged, Krew finally turned and sat on the sofa across from her. "You are going to cause some issues with filming."

"Me?" She crossed her legs and settled back like a content kitten. "I never cause issues. I am issue-less. Completely innocent."

Krew choked on another sip. "Not so sure about that, but I'll never argue a woman's mind. So, what brings you here so bright and early? Beyond the juice."

"Promise you won't push me around anymore?" she asked with a touch of a pout to soften her query.

"Push you— Oh. Sorry. I panicked. I didn't want them recording what was a purely innocent moment."

"It was. So you shouldn't have worried."

"I've seen the results of what me and my fellow Art Guys had thought was merely boring everyday work. Hundreds of hours of film can get edited down to minutes and in a manner that reads so different than what was originally shot."

"I suppose that is the art of creating a television show that viewers will watch."

"We were number one for months last season."

"Marvelous. I do recall that one episode with The Brawn eyeing the woman in the bikini after a deep-sea dive."

"Joss was mortified."

"Then why do you even have the show?"

Krew pressed his fingers between his brows, then splayed out his hand. "The idea of filming a short-run series was presented to us when Asher returned to the brokerage after a stint away to get his life together. At the time, it also seemed like the next step in promoting our work. Joss and I thought it might be good for Asher to have the opportunity to show his talents on camera. He was quite down on himself for a while."

"I'm so sorry."

"It was a family issue," he offered. "But all is good now. Asher's parents are doing well."

"I'm pleased. It is a lovely show. Educational, even."

"That's the part I enjoy. And the reason we continue filming. I'll leave the action and adventure to Joss and the gushing over pre-Raphaelite masters to Asher. I like to explain how things work."

"Yes, the episode where you took viewers on a tour behind the scenes in the restoration room at the Sistine Chapel was so informative."

"Fascinating, right? I admit, I also take a personal thrill in being granted admittance to such off-limits locations. It's a treat that most in our business will never be granted. We've already been slated to do an episode on Notre Dame in Paris as soon as the restoration is complete. And we're planning to do an episode on how forgeries work their way into the world through faked provenances, where I'll get the chance to interview some forgers. I'm looking forward to that one."

"Aren't the forgers behind bars?"

"Some of them. Some can elude the law with an uncanny ability. As you may know it's estimated that over twenty percent of the artworks currently in museums could be forgeries. And what museum is going to reveal that the masterpiece they've displayed for decades is actually a fake? It would destroy their reputation and hinder their ability to acquire more art. So the forgery remains on display for the world to believe otherwise. It's a weird crime."

"Not victimless."

"No, but oftentimes the ones buying the forgeries can afford the loss. I mean, well, I'm not justifying the crime. I hate forgers. Anyone who lies, really. I'm not good with dishonesty."

"That's refreshing." Peachy sipped the green juice. Truth was important. Telling a little white lie as she'd done in the pastry shop was about all she could muster. "But also telling. Have you been lied to?"

"Why do you ask that?"

"Usually the thing a person despises is what has hurt them in the past in some manner."

Krew leaned back on the sofa, stretching an arm along the dark leather. He was trying to appear relaxed but his jaw pulsed. His calm demeanor shifted so subtly. "I mean, hasn't everyone been lied to at some point in their life?"

"I hope not. Though I think my mum believes I don't know about her affair with Heinrich."

"Hammerstill?" He winced, then shook his head and laughed.

"I know. But they've known one another a long time. It was bound to happen. Mum is a bohemian. A free spirit. Always starting new projects. Or taking new lovers. Dancing barefoot through life. Taking off on travels with nothing but a bag and curiosity. Heinrich appeals to her creative side."

"So she's on a universal quest for love?"

Peachy nodded, realizing she'd never thought of it that way. Her mother had had so many lovers over the years. Had she loved them all? Yes, in her way. Was that why Peachy felt offended at the very thought at being so free with her emotions? With love? She didn't want to stretch her love so thin. She just wanted *one* beautiful, long-lasting, forever love. Was it even possible?

"Peachy?" he prompted.

She shook her head, banishing thoughts of romance. "Are you really going to sit in here all morning when there's a little gallery down the street waiting for two hungry art dealers to come sniffing about?" she asked, desperate to change the topic.

"I had noted the gallery when arriving but thought it was closed."

She stood abruptly, gripping the cane to steady herself. "Let's go investigate!"

"And risk being filmed?"

"Doing what? Looking at art?"

He splayed out a hand. Exhaled. Then he said, "I don't know…"

Her smile dropped. She did understand he was trying to avoid a scandal. And certainly she didn't care to have any attraction she was feeling toward the man broadcast on the telly for the world to see. But she had a few hours to waste before the auction, and she did not intend to sit in her room. Alone.

Walking up to him, she stroked her fingers down his tie. "An Eldredge knot. Perfect for a morning like today. The sun is shining. The air is filled with delicious scents. Let's make an escape out the back and go look at some art." She trailed her fingers to where his tie was tucked behind his tweed vest, then back to wiggle the knot. "If you dare."

The man's mouth opened. Green eyes danced with her gaze. She sipped her juice until the scraping sound of plastic against plastic, combined with a silly crossing of her eyes, made her giggle.

With a laugh at her theatrics, he then said, "Challenge accepted."

CHAPTER EIGHT

SNEAKING OUT OF the hotel's back door felt surprisingly invigorating to Krew. With a side of stealth. To judge Peachy's bright smile, she also enjoyed the sneaking around. He was cautious not to walk too quickly, having noticed she used the cane when approaching a curb or if the pace was too brisk.

They made the gallery without sighting the Daves. Yet they were both disappointed to find it was closed for remodeling. So they continued their stroll.

"They sold modern art," Krew commented. "I wouldn't have found anything of interest anyway."

"For a client or your personal collection?"

"I don't collect canvases."

"What? I can't believe I just heard an art dealer say such a thing."

"Why would I? Art should be shared with the world. I have one wall where I hang my current passion. Right now it's a Matisse. I've had it a few months. When I've tired of looking at it, I'll donate it to a museum, then look for something else to make me smile in the mornings."

"I like that."

Peachy clutched his arm, which was about the best feeling. He liked when a beautiful woman made herself at home in his space. Even more when it was a woman with whom he enjoyed spending time. They seemed to have the same passion for specific artists—for the most part—and she really listened to him when he spoke. Refreshing.

"Let's go this way. Stay off the main streets. Out of the Daves' sight." Turning down an alleyway, he slowed to a stop and Peachy leaned against the brick wall. "Am I walking too fast for you?"

"No, I'm good. Just need to pace myself sometimes." She clutched the cane to her chest and smiled at him.

"Sorry. I'll be more cognizant of our speed."

Hair spilled over her face and before he could stop himself, Krew brushed it away. It was soft and bouncy. Fresh and free like he felt right now. When had he last engaged in subterfuge with a beautiful woman?

"You surprise me," she said.

"Why is that?" He danced his gaze over her face, taking in her lush lashes, the scatter of freckles across her nose and high on her cheeks. Her irises were warm brown but now he noticed the gold highlights circling that rich warmth.

"This isn't your manner," she explained. "The Brain always takes a limo to get around a city. And he'd never be caught dashing down the street to elude a curious film crew."

True. And yet...it had been a dare she issued. "Then I guess you don't know me very well."

Much as he never missed a weekly jog around Covent Garden, and he stayed fit working out, this silly escape was just... *Silly* wasn't the word. It was much needed. Truly, a step outside his comfort zone. Would he have done such a thing had Peachy not been along, colluding? Of course not. He'd have called for the limo and made a quick summation of the closed gallery from the back seat. On to the next gallery.

How many times had he missed an opportunity to stroll

alongside a pretty woman because of his propensity to emulate his father? He never used to compare himself with Byron, but as the years passed it grew more evident their similarities could grow if he wasn't careful. Already he never seemed to stretch a relationship beyond a week or two. And that was not acceptable.

Peachy wanted a home in the country with kids and a garden? And a husband who could ensure that slow-paced yet also luxurious lifestyle? Krew had always wanted to acquire some land, but he'd never thought beyond the idea of owning a place away from the city. Moving in a wife and starting a family? Byron would cheer him on and then place bets on how long it would last. Seriously.

"I feel like I saw another museum on the drive in. Maybe that direction?" Peachy pointed down the alleyway then shrugged her fingers through her hair. So naturally undone. And effortlessly sensual. A tug at her lower lip with her teeth attracted his attention. Red lips that looked eminently kissable. "Krew?"

He realized he'd rested his hand against the brick wall, and he stood so close—their bodies were but a breath apart—but he didn't pull away. Partly to support her, but more so because...he wanted to be near her alluring Peachyness.

"Yes?"

Mouth parting, she slid her gaze down his face, taking in his tie—that she knew all the knots fascinated him—and then lower. He'd not worn the shirt with the rescued button today but he'd never part with that one now. It had been transformed by her alchemy. She had stitched her very being into it.

She clasped his forearm. An intimate move. Grounding. The bare warmth of her turned him on. The low-cut dress revealed beautiful curves. Her neck a long line of pale marble. A sculptor's masterpiece. And when his gaze landed on her star-speckled irises, a kiss felt imminent.

The thought startled him.

Krew stepped back. Yet as he pulled his hand from the wall, and her grip loosened from his forearm, for a few seconds, their fingers glided along one another—fire and desire sparkling through his veins—and then parted.

"Right." He gave his tie a tug. "Just ahead?" He crooked out his arm for her and they strolled, side by side.

He'd almost held her hand. Krew did not care for *almost*. He liked solid, sure outcomes. Yet that *almost* had felt more exciting than actually doing so.

They wandered down the cobbled walk studying the shop fronts. This was an older part of town and the street curved around a town hall which featured an astronomical clock that mastered a main courtyard. Building fronts were brick and the diamond-patterned cobbles were well swept. The nearby river offered ferry rides but the auction began in two hours, leaving not much time to indulge in sightseeing.

Krew paused to check a text notification, while at the same time Peachy's phone pinged.

She read her text. "The auction is rescheduled?"

"Due to systems malfunction." They'd gotten the same text: Please note it will be held tomorrow at 6:00 p.m. Classic evening attire. He tucked away his phone and waited for her reaction.

And got an effusive smile.

"You're happy?"

"Evening sale! Goodie!"

"Goodie?" A visceral shiver clutched his neck. "I abhor evening sales. They're so…"

"Glamourous? Elegant? Dripping with champagne and diamonds?"

"Fussy," he decided. "You've probably not packed for it."

"I'll manage. A woman is always prepared for last-minute glamour."

"I imagine you are." Though she was glamorous all the time, whether in polka dots and heels or with her hair drenched by the rain.

"What will we do with ourselves now? I rarely get a chance to wander the city when I travel for gallery business."

Spending more time with Peachy did have its appeal. Unless of course, she thought to go off on her own. And really, what was he thinking? Getting cozy with the enemy had turned him into someone he didn't even recognize. He hadn't spent any amount of time trying to get information from her or learn her auction tricks. He had lost himself in studying her, listening to her voice, taking in her soft brown eyes and red lips as if a balm to…something he hadn't realized he'd needed. But he just knew he did.

"I understand the walk along the river is lovely," Krew commented. "How are you with longer strolls?" He looked to her cane.

"A slower pace is manageable. Though I should have worn shoes without heels."

"We'll table the riverside stroll for now. How about…?"

There were a wealth of museums in Prague. And one in particular that he felt sure she would enjoy.

"Do you want to visit the Mucha Museum?" leapt out of his mouth before he could think it through. Alphonse Maria Mucha was Prague's hometown artist.

She slid her hand into his. "You said his work was pedestrian."

The woman did not forget a single detail. He'd not begrudge her that habit. It was an excellent skill. "It is, but—Well, have you been?"

"No, and I would love to."

"Hand me your bag." He texted his driver. "I'll have the driver pick us up then bring your things back to the hotel."

"I like a man who takes control."

He tilted his head. "You do?" He could imagine so many things he'd like to control about her—but no. He didn't want to tell her what to do. Nor did he expect her to conform to his expectations. The surprise of Peachy Cohen was her appeal.

"I do." She clasped his hand and swung it gaily.

Right, then. He wasn't about to order her about, but he could direct the rest of their day. He rather enjoyed treating a woman who had no expectations of him. And he would.

CHAPTER NINE

Peachy took in every painting, every poster and lithograph, every advertisement in the Savarin Palace, which housed the largest collection of works by the Czech artist Alphonse Mucha. She loved the curves and colors and the clean lines. Mucha was the classic starting point for many who didn't even know they liked art, and his commercial appeal had led to his paintings being used through the ages to sell everything from baby products to theater productions. The Art Nouveau style also boasted a huge hippie following. Which was probably why a love for him ran through Peachy's veins. Her hippie mother lived and breathed the man's artwork.

She sensed that Krew, despite his own feelings about the art, was even taking it in, not simply wandering past things, but rather really looking. Asking her questions. Pointing out the growth in the artist's style.

They entered the room that displayed photographs Mucha had taken of studio models for his works, and even some of his famous friends, and Krew took his time looking over the images.

"Paul Gauguin," he said of the photo taken of the artist sitting in just a suitcoat and shirt before a piano fronted by a bearskin rug. "What do you think is the story behind the missing pants?"

"I hope it's something juicy."

Peachy wandered to a display case where fantastical jewelry drawn by Mucha had been crafted in gold and precious gemstones by the legendary Parisian artist Fouquet. They'd been designed for the 1900 Paris Exposition. She particularly favored the diamond-and-emerald brooch featuring maple seed pods that looked very dragonfly-wingish.

"Brooches have sadly gone out of style," she mused. "But I still like to wear them occasionally. They are so romantic, don't you think?"

"There's romance in jewelry?" he asked.

"There's romance in everything." She wandered into the next room. "Life isn't worth living without romance."

"Not everyone is so fortunate to have romance."

"Maybe. But what a sad life." She wandered the tiled hallway where Mucha's works hung on both sides. Her heels echoed as they seemed to be the only two in the museum. She turned to look over her shoulder at him, casually following her, his hands tucked in his pockets. "I know you're sour on love, but I can't imagine a man can develop a distaste for something unless he's first had it. Yes?"

He waffled, casting his attention to the series of paintings.

"Darling, please, I can't imagine a man like you never once experiencing love."

"A man like me?" His smile was almost there. He wasn't hating this conversation.

So she continued. "Smart, rich, elegant, caring and kind."

"If you say so."

"Anyone watching the telly knows that much. I know all three of The Art Guys are single…though isn't one engaged?"

"That's Asher. He's getting married any day now. They want to do so before the little one arrives."

"They're having a baby? How wonderful! I do adore little ones. And the other? The Brawn?"

Krew shrugged. "He's got a pretty librarian who just said yes to his proposal."

"Oh, how romantic. A wedding!"

"I'll grant you that is romantic."

"I'll take it. So what about The Brain?"

"Are you asking about *my* love life?"

She gave him a shrug and tilted her head. "I'm nosey."

"You are. But... I was married for a year," he stated, followed by a tug at his tie. "We divorced. Amicably."

She'd not known that. It had not been mentioned on the television show. "Recently?"

"Six years ago."

"Was it a love match?"

He stepped over to her side. Looked her up and down. Assessing whether she was trustworthy to reveal some of his secrets? The best secrets involved love. Though she suspected men took the loss of it much harder than women. Perhaps because her mum was so free with her love, Peachy understood it wasn't something one should place all their hopes on. And yet, she was ever hopeful. And she knew it would come to her some day. Love could be all-encompassing and focused solely on the one. It had to be. She wouldn't want it any other way.

Finally, Krew offered, "*I* thought it was love. She didn't think so. So there you go. I've experienced love. Or what I imagine love must be. As I've said, I wouldn't recommend it."

With a moue of sadness, Peachy turned to walk in front of him as they entered a bright two-story room. The walls, ceiling and floor were covered with Mucha artworks, projected from a place she couldn't see. A bench at the center beckoned, and she walked toward it, noticing that the digitally reproduced paintings were slowly shifting, moving along the walls, and that when she held out her hand, petals from an image appeared on her skin as if fallen from a tree overhead.

How magical. Tilting back her head, she stretched out her arms. A spin would feel wonderful, but she didn't want to wobble and crash before Krew. Slowly, she curled her hand above her wrist, a flamenco move, and brought it down to one side. The movement stirred memories of dancing. Of a time when she'd felt free and whole. She wasn't sure what could return her to that feeling of utter freedom in her body now.

"How did you become so enthusiastic about love?" Krew suddenly asked. "If I can ask."

"Well, you wouldn't expect it growing up in a house where my mother was so free with her love. So many lovers. And so easily discarded. I grew to understand that too much of a good thing could spoil the magic of what I thought real romance should be. But I'll tell you my secret." A teasing smile could not be avoided. "It's because of two nuns."

Krew's brow lifted. "*Nuns* turned you on to love?"

She nodded. "After my accident, while I was recovering in hospital, a sister visited me. She was old and had the sweetest apple face. Whenever I think of her I can still feel her holding my hand. Her skin was so soft. After consoling me over my injuries she said such a terrible accident was tragic, but that I shouldn't allow it to darken my heart. That we are all here to love and be loved."

Krew managed a smirk. "A nice sentiment."

He really did fight romance with every breath! "It's only a sentiment if you make it one. You have to *absorb* love into your system. Let it in!"

"If you say so. And the second nun?"

"Ah! She was one of my physical therapists. A former

nun, actually. Built like a rugby player with ruddy skin and a harsh voice. I was on the treadmill, floundering along, and some stupid commercial with lovers was showing on the telly. She noticed my disdain. With a nudge to my arm she said, 'Just love, girl. Be open to it.' And then she clapped her hands together and said, 'Now stop slacking! Pick up the pace!'"

How could a person *not* recommend love? She imagined it was the greatest feeling in the world besides dance. Despite his dismissive statement, Krew's marriage must have been terrible if it had scarred him so deeply.

And yet... Well, despite her cheerleading, for love her quest for romance continued to be fruitless.

"You think you only get one love in your lifetime?" She followed a curving line along the floor that framed the image of a spring dancer swathed in pink fabric, her hair coiling to mirror the frame. "Oh, Krew, we can have so many loves, in so many forms, it's endless!"

He paused beside the bench, hands in his trouser pockets.

"I'm in love every day," she said, turning to him. And it was true. It was the attitude that had allowed her to move on from dance and to embrace the art world. "I love my mother. I love myself. I love my tiny studio in Mayfair. Well. Mostly. It's *very* small. Confining. And I love that I found a new profession after losing dance. I love..." She turned to face him and when she wanted to tap his tie she instead drew a finger down her dress bodice, a subtle dance move. The feeling that they were the only two people in the world curled around her shoulder as if a hug. They floated in one another's orbit and nothing else existed.

"I love making new connections with interesting people who challenge me and teach me new things."

Krew's hair, face and shoulders danced with the digital

flower petals. He splayed his hands. "So we're talking love in general? Not necessarily romantic? I love my life too. I have good friends, a job that I love."

"There, you see? You've not had only the one love. Romantic or otherwise, you just have to live life to its fullest."

"Good to know. But I'll take the other option, if you don't mind. I've given up on romance. Let no nun try to convince me otherwise." He sat on the bench and patted it for her to sit beside him. She watched the digital flower petals dance across his face, knowing the same must be on hers.

"Since we're getting personal...what about you?" he asked as she settled beside him. "You must have a significant other."

"Not at the moment." Her last brief relationship had been filled with sex and late nights eating takeaway before the telly, but he'd had a job as a traveling correspondent for an independent news service so when called to his next assignment they'd made a clean parting. It had been romantic, in a manner, while it had lasted. "It makes me sad to hear you've given up on romance. But I promise, romance hasn't given up on you."

"Is that so?"

It had to be that way. For her sake. "It just may surprise you one day."

"Doubt it." He tugged at his tie.

"Exactly." She clasped the tie knot. A wriggle judged it was tightly cinched. "No romance can get beyond your shield of protection."

"Maybe it is my shield, Peach." He placed his hand over hers. Then he surprised her by stroking a finger across her cheek. "So many freckles. Like a constellation."

"I love those too," she said softly. "I have a love affair with each and every one of them."

His smile creased the corners of his eyes. "All right, I'll give the nuns a pass. You truly are open and embrace everything about life. I like that." He glanced aside and over his shoulder. "We've got the place to ourselves."

She didn't want him to stop regarding her. To take his fingers from her cheek where he traced from freckle to freckle. She didn't want to exhale because he might flutter out of her proximity like a stray flower petal.

So what *did* she want?

"I want romance," she said softly. "I want to find love. I want a home of my own where I can feel stable and peaceful. I want it all. And I know I'll have it."

"I think you'll have whatever it is you seek. You're very optimistic." His finger moved to the bridge of her nose. "These form a map of you."

That he might follow to her heart?

What was she thinking? The moment was utterly romantic, but truly, she was not so talented at recognizing truth and loyalty in men. They generally seemed to want but one thing from her. And when received? Bye, bye, on to the next.

Krew's head tilted. He studied her eyes. "What just went through your mind? I saw it."

"What did you see?"

"A shadow." He frowned. "You're safe with me, Peach."

No man had ever made such a declaration. She almost wanted to believe it. Her heart always leaped for the prize and was then tossed aside with a tattered participation ribbon. The men inevitably leaving to find someone else. Someone whole. But good riddance, because if a man had no interest in romance, he could never be true, and he wasn't the one for her.

But then why must her heart insist on such high standards? And did she need to be so cynical? Perhaps it was possible a man could be interested in her for more than what was on her surface?

When he bowed closer to her, and their noses touched, she closed her eyes. His lips touched hers gently. As if a real petal had fallen from above. Cautioning herself from grasping him and pulling him in so she could hold him, keep him, claim him for one moment of elation, she tilted her head and followed his careful, devastatingly erotic movements.

A hug of their mouths. His warm breath seared her lower lip. Marking his place. Studying her. The scent of him filled her head with an intoxicant she could grow addicted to. His hand slid along her neck, tickling, tracing, taming her wanting skin. A firm grasp along her jaw, his thumb brushing her skin. His fingers entwined within her hair, supporting the back of her head as his kiss grew more demanding. Taking control.

And when he deepened the kiss, Peachy free-fell into a mindless plunge. Not wanting to grasp for a hold. Arms figuratively splaying wide to allow it all in. He commanded her with this kiss. No question who was in control. The man with the protective shield knotted at his throat had just plundered her defenses with a weapon no more deadly than sighs and touches.

When he pulled away, his hand sliding to caress her chin and hold her there while he studied her gaze, she tugged in her lower lip and entreated him silently. And he understood her plea.

Another kiss pulled her closer to him on the bench. He held her as he wished, and she responded with her entire body. Parts of her were climbing all over him even as she remained beside him. Anyone could walk into this room at any moment. And she was well aware that a camera could pop in to record it all.

Let them look.

Her desire went from a slow simmer to a heady want. Oh, how she wanted to slide her hands up under his shirt. Explore and take her time learning his skin and muscles. And then allow him to do the same to her. Inappropriate to grope in such a public place, though.

Suddenly Krew straightened, glanced around. He whispered on a passion-laden breath, "Not the enemy after all."

No, and that could prove dangerous tomorrow evening at the auction.

Peachy's phone pinged with a text and she ignored it. But Krew sat back, legs spread and arms resting on the bench back. "Get it."

Disappointed in their lost connection, she reluctantly tugged her phone from her purse and saw her mum had texted. She must have thought the auction was finished and wanted a report.

"It's my mum. I'll call her back."

"You sure?" he asked, getting up to wander to one of the windows.

At that moment another couple strolled into the room, gasping in delight at the digital figures moving about the walls and floor.

"Let's take a limo back to the hotel," he said, returning to her side.

Back to his room? For the usual expectations?

"Unless you want the Daves lurking outside by the tree to film our leaving?" he prompted.

She walked over to look out the window he gestured to and spied both men, who waved sheepishly at them. Maybe not the usual routine.

"Limo it is," she said, with hope.

CHAPTER TEN

AT KREW'S REQUEST, the driver took them on a tour of the city on the way back to their hotels. The entire roof of the vehicle was glass so Peachy leaned back and took in the buildings, loving every moment.

That was mostly due to the fact she sat in the middle of the back seat, right next to Krew, who held her hand. He hadn't kissed her again. Fair enough. She wasn't much for making out with a third person nearby. And she was still a little leery this day would end in Krew's room, him with his expectations. And her only wanting to please him and not strong enough to refuse the opportunity for intimacy.

Krew pointed out various building spires that jutted over the other rooftops. He explained that he'd only been to Prague a few times, but he liked to page through travel guides whenever he had a moment to relax. As he retained everything he read with ease, it helped for when he was visiting a new city.

"You really are The Brain." She snuggled her head against his shoulder. "How many languages do you speak?"

"Half a dozen. French is my favorite. I find it's easy to pick up the basics when immersed in a culture for a few weeks. Though generally my travels only see me in a city for a day or two for an auction or to visit an artist or client. You must travel a lot for Hammerstill."

"Not as much as you would think. The gallery is small and Heinrich's focus on the classics can generally be fulfilled through the London auctions."

"When you get your home in the country, will you still work in the city?"

"I suppose." She loved that he remembered her goal. "I'd still have to work to support myself. Maybe I'll get chickens and sell eggs?" She laughed. "Selling art was never my goal."

"Dance," he said softly. "I'm so sorry you were not able to pursue that dream. You're so graceful."

"You think? Even with this cane?"

"I've already forgotten that you need to use it. Will you tell me about the accident?"

She didn't mind sharing the struggle she had been through. While stealing something important from her, it had also reshaped her. And if he didn't notice her cane? Maybe that reshaping wasn't such a terrible thing.

"It was in New York City. Our dance troupe had won the British finals and the international competition was held in New York that year. Dance was my life starting from when I was little in those silly dance recitals with the ridiculous costumes. But, oh, did my mum love to sew the costumes! In my teens I began to focus on my skills and had a goal to go professional so I joined the troupe. We spent the first day in the US touring Times Square and tasting all the American fast foods. It was great fun. And I fell in love with Twinkies."

Krew laughed. "Those are terrible."

"They are. But oh, so soft and squishy. That's my best memory from the trip."

He took her hand and gave it a squeeze, seeming to sense she needed some fortitude.

"The bus ride to the competition was when we were hit by a semitruck," she said. "Cut the bus literally in half. I was pulled out with a jaws of life. I was taken to the ER and had emergency surgery that same evening."

He put an arm around her and pulled her against his chest. The comfort in that move stilled the tears that wanted to fall at memory of that terrible time.

"After about ten days in hospital I was able to return to London. Had another surgery months later."

"On your hip?"

"Yes. They did a bang-up job on it, but it's not much good for dancing now. Took me a good year or two to accept that. Thank goodness my mum was such a strong supporter. She was the one who suggested I study art online while I was healing and signed me up for classes. I wouldn't have the job with Hammerstill Gallery if not for her."

"You are an incredible woman, Peach. Even after something so devastating you found a new way. Not many can do that. Those nuns certainly implanted something to make you so positive."

"Are you naturally sweet or do you have to work at it?"

He chuckled. "Ask my coworkers and they may laugh at that. Something about you brings it out of me. You seem to get me. I enjoy spending time with you and this day has been awesome."

"I get some parts of you. But you keep so much more hidden." She tapped his tie. "That's okay. I've decided I want to discover as much as you'll allow."

"I'm good with that."

"You are?"

His eyes twinkled as he looked down at her. "You don't believe me?"

Why was being with Krew so easy? And why was her

romantic heart rushing forward with arms wide open? This could never be more than an affair, a few kisses that got her heart beating and her pulse racing. Because men like Krew did not have serious relationships with women like Peachy Cohen. Did they? No, they used her then tossed her aside. While never even imagining how much love she was capable of giving.

"Peach?"

She lowered her lashes and nodded. "I want to believe you."

He kissed the top of her head. "I get it. We both guard our hearts."

Yes, they did. But his confession went a long way in reassuring her that perhaps this man was different from the rest.

Krew walked Peachy up to her room. With the door open, he remained at the threshold. She swiveled her hips to face him but he noticed her misstep and lean onto the cane. The green polka-dotted dress snugged every curve of her and was cut to reveal the delicious mounds of her breasts that he…wasn't going to focus on. Not if he wanted to remain professional.

You did kiss her.

And that had been a mistake. No. Yes. Hell, he didn't know what to label it. It had happened in the moment. A good moment. So why label it as wrong? And he'd held her hand in the car on the drive here. Her body hugged against his as she revealed some deeply personal information about the accident. Another in-the-moment that he didn't regret.

She wanted to learn more about him? Why not just go with it?

With a lower of her head, and a flutter of lash, she turned and strolled inward. Krew took that as an invitation to follow her out onto the terrace where the night air was sultry and steeped with savory scents from a nearby restaurant. Much as he desired her, he didn't intend to take things any further than a conversation. That wouldn't be a wise move for a man who had just confessed to guarding his heart.

After stepping out of her shoes, Peachy leaned her elbows on the wrought iron railing and scanned the city skyline. It was a Maxfield Parrish blue, underlined by streaks of violet. "Today was lovely. Thank you."

"I noticed you limped just now. I hope I didn't take advantage of your injury with all the walking we've done."

"No, it's just my hip sometimes aches after a long day on my feet."

He wanted to brush aside the hair from her eye, which always tended to snag on her lashes, but he waited while she smoothed it away herself and recovered from the inner sadness he could see traces of in her expression.

"So the cane is because your hip aches? I thought you'd mentioned something about your proprioception?"

"It's a bit of both. The pain is from the scarring in my muscles that stretch as I walk. I can no longer hyperextend my leg, and quick movements are absolutely out. It's the inner ear thing that makes it impossible to do a quick turn or, heaven forbid, a spin. And I really have to pay attention when taking stairs or uneven surfaces like cobblestones."

Her sigh cut into Krew's heart. To have something she loved taken away from her in such a cruel manner? Devastating.

"Anyway, you've heard my sob story," she said with more vim. "And look where I am now. The top dealer at Hammerstill Gallery. Holding my own at auction against the famous Krew Lawrence."

"You do offer a challenge." More so because he couldn't

keep his eyes off her. And yes, he'd also grant her some skill at bidding. "Do you enjoy working for Heinrich?"

She shrugged. "You know his reputation. No one would ever describe him as amiable. But amiable never cuts it when buying and selling valuable artworks. I do worry about his health though. He's certainly not getting any younger."

With a wince, she turned to face the cityscape.

"What is it?" He leaned on the railing beside her, shoulder to shoulder.

"I need those remaining paintings, Krew. Heinrich is depending on me. We made a deal. My commission rate will go up if I bring back all four paintings. That will go a long way toward my dream of owning a home, so I *will* strive to win them all."

Of course, he would expect nothing less. But.

"I, as well," he stated, "strive to be the best, and will win the items on my list. My dad's pride is on the line."

"Oh, darling, men tend to confuse pride with ego."

"I, well…ahem. Just know, I intend to make you another offer on those you've already won. I won't lose. I can't."

At the determination in Krew's voice, Peachy turned to face him. They stood close enough to kiss, but the tension strung between them felt like a silk tie knotted many times along the length. Each had thrown down a gauntlet of sorts. From her tally, she was winning. But she did not doubt he would go to extremes to win the next paintings. And should he make an offer for the ones she had, she would never accept.

"All's fair in love and war, eh?" he casually tossed out.

"Are we engaged in both?" she teased, finding the need to change the mood. She touched his tie. "You intrigue me, Krew."

"Both love and war are necessities to life, I suppose. I'm

at my best when warring against another dealer in the auction room."

She turned to lean her elbows on the railing. The man was a challenge. He could be distracted by a wink, or a trace of her tongue along her lips, even an exaggerated sexy walk, but he was learning her, growing impermeable to her weapons. And that didn't offend her so much as make her want to strive to meet the challenge of him. How to penetrate his protective shield? And once inside, could she settle in and make herself at home? Did she want to? Why was she allowing flirtation to distract her? She should be focused on the goal. And really, she didn't want this night to end in a lackluster romp in bed that would result in him leaving her never to be seen again.

"It's getting late," he said. But he remained at the railing, his elbows propped behind him and his body turned toward hers.

"It is. We have, uh, what *do* we have here?"

He seemed to consider the suggestion for a moment then shook his head. "You undo me, Peach. I'm running through all the things I need to accomplish before tomorrow's auction, yet at the same time trying to figure how to avoid that work and just be with you. I like spending time with you."

"Same. I also like kissing you."

"Yes, that was…better than admiring Mucha's *Slav Epic*."

Peachy arched a brow. Quite the statement, considering the *Slav Epic* was a phenomenal work. Even for a "pedestrian" artist. She wet her upper lip with her tongue and he followed that movement. "Kiss me again."

He slid closer along the railing. Touched the ends of her hair. Then trailed his finger to her shoulder and along the edge of the neckline of her dress. If he ventured lower, and closer, she might lose her careful control and grab him.

A moment later she found herself pinned against the cool brick terrace wall. He did like to press her against a surface. To keep her there in his space? To control her? She found she didn't mind when it was so gentle, even if there was always a touch of command underneath the movement.

Bowing his head, he kissed her nose, and then her mouth. His fingers glided about her waist and to her thigh. Exploring while he kissed her.

The man surprised her at every turn. Just when she thought he had assumed business mode he released his shield and took her into his powerful grasp. Destroying her will to protest. Taking in her gasps. Moaning against her ear as he hugged alongside her body. If only he would press his chest and hips to hers and then she could feel him...

Suddenly he pulled back. His mouth parted, red from their kiss, as he smirked. "I, uh, shouldn't begin what needs to end right now."

What did that mean? She wanted him back at her mouth. His hands roaming her body.

"I've got some work to do that should have been tended to earlier," he said. "Mind if we call it an evening?"

Disappointment rising, Peachy nodded. It had been a long day. And she herself knew moving beyond a kiss was the wrong move. And yet the kiss had been...everything. Had she done something wrong?

Damn it, here it was. The toss her aside part of the deal. And they'd not even had sex! And she'd thought Krew was different than the rest of the men.

"Of course." She clasped his hand. "I'll show you out."

That kiss in the museum had been an in-the-moment sort of thing. And now? Another quick taste. A tease. Or maybe just a digestif to end the night. Now, it was back to business as usual for the man.

As it should be for her.

Krew stepped across the threshold, and just when she thought he would chuckle and apologize for his silly retreat, then ask to stay, his fingers traced across hers, not quite catching a grasp, but rather seeking the touch just for the sake of it.

Her heart nudged her to ask, "You thought we were beginning something?"

He lifted his chin, his jaw tightening. Not the reaction she'd expected.

"I mean," she quickly added, "if so, it was a lovely beginning."

"Yes, it was lovely." No emotion in his tone. Not a single nuance she could read as either positive or negative. And he'd said *was*. As in it *had been*, but wasn't anymore. "Until tomorrow?"

So that was it? Move on, people, nothing to see here!

"Tomorrow then," she said.

"Good evening, Peach."

Watching him walk away, wishing for so much more, she knew that if she were to be in top form tomorrow she had best follow The Brain's tactics and keep this professional. Yet her heart ached, Krew pulling at it with every step he took away from her. He didn't want to stay and kiss her longer. Talk. Get to know her. Maybe make love. She had merely been a distraction. Nothing more.

As usual.

"May the best man win!" he called.

Peachy huffed out a disappointed sigh, then mustered, "Oh, the best woman will win!"

She closed the door and sank down against it. Since the accident, she'd had to try so hard to be noticed by men. And yet that notice was always surface and short-lived. She'd thought it was different with Krew.

Her gaze fell onto the cane. Krew hadn't seemed put off by it. He wouldn't have kissed her otherwise. Perhaps he'd just been test-driving her kiss? And he hadn't liked it enough to continue?

She swore and tilted her head against the door. "How do you do it, Mum?" Was the key to simply not care if a man waltzed in and out of her heart?

"I can't do that," she said, tears rolling down her cheeks. "I want love."

CHAPTER ELEVEN

Peachy stood on a small circular dais before a tall three-way mirror, watching as the seamstress moved around her, marking and pinning the black velvet gown. She hadn't looked forward to a morning of dress shopping. Off-the-rack items were so hard to fit correctly to her body. Which was why she sewed all her clothing.

Yet the first sight of the gown in the window had lured her inside the cozy shop that sold secondhand items. It had only been worn once, and never sat in, the owner had explained in broken English. It just needed some taking in at the waist to fit Peachy properly and the owner had directed her to an alterations shop nearby where the seamstress called her to the back room, told her it would take less than an hour for alterations and promised she would be pleased.

"You have party tonight?" the seamstress asked in her delightful Czech accent as she stepped back to study her work on the dress.

"An art auction. It's an evening-dress event."

"They sell art and dress fancy at same time?"

"That's how it's done on occasion."

The woman gave an unimpressed shrug.

Peachy stepped down, leaning on her cane, and when the woman directed her to the changing room, went inside and slipped off the dress. A discreet hand reached between the curtains and made a gimmee gesture. Peachy placed the dress on her hand.

"I love Prague," she called as she pulled on her own dress, touched up her hair, then realized as she picked up her purse that the scarf was missing.

She'd...not tied it on the strap this morning as usual. Where was it? She never forgot about it. Could she have lost it somewhere? She'd had it yesterday with Krew. Had it fallen away in the museum when she'd been distracted by his kiss? In the car?

"The city is gem," the seamstress called. The sudden mechanical cycling of a sewing machine sounded. "You find coffee and cake by wall. Sit!"

"Dekuju." Peachy gave thanks using the only Czech word she'd picked up since arriving.

She found the proffered treat and poured coffee, still worried about her missing scarf. Maybe it had fallen off in Krew's room?

The coffee was blacker than midnight. But a bite of dense lemon cake countered the bitterness with a tangy, sweet kiss. Settling on a nearby chair, she pulled out her phone, thinking to text Krew, when...she decided she would just ask him about the missing scarf when she saw him tonight. For now, it was time to learn all she could about the man she would be bidding against.

Scrolling to the Wiki page for The Art Guys, she found a link to Krew Lawrence, aka The Brain. A brief bio told her his family lived in Kensington and had owned the estate for centuries. He'd attended the University of the Arts and King's College London. Had started The Art Guys brokerage at twenty-four, which had grown to a billion-dollar success by the time he was thirty. No mention of his marriage. The featured photos were still frames from the television show. So handsome. And always in a smart suit and tie. His profile photo featured him looking directly at the camera, no smile, yet it was visible in his eyes. Shirt, vest, tie and—she couldn't discern the knot from the photo, but it must be a power knot.

Krew's moods were indicated by the manner in which he knotted his tie. She did know that much about him. His tie was his tell. It revealed his strengths as well as his weaknesses.

Sipping the coffee, and settling against a shelf stacked with fabric rolls, she shook her head. She didn't want him weak. *She* wanted to be the weak one falling into his arms. Kissing him under a real blossoming tree that rained real petals over their faces. Or held up against a wall as he roamed kisses over her skin. She might even be tempted to give up the next painting in exchange for another kiss from The Brain.

Pausing with the lemon cake held before her mouth, she rewinded that last thought. Yes, so much fun to go over. And over. And over again. But really? She had been set on a task to bring her boss those paintings. She would not fail. She had to stay in the game and increase her earnings so that dreamed-of home could become hers sooner rather than later. Because her only other skill was dance and that had been soundly ruled out.

What woman would sacrifice so much for a simple kiss?

But it hadn't been simple. If it had been she'd not be expending so much thought on those kisses now. The man lived rent free in her head and she didn't mind that. Normally she guarded her personal barriers. Handled men before they handled her. Yet she'd allowed those kisses, had wanted them to last forever. Krew could devastate with a touch…

But she hadn't been designed for a man like Krew Lawrence. She was not wealthy, elegant, nor did she run in elite social circles. She did have opportunity to rub shoulders with the wealthy because of her job. It was a skill, emulating the haughty expectations of the rich and famous, the reserved gestures and emotions. But she didn't want to put on an act for Krew, a man vehemently against lies and fakes.

Peachy closed her eyes and tilted her head against the fabric bolts. Of course she cared when a man showed interest in her. And not just any man, but one she was attracted to in return. Because she did have dreams of family. Of a real relationship that would last through the ages. Growing old with someone she loved, trusted, a real friend, would be the ultimate foil to the life she'd watched her mum lead. Not that Doris was unhappy. Her bohemian, free-range-dating lifestyle worked for her.

But Peachy wanted more. When she had children, she wanted those kids to be wrapped in the arms of both a mum and dad. To truly know they were loved. She'd never known her dad; he'd left London when Peachy was three, moving to Alaska, of all places. Mum had said he'd been drawn to the ice and snow as he was an environmental biologist. They'd never officially married, which was why Peachy had her mother's surname. Peachy had no memory of a man she sometimes crafted in her imagination as tall, burly, with dark, tousled hair he might never bother to comb because he was too busy exploring, adventuring and generally avoiding his only daughter.

Why didn't Doris have a single photo of him? Peachy had searched in the cardboard box in which printed photos were tucked away at the top of her mum's closet. Nothing. Nor was there a digital photo stored in their shared family photo cloud. And the name she'd been given hadn't led her to any answers. There were literally hundreds of thousands of Jerry Coopers in the world and dozens of them were environmental biologists. So Peachy had given up a search and settled on the fantasy ideal of an untouchable, slightly adventurous, absent father.

"Miss?"

Peachy opened her eyes to see the gown displayed proudly in the seamstress's arms.

"You try on again?" The seamstress gave the dress a shake, an impatient signal that had Peachy bounding up and onto her feet. Then she pointed to her cane. "You need all time?"

"Yes, it's for my balance."

The woman tapped her jaw in thought. Her face brightened. "You let me razzle-dazzle?"

Whatever *razzle-dazzle* implied sounded too good to resist. "I'd love that."

Krew held the scarf he'd found on the floor by a chair leg to his nose. It smelled faintly of tangerine. He inhaled deeply and crushed the fabric to his face. Soft and silken. Like her skin. Like her lips when he kissed her.

What was he doing? He'd kissed her. Twice. He couldn't bring himself to call her an enemy any longer, but what *was* she? An opponent. A fellow art dealer. An art lover. She had waxed lyrical over da Vinci's works. She'd opened his mind to Mucha's more seminal works, which he marked as a feat.

She even drank green juice to start the day. It was rare he found so many common interests with a woman. Interests that meant something to him intellectually.

She'd asked about what he'd meant by *beginning something* and he'd, typically, brushed it aside.

Why was it so difficult to tell a woman how he felt? To

allow emotion into his everyday interactions? To allow himself to want? Yes, to actually want. To need. To give himself permission to seek that need. They *had* begun something. And it felt promising. Yet it also scared him.

The Lawrence men were not made for romance and love, so Krew had never had an example to learn from. Nor had he experienced romantic love—yes, even though he'd been married. What did a healthy relationship even look like?

He and Lisa were both to blame for lacking communication and not meeting the other's needs. Of course, he took most of the blame. Not there for her? It was true. Their marriage had been at a time when he'd been growing The Art Guys. He *couldn't* be there for her as much as she'd wished. And while he did not recognize that then, he did now.

He did want more. He wanted something…meaningful. He wanted to share his life with someone he cared about. Like Joss and Asher were doing right now. They were lucky to have found the person who made them happy and with whom they wanted to create a life.

Krew had a life. But it was functional and regimented and…lacking in meaning.

Just like Byron's life. The old man was probably already eyeing wife number four. Byron didn't love; he entertained, received, bought and displayed—both art and women—but never gave. He collected the paintings he crowded onto the walls in his house, but rarely really appreciated the individual quirks and aesthetics that made true art exciting.

Whereas Krew liked to look deeper. Learning Peachy's quirks and mannerisms was certainly revealing a more beautiful and unique woman every moment he spent with her.

But Byron must have loved Krew's mum? They'd been married for ten years before divorcing when Krew was six.

Had they had a great romance? He realized he'd never asked his dad if he'd loved Mum. He should.

Because he wanted out of the Lawrence mold. He didn't want a wall full of unadmired artwork and a string of ex-wives. Nor did he desire a heart that never got any use. Peachy was different. And Krew liked that. He…didn't want whatever they'd begun to be just a fling.

He carefully folded the scarf and set it aside. She'd come back for it. And when she did, he'd kiss her again.

CHAPTER TWELVE

Krew entered the auction room and touched his tie. A Merovingian knot. It was unique, complicated. Solid. Tonight he would not be defeated.

When stopping into Peachy's hotel he'd been disappointed to find she had already left. He should have texted her beforehand. Why did it feel as if he'd been rejected in a manner?

A white-gloved server in black attire and white apron offered him champagne, which Krew accepted. The room, which might normally be a fluorescent-lit dull space with chairs lined in rows, had been transformed to a slightly more party-like atmosphere. The chairs were covered with black fabric. An open bar stood to the side of the room. Attendees wore elegant gowns and suits. Jewels glinted at women's necks and wrists. A flash of diamond or silver at men's cuffs. And a low melody played across staticky speakers that were not meant for any sort of formal event, that was for sure.

The Daves had been granted limited access because of the logistics—lower lighting, alcohol and an undefined seating plan—and were occupying a corner at the back of the room.

Krew was mic'd. The producers had yet to use any of his auction audio but he'd complied with the request because he'd already pressed the Daves on this adventure. Best to offer an olive branch.

Scanning the room, he sought not the field of boring suits and colorful evening gowns but rather something— There. Hmm...no bold color today? Not a single polka dot? Was she attempting a new ploy? Something to throw him off his game? Because that dress...

The black velvet was fitted to Peachy's body as if it were a second skin. Strapless, it lunged upward to caress her breasts. He followed the curve of her side down to her waist and along her thigh where the skirt was slit so high he wondered if an incorrect move might reveal too much. But no one would call the dress lewd. It was a work of art on a figure that only Michelangelo could have sculpted.

She'd yet to notice him as she spoke to another woman who wore a hideous lime-green cocktail dress spangled with emerald gems. Krew couldn't look away. To hold her in his gaze felt as though he were claiming her. Making her his. The artist who had sculpted her had made an original that no other could copy. Should her stone effigy be placed on the block, the bidding would set world records, but ultimately, it would be best admired in a museum, where the whole world could share in its splendor.

He didn't want to share her with anyone.

Foolish man. Don't go all romantic because of a perfectly fitted gown.

Her hair bounced against her neck, loose and wavy, but even that seemed tamed, apt to remain calm and not distract a man's eye with a flyaway tendril that might get hung up on a long, lush lash. Nothing to distract from her body enveloped in black velvet.

Pity. It was just about the sexiest thing he'd ever witnessed when her hair spilled across her eye and she seemed to not notice. Why hadn't she sought to arrive here on his arm? He'd thought...

Well. Was he getting ahead of himself? Perhaps she did not feel the same as he did. As if they truly had begun something. He must have read her wrong. Never had he felt so unskilled in the art of reading a woman.

Get it together, Krew.

He set his empty champagne flute on a passing tray and grabbed another, veering for Peachy now that the lime-green concoction had sauntered off.

At the sight of him her eyes brightened. The warm rush of adrenaline that overwhelmed his system reminded him that he did have needs. And there was nothing wrong with desiring a beautiful woman. Touching her. Holding her. Kissing her…

"Mr. Lawrence."

Her acknowledgment dropped his heart in his chest. *Mr.* Lawrence? What had happened to first-name basis?

"Miss Cohen." Krew nodded politely to her. He could certainly work the evening attire. Talk about James Bond personified. Elegant, refined, a touch of GQ model, and a whole lot of do-you-want-to-touch-this-tie? A brilliant pink silk tie.

Something tickled Peachy's nose. Then she realized the effervescent bubbles of her champagne were spitting up at her. She felt caught in a swoon. She didn't care. He was too perfect to look away from.

"You look lovely," he said. When he set his flute on the tray of a passing waiter, it wobbled and the waiter had to catch it. Krew apologized.

Something was off about him this evening. He seemed nervous.

"And you…" Her eyes dropped to his tie. "Not sure I recognize that knot."

"It's the Merovingian," he proudly stated.

"But of course, for your march into battle. Appropriate."

He tapped his lapel, then turned it aside to reveal the microphone. They were being recorded. Kind of him to alert her to that.

"I do wish you luck," she said.

"And you as well."

"Did you—" But really? Must they pretend they'd not groped and kissed and, oh, if she let her mind wander "—spend the day in your room?"

"Yes, so much paperwork to tend." He glanced over his shoulder at the Daves. A subtle hint to keep it professional.

"Of course."

"And you?"

"Shopping." She tilted out her cane to show the two wavery lines of bedazzling tape the seamstress had attached to the upper part of the metal column.

"That's marvelous."

"You think? It's called razzle-dazzle."

"I love it. Er…" He pressed his lapel. Withholding his true feelings so as not to be caught out on camera? "It is a lovely upgrade, Peach."

She tilted her head and a strand of hair fell across her lashes. Krew reached to brush it aside but stopped himself. Out of her peripheral vision she eyed the Daves. Hanging on their every word. Quickly, Krew tugged away.

"I spent some of my free time earlier considering Mucha," she said.

"Oh?"

"Yes." How her first kiss from Krew had been not her first, but the only one she would ever remember. "I love how the artist used petals to create a romantic mood."

"Yes, romance—" He frowned at her. But then something twinkled in his eyes. "I'll give you that. Mucha was a master at the romantic aesthetic. Not the time period but the…mood. I'm sure he's been responsible for spontaneous emotion and romance and…such?"

Was he attempting flirtation while under the watchful eyes of the Daves? Love it!

"Mucha's work makes me feel so alive. And sensual."

"Same— Er, I mean, how interesting, Miss Cohen. But yes, sensuality is a strong theme in that artist's work."

Peachy tugged in her lower lip behind the rim of her champagne flute. Krew's eyes arrowed onto the move. "So sensual," he murmured. And then he checked himself. "Er, yes. Uh…"

The auctioneer announced the bidding would begin in five minutes. Peachy raised her glass to him. "To love and war?"

"To…love and war."

She sipped. But he had no glass to meet her toast. Which was fitting.

Suddenly love and war did not go together in any manner for her. It had to be all for love or nothing at all.

War felt an imperfect foil to the love Krew had thought to avoid but which he now realized he wanted more desperately than anything else. Who would have thought? Yes, his life was sadly missing something Peachy seemed to embrace unabashedly. He wanted that freedom and confidence that she exuded from her every pore. And he didn't even require that desire to be drilled into him by a rugby-playing nun.

He could have it. If he allowed himself a selfless lowering of his armor. But it wouldn't be easy. Not while the Daves were recording his every move.

Peachy sat across the aisle from him. A wise choice. He appreciated that the Daves would not capture them sitting close. If seated beside her how difficult would it be to keep from taking her hand or leaning into her tangerine aura? Impossible.

Had she taken his declaration to war and love to heart? She hadn't turned to acknowledge him since taking her place and crossing her legs. To his disappointment, the high slash in the skirt was on the other side of her body—was she waiting to deploy the infamous and wildly successful leg reveal at just the right moment?

Krew tugged at his tie. The thing was too tight.

Why was he so curious about her mannerisms? Hell, was it possible he was even *more* intrigued by the notion of what he could *not* see?

Though they *had* shared some delicious innuendos. Petals and sensual art? She'd been referring to their kiss at the museum. He hoped. Certainly, the conversation couldn't be construed as anything other than a discussion of Mucha's art on the audio track. Could it?

The audience settled to a hush as waiters moved down the center aisle collecting empty flutes and handing out full ones.

The painting Krew had come for was first lot on the block so as the hammer went down to begin the auction, he focused on the small canvas as it was brought out and set on the easel. *Jar and Flower* was a work by painter Ruilin Tang from the late Ming dynasty. The ink wash style was called *shuimohua*. The small painting depicted a large black flower designed with wide, blunt brushstrokes falling from a vase half the size. The only color was a small red seal in the lower corner.

And so the bidding game against Peachy persisted, despite his growing dislike for such moves against someone he no longer considered an opponent.

With an adjusting tug to his tie Krew glanced across the aisle...to find that the dress had fallen to reveal leg!

So this *was* war. Not love. Cursing inwardly, he forced his gaze from the woman's distracting leg.

He expected the item to go for around one hundred thousand. So he would wait until it reached eighty or so to make a bid. He enjoyed granting his opponents the false confidence of a possible win.

Peachy smoothed a hand along her shoulder, which pushed aside her hair, the movement reminding him how he'd caressed her neck while kissing her beneath the digital petals in the Mucha Museum. And then in her room, her curves had fit against his hand as if made specifically for him. If he closed his eyes he might detect tangerine—

Focus, man!

Right. He could appreciate her beauty later. When *he* paid for dinner as the winner.

With a nod, he entered the bidding. Peachy glanced over her shoulder. No smile. A lift of her chin. Determined.

Her freckles were art. Soft smatters that added a touch of whimsy to her face. Had she enhanced them somehow so he could see them from the distance across the aisle? Big brown eyes fringed by those hair-catching lashes. Her red matte lips parted. Making him long to trace his tongue over that mouth, dipping inside her heat and dancing with her lushness. One squeeze of his hand across her derriere...

Krew's heart stuttered.

She turned to face front.

He licked his lips and...noticed the auctioneer eyeing him.

Krew nodded, making another bid. *Pay attention, man.* He had to keep his head in the game. Couldn't afford to become distracted thinking about what he'd like to do with her freckles and lips and hair and—

Another glance from the auctioneer. What was the bid at? He didn't know. Didn't care. Krew nodded.

The battle was now between him and Peachy. Enthralled by their exchange of bids, he also found it, strangely, sexually invigorating. That woman, so confident she would again defeat him, must be put in her place. But the only place he could imagine putting her was in his bed. She was so gorgeous, delicious…

Krew cursed inwardly, then nodded again. Peachy immediately raised her paddle. He nodded.

Making love to Peachy would undoubtedly satisfy like no other. But would she have him? He didn't know. She was so *much* woman.

She turned to him again, but he avoided meeting her gaze. It would be pleading. Desperate. But also erotically infused with a daring tease.

The auctioneer slammed the hammer to mark the end of the bidding. With a gesture of the hammer he announced the winner, "*Jar and Flower* goes to our visiting television star, Mr. Lawrence."

Now Krew looked to Peachy. The hair tendril fell over her eye. She bowed her head. Sucked in her lower lip. Defeated.

And he'd never in his lifetime felt so cruel.

CHAPTER THIRTEEN

"Winner buys dinner?"

Peachy hadn't noticed Krew lingering by the sales desk as she exited the auction room. She leaned heavily on her cane, seeking to calm the anxiety that made her wobbly.

Now what to do? Talking to the winner, convincing him to sell, was crucial. Yet she felt exhausted, unable to face competing with him again so soon, even if just across the dinner table. He'd proven his skill. In the art world he stood on an entirely different level from her. Way up there. With a budget she just couldn't match. She was foolish to think she could compete with him. And to even consider he'd be interested in her for more than a kiss or two...

Another step and she wobbled.

"Peach? Are you okay? You look...not stable."

"Hmm? Oh, of course I'm fine." She forced herself to smile through the pain of the loss and took his offered arm. His kindness was a balm to her scattered emotions. "You're not required to fill in the receiving forms?"

"I'll stop by in the morning to oversee the shipping, as I usually do. I'm sorry you weren't able to acquire the piece."

"No, you're not," she said softly. Heartbeat fluttering like a wounded butterfly lying on cold stone, she remembered Doris Cohen's mantra, and lifted her chin. "But love and war and all that fair stuff, I suppose."

"I suppose." He didn't look triumphant. Or even pleased. "Let me walk you out."

They walked out onto the pavement, where a car waited for Krew. He opened the back door for her to slide in. It felt as though she were stowing away with the enemy. Yet she could not fail in her mission. So she'd go along with him and see if she could convince him to sell.

Slipping off her shoes, she took some relief. Clutching the cane never helped once sitting but it served as a sort of grounding post holding her secure from flailing.

Krew gave his driver instructions to take them to a restaurant Peachy knew was the best in Prague. Ultraspendy. But he'd won fair and square so she had to be fine with allowing him to buy. Much as it cut her heart in two. And yet…now that she was in the position of loser how would she handle it? Moping and pouting was not her style.

And honestly, she wanted to see Krew triumph. He deserved that win.

"I have something for you." He dug inside his suit coat and produced her scarf. "Forgot about it earlier or I would have handed it to you before the auction."

Having it back in hand brought a tear to her eye. Peachy pressed it to her face. "Thank you. I thought I'd lost it. This was a gift from my mother and it's become a talisman of sorts. If I would have had it at the auction perhaps I would have…" She smiled sadly and shook her head. "Or perhaps it was just my time to lose. I was off my game. The best man won."

Krew loosened his tie. Remarkable. "You are my equal, Peachy. You are a knowledgeable art dealer and sharp in the auction room. A formidable opponent."

Hearing that from The Brain lifted her mood. Thankful for his kind words, she clasped his hand.

He tapped her cane. "Razzle-dazzle."

She laughed. "It's removable. Best only for glamorous events."

"Leave it. It's cool."

"You think?"

She did like the way it flashed when the light hit it. On the other hand, did it call attention to her disability too much? "I'll consider it."

Once seated in the restaurant in the quiet back room before a wall that wavered with candlelight, Peachy exhaled a breath that she felt she'd been holding since the auction. She'd lost. But there was still the one remaining painting. And if she couldn't convince Krew to sell this one to her, perhaps when he saw she'd won three of them, he'd be more inclined to sell.

"I won't apologize," Krew started after the wine was poured.

The candlelight adorned his face, burnishing his skin and highlighting his strong jawline. She could stare into his eyes all night and never grow tired of the view. And that tie was a beacon that shouted Look All You Like! yet it defied any woman to approach too closely. She had done that. She had touched his tie, unknotted it and breached his defenses.

Pity he'd had his shield on at the auction.

"No need for apologies," she said. "It's business. I'm pleased you won."

"You're just saying that."

"No, I mean it. You've not retightened your tie. I don't know that I've ever seen you so relaxed before. Loose. It fits you."

He beamed proudly and touched the knot. Now there was the look of triumph she'd been waiting for.

"Shall we toast?" he asked.

She held up her glass and the scent of earth and raspberries reached her nose.

"To love, war and freckles." He pinged his glass against hers.

She touched her cheek, feeling embarrassment at the weird toast. But then warmth spread through her and she took a sip to hide what must be a rare blush.

"If I'm ever again defeated on the auction floor," he said, "it will be due to your freckles. They distract me with acute precision."

"I don't believe my freckles have ever been labeled as weapons. It's a good thing you have your shield on."

"My shield?"

"Your ties. They are your protective shield."

"I suppose. Though they weren't effective for *Melancholy* or *The Deluge*. Apparently, I've learned my enemy's ways and have overcome."

He knew so little about her. "Krew, please don't continue to label me your enemy. I don't like that."

"Sorry. You're right. The word is too harsh. But we have been rivals. Much as I'd prefer another label now." He set down his goblet and reached across the table to touch her fingers. Just the tips of them.

The unbidden touch brought up more emotion than expected. Sitting face-to-face with the man who had defeated her, and now to be touched so gently by him, and with seeming concern, tugged the muscles at the corners of her eyes. Were tears inevitable? She never usually admitted her defeat to any man. What was going on with her this evening?

"Peach?"

How she loved that he called her Peach.

"Would you excuse me a moment? Just need to freshen up a bit."

She headed for the restrooms and only when she stood in a stall with the door closed did she allow the tears to fall.

Pressing a palm to the back of the metal door, she bowed her head and sniffed. Why must she put herself through this agonizing quest for some paintings?

"Because you want the freedom and peace of owning a home," she whispered. Something different than the life her mother led. Away from the tiny flat that reminded of her room in her mother's home. Always embroiled in Doris's wild life.

But if Heinrich wasn't already aware of her value to the gallery, then gathering a handful of paintings for him now might never change that. She deserved a raise no matter the results of this quest.

And, truly, she was glad Krew had won. She didn't want to be his rival. They'd begun something with that kiss. A something that screamed for continuance.

Out by the sinks, she snatched a towel from the stack. Peachy dabbed at the corners of her eyes, then fluffed her hair. Lifting her chin, she stared down the woman who had taken on the job, filling her mother's shoes at the gallery, because at the time it was the only thing she could do after having lost dance. And she did it well. She didn't hate buying and selling art.

But she didn't love it.

And while she knew it was a waste of time to even dream about dancing again, knowing that she had settled into a career that was simply a means to make a living terrified her.

Why couldn't she be happy? Have a fabulous love affair? Get married? Create a family? Leave work behind and simply be a mother who doted on her children without needing them to be her best friends? Feel…not alone?

What would happen if she took down *her* shield? Was it

truly in the way she carried herself? The way she dressed? Did she allow them to believe she was a silly woman who had no inclinations beyond fashion and makeup? Not their competition? Just a toy to use and toss aside?

That wasn't her.

Was it? It was her means to distracting from the cane, her injury, her inability to express herself as freely as dance had allowed. She liked to dress the way she did. And if men liked it too, then so be it.

But then, she did seem to attract all the wrong men.

Unless she'd attracted a new sort. Krew seemed interested in her knowledge of art. He'd even showed cognizance for her injury, ensuring he walked slowly and helping her when needed.

She tapped the bridge of her nose. He'd been distracted by her freckles. She did have a love affair with them, yet there were times even she thought they were too much. But if he liked them…

And he called her Peach.

Did she dare show him how she really felt about him? Could she trust he would treat her heart as gently as he looked after her physicality? If so, she had best stop nudging around what she wanted. It was time to separate business from the pleasure she desired. The next time he kissed her…she would not allow him to stop.

"Oh, those shoes are lovely," a woman commented as she entered the room.

Peachy lifted a foot. The black patent leather pumps had been a reward purchase after her first sale with the gallery. "Thank you. But rather uncomfortable, truth be told."

"We suffer for our triumphs," the woman declared with knowing, and veered toward a stall.

But Peachy didn't feel as though she was triumphing. And

really, the only sort of triumph she aspired to might be managed by setting work aside. Just one night with the Brain?

No, you want more than that from him. And you can have it.

Tugged from her melancholy, she lifted her shoulders, gave the mirror a wink and headed back to the table where Krew stood to pull out her chair for her. The perfect gentleman.

"This looks lovely," she said of the light salad and brie she'd ordered. Her appetite had returned.

So she'd lost. She wasn't down and out just yet.

She held up her goblet to toast. "To love, war and freckles."

The man's grin could only be interpreted as an invitation.

CHAPTER FOURTEEN

KREW SENSED PEACHY had been upset. Thus the reason for her escape to the bathroom. He had won, fair and square. So why did it hurt so much to see her the loser?

Or was it an act? A means to appeal to his inexperienced heart and perhaps convince him to offer her the painting? He didn't suspect she would be so underhanded. Since getting to know her he had learned everything she said and did was genuine.

"What's your next auction?" she asked after the waiter had removed their plates and brought *becherovka*, a bitter liqueur that Krew knew the Czechs liked to consume after meals. "I assume it's *Dance*?"

"Yes. How did we ever end up with the same list?"

"I don't know." After a sip, Peachy winced. "Whew! That is…spicy, and some sort of herb I don't recognize. As for our lists, we both know they were part of a collection owned by one person."

"Yes, my father's collection. His ex-wife stole them."

Her eyes widened. "I wasn't aware they were related to you in any way when I set out to secure them."

"I know. Claudia absconded with them on the day Byron allowed her into the house to take away her things. It was a purely vindictive move on her part." He tilted the entire liqueur back in one swallow. Didn't even flinch. "I don't understand why Hammerstill wants them."

"I didn't ask." Peachy set the remains of her liqueur aside. "I've lost one of the group. I don't know how he'll take that."

"You still have a chance at the final painting."

She smiled softly, stroking the scarf she'd tied on her purse strap. "So are you headed back to London now?"

"I have a flight out in the morning. It's home for me until my secretary alerts me to the next auction. Have you heard when it is to be held?"

"I'm as in the dark as you are. Hammerstill is only learning the auction locations a day or two beforehand. He has an informant connected to the ex-wife."

"Same." Could they be one and the same? He doubted it. Lucy Ellis didn't seem the type to run in the elite art circles Hammerstill traveled. She was an online beauty influencer. On the other hand, her husband was the world's richest man, so who knew? "Would you like to share a flight home with me? I'm making a stop in Paris but I can have my receptionist book two tickets together."

"You don't have a private jet?"

Krew chuckled. "Bit flashy for me. I don't flaunt my wealth."

"I've come to learn that. Unfortunately, I already have a ticket for tomorrow afternoon. On Heinrich's tally. I really should take advantage of any generosity he slips my way."

Fair enough. Though he would enjoy another chat about art on the flight home. This couldn't be the end. "I'm glad we've had opportunity to get to know one another," he said.

Would it be forward to ask her on a date? He wanted so much more than a few stolen kisses and longing looks.

"Me as well. Even if it was as rivals."

"Rivals don't kiss," he said.

"No, they don't." She stood and moved around to sit on the chair next to him. She touched his cheek, smoothing the back of her hand against it. "You can kiss me anytime. Anywhere. Just promise you'll always mean it when you do."

"I promise."

"Is this still on?" She tapped his lapel.

"No, I tucked the mic away in a pocket when we came inside."

"Good, because... I want you to kiss me again."

He kissed her. Public displays of affection were usually absolute no-no's, so he made it quick. But just a taste of her lips was not going to satisfy tonight. "Will you come to my room with me?"

She'd heard the invitation many times before. But never had she felt so worthy, so ready, to take a chance that this time it might be different.

They kissed in the lift, and all the way into Krew's room. Always aware of her need to use the cane, he managed to direct their fumbling walk toward the terrace doors while also supporting her when their motions tilted her. Once the doors were opened to allow in the summer breeze, Peachy directed his attention back to her mouth. The man knew how to kiss. Or rather, he knew her mouth and made sure it received the exacting attention she desired. Gentle and lingering, then forceful and deep. She liked all his moves and learned that a gentle nip to his lower lip could make him growl.

His hands slid down her hips and pulled her forcefully against his body. Always he was a little demanding. Though never dangerously so. She loved it. The masculine control pushed her to the edge of cautious desire and flung her into all-out passion.

As Krew's kisses strolled down her neck she said on a gasp, "We're not dueling art dealers tonight."

"Agreed."

He lifted his gaze to hers. Emerald irises danced as if seeking her rhythm. In that moment she gauged his breaths with her own. Wanting, a little faster, needy. Dare she ask to make love? Would it happen naturally? It hadn't last night. He'd pulled away. She still couldn't be sure where she stood with the man, and it frustrated her while also drove her crazy with desire. He could not be pinned down, and that was exciting.

She wanted him. Come what may.

Tugging at the Merovingian knot, she wriggled it loose and he allowed her to pull it completely undone. Relenting his shield to her? She'd take the win.

He pushed her against the wall. Not so gently this time. His hands clasped over her wrists, pinning her there. What a thrill!

"You're the finest piece of art that I've ever put against the wall, Peach."

"Oh, lover."

Gripping his shirt, she unbuttoned it to his vest, then kissed him hard. Deep. Unleashing her passion. And he didn't relent, following her pace with his own wanting actions. His hand pressing the wall over her shoulder caged her in.

Everything she desired was in this kiss. This man could own her if he desired. And she would surrender to his every wish. Forget romance—she just wanted this man tonight. Any way she could have him.

He kissed down to the tops of her breasts. "I want you."

"Yes," she said and followed with breathy gasps.

The dress was fitted tightly, so he'd have to unzip— He found the zipper behind her and tugged, releasing her breasts to his ministrations.

A kiss there. Oh. She sighed while raking her fingernails through his hair. He took his time, laving a searching path across her skin. Making her nipples so hard. Her heartbeats pounded. Her fingers struggled to find purchase on some piece of his clothing that might be easily torn away.

With a graceful movement, he turned her and gently laid her on the bed.

"Didn't want to spin you," he said. "You left your cane over there."

He was so considerate! Not once had he made her feel disabled or different because of her injury. He even loved the razzle-dazzle.

Now it was time for a little razzle-dazzle of their own.

As he kissed along her neck and shoulders the rough stubble of his beard tickled and teased. Everything about him was raw and wild, so unlike the calm, stoic costume he wore beneath the knotted shield. She trailed her fingers down his taut stomach and to the top of his trousers.

Yet all of a sudden, Krew pushed away from her, leaning on an elbow and crushing his fingers through his hair.

She sat up, discombobulated at the loss of his frenzied touches, his hot tongue tasting her skin, his fingers mapping her lines, angles and curves. "What is it?"

Krew swore softly and flung himself back onto the bed, arms up by his head and head shaking.

He was obviously upset. Was it something she'd said or done? Had she moved incorrectly? Why was it that he never seemed to want to move beyond kissing her?

"I don't know what I'm doing wrong, Krew."

"It's not you," he barely muttered.

That was the worst line a woman could ever hear.

"It's..." Again he swore. "You're so different, Peach."

The second-worst line, surely.

Peachy tugged in her bottom lip with her teeth. She slid alongside him, gliding her hand over his bare chest. The muscles were solid; the protective shield extended. A shield she thought she had permeated. He panted. It was difficult to come down from such a hot and heavy make-out session. And she didn't want to. But something was bothering him.

"Are you sure I didn't do something wrong?"

"Never," he said.

"I thought we'd agreed we are no longer enemies." She glided her finger down to his trousers where she'd been so close to unzipping him. The man was certainly ready to go. But how to rev up his engine again? "Talk to me."

He exhaled heavily. Sat up onto his elbows. "I like you, Peach. But this feels so different."

"You've said that. I'm sorry, but you do know that different doesn't sound very appealing."

"Huh? Oh. No! Different is good. Amazing. You're perfect. And I just feel like…"

The man whom the world knew as The Brain—rich, famous and one of the most talented art dealers she'd ever crossed paths with—had just called her perfect. That didn't track.

"Don't say that. It's just little old me, Krew. There's nothing perfect about me. I can't even walk without a cane. Why are you threatened by that?"

"The cane doesn't bother me. It's part of you. And it's a little sexy, actually. It adds a touch of vulnerability to your strong and sensual persona. Peach, I'm not threatened. It's just…" He sat up and stroked her shoulder, tangling his fingertips in the ends of her hair. "You want real, romantic, passionate love. I…don't know if I can give you that."

Clutching her loose dress against her breasts, she kissed him before he could say more. She moved to straddle him and he fell back to lie on the bed again. She stroked his hair. Tapped that cute little mole above his eyebrow. His eyes, so liquid and green, pleaded with her.

"Let's take this slowly, shall we? Romance isn't even tops on my vision board. Right now? I just want to have sex with you. I don't want your crazy-good kisses to stop tasting my skin. I want your hands all over me. I want…"

He tilted a look at her. "No romance tonight?" His sweet expression held her heart. This man was one in a million.

"I don't think I could concentrate on anything else but how you make me feel."

"Same. I want you, Peach."

And despite her wanting to plead that it mustn't be only one night, Peachy stuffed away that unrelenting desire and kissed him.

And Krew spun her to lay on the bed, tearing her dress lower and making sure any stray thoughts about romance were quickly sidetracked to the real and exquisite now of making love.

CHAPTER FIFTEEN

KREW ROLLED OVER in bed beside the most beautiful woman in the world. Once he'd gotten beyond the worry that she was only looking for romance and roses, and could focus on enjoying her body, the two of them had really synced. In proof, he had sent Peachy into delicious convulsions of ecstasy. He'd had a few orgasms of his own.

Making love to her had guided him beyond her surface and into a deep understanding of how she worked.

And he wanted more. All of her. All the time.

He was moving ahead too quickly though. Last night had been the result of their flirtatious few days together. Did she want more from him? Could he give her more? He knew she wanted romance. And he, well...

He checked his watch. Not even 7:00 a.m. He had some time before his appointment to sign off on the *Jar and Flower*. And then it was off to Paris. A side trip Maeve had scheduled so he could stop into a client's home and oversee the delivery of a sculpture. The client, ever in need of coddling regarding where and how to place the art they purchased, eagerly awaited Krew's direction.

He nudged his lover gently and kissed the curve of her shoulder, noticing more freckles there. "Peach?"

"Morning," she muttered drowsily. "I was lying here with my eyes closed absorbing the heat from your nummy body. So delicious."

She sat up and he tickled his fingers up her back. More freckles here and there. She had them everywhere.

"Is your flight to Paris this morning?"

"It is. First, I need to stop by the auction house to supervise the packing of *Jar and Flower*. Still, that gives me at least another hour."

"Well then. Let's find a way to spend an hour."

"I have a few ideas. Shall we…do something salacious?"

Peachy would have liked to cancel her flight and fly with Krew to Paris for a day but her ticket home was already paid for. Now she was left to wonder at what came next. Had last night been a fling? The culmination of their flirtations? Would he, soon enough, decide he'd had a taste of her and wasn't satisfied? She shouldn't be so hard on herself, but her dating history made it impossible not to consider.

Best to not get too attached and just be thankful for the time she did get to spend with Krew. Once again, she was settling for what she felt others wanted and not grabbing what she desired.

Now she had the tough task of letting Heinrich know she'd failed. Back in her room, she picked up her phone and scrolled to Heinrich's private number. He answered after one ring.

"I'm sorry," she said, "I wasn't able to acquire the *Jar and Flower* ink wash."

A heavy exhale rumbled over the connection. She knew that growlish sigh. He was angry.

"Who got it?" he asked.

"Mr. Lawrence. The Art Guys—"

Hammerstill's outburst of swear words surprised her. The old man did have a tendency to punctuate his conversations with oaths, but it was usually *bloody this* and *bloody that*, not the extreme words he let fly now.

After a fit of coughs that made her wonder if he needed water, he hissed out, "He is the last man on this earth who should have that painting." *Cough, cough.* "You must get it from him." *Cough.*

"I tried. I can make another offer if you'll let me know how high I can go. What is the urgency in getting these specific paintings? I don't understand."

"Because I told you—" *Cough.* "Your damn mum! Why do I continue to do so much for Doris after all the trouble she has caused me? Where's my…?" She heard something scatter in the background and crash. He must have knocked things off a counter. "Winded," he said.

Yes, and he didn't sound good at all. "You need to lie down, Heinrich. I didn't mean to upset you. I'll talk to Mr. Lawrence about purchasing the *Jar and Flower*."

"Have to…hang up. Get that painting!"

The line went dead.

Peachy stared at her phone. What on earth? The man had sounded one step away from complete heart failure. And so angry. And why had he mentioned her mum? What trouble had Doris caused Heinrich that was related to the paintings?

She knew her mum had originally sold the paintings. She'd been working at the gallery right around the time of Peachy's trip to New York with the dance troupe. But what did that matter? What was going on with these paintings that Heinrich had a conniption over the loss of one?

Scrolling to her mum's contact, Peachy waited for her to pick up. No answer.

She left her a message. "Mum, there's something we need to talk about."

***

The Daves merely waved as they met Krew at the doors to the auction house. Yes, folks, the behind-the-scenes stuff was never interesting. Overseeing the packaging of an artwork? Why even bother sending the crew?

But they were merely doing as expected. So he intended to be quick about it. Then they could hop on the flight to Paris with him. His client there was always thrilled to be filmed and hammed it up with hopes to appear on-screen.

Probably a good idea Peachy hadn't come along. Give her a rest away from the camera. He wouldn't see her for two days. It would be a challenge. When he'd vacillated over a tie this morning, he'd gone with the pink one. Because it held a subtle tangerine odor. Wearing her scent against his skin was the next best thing to being close to her.

Krew had asked to look over the *Jar and Flower* before it was packed for shipping to the London office. It was laid out for him on a table in the packing room.

He'd already started The Art Guys when Byron had acquired this from Hammerstill, and he'd only glanced at the painting a few times when it had hung in the living room at his parents' estate. It was small and had been tucked beside the mantel where a massive Ming vase had partially blocked the view of the piece if one were standing at a certain angle from it.

He leaned over the table to reacquaint himself with the work. *Shuimohua* painting was not his forte. The canvas was generally paper or silk. The actual painting was more about the emotion than a precise depiction of a particular object. Only black ink was used. The vase was created with one quick line; a downstroke, then a twist to the right, and then upward to form the rectangular receptacle. The flower was formed by a thick brush; a dab and pull there, there, and there for the petals. The intricately drawn name along the lower right corner was accompanied by the trademark red seal Tang put on most of his works, but not all of them. Krew had viewed a few of his works over the years and the brilliant crimson seal was almost a work of art in itself.

Then he saw it. Something about the seal...

He nudged the edge of his littlest fingernail next to the curved corner of the seal. It was...raised. It should not be. The ink should have permeated the paper. Especially on a centuries-old work... The paper did still have noticeable tooth to its texture. So he tested his fingernail along another corner of the seal. It wasn't removable; it had been printed onto the paper. And yet...

The smell of ink was oddly prevalent. And the red had altered slightly, showing more of an orange tinge to it. Almost as if the crimson had faded.

Snapping his fingers with irritation, Krew gestured toward the clerk. "Hand me that loupe."

A small viewing magnifier was placed in his hand. Krew leaned over the painting, eyeing the details of the tiny seal. But he didn't need the loupe; the differences in brushstrokes and paint tones were obvious. This seal was almost a deep orange. And it showed evidence of fading, which was never apparent in Tang's other works. So obvious he should have recognized it when it was on the bid floor. Why had he not—

That tendril of hair falling across her lashes. Her red matte lips parting. Desire had overwhelmed him, challenging his ability to focus.

Krew swore under his breath. Once again she'd distracted him. Yet why? Could she have known the painting was a forgery? No, she'd wanted it as much as he had. He should have examined it before auction. But this painting had been in the previous owner's care for eight years.

Byron Lawrence had owned a forgery? Had he *known* it was a forgery? Was that the reason he now wanted it back? It was worth absolutely nothing.

No, his father couldn't know. Byron had never had the skill to judge a fake from the real thing. Krew had once stopped him from purchasing a Renoir for that very reason.

"Where's the provenance?" Krew snapped, not caring that it sounded rude.

"Here, sir."

Krew took the packet and sorted through the papers. A digital scan of an invoice, gallery consignment report, a few photographs. It had once been part of a rotating collection of the artist. It listed a half dozen museums worldwide it had toured. Until one of the museums had offered it on the block to raise funds for new construction. That dated to about eight years ago. It listed Hammerstill Gallery as the seller to Byron Lawrence. As for *where* Hammerstill had acquired the work before the museum auction there was no other listing. A period of about a decade was not accounted for.

Was Hammerstill selling forgeries? There was a possibility Heinrich had not known. Much as the gruff old man with a penchant for seeing The Art Guys fall had become a stick in their craw, Krew honestly believed he wouldn't purposely sell something he knew was a fake. It wouldn't look good for his gallery.

He and Peachy were on the hunt for four specific paintings. So perhaps it was just the one that was forged. Made the most sense. It would be incredible were all four were fakes.

Leaning over the painting, he fisted his hands either side of the work.

Behind him Dave asked, "Can you narrate your concerns, Lawrence?"

Right. He'd forgotten he was being filmed.

And yet, what might be the implications if he revealed the fake? Would it smear the auction house? Trace it back to Byron? And ultimately...him.

He touched his tie. The lavalier mic was on. Actually, this...was an opportunity.

"Is there a problem, Mr. Lawrence?"

A new voice. Karlson Richard, the owner of the auction house, offered his hand to shake and Krew did so. In the next few moments Krew worked the angles in his head. He could reveal that the painting was a fake, possibly embarrassing the auction house on camera if they did not know. If Mr. Richard did know, then he would be implicated in a crime that neither of them would want to be involved in.

If he didn't say a thing, and walked away with the painting...

Truth was, he couldn't just declare it a fake without sending it to the lab for a forensics examination. He had a man in London whom he employed for that. It could take weeks once he had the painting in hand. So until then, he wanted to keep this close to the vest.

Out the corner of his eye, Krew sighted the camera crew. Diligently filming.

Mr. Richard waited for his reply.

"Uh, just checking all the paperwork."

"You know we assure that everything is in order."

But had they encountered a forgery before? In the years Krew had been in the art world, he'd never experienced a bad deal with the Arthouse. And Richard was the utmost professional.

"Send this one directly to my office," he instructed the manager.

"Not to the usual holding house?"

"No, I want it sent to the London office."

"Of course, Mr. Lawrence. Will you be overseeing the packaging?"

"No. But do give me a few more minutes with it alone. The crew will want to get some shots." He gestured to the Daves. Krew tucked the paperwork under an arm, and again shook Mr. Richard's hand before he strolled out.

Now he muttered to the mic, "Guys? I think we've got something here."

David, manning the shotgun mic, lifted his head and zoomed over to Krew's side, followed by the cameraman. "What is it?"

"That segment we planned to do on forgeries?" Krew nodded to the painting. "I believe we can start right now."

CHAPTER SIXTEEN

THE PARIS STOP took the entire afternoon and into the evening so Krew's client invited him to stay for dinner, which he did. He'd also invited the Daves, much to their thrill. They rarely got to participate in the rewards of what the camera recorded. Many times he and his colleagues stopped for a bite to eat at a street vendor or attend a cocktail party hosted by a collector and he'd notice the Daves' hungry looks. Well, for once he was glad for the meal and the shared camaraderie.

Now that they'd arrived at Heathrow airport, Krew sighed as he waited for the pilot to announce that passengers could deplane. One more painting left to obtain for his father. Or really, three. He had to get those other two from Peachy. Why was he doing this? To help the old man avenge his pride? As Peachy had said, men had a manner of confusing pride and ego. And truly, it was all ego for Byron Lawrence.

Just as it had been a matter of ego for him back in the Prague auction house. He'd walked out with a possibly forged artwork. He hadn't wanted to implicate the auction house or make any accusations until he had proof, but the move didn't sit well with him now. Ego. Pride. Yes, they were two very different things but also easily confused. Pride would have seen him walking away from the forgery, reporting it to the police.

Had he slipped up? No. The forensic examination would

prove him correct, and only then could he feasibly look toward reporting it as a crime.

And he was growing more inclined, day by day, to let Peachy have the remaining painting. She wanted to advance at the gallery and earn more income so she could create a little country life for herself, something a woman who had lost one dream through a terrible accident really deserved. A place to feel at home. At peace.

Krew could grant her that wish with a slash of his black credit card. The expense would barely matter to him. Buy her some land, build her that cottage. Add in some chickens and…the family. But that was ego thinking. It would polish his ego to know he'd helped her in that way. Pride would see him standing hand in hand with her, giving her help if she asked, and if not, cheering her on.

It was a monumental realization.

He did hope Peachy could have the family she desired. And something nudged at him that maybe he could be included in that dream. Was he getting romantic again? She tended to bring that up in him.

And he didn't mind that at all.

Following his fellow passengers out of the plane, he called Peachy as he strolled through the jetway. She didn't answer so he texted.

Back in London. Can I stop by and pick you up for an evening at my place?

By the time he reached the curb for pickup she'd answered.

See you in a few hours. The Kelvin knot is appropriate for an adventurous evening inside.

Smiling and telling the driver to take him to Mayfair, he tugged loose his tie and began the Kelvin knot.

As Krew's limo pulled up outside Peachy's place, a cheery red-polka-dot dress was the first thing he noticed and his smile was irrepressible. Peachy slid into the back seat and kissed him. Soundly.

"I missed you..." It had only been a day, but yes, he did. He intended to tell her about the forgery but it could wait until he had solid forensic proof. The driver began their route home.

"I missed you as well." She snuggled up and hugged him. "So how was Paris?"

"I don't know. Took the limo to the client's home in the sixth, and then headed straight back to the airport."

"Pity. I understand the d'Orsay is exhibiting Degas for a few months."

"I do know that. I'll jet over one night to sit and enjoy it when I don't have to worry about the Daves following me around."

"You act like you merely tolerate them, but they're your friends really."

"Yes, I suppose. Whenever they're up for pints, I rarely refuse. And we did have a nice dinner with the client."

Later, after a round of lovemaking that had begun the moment he'd closed his penthouse door behind them, they sat in the kitchen sipping wine. Peachy sat on the counter before him, wearing nothing but his shirt. The one she'd sewn the button on. She smelled like tangerines, sex and wine. Sitting before her on a chair, he pressed the side of his face along her bare leg and closed his eyes.

"Best. Place. Ever."

Peachy stroked her fingers through his hair. Always making contact.

He liked it. Hell, he craved it. She made him see the world in a new way. She allowed him to see himself in a new way. Maybe romance could be a thing for him. He did not have to be destined to become a womanizer like Byron. Because he couldn't imagine brushing aside someone like Peachy Cohen as just another pretty face to keep on his arm and then discard when he tired of her.

"Have the Daves ever followed you home?" she asked.

"Not allowed to." He kissed her thigh then stood and fit himself between her legs as he nuzzled into the warm nook between her hair and neck. "Does it bother you? Them following me?"

"I don't want to be a television star," she said, "so I hope they'll edit out anything with me before putting it out for the world to see."

"No hunger for fame?" He straightened and she stroked a fingernail down his bare abs to the top of his boxers. Mmm... "What about your dancing? Did you not aspire for shows, the stage?"

She set her wineglass aside. "I had an aspiration to dance on that television show that couples dancers with stars. And then there was the summer I intended to study in Spain. But now...it's just easier to leave that dream in the past."

He kissed her neck. Her wanting moan fueled his growing desire. Yet it was countered by his genuine concern for her. He'd never cherished a person in his life. No, not even Lisa. Not properly, anyway. But he did now.

Her cane was hooked on the end of the counter. He liked that she'd left the razzle-dazzle on it. "So now the dream is having a country cottage with kids and goats?"

"I never mentioned goats."

"I know. But aren't they cute? A guy could have a goat or two."

"Could a guy?"

"Yes."

"I don't think they'd like living in this penthouse, and I wouldn't rule out a country property." He sensed he'd just jumped too far ahead in the narrative. Is that what romance did to a guy's head? He'd take it. "So tell me about Spain. You studied there for dance?"

"I was supposed to go there the summer following the accident."

"Oh."

"The flamenco style of dance is a passion of mine." She stretched up one long arm, her wrist twisting in what he knew was a flamenco move. "Or it was." Her shoulders slumped and she teased at the band of his boxers. "I had paid for a year of study with a private school. I never did get a refund because I was so embroiled in my injuries and healing for that summer that it didn't even occur to me to ask for one."

"Is that where the polka dots come from?"

She smiled curiously. "You think?"

"Well, the style of your dresses, so fitted and with a flirtatious ruffle here and there, have a touch of the flamenco to them."

"You're right, my clothing is inspired by the dance. I'd actually made myself a *bata de cola*, the traditional flamenco style of dress, and had hoped to take it to Spain with me. You're so smart, Krew." She hugged him. "Do you like the tango?" she asked suddenly.

"I've never danced. But I do enjoy watching others dance the tango. It's very…"

"Push and pull," she provided. "Love and hate. Like us."

He was convinced that strand of hair was designed to fall over her lashes specifically to tease him. Krew brushed it aside, then traced the galaxy of freckles from one of her cheeks, across her nose and to the other.

"We're not so extreme, are we?" he asked. "I don't believe I could ever hate anyone."

"What of love? When love strikes, it's not because you allowed it."

"You think so?"

"I know so." She wrapped her legs around his hips and he hugged her closer.

This felt intimate and right. But could it ever be love? Despite what Peachy believed, Krew knew that love hurt. But there was nothing at all wrong with enjoying the company of a beautiful woman whose touch made him relax and feel comfortable in his own skin for the first time in a very long time.

He brushed the hair from her forehead. "You make me forget about everything but the present. I need that. I need… you." He surprised himself with that statement. "I mean, yes, I feel like now that you've been in my life these past few days, it's as though my entire body is exhaling, relaxing. Taking you in. I like you, Peach."

"It is nice between us. I feel safe with you."

"You've not felt safe with others?"

She shrugged. "I've never been physically harmed by a man, but sometimes they can be so callous. Especially about my injury and the cane."

"I like the razzle-dazzle." He kissed her forehead and then her mouth. "We've done salacious—now how about we try…untoward?"

CHAPTER SEVENTEEN

THEY'D WOKEN TO watch the sun rise. And while Krew was in the shower, Peachy reclined on the big leather sofa sipping the juice he'd blended for them. Extra ginger provided a tangy bite. Wrapped in but a blanket from his bed, she had no desire to dress. But he had to head into the office soon, so she should consider it.

Her attention strayed to the Matisse on the three-story-high brick wall before her. It was a small painting depicting a French country scene. Such a marvel that the man had the discipline to own but one painting. And then to donate it to a museum when he tired of it. More collectors should do the same, she decided. Art truly was something that should not be owned but rather shared with the world.

She had only prints in her tiny flat. Spending money on art wasn't in her budget with the dream of home ownership in her future. But she'd get there.

Krew breezed out, bringing his subtle, darkly sweet scent along with him. He settled onto the sofa, nuzzled into her neck—oh, did she love it when he kissed her there. It sent the best kind of tingles throughout her body. Her toes curled under the blanket.

"I hate to leave so quickly," he whispered. "My car is already waiting," he said after the kiss. "You take your time here. The door automatically locks when you leave."

"Are you sure? I can grab my things so you don't have to worry about leaving the place to me."

"I don't mind. Do you?"

"No." She glanced to the Matisse. "But I may have to spend a little time with her before leaving."

"Take all the time you want. I like to sit and stare at her as well." He kissed her quickly. "I'll text you when the viewing is finished…?"

"Yes."

He grabbed his stainless steel travel mug and headed for the door.

Peachy leaned back, her bare legs jutting out from the blanket. She lifted a leg and pointed a graceful toe. He whistled. And she laughed, not realizing it had been a sexy move, but apparently it had been.

"Bye, lover!"

He'd left her alone in his home. Half-naked and nestled in his blanket. In the presence of a gorgeous Matisse that truly did demand long and relaxed observation. What dream had she been dropped into?

What had begun as a rivalry had taken a sharp turn to the right. And that right felt so good. Dare she believe that love might have found her? Only a nun could tell her for sure.

Her phone, left on the coffee table last night, rang. With a smile from the thought about the nuns still tracing her mouth, she picked it up. "What is it, Mum?"

"Oh, darling, I just heard your message."

"That was sent a day ago, Mum."

"My phone has been weird lately. Losing the charge. No matter. How did the auction go?"

"Mum." Who cared about the auction? That she had lost! There was something more pressing to discuss. "Why is it Heinrich is so hell-bent on recovering these paintings?

And why is Heinrich so enraged about something *you've* done that he calls trouble? What is it you are not telling me? What's going on?"

A heavy sigh was so out of Doris's range. Peachy shifted on the sofa to lean on the thick arm. Soft morning light streamed into the room, highlighting the bookshelf in a corner that she intended to snoop through later. "Mum? What is it?"

"I suppose I must give you the details."

"Details? What is going on? I suddenly feel as though you and Heinrich are plotting something."

"Perhaps a bit."

Peachy's jaw dropped open and she stood, clutching the falling blanket against her bare breasts. She wandered back toward the bedroom as her mum spoke.

"Did I ever tell you about Richard Francis?"

Peachy shook her head, not following this sudden conversation detour. "Who?"

"The man I was dating when you were a teenager. Right around the time you joined the dance troupe. Remember Dickie?"

Oh, him! How could she forget? Her mum's lover for three or four years. The hippie who had sported a long, uncombed beard, linen kaftans, with a penchant for spending hours secluded in their shed while he painted his next "great opus," as he'd so often put it. As a teenager she'd never been compelled to get to know him, converse with him. Too busy with the dance troupe and chasing her dreams.

"I remember those awful striped kaftans. And he always wore sandals," she recalled. "What does he have to do with me getting these paintings?"

"Everything, darling. Everything."

That sounded so ominous Peachy felt her equilibrium

tug. She aimed for the unmade bed and landed on it just as a wave of dizziness overtook. Whatever her mum was about to say, perhaps prone was the best position to be in to hear it.

"It was right about the time of your accident, darling. I was struggling at the gallery. Hadn't made a sale in months."

"Oh, Mum…"

"Now listen, I panicked. And I needed to make some quick cash, so I went to Dickie and he was very willing to help. He did adore me so."

Peachy stopped herself from rolling her eyes. It was Doris's manner to believe most men who walked the earth should adore her. And…who knew, perhaps they all did.

"At the time one of our clients had a wish list of sorts," her mum continued. "Works that he wanted me to keep my eyes peeled for. It was long, but I thought to help him with a few if possible."

"Mr. Lawrence?" Peachy asked, dreading the answer. The only obvious guess since she knew her list was specifically paintings Krew's dad had once owned.

"Yes, Byron. Handsome man. Old money. Entitled. He was always giving me the eye and asking me out for cocktails."

Had Krew's dad dated her mum? The horror! "Did you… date him?"

"Oh, darling, no. He was not my type. Too stodgy."

Krew thought he was like his dad. Obviously not. There wasn't a bit of stodge in Krew. Yet, her mum did have a thing for Hammerstill. And Peachy would label Heinrich as stodgy as they came.

"Anyway, I showed Dickie the list, and… Well, he was able to help me."

"How? I'm not following you at all, Mum."

"Darling, Dickie was a professional forger."

Peachy rolled to her stomach on the bed and clutched the loose sheets. She didn't have words.

"That's why you were never allowed in the shed, darling. He was a marvel with a paintbrush. Taught me so much about light and which brush to use for the desired effect. He managed to whip up a few things on the list rather quickly."

"Whip up...?" Images formed of a hippie in a linen caftan slapping paint across a canvas. And yet, if he'd produced something on Byron Lawrence's list...it would require such skill.

"You know Heinrich never paid much mind when I brought in new works to be sold. He trusted me so long as the provenance was shipshape. Well. He adored me. Always has, always will. I could do as I pleased. And doctoring provenances is a sort of talent of mine, I suppose."

Even more shocked, Peachy could but gape and shake her head. She didn't want to hear this!

And she did.

"Dickie created three of the works on the list. I, in turn, sold them to Byron Lawrence over a period of about a year. Safer that way to stretch it out. Didn't want it to look suspicious."

Suspicious? Peachy gripped a pillow. She almost dropped the phone. Her body shivered. It felt as though her mum had just physically punched her.

"Darling? Peachy, you can't blame me. I did what I had to do. No one was the wiser. But now that they've come back on the market, Heinrich insists we get them back in hand."

"He *knew* they were forgeries?"

"Not at the time of sale. I eventually told him one night while we were...ahem."

Peachy closed her eyes tight at that *ahem*. Her mum had never thought it embarrassing to share occasional sexual details with her over the years. But anything involving her boss was best blocked for fear of lifelong trauma.

"He was upset with me, but not for long," Doris continued. "We'd thought we'd never hear another thing on it. That the paintings would hang in the Lawrence estate forever and either the gallery would close or we'd die before they ever went on the block again."

"Mum, you sold forgeries to Krew's dad. Krew Lawrence. A world-famous art broker who has a show on the telly!"

"You think I would purposely put out those works knowing I might get caught? I had to do it, darling. All those medical bills— Oh. Oh, dear. I swore I would never tell you that."

"The medical bills?" That could only mean *her* medical bills. Her mum had never mentioned a financial hardship at the time of her accident. "Mum?"

"Well, yes, Peach dear. The National Health Service covered your final surgery after returning to London. But the bills incurred while you were in America…"

At the time, she'd asked about the bills that had tallied up in New York and her mum had brushed it aside. *Don't worry about it, darling.* And so, she had not. All her focus had gone into recovery. She'd been determined to walk normally, to even regain the ability to dance. Unfortunately the inner ear injury had other designs on her future.

"We just didn't have enough," Doris finally said. "And I've told you I wasn't selling much at the time."

So paying a medical bill would have been an incredible hardship. And Peachy knew the medical system in the US charged exorbitant amounts. "Mum, why didn't you tell me?"

"It had to be done. Peachy, don't get maudlin now that I've told you. I didn't want to give you another worry, more stress when you needed to be strong to heal."

"Oh, my god."

"And now we're making it right," Doris said with a lilt.

Her mother had committed a crime? To cover her medical expenses. And Dickie… "Where is he? Richard. Dickie. Whatever his name was."

"Oh, darling, he passed a few years ago. Cancer. Nasty stuff."

Peachy crossed her legs, sitting on the center of the bed, feeling so far away from the delicious lovemaking she and Krew had shared in this space just hours earlier. Life had punched her again. And this time she had no clue how to lift her chin and deal with this one.

"Those paintings mustn't fall in anyone else's hands," her mum insisted. "We need all three returned. Then Heinrich and I intend to burn them. End of story."

"Burn them? Three? But…there are four paintings on the list, Mum."

"Yes, well." Doris sighed. "One of them *is* an original. I needed some means to bring in a larger sum beyond the commissions I made on the others. I want you to find it. To bring it back. To place it where it belongs."

Which was where? And which one was original?

This was so much to take in. Peachy felt as if she'd stepped into a new timeline. Another world. Her mum and Dickie and Heinrich were all involved in something so impossible. Yet horribly real.

Which meant Krew may have just won a forged work of art—if it had been one of the three, which, doing the math, was likely. The Brain was known for sleuthing out forgeries. How had he not known before bidding on it? *Had* he known? No. Couldn't have. There had been no public viewing beforehand and she had spent most of the preceding day with him so knew he'd not privately visited the auction house.

A thought struck her. "Is Claudia involved as well?"

"Oh, no, darling. She just happens to be a friend of mine. She's rather crafty, yes? Getting revenge on her ex like this. I'd admire her if it wasn't such a travesty for Heinrich."

"If she's your friend why didn't you offer to buy them from her before they went to the block?"

"Heinrich did. She wasn't having it. Seems she wants to revel in watching her ex lose out on all the paintings. She knows his dealer is after them and is being as elusive as possible. But I also believe she wants him to bid on them. Just to see him have to buy them all over again. Brilliant, actually."

"Mum, that's awful. The woman is awful. What you and Dickie have done is…" So awful!

"Yes, yes, but I did it for you, my dearest one."

Peachy swore inwardly. Putting the blame on her? That was incomprehensible.

"You don't want the gallery to be embroiled in such a scandal," Doris said. "Heinrich's heart couldn't handle it."

Peachy recalled the man's erratic breathing and coughing when she'd spoken to him.

"I think you should check on him," she said. "He didn't sound well when I spoke to him yesterday. And…" She caught her forehead in hand. "I've got to absorb this information. I'm at…"

She stopped herself. There was no reason to tell her mum she was at Krew's home. It wasn't necessary. And really, she didn't want to share the best thing in her life with her mum right now. Because it felt as though if she did, her mum would find a way to ruin that.

If she hadn't already done so.

"Goodbye, Mum."

She clicked off even as Doris was speaking. Tossing her

phone onto the bed, Peachy caught her head in her hands and yelled into her palms.

She felt as though she might crumble if she moved the wrong way. No cane could provide support to the upset she'd just received. Her world had just been shoved, and she wasn't sure how to balance anymore.

She needed some advice. But the only one she trusted was also the man who had more than a few times proclaimed them enemies.

Enemies who set aside their business rivalry and had allowed their hearts to intrude. So much for her hopes for romance. This information would spoil any future they may have had.

She touched her lips, recalling Krew's gentle touch. A touch that had grown masterful and knowing with every moment. Had she ever had a man trust her so completely that he'd allowed her into his shielded heart?

No, never.

If she told him about this forgery mess he'd never look at her the same again. She had lost him. And she'd only begun to realize she may have caught him.

On the way back to the office, Krew took a call from Chuck, the producer. He was excited about this discovery of a forgery and wanted to film every move Krew made around it. It would be days before the painting arrived in London but the forensics scientist had already made time on his schedule and agreed to allow the Daves to film his process.

Chuck was less willing to budge in other areas. Krew had asked him to leave Peachy out of the segments, saying she wasn't necessary to the forgery angle. Chuck refused.

"Why would a dealer from Hammerstill Gallery want to obtain a forgery?" Chuck asked.

"I don't believe she knows it is a forgery."

"Or maybe she does and she'd hiding something. I've seen the preliminary footage. That woman is a bombshell. We need her."

"I feel as though you're trying to leverage her to achieve something that's not true. I'm very willing to expose myself for having bought a fake, but I will not allow you to use Miss Cohen to increase ratings."

"Just stay in your lane, Lawrence. We need to investigate all angles of this. She may be innocent, as you've said. And if so, she'll come out smelling like roses in the edits. But if not…"

Krew blew out a breath and shook his head. Before he could reply, Chuck said "Cheers!" and hung up.

And Krew swore as he tucked away his phone. The last person he wanted to get hurt by this discovery was the only woman he cared about.

Yes, he cared about her.

But could he if she *did* know something about the forgery?

After arriving in her loft and unpacking her things, Peachy's mind was fixated on the news her mum had just laid on her. A crime had been committed—many crimes, in fact—because Doris had needed to cover Peachy's medical bills. The feeling that it was all her fault was immense.

Would Krew pull up his knotted shield should he learn the truth behind the paintings? Of course he would. He was just and upright and would never tolerate such a crime.

Her phone pinged with a text notification from her mum. Not willing to call and talk to her directly?

With a huff, she opened the message app.

Claudia has released Dance to this auction house in Andalusia. Auction tomorrow. You must reclaim.

"Andalusia? Bloody..." It was the absolute last place in the world she wanted to visit, even if only for a day.

Peachy tossed her phone aside. Because of her mum's foolishness she was now forcing Heinrich to buy paintings he couldn't even resell. That *she* couldn't resell. The paintings would have to be destroyed. There went her hopes to make big commissions. To gain a raise. To start looking for a home of her own. She'd already spent close to half a million on the first two. So much more than she imagined her hospital bills could have ever tallied.

Doris should be the one attending these auctions, trying to retrieve her crimes and tuck them away.

On the other hand, Peachy did owe her. At a time in her life when she could barely support the two of them, Doris had done what she had to to make it work. Peachy couldn't fault her that. But if she'd told Peachy about it at the time they could have taken out loans, made it work. Legally.

She texted back: Is this one a forgery?

No answer. If *Dance* wasn't the forged painting, then why bother to retrieve it? So it must be. Peachy punched the air in frustration.

She turned to face the wall where she had pinned photos and pictures that made up her vision board. A stone country cottage laced in climbing roses sat at the center. Surrounding it were images of grassy fields, hedgerows, children laughing, some delicious vegetables piled in a basket. A few of her favorite works of art. And there, right beside the country cottage, was the photo of The Brain.

She tapped the picture. Inspiration. And admiration. She'd been trying to manifest her future life. A home to call her own. A place where she could be happy, peaceful, fulfilled.

A tilt of her head took in Krew's brilliant green eyes. Had she somehow…?

"Did I manifest *you* instead?"

A thrilling shiver traced her neck and cheeks. But only for a moment. Because even if she had manifested the best thing currently in her life, it couldn't last.

She hadn't heard from Krew all day. He must be busy… learning the painting he'd just won was a fake?

She had to tell him. He'd never forgive her if she did not. But if she did, could he forgive her her mother's crimes?

Either way, it wasn't going to be good for her.

CHAPTER EIGHTEEN

THE FOLLOWING MORNING Krew called Peachy.

"Sorry, I've been so busy," he said. "The next auction is in Andalusia."

"I know. My, uh, er… Heinrich's contact came through with the info."

"As did mine. I've booked a flight for us this afternoon. I'll send a car to pick you up. I have more filming today as we receive the *Jar and Flower*, so I'll see you in a short bit. And kiss you then."

He'd taken care of everything. The perfect gentleman.

"That's sounds perfect. I'll see you later. Thank you, Krew."

They hung up and Peachy went to her closet to pack. She would tell him… Hell, when, *how* could she tell him? If he were filming the receiving of the painting today then he would surely discover its secret. Unless it wasn't the forged piece. According to her mum, one of the four on her list was apparently an original.

She hoped the painting Krew had won was the original. She needed all the delay she could get before she had to rip out her heart and toss it to the ground before him. Because he wouldn't respect her after he learned the truth. And for as much as he admired her differences, this new truth about her very different life certainly couldn't overcome the crimes that had been committed.

* * *

Krew took Peachy's hand as the plane began its descent toward the Seville airport. She'd been quiet most of the flight. Extremely out of character for her.

"Are you okay?"

A heavy sigh preceded a nod.

"You're not," he concluded, which he'd discerned from the absence of a smile. "Tell me what's bothering you? Is it your hip?"

"No, it's fine. It's… Andalusia."

"The city? What about it?"

She turned to face him. The sun shining through the window highlighted the freckles sprinkling her nose. "Remember I told you I had signed on to spend a year studying dance in Spain? It was here in Andalusia. And I thought I'd be okay with coming here, but I'm feeling out of sorts. Thinking about what I lost and what I'll never have again."

"Peach, you should have said something earlier." He traced his thumb along her jaw and cupped her cheek gently.

"Wouldn't have made a difference. I need to attend this auction."

"I'll be at your side, holding your hand. Promise."

"That means a lot to me. But I feel as though if I see a flamenco dancer I might burst out in tears."

"Nothing wrong with that. Tears are okay."

"Are they? I can't imagine you've ever cried."

"We men don't do that sort of thing," he joked.

"But it's okay for us weak women?"

"Wow, you really are feeling down on yourself. Come here." He pulled her close and gave her a hug just as the plane's wheels touched the tarmac.

Peachy buried her face against Krew's neck and inhaled, losing herself in him instead of in the anxiety that threatened to overwhelm. It worked for about thirty seconds. When the flight attendant announced they would soon deplane she recalled the other anxiety-inducing information that she needed to tell him.

It had to happen soon.

Krew checked his watch. "We'll go straight to the auction house as we only have an hour before it starts. I booked us a room and can have the driver deliver our things there. You going to be okay?"

She smoothed out her dress skirt and nodded. "Are you sure you want to spend the night with me in a hotel? What if I win this one?"

He kissed her. "Then you buy dinner."

They arrived at the auction house with about twenty minutes to spare. Peachy had touched up her makeup in the car and as they got out, Krew handed her the cane, still razzle-dazzled. Out of the corner of his eye, he saw that the Daves, who had also just arrived, were going through their gear half a block down. He acknowledged them with a nod but Peachy didn't notice as she fussed with the scarf tied to her purse and then gripped both hands on the head of her cane.

"You seem out of sorts, love," he said. "Is it still being in the city that's unnerving you?" They had driven right by the school that she'd been slated to attend. He'd held her hand and had felt her heartache deeply.

She shook her head. "Seeing the school was difficult, but I'm stronger than I realized. It's just… I can't keep this inside any longer. I should have told you during the flight but it was so nice just to sit there and hold your hand."

"Peach?" He smoothed a hand up her back and finally she met his gaze. He'd kiss her but he couldn't be sure the Daves wouldn't capture that on film. Well, he knew they would.

"There's something you need to know about the *Jar and Flower*. All of the paintings on our lists. Or actually, three of them."

But that could only mean... She knew? Krew's heart dropped.

He started to speak but she put up her hand. "Please, just listen. I spoke to my mum yesterday. Oh. Your tie is crooked."

She adjusted his tie. And...he allowed it because her touch was always welcome. This small intimacy felt like his very breath to him. Yet, it cut him to the bone anticipating what she was about to say.

"Mum told me something devastating. I have to tell you. I won't keep secrets from you. *Jar and Flower* is, or rather could be, a fake," she said. "Hammerstill wasn't aware until— Well, it was years after my mum had sold the paintings to your father that she finally revealed the forgery scheme to Heinrich. So he's not to blame either."

"A forgery *scheme*?" Sounded so much bigger than one single painting.

"I swear to you, Krew, I had no clue."

"I studied the ink wash the morning after the auction and determined much the same."

"You— It *is* one of the fakes? But why didn't you tell me?"

"I—" Yes, why not? Because part of him had suspected her? Or because he'd hoped she wasn't involved and it could all be brushed aside, leaving their relationship untarnished? He so wanted this to be real.

"I didn't want to say anything to anyone until my suspicion was confirmed," he said. "It's currently at the lab undergoing a forensic analysis. But now, you've just gone ahead and outright confirmed it."

The Daves were filming and getting much closer now. Krew took Peachy by the arm and turned her away from the camera. He'd not yet turned on the microphone he wore on his lapel, thank goodness.

She gripped his forearms. "You have to believe I had no clue. It's a— Oh, Krew, it's a twisted and tangled thing. One of my mother's old lovers forged the paintings so she could…"

He wasn't sure he wanted to hear more.

But he needed to hear it all.

"Could what? Profit off my family?"

"No, that's not— Well. Yes, it could be viewed in that manner. Mum needed money to pay my medical bills. Her lover offered to fake some of the items on your dad's wish list."

The confession was insanity. The Daves had drawn closer. He should tell them to back away, but Krew's instincts switched toward getting this information on film. It was all linked to the forged artwork. He subtly turned his mic on.

"There's more than one fake?" he asked, needing her to confirm it on record.

"There are three." Her lip wobbled.

His heart did a dive. "Who was the painter?" he asked her.

"His name was Dickie. Richard something or other. I knew him vaguely. At the time I was young and hadn't much interest in conversing with any of my mother's lovers. Mum said he died a few years ago. But Krew, it makes sense to me now why Heinrich insisted we get all these paintings back in hand. He wants to destroy them so they are taken out of circulation."

"He didn't seem so concerned about the forgeries when my dad bought them."

"I told you, he didn't know! My mother didn't tell him."

"How could she have slipped a forgery by Hammerstill?"

"Well, you don't know my mother. She's very...not so much manipulative as...beguiling?"

Krew gave her a gobsmacked stare. Seriously? Of course she would soften it to make it sound as if her mother were merely some sort of misguided honeypot. *She's a honeypot... Too bad she's broken.* Cruel words spoken by that dealer at the first auction.

Had the daughter the same inclinations as her mother? Could he believe Peachy had nothing whatsoever to do with this crime?

"Heinrich has always had a crush on my mum," she continued. "When she was with the gallery she had free rein of the place. And...apparently, she had a talent at faking provenances."

Krew winced. He did not want to hear this even though he needed to hear this. How could Peachy get involved in anything so...illegal!

"So it's your mother who should be prosecuted for the crime."

"No! Krew, don't you see? If we destroy the paintings it all goes away."

"Save the cash my dad laid out for forgeries. Four of them, Peachy."

"No, mum said there were only three. Which makes no sense because there are four on my list."

"Is *Dance* a fake?"

"I don't know. Mum didn't specify which one was the original of the four."

"Peachy, I just spent one hundred and twenty thousand euros on the Tang. I know it's a fake because the seal was poorly reproduced."

"We'll buy it from you. I'm sure Heinrich will insist."

"Buy it? This is a crime, Peachy. I've already begun recording details about the painting for the—"

"The show? You're going to implicate my mum? Me?"

"No, I…"

Peachy clutched his forearm. "I just wanted you to know the truth. I thought I could trust you to keep it between us." When she looked to the side, she gaped. Having sighted the camera crew, she shook her head. "That can't go on record. It's not necessary to tell the world if it's a problem we can easily solve. Your dad will be compensated. And it's not as though she did it for malicious reasons. Mum did it to pay my medical bills. Our insurance didn't cover the stay and surgery in New York."

Krew wasn't sure how to process this information. Her mother had been knowingly involved in a crime to help her daughter. A daughter who apparently had no idea what had been going on behind the scenes.

"I need to think about this," he finally said.

Peachy stepped back. "I want to always be truthful with you. We've…" She glanced to the Daves. "Well. I had thought we'd become…close."

They had. And he wanted that. More than anything. But now that hopeful future had been intruded upon by something that he could not fathom. A massive lie that had involved not only him but also his dad.

Slipping his hand inside his suit coat, he pulled out the lavalier mic and shoved it in his pocket. Without a glance to Dave, who he knew was having a conniption, Krew leaned in and whispered to Peachy, "You are a complication."

And as he drew away from her sweet tangerine aura he winced. Wanting to kiss her. He made a silent promise to them both that he wasn't walking away, that he just needed some time to process it all.

"We should get inside."

"I don't know if I can."

"You have to. We'll figure this out."

"Okay. I'll be right in. I need to...check my makeup."

Peachy stood at the curb, head down. She shrugged one palm up her opposite arm then kicked at her cane.

Krew's heart was torn. And that was a feeling he'd sworn to never again experience. Damn romance.

As the Daves followed him in, Krew kept turning to where Peachy stood at the curb. She lifted her chin, hearing her mother's words. *Darling, lift your chin. A good fake can get by with so much.*

How telling that statement was now. Never in her life could she have imagined what it would eventually mean.

You are a complication. How it hurt for him to label her that way. But it was true.

Involving Krew further in the mess her mother had created was the last thing she desired. But she'd had to tell him. She wanted Krew untouched by the wickedness of it all. Too late. Had she thought secrets delicious? Ugh! This one was awful and heart-wrenching. If she could reverse time and go back and ensure he hadn't won *Jar and Flower*, she would. The man had never asked to be involved in scandal. He was good and just and the best thing that had ever happened to her.

And her mum had messed that up beyond repair. There was nothing she could do to convince him otherwise. And really, now he had excellent fodder for his show. At her expense. He'd not said he'd protect her. Stand by her. Be there for her.

She wanted him to pull her into his embrace. To kiss her. To reignite the passion that had seen them through nights with barely an hour of sleep.

But she'd lost him with the truth. Perhaps it was for the best. He was too good for someone like her.

Krew had chosen his side. And it was not hers.

CHAPTER NINETEEN

PEACHY FELT NONE of her usual confidence as she walked down the aisle between folding chairs, relying heavily on her cane for support. Instead of her usually fun polka dots and ruffles, she'd worn a plain emerald dress today, still fitted, but the only detail was cream buttons at each of the cap sleeves. She hadn't wanted to dress in anything that reminded her of what she'd lost. Once in Andalusia, she'd thought to experience heartbreak all over again by being in the city she'd never gotten to visit. A city that might have been her home while she had honed her skills and furthered her dance study.

Yet the real heartbreak was even more devastating. Here she'd lost the trust of her lover. The only man she cared for. They had begun something. And now it would end.

She found an aisle seat and crossed her legs. Touched the scarf on her purse. Looked over her shoulder. She didn't see anyone's face or if they noticed her because her thoughts raced.

She clutched her cane. While not experiencing a dizzy spell, she felt out of balance with the world.

"Is that seat beside you taken, sir?"

At the male voice she looked across the aisle to find a dapper gentleman with a smart tie waiting for a reply from an elder gentleman sitting one seat in. The older man removed his auction catalog from the folding chair and nodded that Krew could sit.

Peachy glanced down the row to her right. All seats empty. He could have sat next to her. Instead the enemy had seated himself in the most opportune position to go to battle.

Her heart dropped to her gut. But she was cognizant to lift her chin. She smiled at him.

He nodded once. Then adjusted his tie and took in the room. She hadn't noted what type of knot formed his shield today. She was really off her game. Now all eyes were on them. Whispers she couldn't quite make out and glances back and forth between her and Krew made her more nervous. What did they know? The film footage hadn't been aired, and no one could know of their relationship. Had Krew already alerted someone to the crime she was desperately trying to cover up?

She twisted at her waist and spied the Daves at the back of the room. Dave nodded to her. Gave her a thumbs-up. Krew had mentioned they'd begun filming for a show about forgeries. The Brain could bring in big ratings for the show by revealing the forgery to the world. While also implicating her. How could he possibly keep her out of it?

Pressing a hand over her erratic heartbeats, Peachy turned to face front and uncrossed her legs. She felt undone. Out of sorts. Not at her strongest. This was not happening. She was trapped. By the one man she had thought to trust. A man who had promised to stand at her side and hold her hand.

From the corner of her eye, she saw the cameraman move as close to the barrier as possible and adjust his lens. Zooming in on her?

On stage the auctioneer announced they would begin. The hammer landed on the wood auction block and the first lot was brought out to display.

There were a dozen items before the final *Dance* painting, but the bidding went swiftly. Forty-five minutes later, as the audience, now dwindled by half, waited for the final item to be placed on the block, Krew glanced at Peachy. She couldn't read his expression, though if she were telepathic she could likely sense him asking her to surrender. To give up. Make it easy on herself.

"Ladies and gentleman," the auctioneer said, "we've had to pull the *Dance* because of an unexpected issue. The auction is now concluded. Thank you all for attending and your generous bids." With one final tap of the hammer he brought the sale to a close.

Peachy mouthed to Krew, "Did you do that?"

He shrugged. "It wasn't me."

CHAPTER TWENTY

Krew had not attended an auction where a lot was pulled moments before it was scheduled to go on the block. Sure, there were occasions where an item may be crossed out of a catalog because for various reasons it was no longer available. What had happened that they'd pulled *Dance*? Had it been confirmed as a forgery as well?

Peachy had said that there were three forgeries. But she had four paintings on her list. How could he know which of them was the real thing if he'd not held *Melancholy* and *The Deluge* in hand and examined them?

Now that the auction floor had cleared of the dealers, the film crew made its way past the barrier and stood but four feet from Krew. Peachy had swiftly exited. All he wanted to do was rush after her. Because he cared about her. And he wouldn't put up a shield or pretend otherwise. If they whispered about The Brain having an illicit affair, then so be it. Because it wasn't illicit to him. To him it was a joyful thing. And he was all in for protecting Peachy.

And yet, he'd come here today to win. And he was determined not to allow the Hammerstill Gallery to get away with selling forgeries. One of Heinrich's dealers had purposefully introduced forgeries onto the sales floor.

On the other hand, while he felt the mother should pay for her crimes, if the paintings could be gotten and kept out of the public's hands—destroyed—it would cause no one harm. And there was the fact that the real criminal, the forger, was dead.

Krew gestured to the Daves as he strolled down the sales floor. "We're done here. Why don't I buy you lunch across the street. Meet there in twenty minutes?"

Both men exchanged looks. "Miss Cohen hasn't left. We're staying."

Ahead, he spied Peachy in a plain green dress. No polka dots. It hadn't occurred to him during the flight how uncharacteristic her attire was. She was on the phone talking with someone and seemed agitated.

"She hasn't granted us permission for use of her image on the show," he said calmly to the men.

"You can handle that for us."

"That's not in my job description."

With that dismissal, the Daves conceded and left the sales floor.

Krew turned but had lost sight of Peachy.

"I'm here at hospital now," Doris Cohen said over the phone. "The ambulance picked Heinrich up a few hours ago. Oh, darling, I'm so worried for him."

Peachy's mom had just explained how Heinrich Hammerstill had been found in the back of his gallery sprawled on the floor. He'd suffered a heart attack. Her mum was frantic. She was never good at handling trauma. Whenever Peachy had skinned a knee or cut herself as a child, she'd been left to do triage while her poor mother had to lie down on the sofa because the sight of blood gave her nausea.

"Do you want me to return to London?" Peachy asked. She glanced over her shoulder, spotting Krew talking to the Daves.

"Would you, darling? Oh. I really need you."

"Of course, Mum. I'll hop the next flight. I should be there after supper."

"Did you get the *Dance*?"

"Uh, no. It was pulled from the auction. Do you know why they would have done that? Is Claudia behind this?"

"I have no idea. It's not even… Well, it's an original."

"This one is the original? But then why have me go after it?"

"I feared if you knew that you would drop the quest to retrieve it. It's *my* original, darling. Please, Peachy, you must get it."

"Your original. You mean, *you* painted it?" The story behind her quest just got crazier and crazier. And yet, there was no denying her mother was a painter. She'd been painting for all of Peachy's life, her swirly abstract style one that Peachy knew she would recognize instantly. "You didn't copy another work?" She hadn't seen the painting but the auction catalog had described it as an abstract Spanish dancer.

"No, darling, it's my own work. I promise."

"But they've pulled it. I don't have a clue why or where it's being held." And with Heinrich in the hospital the crazy just increased. "Do you want me to come to London or not?"

"I do. Maybe you can have your Mr. Lawrence nab it for us?"

Of all the audacity! "Mr. Lawrence will not be involved in anything remotely criminal, Mum. Now I'm hanging up. I'll…see you later."

Peachy tucked away her phone with a huff. What a bloody mess! And while she wanted to run to Krew for support, a hug, a solution to this problem, she knew she couldn't ask that of him.

She spied Krew still talking with the camera crew. The conversation they needed to have could not be done in public. And...she wasn't prepared for a private one either. She had to get home to London. She'd figure out what to do then.

"Mr. Lawrence!"

At the prompt from the auction manager Krew paused in his pursuit of Peachy. He'd asked to speak to the manager but this was terrible timing. Would Peachy leave without saying goodbye? Or course, he'd not handled her revealing the truth behind the forgeries well at all, even if she did have every right to expect animosity from him given what she'd told him.

"I have a few moments," the manager said and nodded that Krew should join him. "I understand you have questions about *Dance*."

Down a short hallway they turned to enter a room where the lots were held before going on the block. They now awaited packaging and shipping instructions from the winners.

The manager stopped before a painting that featured a dancer. Or the idea of a dancer. It was modern and the entire work was circular, a sweep of paint strokes emulating a figure in a violet-and-pink swirl. He'd noticed it a few times when visiting Byron. Loved the colors, and the allusion to a flamenco dance.

"*Dance*," the manager said. "Artist unknown. I've been unable to match it to any current artist's style."

"Why was it pulled?" Krew leaned in closely to inspect the canvas. It wasn't ugly nor was it masterful. The movement in it was delicious though. Truly a dance.

"The seller called. She's, well, she's..."

"Claudia Lawrence," Krew said. "Or rather, she's taken her maiden name again. Claudia Milton."

"You know her?"

"She's my dad's ex-wife."

"I see. Apparently, she wasn't happy with the venue. That was the only reason she gave. Quite unacceptable. But we do strive to keep our clientele happy."

"Are you aware that the former Mrs. Lawrence stole this painting from her husband, along with three others, and is selling them in order to get back at him in some vicious manner?"

"I never involve myself in the personal minutiae behind the sale."

Krew gave the man a dressing-down. "Well, you should. So far my father has not gotten the police involved, but should he…" He let that loose threat hang for a moment. No one wanted to get involved in criminal or legal action. "How much did Miss Milton want for the work?"

"A hundred thousand. But it's no longer for sale."

Hardly worth that amount. Maybe twenty or thirty thousand at best. The woman truly was greedy.

"Everything is for sale."

Krew stood back and gave the painting a long perusal. Amid the swirls he could make out the faint white dots that must be part of the dress. A graceful hand swept above the head. And then it struck him. The figure was…familiar.

"Are you making an offer under the table?" the manager asked. "The provenance states it was created less than a decade ago. And there are no other known works by the nameless artist. Why is this work so important to you?"

"My father was devastated by the loss of these much-loved works of art. I did try to make this go smoothly, away from leering media, by snagging the painting at auction, but..."

It was a gentle but meaningful threat.

"A hundred fifty thousand," the manager said. "I'm sure the seller would be very pleased with that. And I'll have *Dance* wrapped and shipped directly to your London office."

That was highway robbery. And he suspected Claudia would not see any more than sixty percent of that price.

Peachy's mum had been trying to pay off her daughter's medical bills?

Krew cursed inwardly. He tugged at his tie knot. A circular Aperture knot. He'd thought it fun, relaxed, something Peachy would like. She hadn't even commented on it.

He should have gone with the warrior-like Merovingian.

He held out his hand and the two men shook. "Deal. But I'll take it with me today."

CHAPTER TWENTY-ONE

PEACHY ARRIVED AT the Royal London Hospital and was directed to Heinrich's room. As she walked through the hallways a shiver enveloped her. Last time she'd been here she'd been a patient. A fond recollection of the nun with the apple face and soft hands lifted her chin. *Just love.*

She'd thought to touch love, but it had been fleeting.

She found her mum sitting beside Heinrich, holding his hand. The hand-holding thing shouldn't be weird. Doris was consoling the man. And yet, the vibe Peachy got was more than friends. Not unexpected, but—everything in her life just weirded her out lately!

She set her purse on the end of the bed and leaned down to hug her mum. She smelled of the rose soap she crafted and sold at flea markets and her soft linen dress had been misbuttoned up the front. She'd fix it for her later.

"How is he?"

Doris's loosely braided silver hair frayed out around her face. The last time Peachy had seen her looking so weary was when she'd been in hospital. The woman wore her heart on her sleeve and took in the emotions and pains of others so easily. Of course, she would have done anything for her only daughter. Even sell forgeries to pay the hospital bills.

"He had triple bypass surgery last night. The docs said they expect a complete recovery, but that it could be slow going."

"I'm so sorry, Mum." She tugged a chair over to sit beside her. "He means a lot to you, doesn't he?"

"He does, darling." She patted Peachy's hand. The gentle swoosh of some medical device was audible from behind the bed. "Heinrich and I have been... Well, I'm sure you've intuited that we have a thing."

"I've suspected."

"He's not a boyfriend, more like a lover. But a permanent one, if that makes sense."

It could only make sense in Doris Cohen's life. "I understand, Mum. It's nice to have a companion."

"I love him. But how are you? You didn't get the final painting?"

"It was pulled from auction. I'm not sure why. And I wasn't able to speak to Mr. Lawrence."

She could have. She just hadn't the fortitude to stand before Krew after she'd accused him of not being on her side. A side that was in no way, shape or form a side the man could ever take. He was upright, honest and had a sterling reputation. The last thing she'd want to do was tarnish it.

"Don't worry about it, Mum. I'll find a way to pay you back for the hospital bills. If you would have told me sooner—"

"I don't need repayment, darling. Those are taken care of and in the past. That's not why I wanted those paintings off the market, and you know that. I just don't believe I'd be able to pull off prison stripes."

"Oh, Mum." Peachy hugged her.

"Does your Mr. Lawrence know? Did you tell him?"

Peachy didn't want to lie to her mother but she should have never let another person in on the secret. Especially one who had a penchant for doing the right thing when it came to art.

"You did." Doris nodded. "You have fallen in love."

"I haven't—"

Her mum lifted her chin, eyeing her with that sparkle that told Peachy she knew her daughter's heart better than even she did at times. And besides, she may have actually manifested him into her life.

"I needed a confidant. I'm sorry. I just... This is too much, Mum. It's a huge secret to keep."

"You owe me, darling. We Cohen women are strong. At the very least, you can do this for me."

It was a rare sighting of the other side of Doris Cohen, her cold lack of empathy and determination to get her way. Or perhaps it was a mother's instinctive need to protect her child at all costs.

"When will he be in condition to go home?" she asked of Heinrich.

"I don't know. Probably weeks."

"Someone will have to oversee the gallery while he's away. I'll do that."

"Of course you will. Heinrich would expect it."

So many who expected her to do their bidding. It was tiring. Defeating. Peachy felt as though she had given all she could with no return. She could never sell those paintings, and would Heinrich even acknowledge, let alone honor, their agreement to raise her commissions?

"I'm going home to relax. I came here straight from Heathrow. I'll text you later?"

"Of course. Do let me know when you've secured *Dance*."

Peachy stood and wandered to the door, unwilling to reply that she'd be right on that task. Her mother could bear to share some of the worry over this fiasco. Yes, even with her lover lying in the hospital.

Once home, Krew set the unwrapped painting by the brick wall between the two floor-to-ceiling windows that looked over central London. It was midnight. A crescent moon sat high in the sky above Big Ben, mimicking the curve of the lighted clock face. The flight home had been turbulent. And Peachy had not been sitting beside him. A text inquiring where she had gotten to hadn't been answered.

He tugged off his tie, tossed it to the floor and wandered to the liquor cabinet in search of something to ease the stress. There, at the top, sat a sixty-thousand-dollar bottle of single malt Scottish whisky, purchased from the maker whose family had been distilling the liquor for centuries. It had been a goal when he was a teenager for Krew to purchase the whisky. Something his father would admire him for. Yet he'd still not told him he owned it.

Byron Lawrence had always kept his prized bottle of whisky high on a shelf in their family room. When he was little, Krew would watch his dad dust the thick glass bottle. Say things to it. Pat it. He'd doted on that damn bottle more than on his son. And Krew had known then that it had meant more to his dad than he did. He'd always known his father's love was conditional. Byron Lawrence was distracted by things and not sentiments.

Now, as he held the bottle, unopened, he couldn't quite touch that sense of victory he'd experienced when first purchasing it. The feeling he'd bested his dad. *Look! I too can own a ridiculous bottle of alcohol that I keep on my shelf and dust.*

Krew couldn't imagine having a child and showing an inanimate object more love.

Setting the bottle on the kitchen counter, he leaned his palms on the cold marble and bowed his head. So much he'd lost in the past days. But nothing hurt more than watching Peachy walk away from him after the auction. He'd give a thousand bottles of expensive whisky to see her walk back into his arms.

He didn't want to value *things*. Nor did he want to run from romance. From love. As the nuns had told her, people were indeed here on earth to love and be loved. And it was time he started believing that as much as Peachy did. He only needed her. In his arms. In his life. He could be there for her.

And yet, he had not been there for her at the auction when she'd likely most needed his support. Once again, he had failed a woman he cared about.

He smiled a little. Her dreams of country living had permeated his being. He imagined sharing that dream alongside her.

Peachy hadn't purposely lured him into this mess. She hadn't even known about the forgeries. Her mum had sold them to Byron to pay for her daughter's medical bills and he could imagine it had felt like the only possible way at the time. Not necessarily right but something she could do to get by. Peachy had described her mother as bohemian, a beguiler. She may have thought the fakes were so good they'd never be discovered.

And they had not. Krew had walked by those paintings many times, looked at them, studied the *Melancholy*, for heaven's sake. He'd never noticed anything off.

Of course, he hadn't been looking at them with a trained eye at the time. And any forgery could slip by the most skilled dealer if that person were not intentionally looking for a fake.

Truly, Peachy was not to blame in any of this mess. Her only guilt was in opening his heart and stepping inside with her natural sexy confidence.

Straightening, Krew knew he had to make a bold step. He must protect all those he cared about. And he would.

He peeled the red sealing wax from the whisky bottle and loosened the cap. It smelled...like the best whisky he'd ever known. Like something Byron would admire and attend to without concern for those things in life that were real, honest and, yes, family.

Tilting it over the sink, he watched as the golden liquid glugged out and down the drain. He didn't even wince. It didn't matter any longer that he had the upper hand over some silly competition he'd created between him and his dad.

What did matter was that Krew Lawrence was going to stand up for the one he cared about.

Wandering over to the packaged painting, he carefully peeled away the brown paper to reveal the canvas. And when he stepped back, he saw what had been evident, for the first time, in the auction house.

Now he realized why, during that first auction, he'd thought Peachy looked so familiar.

Krew shook his head and chuckled. "Oh, Doris, I do love you."

CHAPTER TWENTY-TWO

THE NEXT MORNING Krew went over things with the crew as they filmed *Jar and Flower*. They'd taped him talking to the forensics scientist, getting a short, easily digestible lesson on how they took microscopic flakes of paint and canvas from the work and used radiocarbon dating to determine age. The Daves then followed the scientist to the room where a high-resolution digital scanner waited.

Krew gestured he'd be right in. He wondered now if he should buy *Melancholy* and *The Deluge* from Peachy so he could have them analyzed as well. But really, Peachy had already confirmed they were forgeries. Today's filming was merely for the benefit of the show. He knew what the results would ultimately show.

And he guessed Hammerstill would never sell. The paintings would be burned. End of story. Hammerstill would be out hundreds of thousands for that trouble.

Krew could step in and lessen the financial burden. If he wanted to. He didn't owe Heinrich a thing. Not a single pence. But that the old man had employed Peachy, and her mother did mean something.

His phone pinged with a text from Peachy saying she wanted to call but wasn't sure he wanted to hear from her. Shaking his head, he pressed her number and she answered on the first ring.

"I'm sorry I had to leave Andalusia so quickly. It's Heinrich. He's had a triple bypass," she said, followed by a heavy sigh. "He won't be able to work any longer. He's said he wants to begin paperwork to hand the gallery ownership to me."

"That's remarkable." But he realized the enthusiasm was not appropriate. The old man had had a heart attack. "I'm so sorry about Heinrich."

"Thank you. I, uh, have been thinking about the forgeries we've purchased. And there is still the issue of the painting you won. *Jar and Flower* must never be resold or placed in a museum. But you are aware of that, I'm sure."

"Yes, the painting will never be placed before the public again. But we will use it for a show. I don't want to talk about that right now. Can we meet? I want to see you, Peach. Come to my place?"

"I can stop by this evening," she said.

He'd called her Peach. She wanted to cry. To believe that she could really have him in her life. To know that their future had not been destroyed by some hippie named Dickie who had thought to help out a woman who had only been trying to survive and take care of her daughter.

Nervous about seeing Krew, Peachy paid attention to her hair, her dress, her shoes. Her lipstick seemed to be the wrong tone so she switched it up for something a little redder. That went well with the red dress. Polka dots as usual. She liked them. They were fun.

But did she appear too flirty, too much the toss-aside woman for what could be the we-can't-do-this-anymore talk they might have? Krew had every right to walk away from what they'd started. She was involved in a ridiculous forgery scheme. Not by choice. But…whew!

Lift your chin, she coached as she headed out to catch an Uber. *Get through this night and then move forward tomorrow.*

If tomorrow didn't have Krew in it she would be devastated. No little house in the country would matter if the one person she cared about most were not in her life to share it with.

The driver stopped before Krew's building and she got out. Taking in the building front, she tilted her head all the way back. His penthouse overlooked the Thames and the city center. Thanks to his success, the man could have anything he desired. And for a moment, she'd thought to be included in those desires.

She touched the scarf she'd tied about her neck. She could do this.

The lift moved so rapidly she clutched her cane and placed the other hand to the wall for stability. When the doors opened, she held her finger on the open button and took a moment to regain her equilibrium.

Before she could even knock on Krew's door it opened and his smile grabbed her nerves by the scruff and flicked them away. He took her hand and led her inside. The cool brick-and-wood exterior was so masculine. Perfectly him. With a glance over her shoulder, she eyed the Matisse. The country scene seemed a little too sprightly for the dread that lingered just below her throat.

He kissed her on the cheek. Not the mouth. Did that mean…? Her nerves sat up from where he'd tossed them and decided to stick around for a while.

"How's Heinrich?" He gestured she sit on one of the leather sofas.

She went to the sofa and sat. "Mum is there with him. He'll need some time for recovery."

"And he's asked you to take his place. That's what you wanted, right?"

She leaned against the back of the sofa, setting her cane aside. The floor-to-ceiling windows brightened the room filled with brick, leather and dark woods. Between the two windows sat a canvas covered with a sheet. She was curious about it, but more curious about their relationship right now.

"Taking on a managerial position will help me get closer to that country cottage," she said. They needed to move beyond polite chat before those nerves of hers did a dance about her system. "What will you do with *Jar and Flower*?"

"I'll be using it as a teaching example for the show. Forensics just confirmed it was painted less than a decade ago."

"Which I've already explained to you. But how can you put it on the show without explaining provenance, which will trace it back to the Hammerstill Gallery?"

He shifted, propping an elbow on the table, and faced her. For a man so uptight and astute his posture was downright casual and open. And then she realized he wore a shirt unbuttoned at the top. And no tie!

"Wait." She leaned forward and tapped the base of his neck, then tugged at the shirt collar.

"Right?" His smile was so broad now she knew something had changed significantly in Krew Lawrence. Maybe he was sick? He was certainly not feeling his normal self. "This is the one with the button you sewed on for me. I cherish it. And I can do casual, Peach."

He'd called her Peach. And he cherished the shirt. That lifted her shoulders.

"I like you casual," she said. "But it'll take some getting used to. I have no way to judge your mood without the tie."

"My shield?"

She nodded. "No need for a protective shield today?"

"Not at all. As for the ink wash, I understand that the gallery could be implicated in a crime and... I don't want to do that to the old man. He's having a tough time of it as it is. And with the forger dead there's no one to prosecute. Save, well... Anyway, I spoke to Byron. He's upset about the loss, but also unwilling to take forgeries back into his home. I intend to cover his losses. Which means there's really no need to pursue legal action. I've discussed it with my producer and he understands as well. We'll use the painting but it's not necessary to divulge the details as to names and locations of any galleries or owners' hands it has passed through."

"Really? That would mean so much if you can do that. But you shouldn't have to pay your dad for the loss."

"It's best for us both. Erases any sense of monetary obligation I may feel toward him. Keeps the old man happy. Besides, I'm doing this mostly for you, Peach."

"You're doing this for *me*?"

"Of course." He slid closer and took her hand. "I decided you should be the winner of this round. And really, it's not going to affect me or The Art Guys if we use this as a teaching moment on the show. The editing team has already remarked that they are going to make it look as though I was specifically on a quest for a forged work. I think it'll work. Though they still insist on using our interactions. Are you good with that?"

"I am. As you've said, there was nothing untoward between us. At least, not that was filmed. But what about the two works I've won? Those are forgeries. And as far as I know, Heinrich wanted them burned."

"Then we'll burn them."

"As simple as that?"

"Of course, but not until you allow me to buy them from you first. Heinrich won't be out any money that way."

"Why be so kind to a man who has been the thorn in The Art Guys' sides for years?"

"I'm not vindictive," he said. "Not like..." He sighed. "Byron's ex-wife did a mean thing. It was calculated and cruel. But Byron going after the paintings was just as selfish in different ways, not to mention a little childish. He's an art hoarder. He doesn't buy things to admire and cherish—he buys them for status and boasting rights. 'I have the most and you don't,' that sort of thing. I'm not like that. I don't need to prove I'm better by owning more. Nor do I need to bring another man, like Hammerstill, down because it'll make me appear the better. That's not being better."

Peachy leaned forward and he bumped foreheads with her. For a moment they sat there, taking it in. Skin against skin. He was a true gentleman. Her calm warrior of the shielded ties. She could love him.

She did love him.

"If your mum will verify that only three forgeries were sold to my father, I'll trust her," he said. "I'll want to speak to her, of course."

"She will. I'll make sure of it. She promised me there were only the three."

"So, that leaves the final one on your list. *Dance*."

"Mum tells me it's not a fake."

"Yes, I have determined that."

"You have?"

He nodded to the windows where the sheet covered a canvas. "Let me show you."

He took her hand as she stood. "You got it? I thought it had been pulled from the auction."

"Another sneaky move on Claudia's part. I spoke to the auction manager, explained the situation and...offered him double what Claudia was hoping to get for it. She immediately accepted the offer. Come take a look."

As they stood before the sheet-covered canvas, Krew took both her hands. "Before I show you this, I want you to know something. You've changed me, Peach. And I don't want to go back to what I was."

"You are a fine man, Krew. You don't need to change anything."

"But I do. You've taught me about love. How it can be so many things. That I am worthy of it. You've altered my heart. Tugged away my protective shield."

"I adore your various tie knots. It's the best way to read you."

"It's a language only you know." He slid his hand along her jaw and stroked her cheek. "Peachy, I love you."

A feeling no master could ever do justice with paints or inks trilled through her insides, stirred in her belly and burst through her being. Clutching Krew's unbuttoned shirt, she said, "I love you too. But with the secrets, I...didn't know if we'd have a chance."

"We do. If you want us to."

"You're the best thing to come into my life, darling."

"Good, because I only want the best for you. And... I want to help your dreams come true. This might be fast, but I want to help you look for land. Maybe a place we could share together?"

That *was* fast, but... She thought of her vision board in her tiny studio apartment. Krew's photo had been close to center, right beside the cottage photo.

"Sounds like the dream I've been chasing for years."

He pulled her close and they swayed there for a while. Dancing the only way she could. In the arms of the man she loved.

"You'll always have dance," he whispered. "Just like this."

"Only with you. Forever."

With a kiss to the crown of her head, Krew stepped over to the covered canvas. "Take a look at *Dance*." He pulled the sheet from the painting and Peachy approached it. "Your mum is the artist, yes?"

"Yes," she said quietly. There was no doubt. The brightly colored abstract swirls were undeniably Doris's unique style.

"And the model?"

Peachy touched her lips. The abstract clearly showed a female dancer and though her face was blurred it was apparent she had freckles. And dark hair pulled back. The dress was a polka dot *bata de cola*, a traditional flamenco dress, in Peachy's favorite shades of red and pink. Was it really…?

"Me?"

Krew wrapped his arms around her waist. "This painting hung in the hallway at my parents' home. On the occasions I'd visit Byron, I used to sit on the sofa, so far away, and notice that viewing it from a distance the dancer looked so clear. And I remember when I first saw you at auction you looked familiar. That is you, Peach. And this painting, I believe, is a love letter from your mother to you."

Catching her breath, Peachy felt a tear begin to spill down her cheek. It was lovely. And if Doris had painted it to make money to cover her bills it had to have been created about the time she'd lost her dream of dancing. Of studying flamenco in Andalusia. Truly, this was a mother's tribute to her daughter.

"I don't want to give it back to her," Krew said. "I'd like to keep it. Place it on the wall where the Matisse is."

"You'd trade a Matisse for a Doris Cohen?"

"In a heartbeat. But I won't trade you for the world, Peach."

EPILOGUE

Six months later...

Joss and Ginny's wedding reception was held in a flower-festooned gazebo in the least-expected place for a wedding, Transylvania. The guest list was small, private, but perfect for the ceremony held before the lake. Having met Ginny a few times previously when the three Art Guys had gathered with their significant others, Peachy had grown to adore her. She was giggly, fun and smart, and the bright yellow and orange flowers appliquéd on her white dress matched her personality. She and Joss had fallen in love while on a job to appraise a dusty old library in Transylvania and everyone was now jokingly calling her Mrs. Brawn, and she loved it.

Sipping champagne and taking in the fresh air tinted with the smell of pine needles and the sound of vibrant dance music, Peachy looked around for her Mr. Brain. Well, The Brain. She'd moved into his penthouse two months earlier, after four months of dating. Finally, she had found real love.

They'd looked at a few different plots for sale outside Bath. It was a bit farther from London than Krew had planned on, but he loved the area, as did she. Krew was all in for building a little cottage and having goats. She still wasn't so sure about the goats, but she did like to indulge her lover.

Bumped from behind, she turned to find Krew's back to her. He was rocking gently...

"Oh, my gosh." She turned around before him. "Is that…? Darling, what are you holding?"

Her handsome lover had chosen the Desiderata tie knot to go with his groomsman attire this evening. He was truly her heart's desire.

"This," he said plainly, "is a baby. They are common throughout the entire world. A miniature version of human."

What a joker! "Fair enough." It was Maeve and Asher's daughter. Peachy had been eyeballing the tyke all evening. At two months she was so tiny and adorable.

"Smell her head," Krew offered, lifting the baby to her nose.

Peachy pressed her nose to the baby's tuft of thick black hair. "Mmm, smells like…"

"Heaven?"

"And like sweets and your favorite memory."

"Right?" He hugged the baby and continued rocking. "I like her."

"Oh dear." Maeve suddenly intruded, reaching for the baby. "That's where Scarlet got to. It's time for your bottle, love." Then she said to Krew, "I'm not even going to ask what you're doing with my delicious little nugget. I know she's been circulating."

Both Peachy and Krew laughed as Maeve wandered off, bouncing Scarlet gently.

Krew slipped his hand into hers. "Babies are nice."

They'd not discussed children, how they felt about them or if they would like to have them in their future. If they even moved toward that future. But Krew's simple statement blossomed in Peachy's heart and she tilted her head to his shoulder. "They are. I'd like one."

He nodded. "Yeah? Me too."

With a whistle, the crowd settled. On the dais under the floral arch, the bride stepped up and swung her bouquet. "Time to toss the bouquet!"

"I'm out of here." Krew gave Peachy a nudge as he quickly left the dance floor.

Leaning onto her cane to keep from toppling, Peachy looked for a quick exit as well, but a half circle of women had formed, and for some reason she stood in the middle. She wasn't one for such theatrics. But the bouquet, brimming with white roses and eucalyptus, was beautiful. What was it they said about the woman who caught the bouquet—she would be the next to marry?

"Worth a try," she whispered. Though Krew's fast escape did not bode well for that future.

Ginny raised the bouquet, turned her back to the crowd and gave it a toss.

And…without stepping forward, Peachy suddenly felt the heavy bouquet of flowers land against her chest. She caught it with one hand. Cheers erupted around her. The fragrance seeped upward like expensive perfume. So gorgeous. Did that mean…?

Turning to look for her man, she startled to find Krew standing right behind her.

"Krew?"

"Peach."

When he went down on one knee, Peachy caught a gasp at the back of her throat. This was…so unexpected. And yet, he held up a ring and she could barely hear him speak as the crowd again clapped and cheered.

"You've taught me that love is all a person needs. I love you, Peach. Marry me!" he shouted so she could hear.

She nodded. "Yes!"

Krew slipped the ring onto her finger. He kissed her to renewed applause. Together they would touch their dreams.

* * * * *

MILLS & BOON®

Coming next month

SECRET ROYAL'S NAPOLI REUNION
Nina Milne

Sofia's tummy went into freefall, instincts colliding, fight versus flight, but her feet seemed rooted to the pavement, the two of them caught in an immoveable tableau of shock.

Could it really be Marco? But stood here, looking at him, every bone in her body told her it was. Even though this man was a far cry from the young man of yester year. The overlong hair was now ruthlessly short, his features seemed harder, the jaw more pugnacious, the grey eyes now full of shock, seemed harder. Now her gaze lingered on his lips, set in a firm line. Lips that had given her such joy in that one glorious kiss.

'Marco?' the more her gaze drank him in the more familiar he looked and for once all the years of royalty, of knowing the right thing to say at the right time, the correct smile, the things drilled into her in lieu of an actual education, deserted her and she knew she resembled nothing more than a puffer fish. 'I...'

Continue reading

SECRET ROYAL'S NAPOLI REUNION
Nina Milne

Available next month
millsandboon.co.uk

Copyright © 2025 Nina Milne

MILLS & BOON TRUE LOVE IS HAVING A MAKEOVER!

Introducing

Love Always

Swoon-worthy romances, where love takes center stage. Same heartwarming stories, stylish new look!

Look out for our brand new look
COMING SEPTEMBER 2025

MILLS & BOON

COMING SOON!

We really hope you enjoyed reading this book. If you're looking for more romance be sure to head to the shops when new books are available on

Thursday 25th September

To see which titles are coming soon, please visit
millsandboon.co.uk/nextmonth

MILLS & BOON

FOUR BRAND NEW BOOKS FROM
MILLS & BOON MODERN

Indulge in desire, drama, and breathtaking romance – where passion knows no bounds!

BILLION-DOLLAR TEMPTATIONS
Melanie Milburne · Kali Anthony

GREEK Scandals
Abby Green · Caitlin Crews

SEXY RICH BOSSES
Maya Blake · Tara Pammi

One Night, Nine Months
Heidi Rice · Emmy Grayson

OUT NOW

Eight Modern stories published every month, find them all at:

millsandboon.co.uk

afterglow BOOKS

Afterglow Books is a trend-led, trope-filled list of books with diverse, authentic and relatable characters, a wide array of voices and representations, plus real world trials and tribulations. Featuring all the tropes you could possibly want (think small-town settings, fake relationships, grumpy vs sunshine, enemies to lovers) and all with a generous dose of spice in every story.

@millsandboonuk
@millsandboonuk
afterglowbooks.co.uk

#AfterglowBooks

For all the latest book news, exclusive content and giveaways scan the QR code below to sign up to the Afterglow newsletter:

SCAN ME

afterglow BOOKS

Let's Give 'Em PUMPKIN to Talk About
She's grumpy. He's sunshine. Will love grow?
ISABELLE POPP

The Secret Crush Book Club
Could this be the start of a new chapter?
KARMEN LEE

- Grumpy/sunshine
- Small-town romance
- Spicy

- LGBTQ+
- Small-town romance
- Spicy

OUT NOW

Two stories published every month. Discover more at:
Afterglowbooks.co.uk

OUT NOW!

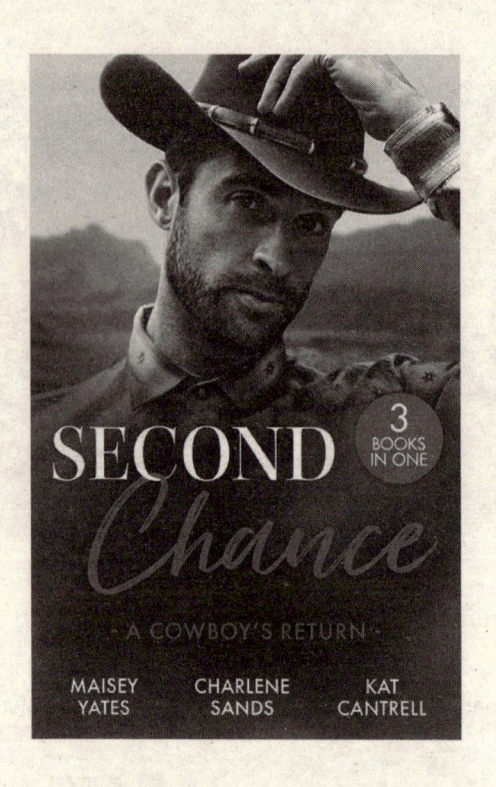

SECOND Chance
A COWBOY'S RETURN

3 BOOKS IN ONE

MAISEY YATES · CHARLENE SANDS · KAT CANTRELL

Available at
millsandboon.co.uk

MILLS & BOON